On a Sundown Sea

On a Sundown Sea

A Novel of Madame Tingley and the Origins of Lomaland

Jill G. Hall

She Writes Press

Published in 2025 by
She Writes Press, an imprint of The Stable Book Group

32 Court Street, Suite 2109
Brooklyn, NY 11201
https://shewritespress.com

Print ISBN: 978-1-64742-988-1
E-ISBN: 978-1-64742-989-8
Library of Congress Control Number: 2025909427

Interior design by Stacey Aaronson

Printed in the United States of America

This book is dedicated to my siblings,
Todd, Sandy, and Leslie
because you grew up with the rumors too.

Chapter One

March 12, 1888
Manhattan

To Katherine's surprise, snow drifted upon her shoulders, and she pulled the cloak's hood over her head. It had been a mild winter, with many days even in the fifties. A steady rain had fallen overnight, and without warning the temperature plunged. Surely the sun would come out soon and warm up the morning. At least the wet weather would clear the odious soot that fumed from factory smokestacks. How she longed to live in the country where fresh air filled her lungs and nature abounded. But her work was here. And here she must stay to aid the poor. Even though she couldn't save them all, she remained compelled to help as many as she could.

By the time Katherine arrived at her Do-Good Mission, located in the bottom floor of a tenement building, her mood resembled the dark clouds overhead. There wouldn't be nearly enough to feed the hundreds of starving women and children who wailed and waited in front of the five-story brick building with ornamental cornices. Like so many others nearby that held the clandestine truth of the impoverished immigrants who rented the apartments inside.

Last year the cloakmakers' strike had dragged on. The brave workers had held out for what they felt were their rights. After their jobs were given to others, the destitution became even more terrible. In addition, refugees continued to pour in across the harbor from Ellis Island. And so the downtrodden outside the mission, with their spoons and tin cups, increased daily.

Katherine clasped her beloved grandfather's watch tightly. Even through her glove she could feel his loving strength help her carry on. Anger incensed her at the factory owners who turned their backs on the workers, while they lived in their massive mansions, rode luxurious carriages, and sported extravagant apparel. A small hourly increase and better working conditions would have made such a difference. Yesterday morning a baby had died in his mother's arms on the mission doorstep. Katherine prayed for the woman's pain to ease and for the infant's soul.

She pushed through the throng, frowned at the empty table, slid inside the building, and asked, "Why haven't you started to serve?"

Grace Gergen ran a wrist across her forehead with tears in her eyes. "Sorry, Mrs. Tingley. Mabel didn't show up. Shorthanded, the soup's not ready, and the baker hasn't delivered the bread."

Katherine touched the young woman's shoulder. "Don't feel bad, dear. It's not your fault." Since the day Grace arrived, tall and elegant, with sad eyes and an armload of cast-off clothes, she'd been a godsend. A dependable volunteer to do whatever she could to help.

Katherine put an apron on over her cloak and stirred the earth-scented concoction. Too bad she didn't have enough funds to add meat for these hungry souls. At least Friday's potato donations from the grocer had stayed fresh enough. From outside, shouts of despair rang in Katherine's ears. She had to do something.

"I'm going out. Bring the soup when ready." She carried a crate through the door, placed it upside down on the sidewalk, and climbed atop it. Lowering her hood, she waved her arms until the crowd quieted. As loud as possible, she called, "Be patient. I promise we'll feed as many as we can."

Shoulders slumped as the hungry families huddled together for warmth. Katherine's heart was almost at a breaking point to see so much misfortune and know she could do so very little.

Grace lugged out the vat and set it on the table. The crowd parted as the breadman pulled through in his cart, and Grace rushed out to greet him. Katherine climbed off the crate and motioned at the front of the group to form a line. She stirred the soup and nodded to a woman whose baby fussed in her arms, three children with red-rimmed eyes beside her, shivering, half-dressed. To eke out cash, like many mothers, she'd probably pawned most of their clothes. Too bad castoff donations to the mission had recently been paltry.

Quietly, Katherine filled their cups as Grace handed out smidgens of bread.

"Please, ma'ams, may we go inside for warmth?" the mother begged as she joggled her crying babe.

Katherine considered letting some inside, but the landlord had warned that more than fifty bodies could cause the floor to collapse into the cellarage. She counted five times that many out here. If she allowed only a portion in, it could cause a stampede.

Grace and Katherine exchanged glances. She couldn't abide it. "We'll do half-hour rotations allowing less than fifty in at a time."

Grace opened the door and let in the first family. Katherine dipped the ladle in the soup again. "Next," she said to the Levi boy wearing threadbare jacket and trousers. His cup filled, she handed it back to him. "Where's your mother today?"

"Don't know, ma'am. Probably upstairs with the young ones."

Katherine held back a sigh. Last time she'd seen Mrs. Levi she'd been quite ill.

"A bit for him too?" the boy asked, nodding to the mangy dog tied with a frayed rope about his waist.

Katherine's impulse was to say no, but she smiled instead. "Animals are God's creatures too." She nodded to Grace, who handed a bit of bread to the lad. "Take a seat inside and warm up," she told him.

He took the piece Grace offered and plodded toward the door, the dog trailing as he spoke. "Those are some nice ladies. Wouldn't you say so, chuckaboo?"

Katherine scooped the ladle again. Suddenly, she felt unsteady as flashing lights glittered and spun overhead. She dropped the spoon into the pot. Not now, not a vision! Snowflakes fell minute by minute as the throng disappeared under piles of eiderdown snow. The wild wind and whines of the hungry ceased into silence. The tenement buildings across the street faded away. Soon the whole world was white.

After what felt like an eternity, she blinked, the snow vanished, the buildings became visible again, and the multitude of anguished voices filled her ears once more. Hopefully, this wasn't a premonition that this storm would rage on into danger. From an early age, Katherine had seen things others could not.

She waited to regain her senses and returned to the soup. Cup after cup filled, bread bits were handed out, families rotated inside, snow continued to fly, and drifts piled up around them. Icicles had begun to form under the building's eaves and on the electric wires that crisscrossed overhead like hundreds of laundry lines.

Bone-chilling cold seeped beneath Katherine's layers of clothes, and she felt sorrow for those waiting. The pot grew low, and she scanned the crowd. Her attention was caught by a man under an umbrella staring at her from the outskirts of the crowd as if he knew her. Coat collar turned up and buttoned around the neck, while a stiff-crowned fur hat covered his head—clearly not one of the garment strikers. A gentleman with a neatly trimmed beard and mustache. Perhaps he had been recently reduced to poverty and was too ashamed to come forward with the rest.

She returned his gaze, and their eyes connected. Despite the cold, a warm sensation spread through her whole body, and she found it hard to breathe. He seemed familiar. She couldn't explain the eerie feeling, as if he could see into her soul.

A tug on her skirt broke the reverie, and she looked down at the tiny redheaded lass holding up her cup. "Can I have some, please?" Her face was grimy with an endearing grin.

"Of course, sweetheart." Katherine took the girl's cup, filled it, and handed it back.

Katherine pointed to the back of the crowd and said to Grace, "Please ask that gentleman to come up next."

Grace peered across the horde. "What gentleman?"

Katherine searched for him again, but he'd disappeared.

Chapter Two

Katherine and Grace continued to serve the rest of the victuals and rotated folks inside the mission while wind gusts howled and snow fell. Katherine's gut wrenched. She feared the white vision had been a premonition. All her life, she'd tried to understand where they came from, but as she grew older, she'd learned to just accept them.

By early afternoon, the storm had become a full-blown blizzard, and Mr. Thomas, the landlord, arrived. "Get home to your husbands," he said.

"Yes, sir." Grace pulled her toque hat farther down and fingered the blond fringe over her forehead.

"I'd rather stay." Katherine felt no need to grovel to Mr. Thomas, who'd never known a hungry day in his life.

He glared at her. "Aren't you a surly one, Mrs. Tingley? Go now before the roads are impassable."

Reluctantly, Katherine acquiesced. Nothing more she could do here anyway. Besides, Philo, her husband, might be worried about her. Arm in arm against the squall, the two women supported each other and trudged through the snow to the elevated train a few blocks away. Jolting through the crowd pushing up the slick stairs to the platform, Grace caught Katherine just in time as her foot began to slip. They climbed inside a car as the conductor called down to the stairs, "Folks, snow's piling high. This is the last car today."

Grace clutched a strap, and Katherine held tight to her waist in the packed car. The conductor shut the door on the angry crowd, who banged on the El as it pulled away. Katherine clung to Grace in relief. Slow going, the locomotive slogged along, spewing coal soot. The train made several stops, and people descended. Grace and Katherine took seats on an empty leather bench.

"You were brave today," Grace said. "I could never talk to a man the way you did to Mr. Thomas."

"Our people are in trouble and need us." Katherine rubbed her gloved hands together for warmth. Grace, too timid to understand the difference between following a rule and following her heart, had probably never contradicted a man in her life. Still, Katherine liked her, admired her help at the mission. Most other wealthy New York women didn't veer from their teas, operas, and balls.

Outside, blowing gusts could be seen. Katherine hoped Philo was safe at home, and she worried about the dear ones she'd left behind at the mission—and the man who had disappeared. Who was he? His gaze had given her shivers like she'd never experienced before.

"That man today," Katherine asked Grace, "did you see him?"

"What man?"

"Standing at the back of the crowd. Well-dressed, not asking for food."

"A patron, perhaps," Grace suggested.

"I don't think so. It's strange. You're sure you didn't see him?"

Grace shook her head.

The train came to a sudden halt.

The conductor walked through. "It's stuck! Everybody out."

"Can we stay in here for warmth?" a man bellowed.

"Please." A woman with a baby in her arms sobbed.

Nonetheless, the passengers peacefully climbed out and helped each other down from the tracks into the white wildness. Katherine and Grace held on to each other until they reached the younger woman's home safely.

"Come in and stay with us," she offered.

"No," Katherine responded, "I must get home to Philo and the dog." They hugged briefly, and Grace escaped inside.

Katherine trudged another half hour with the wind whirling and snow piling high around her; she'd never been so cold in all her life. She looked forward to a cozy night with Spots at her feet beside a warm fire. Perhaps Philo had put dinner in the oven.

It was the twilight hour when she finally reached the house at 373 West End Avenue. Its dark façade loomed like a castle; arched windows adorned the front, curved balconies hung on the side, and crenellated teethlike projections pointed along the roof's edge. She imagined the Hudson River below, iced over and covered in white. Due to Philo's bad business venture with the wheelie-chair contraption, they'd had to vacate their downtown apartment. Blessedly, her friend Cora, one of the mission's benefactors, had offered the use of the ground floor of her mansion while away in Europe on her honeymoon.

Katherine mounted the stairs, kicked snow out of the way, and pushed the front door open. Spots greeted her with a bark and barreled out into the cold.

"Philo, haven't you let the dog out?" Katherine hollered.

All was quiet. Where was that man? Even though she worried about his safety, she couldn't suppress annoyance over the cocker spaniel. Spots popped in and out of the snowbanks in circles until night darkened and his little black body grew invisible. He followed her back inside, ran down the tiled hallway, and rolled around on the salon's Persian carpet to dry himself.

Inside the freezing house, Katherine shoved the door closed and lit the sideboard lantern. She dropped her soaked boots to the floor, hung her cloak on the hall tree, and wrapped herself in Cora's sable coat. In the mirror, she smoothed down her damp jet-black curls. With no gray in sight, most didn't realize she'd just passed her fortieth year, and people never guessed Philo, her third husband, was ten years her junior.

She carried the lantern down to the kitchen, filled Spots's bowl, and he gobbled it up. She planned to build a fire in the parlor; however, there was no wood. Down the shadowy hallway, she called Philo's name, knocked on the study door, and opened it to emptiness. Spots followed her inside and curled up into a ball on the rug. A strong mint odor hit her nostrils. Philo must have bought new aftershave. She hoped it hadn't been pricey.

Before they wed six months ago, he'd led her to believe his job with the Red Ball Steamship Company was secure and had alluded to the fact he'd other means as well. Soon she learned that both claims were false. Within two months, he'd run through not only his own meager funds, but most of hers, too, on his cockamamie inventions.

Katherine held up the lantern and shook her head at the partner desk. When he'd had the monstrosity delivered, he'd had the men move her own desk to the parlor, telling her they could both work together facing each other. When she'd protested, Philo had tried to convince her to take the sheets off the furniture on the top floors. Katherine had refused. Cora could return at any moment. It would be disrespectful to her friend after her generosity. Soon, though, he'd pushed her chair into a corner, and covered the entire desk's surface with his concepts. Just as well. His pencil flicking and constant humming drove her to distraction.

She picked up a stack of papers and ruffled through his sketches: a cigarette holder, a cream whipper, a wave-harnessing machine. These detailed drawings and descriptions were overdone, verbose. Could even be unadulterated hogwash. A drawing she hadn't seen before caught her eye: a garter with a metal heart attached to the clasp. She held it closer to the lantern. Philo had labeled the drawing *Man's Garter*. Ha! Leave it to him to design something so silly for a man.

Spots whined, pushed his nose in the trash bin, and tipped it over. Wadded papers spilled out along with an empty bottle that exuded a hellish medicinal odor. That wasn't aftershave. Had Philo been feeling ill? Katherine picked up the bottle and read the label: *Rumple Minze, peppermint schnapps*. Had she been bamboozled? He'd claimed he was a teetotaler like her. She positioned it on the desk in front of his chair where he'd see it.

Spots in tow, she shut the door behind them, carried the lantern to her bedroom, hung it on a hook, and removed her damp stockings. Underneath the blankets, still in the sable coat, she tried to warm up. Spots jumped up beside her. His now dry fluffy ears and silky back warmed her body. At least now that they lived in the mansion, they could each have their own bedrooms like civilized people.

At midnight, snow continued to fly and wind gusts blew louder than a locomotive. She turned off the lantern and closed her eyes. Worried about the poor families huddled in doorsteps, sleep eluded her. Guilt tapped at her for being warm in a bed with three thick blankets atop her and Spots snuggled beside her. And where was Philo?

Her first two marriages had ended in disaster, and she feared she'd made another mistake. Naïve at twenty, she'd wedded and within two months, unable to live up to her wifely duties, she'd fled from Savannah to New York and scurried away on a ship to London. There she'd joined a theater troupe. Her knack for memorization, dramatics, and mediumship skills enhanced the group's entertainments, which helped sell tickets across Europe for over half a decade.

Back in the States, she never shared she'd been an actress. They were compared to harlots. Spiritualists, though, were all the rage. She'd gotten by in New York City by doing occult readings and fallen for another man. After they'd been married six years, she'd been distraught to discover he'd used the income she'd brought in by mediumship mail, private seances, and public presentations on his mistress. She vowed never to marry again. But society didn't take kindly to unmarried women, and she'd convinced herself matrimony with Philo, who seemed to understand her, would be a wise choice. She'd never admit to others their marriage was anything but happy.

Now, to help her drift off to sleep, she put her hand on Spots's back and imagined being at the Laurels in Newburyport, Massachusetts, her childhood home. There the sun shone through oaks as she walked along the path above the flowing Merrimac River. Her thoughts then shifted to her ongoing dream of a white city in a golden land overlooking the sundown sea. An enchanting place where people from around the world lived in harmony. Her whole life she'd longed for that place. Her last thoughts before nodding off were filled with curiosity about the mysterious man at the back of the crowd.

Chapter Three

The next morning, Spots curled up beside her. Winds blew and snow continued to fall. She'd heard Philo come in very late. She picked up her grandfather's watch from the nightstand. Past time to go to the mission, but she wasn't ready to face Philo yet, so she lay back and rubbed her thumb across the crystal, remembering the first time her grandfather let her hold it.

Sitting above the river under Shady Fellow, their special giant oak, she begged, "Please!" Now five, this had been their running game since before she could recall.

Her grandfather teased, "No," then smiled at her and said, "I suppose so. You're such a fine young lady now."

She clapped her tiny hands and put out her palms, and he gently placed the timepiece in them. It weighed no more than a songbird. She touched the glass above each number and counted: one, two, three, all the way up to twelve.

"That's right!" her grandfather said. "You're so bright."

She loved the rhyme and repeated. "That's right! I'm so bright."

"Want to wind it?" he asked. He twisted his fingers and demonstrated. "Gently now, one, two, three. Three times only."

She followed his directions. "Gently, one, two, three." She put the watch to her ear, listened to the *tick, tick, tick,* and synchronized the sound with her heartbeat. She turned it over as sunrays glinted off his fancy initials on the gold back.

Now Katherine sat up, pulled her purple dressing gown from the armoire, tied the braided cord around her, and stepped into slippers.

Her grandfather had always believed in her. As a Transcendentalist, he'd recognized her powers and believed in the divinity of nature. He'd agreed the Laurels were filled with magic. He'd agreed rocks, trees, and flowers had voices and the big man who occasionally appeared to her was real too.

Spots clicked down the hall behind her. The study door was open, but Philo wasn't inside. He sat at the kitchen table with a cup in his hand staring out into space. His unbrushed hair poked up like a Roman soldier's helmet bristles. He didn't resemble the man she'd first seen at one of her Do-Good benefit auditions. His resounding tenor range had filled her heart. Enamored by his tall physique, dark hair, neat beard, and dapper silk suit, she'd taken a liking to him. He'd begun to frequent her readings and occasionally even helped at the mission.

He sheepishly looked over and didn't mention the schnapps. "May I make you some eggs?" Unlike other men, at least he cooked sometimes.

"No, I need to rush off to the mission."

He laughed. "You're not going anywhere."

"What do you mean?"

"You can't get down to the street."

"Would you shovel the snow for me?"

"The door won't open."

Spots on her heels, she rushed to the foyer and pushed hard on the door, but it wouldn't budge. The back door wouldn't open either. She sat at the table with a thud. Her vision had certainly been a premonition after all!

"Where were you last night?" she asked.

He yawned. "Trains were down. I tried to check into a hotel. They were all booked; people even bedded down in the lobbies." She wasn't sure whether to believe him or not. She'd never heard of such a thing.

"I hiked home, almost didn't make it." Philo sang, "Today the roads must all be closed. No way to get anywhere. No wagons, horses, trains, hacks, sidewalks, paths, just snow."

She couldn't help smiling at his made-up song. He scooped a pile of marmalade on a piece of toast the way she liked and put it on her plate. The kettle whistled. Philo made her a cup of tea and put it before her.

"May I have some milk, please?" she asked.

"It hasn't been delivered."

"Did you call?"

"The phones are down and no newspapers either."

She dropped two sugar cubes in the cup and stirred it with a spoon. "Those darn utility companies! It's pure greed." The owners had ignored the law for all wires to be put underground.

"The weather service isn't open on Sundays, so they couldn't predict it," he said.

"I knew," she said sadly.

"Did you have a premonition?"

She nodded and told him about her vision in front of the mission.

"Why didn't you warn anyone?" he asked.

"I wish I had. No one would have believed me. Besides I wasn't sure when or if it would really happen."

She bit into a piece of toast and swallowed. "I see you've been drinking."

"What? You mean the schnapps? Peppermint helps soothe my throat for singing." He smiled at her.

She wanted to believe him. He kissed her forehead, patted her arm, and rambled down to his study. She moved to her desk in the parlor and caught up on mission donation requests. A few minutes later, hammering clanged from Philo's office. What was he making now?

At first, she'd considered him a genius and had striven to be supportive. Now she fretted he might have an obsession. He talked nonstop about his innovations. Embarrassingly, he told others Edison had nothing over him, bragged about the patents he'd applied for, and claimed that someday he'd be filthy rich.

With her savings, he'd started the Invalid Health Company and convinced friends and neighbors to buy stock in it. The hospital lifting-chair protype never worked and the wheelie-chair contraption had made them a community laughingstock. During a demonstration, the brakes hadn't worked; a financier rolled down a hill and broke his leg. The patent was refused, and the irate investors lost their investments, including Cora and the landlady who'd booted them out.

After supper that evening, as snow continued to fall, she tried to entertain her husband by reciting her favorite poems by Emerson, Thoreau, and John Greenleaf Whittier. Philo's eyes began to droop. So she switched to her old standby, *Little Women*. Philo turned up his nose and asked for *Treasure Island*. After a while, though, he yawned and made his way down to his room.

At breakfast the next morning, he hadn't bothered to trim his beard or bathe. After another boasting session about a scooter idea, she couldn't take it anymore and had to speak up.

"Philo, I honor your imagination. It's okay to keep your head in the clouds if you keep your feet on the ground."

"What's that supposed to mean?"

"Get a job that brings in money. Find a place for us to live."

Their financial lives had literally gone downhill. Philo's inventive mind was creative, but it didn't pay the bills. They were sinking.

"When's Cora coming back?" he asked.

"I don't know."

"Some people have all the luck. Fancy that, little Cora Slocomb to Countess di Brazza in one fell swoop. She's rolling in it now with her husband's Italian estate." With Philo, it was often about money.

"Don't be crass. Be grateful. She's an heiress in her own right and has been generous to us," Katherine said. "Ask the shipping company for your job back. When home, complete the basic tasks here first and then let yourself go as much as you want with your inventions."

He smiled at her. "Of what tasks do you speak, kitten?"

"Tend to Spots." A month ago, he'd been a scrawny stray who stalked the mission in hopes of a dropped morsel, his fur so dirty she couldn't tell its color. After two days, Katherine had taken pity and handed him a few tidbits.

One afternoon when the trains were down, he'd trailed her as she walked home. Katherine and Philo had bathed and brushed Spots's coat until it felt smooth as silk.

The next morning, she'd released him in hopes a wealthy nearby family would take him in. But he'd laid down on her doorstep and whined. Philo had brought him back in and begged to keep him. He'd promised to feed him and take him out. She'd reluctantly agreed.

"What else can I do?" he asked.

Katherine put her hands on her hips. "Fold the newspaper after you've finished reading it instead of throwing it on the floor and wash your unmentionables."

"If they're unmentionable, why are you mentioning them? Beloved, now that we're married, those are your responsibilities."

She couldn't believe he'd said that. When he proposed he'd told her he admired her beauty, gumption, and gifts. And if they married, she could do exactly as she pleased, and he'd help with the household duties. Her intuition had told her he was too good to be true. However, after a while his attention and compliments had melted those concerns away.

While courting, Philo had escorted her arm in arm on promenades and to events. Once they were married, she'd assumed his physical affections toward her would surge. However, a month after they wed with still no marital relations, she'd believed he must have been waiting for her to give him a sign. One night while he was sketching, she'd sauntered into his bedroom in her nightgown, sat next to him, and gently touched his thigh. He didn't look at her and pulled his leg away. At that moment, it dawned on her. He hadn't married her for love or affection. She was horrified to realize the depths of her mistake.

Chapter Four

By Thursday morning, the snow had stopped, and sunrays glittered through the haze. From the window, Katherine watched Philo clear the walkway and make his way down the street. Worry racked her soul. How many had been lost in the blizzard? Were cold and starved people waiting in front of the mission? Would the benefit scheduled for this evening still take place?

After she dressed warmly to leave, Spots started to bark and there was a knock at the door. She walked down the hall, picked up the dog, and opened the door.

"I must speak with you." The man offered her his card. "I'm William Q. Judge."

It was him, the man with a noble expression from the back of the crowd. "Weren't you at the mission the other day?" she asked.

"Yes, I'd heard about your work and came down to see for myself." The beauty of his Irish brogue rolled off his tongue. He wore the same fur hat. His deep blue eyes had a look of eternity, an inexpressible mystery, like the ocean. Although handsome, he appeared haggard, with a deep sense of sadness—caused by hunger, no doubt. She pulled her eyes from his and noticed the elegant carriage and two striking horses on the street behind him. No, it wasn't hunger. He seemed desperate for some reason, and her heart went out to him.

"Philo told me about you," Mr. Judge said.

Suspicion engulfed her. What was Philo up to now? Did he want her to help him take advantage of this cordial man, to invest in his convoluted inventions or charge for a reading? She said, “I don’t have time to talk to you now. I need to get to the mission.”

“I can imagine. I’m sorry to intrude. You must be worried. This was the worst storm we’ve ever had. They say over twenty-two inches of snow fell. I’m afraid many lives have been lost.”

She paused, trying to take it all in. Spots wiggled; she put him down, and he ran out into the yard.

The man didn’t budge. “Please. I really need to speak with you.” He held out his card again.

She struggled to keep the annoyance out of her voice. “Where did you meet Philo?”

“At the Masonic Lodge. He told us you’d encouraged him to join?”

She’d hoped it would help him improve his ways. “I have a high regard for the Masons. My grandfather was one.”

As she accepted Mr. Judge’s card, she felt heat through his leather glove, as if a warm summer sun spread throughout her body.

“I’m also leader of the Theosophical Society here in America.” He smiled at her.

“The what?” she asked.

“Theosophy. It’ll remove the causes of misery from the world. I believe you’re called to learn about it.”

Called? That term piqued her interest; even so, she stepped back inside. “As you know, my time is consumed with the mission. Now I need to get there.”

He persisted. “Your work at the mission is important, but I perceive you yearn for something that goes deeper and broader to help humanity.”

Such big thoughts. “That’s very nice, Mr. Judge. I really must go now.”

“Think about what I’ve said.”

Suddenly, within a spiral of gossamer light, a vision of a curly-haired babe of sweetness appeared above his left shoulder. Katherine paused, ready to receive a communication. Sometimes she’d feel one in her chest, and other times she’d hear one. It was always different. Had this man once lost a child? She'd often eased sufferings by sharing messages from departed souls.

Mr. Judge turned, and the spirit disappeared. He made his way down toward his carriage, then stopped and looked at her. "Might I give you a ride?"

Tempted, she considered it for a moment. "No, thank you, sir." It might be inappropriate.

"I'll come back another time. It's important to me."

"I understand." She nodded. "I'll see you again soon."

Chapter Five

Katherine's boots crunched through snow-crusted ice as she made her way to the train. A newsboy held up a paper while calling, "Great white blizzard! Hundreds die! Worst storm ever known!"

She gave him a coin and took a copy. He tipped his hat and said, "Thank ye."

Riding toward the mission, she held the paper, not ready to read about the devastation. Outside the window, men were digging out homes where roofs had caved in or had been torn off in the storm. Her thoughts drifted back to the stranger she had now seen twice. Mr. Judge. Who said she'd been called to learn about Theosophy.

What a notion. Her whole life, Katherine had wanted to be called. Called to a sense of purpose. Called to a connection to the world. Instead, she had been called to visions, bad marriages, and despair. Mr. Judge, with his Theosophy, might be no more than a charlatan. Still, she couldn't shake the sincerity of his visit.

In front of the mission, a tattered-hatted busker played a sorrowful accordion drone. The food table hadn't been set out. Only several people hailed her; usually there were many more. She worried how many of her regulars had perished in the storm.

A tearful woman jiggled a howling baby in her arms. "He's sick. Can I bring him out of the cold?" A man in a threadbare jacket quaked. His cheeks red from the cold. "Yes, please let us in!" more folks cried.

Grace opened the door, escorted a group out of the building, and sang,

"Thirty out, thirty in, thirty-minute shifts." She counted from the front of the group. Katherine filed inside behind them and slid an apron on over her coat while the clients found room on the benches.

The room began to warm as the fire grew, and the cedar scent masked the smell of unwashed bodies. "Wherever did you get the wood?" Katherine asked Grace.

"This morning when I arrived, a man in a fine carriage pulled up and deposited several armloads inside."

"Who was it?"

Grace shook her head. "He wouldn't tell me."

"What did he look like?"

"A beard, overcoat, tall fur hat."

Mr. Judge! What kindness. What forwardness. Why was this man continuing to show up in her life? She was both intrigued and afraid of what might happen if he was right.

Grace put her hands on a pile of clothes. "Look what the Presbyterians dropped off too."

Katherine added a blanket from home to the mittens, hats, and coats, and Grace started to sort through them. She held up a lacey wedding gown, and the women laughed at the absurdity.

Katherine gestured to a young woman shivering on a bench to come over. "Try this." She handed her a sweater.

The woman pulled it on over her head, rubbed her hands along the arms and said, "It's mighty soft."

"What's your name, dear?"

"Cynthia." She looked at the stack of clothes. "Might I help?"

Katherine smiled at her and took a handkerchief from her pocket. "Certainly. First let me wash you up a bit." The girl squinted while Katherine cleaned her face and hands. "Good as new. Please dole out to the youngest tykes first."

A baby screamed.

"Grace, please administer to that child," Katherine whispered. "I fear the mother is distraught."

Grace blinked her lovely eyes, nodded, and made her way over to them. As she took the child in her arms, the mother's face relaxed. Then the child screeched more loudly.

"Mrs. Tingley!" Grace yelled. "The baby is burning up and barely breathing."

Katherine felt the child's forehead. "How long has he been like this?" she asked the mother.

"A fortnight."

"I'm taking you to the clinic right away. Cynthia, assist Grace as needed." Katherine took the baby from Grace. "Take care, dear ones," Katherine called as she led mother and child outside into drizzle.

A foul stench of illness permeated the clinic's crammed front room. Patients slumped on benches and on the dirt floor. Katherine told the mother to wait there and carried the baby behind the screen as the doctor finished with a patient. This beautiful young doctor was a wonder. Talk about a calling. Gertie had defied her family and society and despite all odds had made it into and through medical school.

"This is an emergency. Dr. van Pelt, please tend to him next," Katherine pled.

"Of course, for you." The doctor accepted the child. "Where's the mother?"

Katherine brought the mother to her and watched while the baby was examined, dropped coins into Gertie's hand, and rushed back to the mission.

At home that evening, she told Philo about Mr. Judge's visit to the house that morning.

Philo grinned. "Did he ask to see some of my inventions? Maybe he'll invest?"

For goodness' sake! She shook her head. "What did you tell him about me?"

"I don't recall. Probably about the mission. Maybe your readings too. An interesting fellow. A lawyer by trade."

"He appears sickly. What's wrong with him?" she asked.

"Some kind of exotic disease he picked up in South America."

"That's horrible." She thought about the babe's image. "Does he have children?"

Philo shrugged. "No idea."

"What do you think he wants with me?" Katherine asked.

"He's a good egg. You'd better be nice to him. Maybe he'll have the Masons donate to your mission. As you know, there's plenty in those coffers to help needy causes. He's the bursar and controls the money."

"He talked about Theosophy. What do you know about it?"

"They're occultists too. He's said to be a mesmerist. Some even call him the Rajah."

Intrigued, afraid, and a bit confused, she hoped he'd visit her again soon.

Chapter Six

By mid-April, a month after the storm, the city had thawed, geraniums filled window boxes, and the streets resounded with horse hooves *clip-clopping* once again. Katherine believed those who thought their lives would return to normal were foolish. Trenches started to be dug and utility wires put underground. Serious discussions about creating a subway system began. Dubbed the Great White Blizzard, the storm's snow drifts had accumulated over fifty feet all along the northeastern seaboard. More than two hundred ships had been grounded or wrecked, resulting in the death of a hundred seamen.

The Thursday mission benefits had been canceled. However, she'd provided a few private readings at the mansion that brought in some income—not nearly enough, though. She had no idea how she'd pay the Do-Good Mission rent at the end of the month. She continued to manage the mission with Grace's assistance, and others started to volunteer there too. These wealthy women, who had suffered inconveniences during the storm, shared they'd recognized how difficult life must have been for those less fortunate. Philo minded his *p*'s and *q*'s, coming home at a reasonable hour and helping with household tasks. Spots continued to be a cuddle muffin.

One night she dreamt again of her childhood home at the Laurels. The trees' green leaves shaded her path above the Merrimac River. They whispered endearments to her, and deep-voiced boulders murmured love. Sunrays danced through giant oaks, casting delicate decorations on her hands like lace gloves. She twirled maple leaves' *L*-shaped boomerangs that had fallen to the ground and watched them float away. As she touched the pink lady slipper buds, she made shoes for the fairies that flew down to visit her from the wooden castle on the hill.

The tall man who often joined her smiled with admiration. His mesmerizing blue eyes gleamed like the river. "Even when you can't see me, I'll always be with you," he said. "You're going to make a difference in the world."

Katherine woke with a start. Those were Mr. Judge's eyes! That's why she felt she'd always known him. She had! It had been over a month since he said he'd see her again and he hadn't called, at her home or the mission. Intensity tugged at her, the dream something more than just the odd coincidence. She felt drawn to see him and find out if he was okay. She pulled his crisp white card from her nightstand drawer.

William Q. Judge
Attorney-at-Law
American Theosophical Society General Secretary
117 Nassau Street, 4th Floor

The next morning at breakfast she asked Philo if he'd seen him.

"Neither hide nor hair," he said.

Katherine made certain Grace had adequate coverage to run the mission smoothly, then walked down to Nassau Street in the financial district. Miller's Restaurant on one side of the double entry doors and a watch shop on the other were not open yet. A *For Rent* sign hung on a metal balcony near the fire escape that zigzagged over arched windows.

Inside she climbed to the fourth floor and hurried down the hall to the door with *William Q. Judge* stenciled in gold. She knocked, but no one answered. A note strung around the knob said *Temporarily closed*. The office next door was vacant and the other two businesses on that floor were closed as well. Back to the street level, the restaurant still hadn't opened. The clockmaker suggested she try the Freemasons.

She rode the train to midtown and walked to the lodge. Old Glory and the Masonic flag flew above the doors. The ornate French Empire Style building, opened in 1875, had taken five years to complete, costing way over a million dollars. What would her grandfather, who'd been Grand Master for the states of Massachusetts and Rhode Island, have thought about the extravagance? Just like her, he probably would consider all the poor people that currency could have aided. Still, the building was stunning, and she couldn't help but be in awe.

She started through the door, but a burly guard stepped in front of her. "Ma'am, no women allowed."

"May I just speak to someone at the desk?" She tried to look around him to see inside.

"Members only." The guard flicked invisible lint off his red uniform's sleeves.

"My husband, Philo Tingley, is a member."

The guard wouldn't even make eye contact with her. "Never heard of him."

She handed him Mr. Judge's card. "I'm looking for this gentleman. A sign at his office said it was closed. Have you seen him lately?"

He studied the card. "I couldn't say."

"Is he ill?"

"I couldn't say, ma'am," the guard repeated.

"Last time I saw him, he told me it was of the utmost importance that we meet again." She gave the guard a grave smile. "Please ask the desk clerk for his home address."

The guard shook his head. "No."

How callous! Dejectedly, she rode the train home. Arriving there, she knocked on Philo's office door. She could hear noises, but he didn't answer. It wasn't her usual practice to walk in unannounced; however, she was at her rope's end and entered anyway. He wore goggles and swayed a cylindrical cardboard instrument back and forth like a conductor's baton. "Do you like it?" He smiled at her. "I'm creating a special light."

What next? "Yes, dear. I need a favor. Would you go with me to the lodge tomorrow?"

"What for?" he frowned.

"I need Mr. Judge's address. I told you he wanted to speak with me."

"As you can see, I'm very busy. Can't you go alone?"

"I did. They wouldn't let me in. I'm a woman, remember." She put a hand on her hip.

"That's right. They're persnickety about that." He raised his eyes and swung the tube over his head again. "I was going to work on this. Since you need my help, I'll go tomorrow."

The next afternoon, she waited with the guard while Philo went inside.

"I appreciate it," she said as Philo handed her a slip of paper with the address.

"It's in Brooklyn. Shouldn't I escort you there?" He took her arm in his.

She didn't want him along. "Wouldn't you rather work?"

"Suppose so." He nodded.

The sun had begun to depart for the day. She'd wait and go on the morrow.

Chapter Seven

The mission kept her busy the next two days, and on the following, after enough volunteers arrived, she slipped out to find Mr. Judge. At the South Street Seaport, foggy morning dew covered the sailing vessels that filled the nearby docks, their masts sticking up like toothpicks. To hire a carriage to take her across the bridge would be too costly, so she set off in her sunbonnet and boots.

The longest suspension bridge in the world had opened five years before to great fanfare. Prior to that, the ferry rode people across the East River to Brooklyn. She'd always avoided the walking trek. Now, as her boots paced along the wooden planks, she tried to ignore the urgent whispers that regaled her from the beyond. She said a prayer for the laborers who'd been lost during construction, some in accidents and others from diving deep into the depths of the flowing river. Now beneath the bridge, men in rowboats oared through the murky water and cargo ships hauled wares. As she approached the other side, the stench of the sugar refinery, factories, and textile mills accosted her. Like in the city, immigrants from around the world resided in slums of tenement houses, trying to eke out a living.

She walked off the bridge through the poverty and kept going until, closer to her destination, the neighborhood changed. Maple trees provided shade, and window boxes overflowed with color on the front of graceful brownstones. Her spirits fluttered like dove wings at the thought of seeing Mr. Judge again, and she picked up her pace. Even though the morning was cool, she began to perspire, and hair that snuck out from underneath her bonnet clung to her face. After a while, she still hadn't seen Willoughby Street and stopped in front of a home where a family relaxed on their stoop and asked for directions.

A woman pointed. "It's back that way."

Katherine had been totally turned around. She retraced her steps, finally found the street and the address, and then paused. The handsome brownstone had a tall stoop, like all the others, with elaborate carvings over the door. A bay window patinaed with age heralded that someone unique lived there.

Would he be home? Did he live alone? She looked around the quiet street. If invited in, would it be proper to enter? Maybe she should have had Philo come with her after all. Maybe she should have sent a note first.

She tucked her hair back into her bonnet, climbed the steep steps, and tapped on the door. All was quiet. She rapped the brass knocker and waited, but there was still no answer. Disappointed, she turned away, then heard the latch open behind her.

A woman about her age towered with a butterfly-and-bee-bedecked flowerpot chapeau perched on her head. "What do you want?" She scowled.

Could Katherine have the wrong address? She tried not to stare. There was a reason journalists called those hats "hat-trocities." "Is Mr. Judge home?"

"He's not seeing anyone." The woman eyeballed Katherine as if she were a strumpet and began to close the door.

"Ella, who's there?" Mr. Judge came up behind her. Golden rays streamed through the breaking mist, lighting up his face. "You found me." His kind smile and those blue eyes filled her with gladness.

"It's been over a month since you told me you had urgent business to discuss, and I became worried."

"He's been ill since the blizzard." The woman sneered.

"Mrs. Tingley. Come in." He opened the door wider. Even though thinner than before, he was handsome in a brocade banyan that matched his eyes. Could he really possess the same soul as the man who'd walked with her at the Laurels and in her dreams?

The woman crossed her arms and moved to block her. "No, you don't! William's to be resting."

"Ella," he said. "This is Mrs. Tingley. I told you about her, from the Do-Good Mission."

"Do-Good! Bah! I don't care if she's from Kathmandu. You're to go back inside and lie down."

"The doctor said I could resume my work as soon as the fever broke. I feel fine now. Finish packing or you'll miss your train." He coughed into a handkerchief.

"See." She harrumphed and tramped back inside.

"I apologize for my wife's manners. Come in."

Katherine couldn't believe that horrible creature was his wife. If she didn't have a weasel's countenance, she might have been pretty. "You're ill. I'll return another time." Katherine turned and started down the stairs.

He followed her, using the cast-iron railing for support. "Please. I must speak with you." He coughed again and stopped midway down. "It's a sense of urgency."

She turned and studied him. Was he dying? Many people at the end of their lives on earth wanted guidance from her. However, Katherine didn't want to be anywhere near his wife's dreadful forces.

Ella pushed past them, clomping down the stairs toting a satchel. She climbed into the waiting carriage, exposing her big beribboned bustle.

"Say hello to your sister," Mr. Judge called as she rode off.

He sighed. "Again, I apologize. Come in."

"It's inappropriate for us to be alone," Katherine said from the sidewalk.

"Mrs. Buckley, our cook, is here."

Just like the last time she'd seen him, a cherubim's visage appeared above his shoulder.

"Please," he pleaded.

The vision disappeared. Did that babe have a message for Mr. Judge?

"All right." Katherine climbed back up the stairs and followed him inside.

He led her down the hall and poked his head inside the kitchen. "Mrs. Buckley, please bring tea to my study."

"Yes, sir."

He escorted Katherine to a cozy room where a fire flickered in the grate, Oriental carpets graced the floor, and shelves were packed with books. She stared at a corner table draped in silk that held a display of exotic items: a hand-carved Buddha with beads strung around its neck, a brass bowl, a bundle of white sage, a peacock feather, and a few large geodes.

She pointed to a purple gem, her favorite color. "That's exquisite."

"Amethysts have the ability to create deep peace, serenity, and joy." He held it up to sparkle in the light and handed it to her.

She took the leather chair he proffered to her, rested the crystal in her lap, and fingered the smooth pointed surfaces as a sense of calm overtook her. Perhaps only because he'd suggested it.

He sat behind the neat desk with its green lamp and typewriter, leaned over, and ran his fingers over the keys. She wanted to ask him if he was the man in her dreams but didn't know how to go about it. Her foot wiggled as she scanned the watercolors on the wall above his head.

Mrs. Buckley delivered the tea and set it on the desk. "Anything else?"

"No, thank you." William smiled kindly.

The cook stared at Katherine and left the room, leaving the door open. Katherine warmed her hands on the porcelain cup, put it down, and waited for him to start the conversation. A clock ticked on the mantel. William's eyes looked directly into hers. She stirred her tea. The spoon clinked on the cup's edges.

"What can I do for you?" she finally asked.

"It's not what you can do for me; instead, it's what I can do for you."

"What do you mean?"

He leaned across the desk and reached toward her hand. "I know you have many needs."

She jumped up, the crystal fell to the carpet, and she glared at him. "How dare you make advances toward me?"

Yes, she felt lured to him in an unusual way, but any type of liaison between them would be impossible.

"Oh, dear me! I apologize. It seems I've given you the wrong impression." His face turned red, and he raised his voice. "I want to help you with the mission."

Katherine wasn't sure what to do. The schoolboy embarrassment convinced her of his honest intentions. Abashed herself, she retook the chair. They drank tea in silence, and each ate a gingersnap.

"How did you come to open the Do-Good Mission?" he asked.

"I started the Ladies Society of Mercy to visit prisons and hospitals. After a while, I wanted to do more, so I opened the Do-Good."

"It's obvious there are still more challenges than you've been able to fulfill. It'll only get worse as immigrants keep pouring in."

"That's true." She sighed.

"The lodge might aid you to support the mission." His smile was radiant.

Relief swept over her as she thought of the Do-Good rent and unpaid bills on her desk.

"As Freemasons, we're committed to being faithful to our responsibilities to God, country, family, and fellowman. Philo suggested we might choose it as a charity."

How kind of him. "As I mentioned, I have a high esteem for the Masons. My grandfather instilled in me their values from an early age. If I'd been a man, I'd have applied too."

Mr. Judge laughed, a deep belly laugh, and she couldn't resist joining in.

"I'm sure you know they have affiliate groups for women," he said.

"Bah! The Order of the Eastern Star. I tried that." She blurted, "Those demur ladies who kowtow to the high-and-mighty men repulse me."

Mr. Judge chuckled.

She caught herself. "Of course, we'd be ever so grateful for any help you can give us."

"I'll see what we can do." He cleared his throat and drank some tea. "Tell me more about your grandfather."

"We were close. We lived on the banks of the Merrimac River in Newburyport. Grandfather Chase had an estate there called the Laurels."

"I know a poem by that very name. Have you heard it? *From those wild rocks I look today. O'er leagues of dancing waves*," Mr. Judge began to recite.

Goose bumps prickled up her arms. He knew the poem! How on earth was that possible? Who was this man? Overjoyed, she joined his recitation. *"And see the far, low coastline stretched away to where our river meets the sea. The light wind blowing off the land is burdened with old voices. Through shut eyes, I see how lip and hand, the greeting of old days renew."*

As they continued to recite the stanzas, her heart drummed with the poem's rhythm. When finished she said, "John Greenleaf Whittier was a neighbor. He visited the estate often."

"You knew him?"

She nodded.

"Was that poem inspired by your grandfather's land? I've admired Whittier's work for a long time. His nature poems and abolitionist pieces move me."

"Grandfather and Whittier were friends. They were not only Freemasons, but New England Transcendentalists together. They acquainted me with the themes of self-wisdom, nature, and social reform."

He dipped his head. "Now I understand how you came to be a woman such as yourself."

She smiled. "My early years at the Laurels with Grandfather are my finest memories. I'd give anything to go back and see him again."

"Have you tried to communicate with him?"

She laughed. "Of course not, he's been gone for years."

"That's not what I meant." William eyed her.

She looked down at her hands to gather her thoughts. Some were judgmental about her mediumship powers, calling them unchristian claptrap, and aimed to invalidate her. Her grandfather had taught her it was a sacred gift to be used to alleviate suffering of loved ones left on earth who were grieving. At times, it didn't feel like a gift, but like a curse. No matter how much a loved one suffered, she always relayed the truth. However, when she saw a tragedy too horrible to repeat, she held that part back.

William handed her a tiny yellow bow tied onto a silver filigree clasp. "What do you make of this?"

This man was a friend in need of solace. If she could give some relief, it would bring her pleasure. She took the bow, looked up, and concentrated. Within a few minutes, sweetness and light hovered above his shoulder. "Did you have a child?" she asked gently.

His eyes opened wide with the look of hope. "Yes. What do you see?"

Katherine had to make sure this was his babe. "Tell me about the little one."

"A child filled with love." Judge told her about Alice's wavy hair, how she liked blueberry pie, how she used to sing all the time until diphtheria ravaged her body. "She held on for weeks," he said, the emotion catching in his throat.

"Did she have a missing-tooth grin and wear a lacey layette?" Katherine asked.

William's face lit up. "That must be our little girl. I've tried for many years to receive contact from her. Does she have a message for me?"

Katherine paused to listen and repeated what she heard. "She says, 'Thank you, Papa. I'm at peace in a beautiful garden.' She's been with you all this time and will be forever."

He wiped his eyes with a handkerchief. "Bless your soul for this gift from the spirit. I can now move forward in peace. I'm only sorry I can't share this with Ella."

"Why not?"

"She doesn't believe."

"Maybe if we tell her the message, she will."

William continued, "I doubt it. After we lost Alice, Ella became even more Christian. Instead, I became more interested in spiritualism."

"Do you go to church with her?"

"When I have to." He laughed. "What about you?"

"I haven't been in years. Sundays, I'm usually at the mission."

She'd always hated church. Once to stall, Katherine had refused to put on her shoes. Her father had picked her up and carried her instead. The wooden cross, hard pews, and dark shadows above the rafters had swooped toward her. Dripping sconce candles had flickered. The congregation had sung such sad songs. Reverend Fiske had preached sin and damnation to hell. At the time she'd had no idea what that meant but knew it was bad. Oaks outside the window had called to her. Her mother had tried to keep Katherine tightly in her lap, but she'd pulled away and run off into the woods where beauty resided, where she felt safe. If that church had felt as comforting as this room, she wouldn't have dreaded those Sundays.

"Do you have children?" William asked.

She shook her head sadly. "Alas, I haven't been blessed in that way."

William looked at her kindly. "God must have other plans for you."

"Perhaps." She studied her hands and held back tears.

"Do you often have visions?"

"Many when I least expect them. More when I try." She sipped her tea, now cold.

"What does Philo say about them?"

"He says he believes, but other times he seems skeptical."

"You've many powers. However, I believe you're still a seeker," he said quietly.

"A seeker of what?"

"Happiness. You're so committed to helping others you've been unable to reach peace within yourself."

She sat up straight. "What makes you say that?"

"I can sense these things. What is it you want most in the world? I can—" He started to cough, and his cheeks turned red. "I'm sorry. This is infuriating."

She waited for him to gain composure until he gasped, "More tea."

She filled his cup and said, "I'll put a daub of honey in it." She added a spoonful of the amber nectar from the tray, stirred, and handed it to him.

He drank it down, relaxed back, and closed his eyes. "Let me rest a moment."

She picked up the geode from the floor and held it again, trying to radiate calm energy toward him.

He started coughing again.

Mrs. Buckley rushed in and pounded on his back. "Madame, I request you leave now."

"May I do that for you?" Katherine reached her palms to take over.

Mrs. Buckley glared at her. "It is best you go."

Mr. Judge's coughing eased. "Wait!" He selected a pamphlet from a bookshelf and handed it to her. "This is for seekers such as yourself. Read it and return here in a few days for another conversation. I'll be better by then."

"If you wish." She ran her hand over the booklet, skimmed the cover, and saw his name printed there. "You wrote this?" She looked at him in surprise.

"Only published and edited—" He started hacking again.

"Leave now." Mrs. Buckley indicated the door.

"Wait." William stopped her again. "I insist you take my carriage home."

"Are you sure?" Even though she was so very tired, she didn't want to impose. Between his wife and the cook, Katherine already felt hated by the women in his home.

He said through coughs, "Mrs. Buckley, make sure she gets safely in the carriage."

Chapter Eight

Katherine slid into the carriage and gave the driver her address. What an afternoon. Mixed emotions stirred within her. She worried about William's health, but the flicker of a connection with someone who might understand and support her filled her with hope. Whittier's poem still scrolling through her heart, she saw her five-year-old self. The piano bench hard beneath her, her small hands tried to plunk the assigned scales.

Through the paned windows, sunrays shone on the keyboard, and she put her hands in her lap and looked out at the pure blue sky. Crocus blossoms pushed up from the soil, opening their yellow skirts. The big birch tree had sprouted green leaves.

Grandfather Chase passed by going toward the river with his walking stick. She longed to run outside and join him in the forest like the fairies did.

Mama came in the room and put her hand on Katherine's shoulder. "Back to the keyboard. You know what your father says."

Katherine pouted. "Why do the boys get to do anything they want, and I don't?"

"This should help." Mama reset the metronome and returned to the kitchen.

Katherine stared at the wooden box and watched the pendulum tick back and forth, clicking off time. Tears filled her eyes, and she softly trilled her favorite song, "On the River."

She preferred singing and moving to the music than making her tiny hands play piano.

She turned to make sure Mama wouldn't see, jumped up, and ran out the door. She floated away from the house, followed the flowing river, and found her grandfather under Shady Fellow, their favorite oak.

He opened his arms to her. She landed on the soft ground and curled up in his lap. "Grandfather, look at that butterfly!" She hopped up, chased after it, and waved as it flew high into the sky.

"Did you see the blue and yellow?" her grandfather asked. "It's called a swallowtail."

She giggled. "Does that mean it swallows its tail?"

He laughed. "You're a funny one."

She sighed. "I wish I was a butterfly."

"So you'd have pretty wings too?"

"So I could fly away and not have to practice piano." Katherine began to cry.

"What's wrong?"

She crawled into his lap again. "What should I do when Father yells and makes me feel bad?"

"Put your hands over your heart like this." Grandfather demonstrated, and she copied him. "Close your eyes, think about a butterfly, and let those sad feelings float away into the sky."

She practiced it and would try it again tonight if Father came home in a bad mood.

"Look who's on his way!" her grandfather shouted.

Katherine followed his gaze down to the dory being rowed toward them from Amesbury across the river. A straw sunhat sat on the passenger's head.

Katherine ran down the path toward the old ferry landing, waved her arms, and hollered, "Hello, Mr. Greenleaf."

The boat pulled in. He handed coins from his pocket to the oar boy and said, "Thank you for the ride, Tinky."

As Tinky pulled out into the river again, he winked at her. She smiled and hugged Mr. Whittier around the knees.

He ruffled her hair. "Good day to you, Miss Catty Cat-Cat!"

She meowed like a kitten, and giggled. Taking his big hand, she led him up the slope and sat under Shady Fellow with her grandfather.

"Did you find that white city yet?" Mr. Whittier asked.

"No, sir." She reached up and tugged on his silly sideburns.

"Keep looking for it," he advised.

"Perhaps she'll need to find property and build it herself." Her grandfather laughed.

"Is that possible?" she asked.

"Anything's possible, my dear," he said.

Mr. Whittier stood, opened his notebook, and cleared his throat. "Nathan and Cat, I've a new poem to share with you."

She crawled into her grandfather's lap and got comfortable. Sometimes these readings took a while.

Mr. Whittier cleared his throat and began, "'The Laurels' by John Greenleaf Whittier."

She wanted to yell "That's about us," but wasn't supposed to interrupt.

From these wild rocks I look to-day
O'er leagues of dancing waves, and see
The far, low coastline stretch away
To where our river meets the sea.
The light wind blowing off the land
Is burdened with old voices; through
Shut eyes I see how lip and hand
The greeting of old days renew."

He looked up and held his hand out to them with a grin.

"O friends whose hearts still keep their prime,
Whose bright example warms and cheers,
Ye teach us how to smile at Time,
And set to music all his years!

I thank you for sweet summer days,
for pleasant memories lingering long,
for joyful meetings, fond delays,
and ties of friendship woven strong.
As for the last time, side by side,
you tread the paths familiar grown,
I reach across the severing tide,
and blend my farewells with your own.

The poet pulled a pencil from behind his ear and made a few notes on the page, then continued.

Make room, O river of our home!
For other feet in place of ours,
and summers yet to come,
make glad another Feast of Flowers!
Hold in thy mirror, calm and deep,
the pleasant pictures thou hath seen;
forget thy lovers not but keep
our memory like thy laurels green.

Katherine jumped up and clapped loudly.

Mr. Whittier smiled shyly. "What do you think?"

"That's a fine poem," her grandfather said. "The rhythm and rhymes superb. You're the best poet in Massachusetts."

Katherine raised her arms and shouted, "In all of America!"

Now the carriage came to a halt, her reverie broke, and the driver said, "I believe this is your home, ma'am."

Chapter Nine

Glistening the color of Mr. Judge's amethyst geode, the sun began to set over the Hudson. Spots greeted her at the door. Philo was still out. What a remarkable afternoon.

In the parlor, she looked at the pile on her desk. She should compose personal invitations to well-to-do acquaintances in hopes they'd attend the mission benefit at the end of next week. If the event wasn't successful, she'd be unable to pay the mission rent and bills. That was unless Mr. Judge and the Masons decided to help soon.

Too tired, she yawned and walked down to her room. Spots jumped on the bed and watched Katherine at the vanity as she took her hair down and brushed it. Even though drowsy, her brown eyes reflected in the mirror a newfound light. She climbed into bed, under the counterpane, and stroked the spaniel's smooth back. During a full moon, Katherine always felt edgy and had a difficult time sleeping with bright light shining through the window. She picked up Mr. Judge's pamphlet and reread the title:

THE PATH, A MAGAZINE DEVOTED
TO THE BROTHERHOOD OF HUMANITY,
THEOSOPHY IN AMERICA,
AND THE STUDY OF OCCULT SCIENCE

Vol. I *April 1886* *No.1.*

She continued to read: *The first step in true mysticism and occultism is to apprehend the meaning of Universal Brotherhood; without it the magic turns to ashes in the mouth. The Theosophical Society appeals to all who wish to raise themselves and their fellow creatures—man and beast—out of the thoughtlessness of selfish everyday life. Utopia cannot be established in a day; but through the spreading of the idea of Universal Brotherhood, the truth of all things will be discovered. If we say it is useless, nothing will ever be done. The Society has started a beginning. Although philanthropic institutions and systems are being brought forward by good and noble men and women, selfishness, vice, brutality, and the resulting misery seem to grow. Riches are accumulating in the hands of the few, while the poor are ground harder every day as they increase in number.*

Katherine's hand flew to her sprinting heart. That was exactly how she felt. She'd never dared share her innermost heartbreak aloud before. Sadness and guilt often set in as she traveled from the poverty of the slums up to this neighborhood filled with luxurious homes amassed with unnecessary things. Like the white moon outside, hope glowed in her chest. Could Theosophy really be for her, as Mr. Judge said? What a blessing to encounter a whole organization that reflected her own thoughts and beliefs about life.

She flipped through the booklet titles: *The Kabbalah, Seership, Buddha's Religion, A Prophecy about Theosophy.* Many topics with symbols and verbose words were beyond her mind's grasp; others truly spoke to her. A poem, Shakespeare scene, or even a Bible verse she could comprehend within no time and remember the lines word for word. However, philosophical concepts like some of these would always elude her.

Even so, she read slowly into the night until she heard the key in the lock and Philo bungled into the house. She quickly slid the pamphlet under her pillow and turned off the lantern.

She'd never believed in the concept of a Christian heaven. Now this new friend had the capability of explaining the Theosophical view of heaven on earth. Yesterday she hadn't known one person could have so much love in their heart. Now that she'd encountered him and felt his force, life would never be the same again.

Chapter Ten

Katherine rapped on the door, hoping Ella wasn't home. After a week, Katherine had digested what she could of *The Path*. She'd sent Mr. Judge a message to inquire if his health had improved and if he was available for another visit. He'd responded immediately and sent his carriage to pick her up at the mission that afternoon.

His vigor much improved, he ushered her into the foyer, put his hands on her shoulders, gazed into her eyes, and said, "I'm glad you've come." Tenderness flowed from him to her like calm river waters, as if she were the most important person in the world. Now that he felt better, he looked much younger. Possibly only a few years older than her.

"I'm gladdened you look so well, Mr. Judge."

"Call me William."

"All right, William." She liked the feeling of his name on her lips.

"May I call you Katherine?"

"Please do." She glanced down the hall. "Who else is here?"

"Ella is still in Boston. Mrs. Buckley has gone to the market."

"Isn't it improper?" Katherine asked.

"Not in the least. We have much to discuss, and the quiet will be most beneficial."

"Shall I make us tea?" she asked.

"I've already prepared it," he said and escorted her to his study that smelled of lavender and sage. She removed her bonnet, placed it on the desk, and fingered her hair to provide a semblance of neatness.

He sat behind his desk across from her, studied a sketch, stared at her a few moments, and slid the paper underneath a pile. Strange. What was it? Upside down, she'd been unable to decipher the drawing.

He poured tea, cut slices of cake, and plated them. "I apologize for my coughing spell the other day."

"I'm sorry too." Even though Philo had told her about his illness, she wanted to learn more. "What ails you?"

"Since childhood, I've been sickly. Doctors haven't been able to diagnose this recent illness. It comes and goes at random. One day I'll feel perfectly fine, and the next the fever and cough return. I must have picked something up in Venezuela when I was there on business."

"Theosophical concerns?"

"Heavens, no. Mining speculation." He frowned. "It didn't work out how I'd hoped in more ways than one. I believe my days on earth are limited."

No wonder his wife was so protective. "That's horrible."

He sighed. "It's all in the Divine's destiny."

"Do you truly believe that?" she asked.

He nodded. "I am certain of it."

She wished her faith was as sure as his.

"Your brogue is charming. How did you come to live in the United States, Mr. Judge?"

"William." He laughed.

She laughed too. "William."

He told her his mother had died when he was seven and his father had struggled to care for all seven of them. When he was thirteen, in the mid-1860s, his father had brought them here from Dublin.

"We were poor immigrants. That's one reason I admire the work you do." William told her he would have gone into social concerns himself, but he needed to earn a living. "I studied law as soon as I was able."

She held up the pamphlet she'd read front to back three times. "Do you have more issues for me to read?"

He pulled a red tome from his shelf and pushed it across the desk toward her. "Here's Volume One of Madame Blavatsky's *The Secret Doctrine*. It's just been published. Volume Two comes out very soon."

As Katherine held the heavy book, anxiety overpowered her. Trembling, she leafed through the dense pages. "I'd prefer another pamphlet, please." With so much to be done, she didn't have time to sit for hours and read. Plus, she preferred to gain knowledge in smaller bites. The energy she felt staring at the thick book was palpable, and she set it back on the desk. She worried she had disappointed William, but he showed no such sign.

"Certainly." He stacked three more pamphlets.

She wanted to ask him more about Theosophy and what she'd read but didn't know where to begin. The pictures above his head caught her eyes. "Tell me about those lovely watercolors."

"I painted them when I was in India a few years back." He pointed to each as he described them. The Theosophical Society headquarters in Adyar, India. A nearby temple, and his friend Colonel Henry Olcott's residence.

These paintings had heart and emotion. The opposite of Philo's detailed patent drawings. "They look like ancients lived in them. You've captured them beautifully. I'd love to go to India someday." She walked toward a shelf where photos leaned against books. In one, a woman's eyes seemed to follow Katherine like the Louvre's *Mona Lisa.*

"That's Madame Blavatsky, head of the Theosophical Society, who wrote *The Secret Doctrine*," William put his hand on the big book. "In the other picture, under the banyan tree with me is Colonel Olcott."

Katherine blurted out, "With that beard, he looks like Moses."

William grinned. "And here I am on a donkey. They teased me about sitting on my ass."

Katherine laughed out loud, surprised at his bawdy comment.

"A local man took the shots. Next time I'll bring my new toy with me." He picked up a wooden box from the shelf. "These new cameras are quite the innovation. The roll holds a hundred exposures. Mail it to Kodak, and they develop and print them for you."

Katherine remembered Philo going on about the camera. These men with their silly obsession over toys, machines, cameras, and engines. Still, in William's hand, she saw how he might bring the world back to people who'd never have a chance to travel. She sat down. "Tell me more about your Theosophical Society."

"Theosophy comes from the Greek *theosophia*. *Theos* meaning god, gods, or divine, and *sophia*, wisdom. I just call it divine wisdom."

"Is it a Christian religion?"

His face grew serious, and he told her it encompassed all religions of the world. "We study the great teachers who walked our earth long ago, including Jesus. We've also researched Buddha, Muhammad, and many others by reading ancient writings in their original languages, such as Egyptian hieroglyphics, Sanskrit, Persian, Greek, and Hebrew." He raised a finger. "The only religion is the truth!"

Katherine crossed her arms. Wasn't that what all religions said? Christian and Jewish alike claimed to know the truth. She'd always been a skeptic and wanted to believe in something real and not just a bunch of dusty old rules. "How did you get involved?"

"Madame Blavatsky invited me to a salon at her rooms on Irving Place here in New York. Immediately, I was impressed by her deep insight into human nature, marvelous wisdom, and generosity, and began studying under her. Along with Olcott, the three of us founded the Theosophical Society for research into spiritual laws governing the physical universe. For instance, phenomena summoning elemental spirits."

"That sounds similar to the Psychical Research Society." She thought she'd found her community when she'd joined the New York chapter. Other members were mediums and held seances too. However, after a while she realized it wasn't for her. The group focused on proving and disproving the authenticity of presenters. She knew her gifts were true and didn't need or want to take the time to impress anyone.

"In a way. We focus on studying ancient practices to enhance our work. Ten years ago, Madame Blavatsky and Colonel Olcott relocated the society to Adyar, India. I wanted to go too but had family obligations here. Five years ago, I visited and wanted to stay longer; however, Madame Blavatsky bade me to return here. She prophesized in America at the turn of the century a transformation will take place and a great seat of learning will be established in the West. She needed me to prepare the country by adding membership and lodges."

Katherine gasped, put a hand over her mouth, and stared at the woman's photograph. Could she have been referring to her childhood vision?

"What?" He frowned with concern.

"Nothing." Katherine folded her hands in her lap.

He smiled. "Enough about that now. When was the first time you received a message from a departed soul?"

She sipped tea and ate a bite of cake to recover herself. "When I was six, my grandfather handed me a locket to play with, and I ran my fingers over the filigree crescent moon and star." She paused, recalling the sensation. "Suddenly, I smelled roses, looked up, and saw a woman floating above the river. I exclaimed to Grandfather that the lady was very pretty. His gaze followed mine, but he wasn't able to see her."

"I've heard of other young ones who had visions. Were you frightened?" William asked.

Katherine smiled. "Not at all. I asked Grandfather if she was a ghost. He said he didn't think so. Ghosts were stuck, while spirits were free."

"Very impressive." William nodded. "What other types of visions have you had?"

"One in particular." Katherine fidgeted. "You might consider it silly."

"No one's dreams are absurd." He looked at her kindly, and she felt she could tell him anything.

"Ever since I was a child, I've continued to dream of a city with white buildings on a hill in a golden land on a sundown sea. A place where people from all countries would live and children would learn to be true, strong, and noble." She stood up and put her hands on the back of the chair. "Could it be the school Madame Blavatsky forecast?"

"Quite possibly! Tell me more."

"I thought it was a fairy dream until I attended an abolitionist reception and heard Fremont boast about his Mexican-American War exploits in California."

William interrupted, "*The* General Fremont?"

"The very one." The American explorer of the West, Senator, Governor of California, and Civil War general. "Later that afternoon I asked him if he'd seen the western ocean."

"He answered in the affirmative, and when I told him about my vision, his eyes opened wide, and he laughed. 'Golden hills, cliffs, sea? Heck, that sounds like the entire coast. One location though, stands out to me. Point Loma, a peninsula that juts into the Pacific and protects a large harbor in San Diego, the lowermost California town.'"

She smiled at William. "With that conversation, my hopes began to rise at the possibility."

William said, "I believe this premonition is your destiny and one reason Madame Blavatsky insisted I move back to New York. She's esoterically brought us together."

That sounded a bit much, but she asked, "When can I meet her?"

"She lives in London. I'll write her about you tonight. She'll be pleased. This is the spirits working to make the world better. Your revelation reassures me it might truly be possible."

Could he be trying to take advantage of Katherine? Could she trust him?

He reached under the stack of papers. "In fact, I want to—" He paused, then shook his head. "Never mind. We'll save it for another day."

She needed to get out into the fresh air and looked at her watch. "Philo should be home soon. I'd better go."

"How about tomorrow night?" William asked. "We have much more to talk about."

She pulled a flyer from her purse and handed it to him. "I have a mission benefit then with musical offerings and readings. Perhaps you'll come."

Chapter Eleven

Katherine sat in the wings at the Knights of Columbus Hall and checked her watch. Fifteen minutes past time to begin and Philo hadn't arrived yet. He was supposed to be up first, and she needed to make a snap decision. The choir ready behind the curtain, she beckoned Grace over. "Have the singers exit and prepare the orchestra to go on."

Grace nodded and scurried the choir offstage as the musicians stumbled around setting up their chairs and instruments. Katherine leaned forward and peeked into the restive crowd. Prior to the blizzard these Thursday benefits stretched to only half-capacity. Even on this warm evening, paying twenty-five cents apiece, doctors, clergymen, lawyers, actors, artists, and business managers, as well as elite society, filled the auditorium. Probably not to support the Do-Good Mission or listen to the music, but in hopes of receiving messages from the beyond. After disasters such as the storm, where many had died, people were drawn to mediumship.

When out of sorts, she had difficulty discerning spiritual communications. She waved a fan to cool herself, closed her eyes, and tried to focus. She was tempted to skip readings altogether, but the entrance fee alone wouldn't cover mission expenses, and potential donors would be disappointed. At least she hadn't used precious funds to print programs. She'd make changes, and none would be the wiser.

She stood, pulled back her shoulders, and brushed down her purple gown chosen because the long lines made her short stature appear taller and made a dramatic entrance. Center stage, she raised her arms until the audience quieted down. Yes, she knew how to get a crowd's attention.

"Ladies and gentlemen!" She gracefully lowered her arms and scanned the room but didn't see Philo or William. "Thank you for supporting the Do-Good Mission." The audience applauded, and a few patrons nodded. "I'm grateful for your donations to provide much-needed support and sustenance to so many. Sit back and enjoy the selections we've chosen to entertain you this evening. First, Grace Gergen on the French horn, accompanied by members of the New York Orchestra, will play Mendelssohn's overture to *A Midsummer Night's Dream.*"

As the curtains opened, Katherine escaped offstage and sat back down. Next, she planned to recite Titania's monologue. She studied her watch. The orchestration and dramatic presentation, always crowd pleasers, would take up at least fifteen minutes. Philo would certainly arrive by then.

As she listened, her time treading the boards in her favorite play floated back to her. Without those years, she'd never have experienced the fulfillment of theatrical applause and the beauty and power of the arts. Back in the States, donors often asked how she'd learned to manage benefits so adroitly. She laughed it off as a gift from God. If New York Society learned she'd performed onstage, she'd become persona non grata. Actresses were considered the filth of the earth. She'd love to direct a play someday, but for a woman that would be impossible too.

The music subsided, and there was still no sign of Philo. The crowd applauded as the curtains closed. She put her hand on Grace's shoulder as she exited with her horn. "Well done! I'm going on with the monologue. If Philo hasn't arrived, notify Sylvester he'll be singing the solo next."

Grace frowned. "Are you sure? His pitch isn't dependable."

"Do we have a choice?" Katherine scurried on stage. "Let's give the musicians another round of applause." The conductor and orchestra joined her for another bow and then exited. She opened her mouth to recite Titania's monologue but froze when she spotted William standing in the back of the room with a smile on his face. With a sunflower blue ascot beneath his dark suit, he was striking. She smiled back at him.

Instantly, she shifted plans and said, "I'd like to share with you a special piece about another fairy place. 'The Laurels' by John Greenleaf Whittier."

"*From these rocks—*" Comforted to see William mouth the words with her, she continued to recite the poem, pulled her gaze from his, and kept her voice steady and full until the end.

While the audience clapped, the giant doors at the back of the room opened, and Philo, hat askew, staggered inside singing. She couldn't hear the lyrics, but by the grimaces on a few faces in the back, the words must have been lewd. He baltered farther down the aisle until William and a burly man grabbed each of Philo's arms and pulled him outside, kicking and shrieking.

Katherine struck a pose as if nothing out of the ordinary had occurred, then stepped downstage and raised her arms for silence. "The Men's Chorus will now entertain you." The curtains remained closed, and she imagined the singers' surprised faces as they panicked that Philo hadn't joined them. She yelled the cue again and added, "Sylvester Smith will sing the solo."

She hurried into the wings as the curtains opened and the chorus began to sing. Without Philo, "America" didn't have much vitality. She winced when Sylvester hit "The Star-Spangled Banner" high note noticeably off-key, put her hands on her head, and peeked out at the audience. This wasn't what they'd paid for, and many in the crowd fidgeted. She'd forgo the next three songs and skip to the finale.

Katherine coaxed the young lady waiting beside her, costumed in a white gown with a crown on her head and a torch in her hand, to march onstage. The confused singers froze as she posed in front of them, like the statue in the harbor that had recently been gifted to the United States by France. Her crown fell to the floor as the chorus began to sing *God Bless America*, then Katherine motioned for the curtains to close.

Off-kilter, Katherine, who wasn't up to mediumship readings, reentered the stage. "Now I'll recite Titania's soliloquy from A *Midsummer Night's Dream.*" She summoned her anger at Philo to catapult her ire at Oberon.

"These are the forgeries of jealousy:

And never, since the middle summer's spring,

Met we on hill, in dale, forest, or mead,"

A man in the front row scraped back his chair. Others joined him and stomped out too.

"By paved fountain or by rushy brook,

Or in the beached margent of the sea—"

A woman in widow's weeds stood and yelled, "I want to hear from my Johnny."

Another woman's plaintive voice moaned, "I want a message from my baby."

Katherine kept going until a skinny man called, "My wife has words for me tonight. I can feel it." Others now called for loved one's messages. William had returned and from the back of the room stared at her with wide-open eyes.

She had to do readings, or the night would be a total failure. She solemnly stepped farther downstage and waited for the auditorium to hush. "Thank you for your interest in hearing from the spirit world," she said and nodded to the wings. Men carried out a table and set it in front of her. Grace placed a bowl of rose water atop it. Katherine dramatically removed her gloves, washed her hands for purification, and dried them on the towel Grace handed her. Grace blindfolded Katherine with a black satin cloth and picked up a tray from the table.

Katherine heard Grace step lightly down the stairs and instructed, "As Mrs. Gergen walks through the hall, remain as quiet as possible and place your items on the tray. We're gathered here to support one another. I'll give messages to as many as I can tonight." Assembly readings were more challenging than private seances. Without time to calm herself, she had no idea if anything would come through. After a few minutes, Grace put the tray on the table and moved upstage.

Katherine held her arms toward the sky and called, "Those in spirit who have healing messages for friends and family draw near." Silence reigned as she waited but nothing came forth. "Recipients, be open and ready," she said. "Spirits will work hard to be here."

Sharp voices audible only to her clamored for her attention. Audience members began to talk on top of the spirits. Overwhelmed, she couldn't concentrate. "I can't—please wait." She raised her voice, "I must have quiet." Slowly the room grew silent.

She held her stance firmly on the floor, opened her heart, and waited. After a while, her body began to vibrate with the power of a bright light within her. She waved above the tray until her hands trembled to indicate which item to select first. She picked up a handkerchief. The clamoring voices died down. Finally, a visage neared, and she said, "I've a red-headed, small in stature, mustached man. Does this mean anything to anyone?"

The room stayed silent. Katherine continued, "An olive or maybe someone named Olive. Do we have an Olive here?" There was still no reply. She waited for more information from this spirit, but nothing arose. She was failing.

She put the handkerchief aside, waved her hands again, and picked up a ribbon. "I have a woman's energy here. She's wearing a cameo on a velvet ribbon around her neck. If this means anything to you, stand."

Katherine heard chairs scrape along the floor. "I smell roses."

A woman yelled. "I'm Roselyn. My mother called me Rose."

Katherine asked, "What color is the cameo?"

"Pink."

"Everyone else, please sit down."

Katherine spoke rapidly, "Rose your mother wants you to know she loves you and that you were a wonderful daughter. She forgives your elopement. She wishes you well, wants you to have a good marriage with many children."

Rose snuffled. "I've mourned her death for five years and thought it was my fault."

Katherine held up a finger, raised her head, and listened. "It had nothing to do with you. She says her sadness of living without your father overpowered her. They are together now, watching over you."

Katherine heard Rose sob as she sat back down. Grace helped Katherine wash and dry her hands again. A lace remnant was chosen. She shifted her head high again and fought to discern a voice. "I hear a soprano singing

'Brahms's Lullaby.'" Several people stood. Katherine continued. "I have a young girl, about six or seven, here in a red rocking chair. Braided pigtails hang down her shoulders. She smiles and waves hello."

A woman called from the audience, "That's my Sally. She died three years ago."

"No, it's my Rachel."

"Did you have a puppy?" Katherine asked.

The women yelled simultaneously, "Yes!"

"What kind?"

"Great Dane."

"A Dalmatian."

"Thank you. You may both sit." Katherine asked, "Did anyone else have a girl with a puppy?" She saw the letter *L*.

"We had a beagle and lost a little girl." Katherine recognized the voice of Mr. Gergen, Grace's husband.

"What was her name?"

"Sophie."

"The puppy's?"

"Lucy."

Katherine nodded. "Sophie has a message for you. She says, 'I love you, Papa and Mama. Lucy is here with me, and we are both always with you.'"

Katherine heard a gasp from the wings and now understood why Grace often seemed downhearted. Why hadn't she ever told her she'd lost a child or asked for a reading?

Next Katherine picked up a cravat and reflected inward to designate another soul. "I've a young man in a uniform with slicked back hair, grizzly mustache, and beard."

Katherine paused. "He says he has a message for Mary. Is there a Mary here?"

A woman shouted, "I'm Mary. My husband, Billy, was lost in the War Between the States."

"I see an ivory hairbrush with a mirror to match. Do these things mean anything to you, Mary?" Katherine asked.

"Why, yes." Mary gasped. "My husband gave them to me for our first wedding anniversary, right before he left."

"I believe this is your husband. He asks you to forgive him."

"For what?"

Katherine learned he'd deserted the army. Too ashamed to return to Mary, he'd headed out west. After a few months, he missed her dearly and started back to her. The stagecoach had an accident, and he perished. Katherine chose not to convey all that information because it wouldn't help Mary heal her grief and instead asked, "Spirit, do you have another message for Mary?" Katherine listened intently, then relayed, "He lays petals at your feet. Light a white candle for him." Katherine heard Mary weep as she sat back down.

Katherine did two more readings, then the spirits raised their voices and demanded her attention. Overwrought, she was forced to conclude the session and raised her arms. "Spirits, we accept these gifts."

"Thank you all for your excellent attention. If you didn't have a loved one come through, know the spirit of those who have departed are with you. Those who did receive a message will help send positive energy to them." Grace removed the blindfold, and Katherine blinked to adjust her eyes to the light. Many pieces remained on the tray. Audible sighs of regret echoed in the room. Usually, she kept going until most prompts were held. Disappointed in herself, she knew few would donate tonight.

Exhausted, she dragged herself offstage and nearly collapsed into William's arms. Philo was nowhere in sight.

"Where is he?" she asked.

William whispered, "I sent him home in my carriage." He pulled a handwritten card from his jacket pocket and handed it to her. "Please go out there and read this to introduce me."

"What?" She just wanted to go home and crawl into bed.

He gently turned her back toward the stage and said, "Go now."

She reluctantly returned and motioned those starting to leave to sit back down. After the audience resettled, she read from the card. "Mr. William Q. Judge, New York's Masonic Lodge bursar and head of the American Theosophical Society, has a surprise for us."

William strode onstage to a smattering of applause, and Katherine began to exit but he called, "Mrs. Tingley, stay here with us."

With anticipation, she retraced her steps and stood beside him. "How many of you have visited the Do-Good Mission?" he asked the audience. Only a few raised their hands.

Katherine admired William's deep voice and handsome visage as he spoke. "I've been there and encourage you to go too. Your hearts will break at the poverty, but you'll be impressed with Mrs. Tingley and her volunteers as they boldly feed, clothe, and nurture the needy." He pulled an envelope from his pocket. "In fact, the Masonic Lodge has been so enamored that I'm delighted to donate on their behalf this $250 banknote to Mrs. Tingley for the Do-Good Mission."

Astonished, she accepted the envelope, resisted the urge to hug him and said, "We are so appreciative. It'll help us provide services for at least another month."

The audience applauded. William said, "Did you hear? Another month to feed hundreds. Let's try to make it two! Who among you will open your hearts and pockets and help match this sum?" William's far-gazing eyes landed on a gentleman in a dapper suit and tie.

The man stood and raised his hand. "I will!"

"God bless you. Who else will join him?" William scanned the crowd.

"Here!" A lady in an ostrich-feather turban waved. Dr. Gertie van Pelt and even Mr. Thomas, the tenement building's landlord, joined in the fray until five more people had pledged to donate to the cause.

Chapter Twelve

Before dusk a few days after the benefit, Katherine rushed home from the mission for William's visit. She tended to Spots, stepped out of the constrictive corset, and donned her floor-length silk kimono embellished with purple chrysanthemums. She started to take her hair down, reconsidered, and left it piled up instead. Even though William could never be more than a friend, she desired to look her best. With his kind heart, peaceful ways, and loving spirit, she wondered how different her life would have been if one of her husbands had been more like him.

Spots barked and ran down the hall as the front knocker rapped.

"Quiet," Katherine scolded as she opened the door.

William handed Katherine his briefcase and bent down for Spots to sniff his hand. "I remember you," he said and scooped the puppy up in his arms.

"Don't! You'll get hair all over you." Philo didn't let Spots near him when he was cleaned up.

"Doesn't matter." William scratched the puppy behind the ears, and Katherine led him to the parlor. He sat in a velvet chair and settled Spots on his lap. "Where's Philo?"

She put down his briefcase and sat on a settee across from him. "At choir practice. Although after the humiliation the other night, I wouldn't be surprised if they asked him to leave the group. Thank you for waylaying him from making a further scene."

She cut slices of pound cake, put them on plates, and filled cups with tea, admiring Cora's Haviland dishes. The ones with violets.

William's eyes softened. "How long has his alcohol-induced behavior been going on?"

"I'm not sure. Maybe before the blizzard." In embarrassment, she looked down at her hands. "When we married, he assured me he never drank."

"Do you want me to have a word with him?"

"No." She sighed. "I spoke with him, and he promised to stop." She changed the subject. "Thank you for the generous donation and encouraging others to give as well."

"It was the least I could do. You're the one who does so much under such dire circumstances. I was also impressed by your mediumship powers. Philo mentioned them, but I had no idea of their strength."

"I just repeat what I'm called to say." She sipped her tea and put down her cup.

"Have you tried other occult practices?" he asked.

"I attempted table tipping, tarot cards, palm reading, numerology. None were for me."

In Europe, Andre, the traveling show director, had encouraged her to be more histrionic with her readings. So, she'd emulated the old gypsy fortuneteller whose caravan had camped down the road from the Laurels. Katherine had donned a headscarf, ruffled clothing, a paisley shawl, and loads of jewelry. She'd even imitated the woman's Hungarian accent, peered into hands, gazed into crystal balls, and flicked over cards. The props only distracted her. However, when she held items once used by departed loved ones, her messages strengthened. In the end, Andre had suggested flowing gowns and a blindfold to add mystique. She found it helped her concentrate better too.

"I don't like my readings to be referred to as an act. The spirits are truly communicating with me."

"I didn't suggest otherwise. I believe you're a true medium." William squinted and put his hands over his eyes. "Would you mind turning off the gaslights? They can aggravate my headaches."

"Certainly." She stood and walked across the room. "I'm sorry you still aren't well."

"It's just a precaution. Candles are fine."

She busied herself with igniting a few wicks and started toward her chair.

"Sit closer so I can see you more clearly," he suggested.

She moved a dining room chair to face him.

"That's better." He put his hands on his thighs. "I have something very important to discuss with you. You demonstrated at the benefit you have unique skills. The power to heal many and improve the world, but you have obstacles in your way keeping you from following the path put before you."

"I'm following my path," she bristled. "Don't I render considerable aid to those in need?"

"Yes. You're doing much now. However, I feel you're destined for greater things." Candlelight flickered off his serious face as he gazed at her.

"What are you referring to?"

"Like at the benefit. I'm sure I can help you hone skills when connecting with spirits."

How did he know she'd had a difficult time that night? Was it obvious to everyone?

"I'm inviting you to be my chela," he said.

"What?" She'd never heard of such a thing.

"A disciple of Theosophy. In the occult sphere there are three stages." He counted on his fingers. "The highest are the mahatmas or masters, great souls who live on earth and have obtained perfect wisdom. Adepts who understand the deeper mysteries in nature. And chela, the adept's pupils, who have dedicated their lives to Theosophy."

"Which are you?" she asked.

"I'm an adept."

She thought he'd be a master. "What might it entail?"

"The first need of a student is to learn how to use your mind."

She raised her voice. "Sir, are you saying I don't know how to think?"

Spots wiggled. William set him on the floor, and he curled up in a ball at her feet.

"Not at all." He laughed. "In this process, you'd learn about karma and intuition, and acquire more knowledge of the occult, such as eternal life and divine love."

She listened carefully as he continued, "The first step in occultism is the practice of unselfishness. All work for humanity should be performed without thought of self-image or monetary gains. I believe you already do this."

She wished she could say none of the funds she'd earned through mediumship had ever gone into her pocket. If she gave that up, and with Philo unemployed, they really would be destitute. "How does one become a chela?"

"You'd receive a series of questions to ponder for twenty-one days. If your desire remains firm to commit yourself to serving humanity, you'll take on the course I'll open to you." He told her after that, as an apprentice she'd undergo seven years of probation. She'd begin to study the masters and work toward spiritual enlightenment for all humankind in and through the Theosophical Society and in all other modes and planes as best she could. At some point, she may or may not become an adept.

"But I'm a woman."

"All I say of men applies equally to women. We don't discriminate. Remember our founder, Madame Blavatsky, is a woman."

Overwhelmed, Katherine shifted in her chair. "I'm too busy for that type of thing, with my household responsibilities and the Do-Good."

"Are you too busy to fulfill your highest destiny?" He said softly, "The Creator has given you great gifts. With your clairvoyant and mediumship skills you have much promise for the good of all mankind."

"Pish-posh. That's an exaggeration."

He put a hand on his chest and shook his head. "I want to help you harness your skills, raise your confidence, and show you how to help fill the world with brotherly love and peace."

She'd always wanted to do more for the world, but the mission needed her. "Could you just give me more pamphlets? Maybe I could find time to read books later."

"These things cannot be learned by reading. Only guidance from a trained seer like me can show you the secrets of the masters."

"Aren't they long gone?"

"They are still with us, highly evolved, both in terms of advanced moral development and intellectual attainment. Through many years of training, they have long life spans, supernatural powers, and the ability to instantly project their soul out of their bodies to other locations. They preserve the world's ancient spiritual knowledge and represent the Great Lodge, which watches over humanity and guides its evolution. Some live high in the Himalayan mountains and are the source of many of Madame Blavatsky's published writings. Other masters were biblical figures like Abraham, Moses, Solomon, and Jesus, ancient religious figures like Buddha, Confucius, and Lao Tzu, and individuals like Alessandro Cagliostro and Franz Mesmer."

As much as she wished it possible, it sounded too outlandish to be true. She wanted to say so but held her tongue. "What if I fail?" she asked.

"These are the words of the masters: He who does what he can and all that he can, and all that you know how to do, does enough for us. If at any time you cannot work for an unlimited period of unselfish work for humanity, you must resign your chelaship."

"Would you always be there to guide me?"

"You wouldn't always need me. You must be ready to work, wait, and aspire in silence. Your truest adviser is to be found within yourself. Only by experience can you gain its voice."

"It's all too much. I can't undertake something like this now."

"Before you say no, I have something to show you." He lifted a paper from his briefcase.

She accepted it from him. Her face reddened as she studied the portrait sketch. "William, I'm flattered. I believe this looks just like me."

He smiled. "I didn't draw it. Read the corner initials."

She ran her fingers over them. "HPB?"

"Helena Petrovna Blavatsky. Madame Blavatsky," he said.

Confusion permeated Katherine's mind. She heard the door latch open and then Philo's singing echoed from the front hall. "I'll be coming round the mountain—"

She offered William an apologetic wince as Philo stumbled into the room, weaving back and forth. His head shifted to the low candles, then his wife and her visitor. "What have we here?" Philo slurred. "I didn't mean to interrupt anything."

William stepped toward Philo and put a hand on his shoulder. "Good fellow. I'm glad to see you."

"Well, I'm not glad to see you!"

William said, "Katherine, I'll help you get him to his room."

"Katherine, he called you Katherine!" Philo smirked and pulled his fist back, ready to strike William.

She hurried forward and grabbed Philo's elbow. "It's not what you think." She began to lead him toward the hall. He slipped and fell. William led him to his room, and gently laid him on the bed, but he struggled to rise.

"Look at me," William said and stared into Philo's eyes. After a minute, Philo gave him a sloppy grin, sank back on a pillow, and started to snore.

"Do you want me to undress him?" William asked.

"Goodness' sake no." She'd just leave Philo that way.

They returned to the parlor, and William said, "When he wakes, tell him I said he's not to share with anyone I was here alone with you."

She sat next to William on the settee and took a few minutes to catch her breath. Then she picked up the sketch from the tea table. "How did she know what I looked like?"

"Earlier this year in London, while I was helping develop an esoteric course for chelas, she told me to start looking for a special one. A few months later she sent me this sketch."

He flipped over the paper and read aloud the note on the back: "Have you found your chela yet?" William looked at Katherine. "She must have envisioned you."

Shocked, she didn't know what to say. Now it all began to make sense. Him staring at her that first day, his insistence that he needed to speak with her.

"Why did you wait to tell me?"

"I didn't want to scare you off. But time is of the essence. I recommend we get started as soon as possible. As I've told you, my time here on earth is limited. Madame Blavatsky would want you to begin soon as well. We think you're the one."

"The one?"

"When we are both gone, the one to take over the Society. Perhaps even build that great school in the West." He fixed his eyes on hers.

This was too much. She didn't want to offend him by saying no right away. But what if it was possible for her vision to come to fruition? "Leave the questions with me," she said.

He slipped the sketch into his briefcase and handed her another paper. "Contemplate these for twenty-one days. Don't contact me before. It'll feel like a long time, but you'll need it." He took her hands in his. "The stars are aligned for us to be here and now in this slice of time and place. Thanks be to the stars for bringing us together."

A vibrating white light surrounded their bodies, as if they were floating together. Face-to-face with a new type of human nature, an inner consciousness told her William was as perfect as a human being might be and could truly show her how to use her gifts to their fullest to help mankind. She might have finally found her place.

Chapter Thirteen

After William left, Philo snored in the next room like a rusty carriage wheel. Katherine couldn't sleep and moved down to the parlor to think. Was that story of Madame Blavatsky's sketch true? Could Katherine be destined to carry on the Theosophical Society after they were gone? Hope rose in her chest. Was this pathway to establishing her white city on a sundown sea preordained? If so, she needed to do all she could to prepare.

She read over the chela questions and began to ponder her answers. A few were confusing. She rewrote them into her journal and jotted down thoughts:

> *What are my motives for becoming a chela? I'd like to be more like William, calm, kind, and generous of spirit. I want to help humanity and make the world better.*
>
> *Am I willing to work unselfishly for humanity? I feel as if I'm already doing that with the Do-Good Mission. Is it selfish that it makes me feel better too? If I could learn to do even more, that would be marvelous.*
>
> *Am I willing to strive to rid the strength of personal idea?*

This one stumped her. She got up and paced around the room. William had said it meant doing what the spirit desired her to do by using her intuition instead of what she wanted to do. She sat back down and wrote:

With my strong opinions, this will be hard for me. My intuition is strong, but I don't always follow it. Perhaps William will show me the key to this. Is it related to confidence? Am I ready to have a conscious existence separate from that of the body? I already feel separate when lost in the beauty of nature, having premonitions, and doing readings. Is this what's being referred to?

She continued to muse over the questions. The more she thought about them, the more confused she became. She started to read *The Path* pamphlets to further inform her answers. Articles about the Upanishads, ancient theosophical treaties written originally in Sanskrit, the Mystery of Numbers, and Sufism, a religion of the heart, made no sense to her. However, the poems "Inworld" and "Outworld," taken from the *Dial,* an 1842 Transcendentalist magazine edited by Emerson, made her tingle at the beauty of the words and the thought her grandfather might have read them too. Perhaps Theosophy was too intellectual, esoteric, and not for her. She'd never been one to sit still and study.

William had told her she had to wait twenty-one days before seeing him. After a week, though, she had more questions than answers and sent a note telling him she needed to see him as soon as possible. He replied it was necessary for her to fulfill the total twenty-one days. She marked *X*'s in her journal to keep track of the days that ticked by slowly. Another week went by, and she grew more anxious. Insecure and doubting she could become his chela, she sent him another note. He explained again this contemplative time was sacred and she needed to wait another week.

On the twenty-first day, a note arrived informing her that his carriage would pick her up early that evening and take her to his Nassau Street office. Against the heat, she donned a lightweight frock, threw on her hat, and scribbled a note to Philo that she'd be late. He himself had been late most nights anyway.

Waiting, she paced the parlor. If she said no, she feared she might lose William from her life forever. When the clock struck the hour, she waited in the window seat and ran out as the driver pulled up.

When she arrived at the building, dark began to set in, and the heat dissipated. A few patrons were visible though the restaurant's window. The watch and stationery stores were closed. Up the stairs she followed a sweet leathery scent and bizarre bells that chimed and echoed in the halls, growing louder as she climbed.

On the fourth floor, William greeted her in the hallway. "I'm glad your twenty-one days are up." In a white cotton shift suggestive of another land, it appeared his health had greatly improved, and she was glad to see he'd gained weight. She'd missed him so. His eyes filled with adoration, and she wished he'd take her in his arms. He led her into his small office, jam-packed with law books. There was barely room for his desk.

From the next room, the bells rang louder. "What's going on over there?" she asked. "What's that smell?"

"Sandalwood incense. Would you like to see?" He moved two chairs side by side facing the adjoining doors and opened them, indicating for her to sit. "The Buddhists will be finished soon. Let's listen."

Soon the bells ceased, and a mysterious chanting began. *"Om, om, om."* A thin Indian man with a turban wrapped around his head led the group from the front dais. A dozen men sat cross-legged on an Oriental carpet intoning the chant. Their voices grew louder and softer and louder again. She'd never heard anything like it.

William closed his eyes and deeply breathed in and out. She closed hers too, followed the rhythm of his breath, and let the reverberating sounds and sensuous sandalwood scent fill her senses. He joined in the chant, his bass tone deep and masculine. At first self-conscious and unsure whether to join in, after a while she allowed her yearning to take over and she chanted too. Her mezzo intonations fell and rose like ocean waves. Her whole body resonated from the inside out.

One with William, the group, and the world, a calmness like she'd never felt before subsumed her. She flew with fairies at the Laurels above the Merrimac River toward the hill castle. She rode a ferry across a sparkling lake to a miraculous island. She strolled along a cliff on a golden land overlooking an ocean. With no idea how long she'd been chanting, she heard the sound ebb and evaporate, and she opened her eyes. The men silently stood and moved down the hall.

The turbaned man from the dais in a cerulean-blue coat came to their common doorway. The two men put their hands in a prayer position at their chests and bowed. "*Namaste*," they said to each other with soft smiles.

She clasped her hands and said, "*Namaste*." The man bowed back to her and moved down the hall. She didn't want the mellow feeling to end and asked softly, "Who was that?"

"Balarama. He appeared one day and told me a Master sent him to me." William explained many Buddhists lived in America, but there had been no temple and no teacher. Young men had deserted the laws of Buddha or believed the wicked lies against Buddhism told by converting missionaries.

William continued, "The Theosophical Society headquarters had outgrown my legal office." He waved his hand around the tiny room. "I suggested the Society rent the vacant space next door for meetings and share with the Buddhists. It's worked out quite well."

He led her inside. Curly smoke wreaths emitted from an incense pot in front of a Buddha statue lodged in a small niche. "It's kept burning day and night," William told her.

He pointed out the twenty-five shields around the room, one for each of the Theosophical Society branches in America. "The most active ones are in New York, Pennsylvania, Ohio, Iowa, Missouri. California has many lodges too. I'd like to triple the number of lodges within the year."

"How can one man do that?" she asked.

"I've assigned men to give talks throughout America."

Maybe that's what he wanted her to do: give speeches.

He led her to the end of the room. "There's the Theosophical Society seal." He read the motto aloud, '"No religion higher than the truth.' I've intended this room to have a representation of all great religions of the world." William showed her the displayed items and described their origins. Many Indian ones represented Krishna and other gods. Like the intricate designs hand-cut from white paper and placed over colored parchment. A picture of an Egyptian initiation painted with magic colors from pigments Madame Blavatsky had brought back from an ancient stone wall in Tehran. A special Virgin Mary blessed by Pope Leo XIII was so small Katherine wouldn't have noticed it if William hadn't pointed it out. She hadn't known there were that many other religions.

He moved to a table pushed up against the wall. "Here are copies of the *Bhagavad Gita* in English and Sanskrit. You might have read about it in one of the issues I gave you. It formed the basis for Theosophical discussion in America."

William opened a photograph album. "These are Theosophists from around the world."

Katherine flipped through it to a page where a man magically blinked his eyes at her. She jumped back, and William grabbed her elbow with a laugh. "You should feel flattered. He doesn't do that to everyone."

She closed the album and opened it again. The man's eyes didn't move this time. Feeling light-headed, she began to weave. William helped her sit on the carpet. He picked up a shimmery rock from a table, handed it to her, and sat down. "This crystal varies in brilliancy," he said. "It's very powerful. We consult it to learn about society branches. When members of the Inner Circle are present, queer sights and sounds can be heard." He returned it to the table and struck a brass bowl three times, letting the echoes reverberate. He moved to sit facing her. "I'm going to ask you the questions now."

"Should I get my journal from my bag next door?" She started to get up.

"No, just speak from your heart. Let's start with number one: What are your motives for becoming my chela?"

"I've decided I don't have the time." She didn't want to tell him she was afraid she'd fail.

"Could you ask Grace to take over most of the mission responsibilities?" he asked. "The Masons can continue to support it so you can curtail the benefit readings."

"What about Philo?"

"You can't go on like this with his behavior. Either way, it will ruin your reputation. We need to let nothing get in the way of you being accepted as the next leader of the Society."

She asked, "What can I do about him?"

"Let me try to help him mend his ways," William suggested.

"You won't be able to mesmerize him."

He laughed. "I've other means. I'm a lawyer after all. In fact, I even helped Madame Blavatsky in a similar situation. I could send you to Iowa for a while, where it's legal for women to obtain divorces."

Katherine raised her voice. "No!" The last one was too difficult. "Besides, he'd never agree. I'm his bread and butter."

"You're right." He sighed. "Divorce is always a last resort. If Ella approved of my occult interests, how different my life would be. I could never divorce her, though. I took a sacred vow."

"I understand." She really didn't. None of her marriages had been sacred.

"If you study with me, you'll search for your highest calling. With introspection and practice, you'll attain more balance, and your ability to discern better choices will become keener." He smiled. "Let's go back to the questions. Why would you like to become a chela?"

"I told you I can't do that," she said. But she was still unsure. A part of her wanted this commitment. She wanted to feel special. She wanted to believe William. There was nothing she wanted more, and yet . . .

"I do want to learn how to make the world better."

He nodded. "Good. Are you willing to work unselfishly for humanity? Yes, or no?"

"Aren't I already doing that? I've always been compelled to help others. Is it selfish that it makes me feel better too?"

"Just answer yes or no," he said patiently. "As part of the chelaship, we'll discuss all your queries. Yes means you're willing to do your best."

"Okay. Yes."

"Are you willing to strive to rid the strength of personal idea? Yes or no?"

She paused. What was she getting herself into?

"As I've told you, you've so much promise. The stars have aligned." He gazed at her for a few moments.

A calmness soared in her chest. All the reasons she'd told herself it was impossible vanished. There was nothing she wanted more than to be brought into the realm of studying Theosophy with this man. She said, "Yes."

He smiled at her.

She was filled with hope. "When do we begin?"

William's face softened. "We already have."

Chapter Fourteen

Back on Nassau Street a few days later, the scent of sandalwood still permeated the air. Doors wide open, from the office nook Katherine and William chanted along with Balarama and the worshippers. And again, she fell into a sense of peace. As the service ended and the men filed out, echoing bells and the men's energy still pulsed within the sacred space, and the two entered and sat on the carpet.

William said, "As your teacher, I need to know as much as I can about you. Besides the dream of the white city, did you have any other childhood visions?" His blue, blue eyes told her she could tell him anything and he'd listen with an open heart.

"As early as I can remember, I dreamt of woodland nymphs who'd hold my hand while we flew through oaks, pines, and maples at the Laurels by day and into starry skies at night. Of course, those never came true."

"They were true in your mind."

"I'd often encounter a tall man who'd walk the path with me. Sometimes he had a beard, but other times he'd be clean-shaven and wear a turban like Balarama. His eyes were blue." She paused. "In fact, they were just like yours."

William didn't say anything, only smiled and nodded his head.

She waited for his comment. None came, so she asked, "Was it you?"

"Was the man kind or scary?"

"Very kind."

"Then it must have been me." He laughed. "Do you think it was me?"

"I don't know. He told me he loved me and to remember him always. And I have."

"Over time, see what you decide. As you grew, did any other sights come to you?"

She clenched her fists. "At thirteen, I had nightmares with boxes piled high around me, saber-sliced body limbs, cannonballs blowing up fields of horses and soldiers. I can still hear screams."

"That's horrible," William consoled. "The Civil War?"

"Civil," she said, her voice raised. "There was nothing civil about it. Why do people hate each other so much that they have to kill?"

"Did you tell anyone of your premonition?"

She nodded. "I shared it with Grandfather." He'd held her when she cried.

"Not your father?"

"Early on, he forbade me from telling 'devil stories.' I had to learn to hold my tongue. Don't get me wrong, I loved my father; he was quite a wonderful man." That wasn't exactly a lie. He had some fine qualities, handsome and funny when in a good mood. He'd seemed to be a pillar of the community, but as she grew older, she'd learned the truth. Her father had claimed to be the honorable town marshal and Civil War hero, but she knew better. His gambling, bootlegging, violent acts, and questionable accumulation of wealth through illicit activities cannot be shared with anyone.

Her stomach tightened. "I'd a hard time conforming to his wishes. He never understood me and was only concerned with my reputation and potential for a good marriage match. I'm not sure he ever loved me." She'd never told anyone that before.

William frowned. "Why?"

"If he had, he never would have sent me to the convent like he did."

"A convent?"

She nodded. "A few months after the war began, he gathered up a unit of local men and headed south to join the Union army." She remembered how striking he'd looked in his uniform with the big saber at his side. Her brothers, Jimmie and Georgie, had taken turns playing with it and teasing her. "A month after he left, Father procured a mansion in Union-controlled Alexandria and insisted we join him there."

"It's hard to fathom a father would take children so close to the front lines." William shook his head.

"It surprised Grandfather too. He tried to convince Father to let me stay at the Laurels with him, but he refused. There was quite a row. Grandfather, who never said anything malicious to anyone, even called him selfish."

As they said goodbye the next day, her grandfather held her close, slid his watch into her hand, and whispered, "Follow your heart and find that white city someday." He studied her face as if memorizing her features, and that was the last time she'd seen him.

"What did your mother say?"

"She was Father's wife. What could she say? And then there was the incident. After the Second Battle of Bull Run, Father found me in the hospital tent nursing soldiers, and, irate, he sent me away."

"Tell me about it." William gazed at her.

"No." She felt faint as her mind wove into a memory of that day. "I don't feel well."

"Lie down." William helped her roll onto her back. His hand, cool on her skin, made her feel safe. She fell into a deep sleep of remembrance of that day. From an upstairs window, Katherine and Sadie, the family servant, watched ragged, wounded Confederate prisoners being led along the road by Union soldiers on their way to Washington.

Skinny as a cattail, a young soldier collapsed in front of the mansion. Katherine thought her heart would break. How could God let such horrors happen? Hatless, she ran down the stairs and outside toward the boy.

Sadie caught up and dashed in front of her. "Miss Kitty, you know you're forbidden to be out here." The servant's dark skin shone in the afternoon light.

Hoop skirt, crinolines, and all, Katherine evaded Sadie, plopped down in the mud, pulled the boy's head onto her lap, and took his hand. About her age, he blinked his eyes open and gave her a shy smile. "Are you an angel?" he whispered.

"No, I'm just a girl. What's your name?" she asked.

"Johnny."

She tore a scrap from her petticoat and tried to cease the blood oozing from the deep gash on his forehead.

He screamed in pain.

She pulled her hand away. "Sorry, Johnny." She began to sing "Amazing Grace."

He looked at her with terrified eyes and squeezed her hand tightly. After the song ended, his fingers slid from hers and his eyes stared at the sky.

She shook the boy, but his body remained limp.

Sadie placed a hand on her shoulder. "He's gone, Kitty." She closed his eyes and helped Katherine stand. "We'd better go inside."

"We can't leave him here," Katherine hollered. "We need to revere him." She began to recite the psalm she knew so well. "The Lord is my shepherd; I shall not want. He maketh me to lie down in green pastures: he leadeth me beside the still waters. He restoreth my soul—"

When finished, Katherine looked up the road at a hospital tent being erected. Unable to bear the sight of more wounded men streaming by, she said, "Sadie, don't you see their suffering? We must help! Gather as much food as you can carry from the pantry."

After an argument, Sadie acquiesced and hurried into the kitchen. Katherine grabbed the medicine basket, added her father's handkerchiefs to use as bandages, and the two women rushed up the road to the hospital. Inside, the screams and the acrid stench of death met her. She recoiled at the doctor's matter-of-fact attitude as he lopped off limbs as she bound soldiers' wounds, prayed, and sang hymns. Her father found her there hours later, picked her up in his arms, and carried her out. "No respectable young lady can be seen among men like this."

How could a respectable young lady not nurse the wounded? How could God let such horrors happen? At the mansion, her father gave her a sermon on the impropriety of her conduct. In the morning, he broke the news to her. He was shipping her off. At the memory, she started to sob.

"Katherine." William's voice broke into her consciousness, and he touched her shoulder.

She blinked, rolled over, and sat up. "You're here," she said to William, confused.

"Stay within yourself," he said. "Where are you now?"

She closed her eyes as her father's voice boomed as loud as the cannons on the front a few miles away. "I'm putting you on a train north to Montreal. No matter what you say, I'm not changing my mind," he ranted and stormed out of the house.

Katherine plonked on the rug in front of the rocker and put her head in her mother's lap. "I don't want to go. Can't you help me?"

"You're no longer a child. You need to act like a respectable lady. Father has begun to consider possible husbands for you. With a bad reputation, a good match won't be possible."

"But I'm only thirteen!"

"I'm sorry, Kitty. That is the way of life." She put her hand on Katherine's head and said softly, "I can't do anything."

"Don't you love me?" Katherine sobbed.

Tears glistened in her mother's eyes. "I love you more than the world. You know your father makes the decisions. However, I agree with him on this. You'll be safer in Canada."

Katherine looked up. "I was safe!"

"Safe is not being in a tent with half-dressed soldiers in the middle of the night."

Katherine wiped tears on her lace sleeve. "I'll miss you so much, Mama."

Her mother pulled a handkerchief from a pocket and handed it to her. "I'll miss you too, darling." Katherine began to weep again.

William broke her reverie. "That's enough for today. Go home, get some rest, and we'll continue this tomorrow."

At home that night, she crawled in bed with Spots beside her and recalled the memory of standing in front of Villa Maria's ominous stone structure as if she'd been sent to prison. The eerie nun who answered the door held a candle but didn't say a word. She just led Katherine through the mansion filled with tapestries, lush carpets, and ornately carved furniture, up the steep stairs, and down the hall to a small room. The nun handed her the candle and left Katherine there.

The simple room had a mirror atop a dresser, a washstand, a lace-covered screen in a corner, and a rocking chair in another. The open windows overlooked a bountiful garden as dusk fell. She tumbled onto the padded cot, drew up the white chenille bedspread, and blew out the candle. Despite the devastation of being sent so far away, the quiet tranquility soothed her to sleep.

The next day sorrow swept over her. She considered the confinement as penance for upsetting her father and prayed to learn how she could have been a better daughter. After a month, it became apparent there would be no answer to her prayers and daily sittings were a waste of time. She longed to be in the world living a true existence and helping others.

The nuns kept the girls busy from six in the morning until eight thirty at night. Donning multiple skirts the nuns demanded they wear, the students attended mass, studied French, English, penmanship, music, arithmetic, Bible readings, piano lessons, drawing . . . study, study, study. One course called the art of conversation was difficult for her because she knew very little French.

Katherine despised the chapel's cross with blood dripping from Jesus's crown and his stigmatized hands and feet and wondered how anyone could believe this macabre saint should be worshipped. Son of God. Ha! Died for our sins? Bah! In her heart, she knew that wasn't God or even his son up there. She'd felt God's presence when helping those soldiers, working in the convent gardens and orchards, or feeding the chickens and horses. The bounty sustained everyone at the convent. While selling surplus to neighbors, if she sensed a family was especially poor, she slipped them extra.

When meeting a nun in the parlor, the girls stopped and bowed. Special activities like fasts were supposed to be fun, to help them feel closer to God. Katherine cheated and snuck food from the gardens. Her favorite nights were when they studied celestial bodies with the telescope.

She knew she was different from the other girls and kept her visions to herself. Easy because they weren't allowed to talk, even during meals, except during specific times. Strange at first, after a while the quiet allowed her to think more clearly.

Chapter Fifteen

A few days later Ella was out of town, and William suggested they meet at the brownstone. Katherine sat across from him at the desk in his study, and he continued the convent conversation. "Did you miss your family?"

"I sent apology letters to Father and begged to be brought home. He didn't reply. Only Mother and Grandfather wrote to me. I desperately yearned for them."

"What about when you went home to visit?"

"Boarders were allowed to go home for Christmas, Easter, and summer vacation. Mother wrote the journey was too far and Father wanted me to stay at the convent."

"How long were you there?" William asked.

"Four years. Until I was seventeen."

"What was it like when you finally returned home?"

"I didn't."

William frowned. "What do you mean?"

Katherine jumped up and paced back and forth. "Father had arranged for me to marry one of his military cronies. Used to the convent quiet life and safety, I begged the priest to let me stay and take my orders."

"What did he say?" William asked.

She sat down and smoothed her skirt. "He told me God had other plans and I needed to go home and get married. Maybe he knew I didn't believe in all their doctrines and sensed I felt I didn't need a man between God and me but was closest to him in nature."

Terrified of her future, she'd cried the whole way on the train south. As it pulled into Newburyport she'd peeked outside the window and saw her brothers, father, and the old geezer chosen for her waiting on the platform. She'd ducked until the train left the station, with no idea where she was going. Anywhere was better than marrying that man.

"Where did you go?"

With his sympathetic expression, she felt she could tell William anything, but she still held back. "Here and there. Traveled the country in search of others like me." She didn't tell him she sewed neckties to be able to eat, about her marriages, or her time across the pond onstage. "Finally, I landed where the neediest were, New York City."

William sighed. "Katherine, I'm going to be frank with you, I sense something even more horrible happened to you as a child. Memories that have kept you from finding happiness."

"Happiness might not be my lot."

"Everyone has the right to be happy. Did your father ever harm you?"

"Not that I recall. He only had moments of vocal rage."

"Do you want to discover if something occurred through hypnosis?"

"That's never worked on me."

"I've had success when others have not." William waited.

"I don't want to." She folded her hands to keep them from trembling.

He raised his thick eyebrows. "Won't you be brave and let me try?"

She closed her eyes a moment, then opened them. "Okay. It won't work, though."

"Let's face each other." He moved around the desk, turned the partner chair toward her, and she moved hers around too. Knees close, he rang a brass bowl on the desk several times.

"Breathe with me," he said. "Put your hands on your thighs." He rang the bowl again.

She breathed in and out with him as she stared into his dazzling blue eyes.

"My touch on your shoulder will be your cue to go deeper and deeper into a trance." They continued to breathe together. "May I touch you now?"

Her fingers fidgeted. "All right."

His gentle but firm tap brought unexplained tears to her eyes.

"Any sounds you hear around you will help you go deeper into the trance."

Outside the wind blew. The mantle clock ticked. She followed the sound of his melodic Irish accent. Her eyes began to grow heavy and closed. As if blindfolded, no matter how hard she tried, she couldn't open them. Soon the blackness turned to a swirling kaleidoscope of colors.

"My voice follows you wherever you go," he said. "Which allows you to hear my voice and the meaning behind the words. Relax your arms at your sides; feel the chair beneath you."

Her arms fell. She couldn't move them, as if they were bound to her sides.

"You're in a hypnosis state. The next time you choose to go into hypnosis, it will be easier than ever before. You're an excellent subject. You can look forward to all the positive changes it will bring into your life. Allow yourself to relax more and more with each breath."

He touched her shoulder again. "You're an extraordinary woman filled with love for others. You make their lives better. As you go deeper and deeper into a comfortable trance, you'll become more relaxed. You're safe."

She surrendered to the trance and imagined a circle of swords surrounding her body, shielding her with protection.

"As you relax more deeply, you're in a sunny spot with a serene view of nature. There's a breeze against your skin and the colors of water."

She found herself sitting above the Merrimac River at the Laurels.

"Smell the air deeply. Relax while you enjoy the most exquisite trance ever. Now you're in your childhood home."

He paused. "Are you there?"

She nodded. "Yes, at the dining table."

"What do you hear and smell?"

"Dishes rattling in the kitchen. Coffee brewing, bread baking, bacon frying," she said.

"Who's at the table with you?"

She swallowed. "Father, Mama, Jimmie, and Georgie." Her brothers' wheat-colored hair was the opposite of her own dark curls.

"Where's your grandfather?"

"Not here." Katherine shook her head.

Again, William touched her shoulder. "Float deeper into the reverie back to that morning."

Katherine saw the scene unfold before her as Sadie came through the swinging door with a serving tray.

"Lady Susan," Sadie said, placing a tray in front of Katherine's mother; then she served the rest of the family.

Father set down his newspaper. Katherine picked up her fork and dove into the eggs.

"Napkin," her mother scolded.

"Sorry." Katherine obeyed.

Her brothers laughed at her and jammed pieces of bacon into their mouths, teasing her as if sticking out their tongues.

Katherine ignored them, nibbled a bite of eggs, and swallowed. "Jimmie, don't climb Shady Fellow anymore," she said.

"What are you talking about?" he asked.

"You'll fall and break your arm."

"Don't be ridiculous," he spat.

Father looked up from his plate. "What's this?"

Jimmie laughed. "Katherine said I'll break my arm if I climb the giant oak."

Her mother looked at Katherine with pleading eyes and put a finger to her lips.

Father frowned. "Remember you're forbidden from lying."

"It's true." Katherine lifted her chin and looked at Jimmie. "Don't climb him."

"Katherine Augusta Wescott!" Her father raised his voice and hit the table.

"I saw it!" Katherine couldn't help herself.

"In a dream? Dreams aren't real," Georgie scoffed.

"Sometimes they are. Mama, tell him." Her mother knew these stories could be real. Like the time the puppy fell into the fire and when the storm blew over the windmill.

"Just in case, you'd better not climb him." Katherine's lower lip quivered. She didn't want her brother to get hurt.

Father jumped up. "You've been warned!"

Mama rushed around the table and put her hand on her husband's arm. He shook it off, grabbed the Holy Bible from the sideboard, slammed it in front of him, and flipped to the front page filled with handwriting. "Come, Katherine. Find your name."

Katherine crept over to him and with a shaky finger pointed to the "K" for Katherine underneath her brothers' names.

Her father yelled, "If you continue to be such a wicked girl, I'll scribble your name from our Bible as if you never existed."

"I don't want to be in your stupid book anyway," she cried and tried to run behind her mother.

Father grabbed her shoulders. "Tell Jimmie he won't fall from the tree."

"But I saw it."

Her brothers jeered at her as Father shook her over and over again as he repeated what he wanted her to say. She refused because he'd always told her never to lie.

He turned to another page. "Look." He pointed out the clawed devil with scary eyes, horns, and batwings. "You're like Beelzebub," her father scolded.

Sobbing, Katherine squeezed her eyes together and put her hands over her ears. She'd tried to control her visions so Papa wouldn't be so angry, but they returned again and again: glimpses of her brother falling from Shady Fellow, the fairies who played Ring Around the Rosie with her, the man with the kind blue eyes. It was sometimes hard to know which ones were real on earth and which ones were not.

Grandfather had often assured her they were gifts from God, like the shiny stones found on the path, the poems their friend Greenleaf wrote, and their love for each other. "Use your gifts for good and to make the world a better place," he'd told her.

How could she be a devil? She was just a girl. She sobbed uncontrollably. William's voice cut through the pain, and he clasped her shoulder. "I'm going to count from one to three, and when I reach three, you'll open your eyes refreshed and relaxed. Come back more and more with each breath."

His gentle voice commanded, "One, two, three. You're back safe in your chair. Let the scene simply fade away as if you're watching from a distance."

Her shoulders dropped, and she felt the chair underneath her. "I'm sorry. It seems I lost control." She wiped her eyes with the handkerchief William handed her.

"No need to apologize." He poured a glass of water and waited for her tears to subside. "Would you like to tell me what happened?"

She sipped the water and waited for the edges of her emotions to ebb. "It was horrible."

"Maybe it will help to share."

"I just can't." Tears ran down her cheeks. "I need to be quiet now."

Then the memory tumbled out like a restless sea. "Father said I was bad and ugly like the devil."

"How did you feel when he said that?"

"Ashamed, scared," Katherine said. "I know it's not true. Sometimes, though, when I see my reflection in a mirror, I see a devil."

"Everyone has a little devil in them, but you're loved and filled with love."

"I want to believe that."

"Living with him must have been harrowing." William put his hand on her back. "Even so, the bonds of his abuse are still with you. I hope someday you'll be able to forgive him so you can live more fully."

"I tried to be a good daughter. Why couldn't he love me?"

"He loved you in his way."

She wished William would hold her close while she wept. But he did not.

Chapter Sixteen

Two days later Katherine received a note from William: *Last night Philo came to the Masonic Lodge drunk as a wheelbarrow and tried to fight me. He had to be escorted out. To help you reach your potential, your home-life needs to be peaceful. I'll be over tonight to discuss.*

Her face flushed with embarrassment. She should have told him Philo's drinking had accelerated and with it comments that he suspected her of spending inappropriate time with William.

The knocker rapped. Philo yelled, "I'll get it!" He hurried to the door, opened it, and shook William's hand. Spots shot through the threshold, jumped on William's legs, and barked a greeting.

William picked up the puppy and followed Philo to the parlor, where lanterns and candlelight cast shadows against the turquoise walls. As soon as they sat at the oval table, Philo slid a pile of patent applications to William. "Here are a few of my new inventions."

Katherine regretted she hadn't told Philo there was something serious to discuss, but she hadn't had the courage. "Please let William have some tea first," Katherine scolded as she poured and served.

"That's okay." William handed Spots to Katherine and slowly studied the stack. "Very interesting," he said.

She scratched Spots behind the ears and sensed William was preparing for the difficult conversation ahead. As William glanced through the stack again, Philo fiddled with the striped ascot around his neck and raised his eyebrows at her.

William placed one on top and smiled at Philo. "You've been blessed with a keen mind."

"Yes, I know," Philo cut in. "Thus far I have two patents. I'd like to apply for more. If only I had the funds." He sighed.

That wasn't subtle.

"I understand." William nodded. "This one intrigues me." He held up the egg scrambler sketch.

"That's one of Katherine's favorites too. It's handy all right! Do you see the handles?" Philo circled his fingers. "No one has ever thought of that before." He stood, took the paper from William, and pointed to the detailed drawing. "As you can see, it has gears, nuts, and bolts. It can also whip cream."

Oh, dear God. Won't he ever stop? Katherine grew less and less patient with Philo's foolishness. She put wiggly Spots on the ground.

William set the pile aside and listened as Philo began to read, "This invention has for its object to provide a culinary implement adapted for general use which shall be simple and inexpensive to produce—"

William held up his hand. "I'll consider it."

"You won't be sorry!"

"However, we have another matter to discuss," William continued. "Katherine has been unhappy."

"You have?" Philo gaped at her and shifted in his chair.

"Katherine, enlighten your husband," William said.

She didn't realize she'd need to speak. She thought William would do the talking. She took a breath and started in. "I feel betrayed. When we married, you told me you were employed at the steamship company."

"They let me go." Philo looked down.

"Why?" William asked.

"I'm not sure."

"I can only imagine," Katherine said. "You won't search for another job, and we need the money. What if Cora asks us to move out?"

"I'll start looking."

"You told me you admired my humanitarian projects and would help with household chores so I'd have time for them."

"We've been through this. I've assisted more since then."

"Yes, off and on. Nothing I can depend on."

"I'm sorry." Philo spoke slowly. "I'm just so miserable too is all. I thought if we wed some of your goodness would rub off on me." He looked at Katherine. "Obviously, it hasn't."

She was astounded. She'd never seen this side of him.

Philo picked up Spots, who had been pawing under the table, and cuddled him. "I promise I'll do better."

"I'm glad to hear that," William said. "I'd like to help. Will you let me?"

She hoped he didn't plan to hypnotize him. With Philo's temperament, William would never be able to put him under.

"Maybe." Philo held Spots tighter.

"There's something else. Your late nights and public displays of drunkenness."

"Poppycock!" Philo frowned, put Spots on the ground, and slumped in his chair. He folded his arms and pouted like a child. "I'm just having a little fun is all."

William said gently, "You've embarrassed Katherine. Don't you see that kind of fun hurts others?"

Philo shrugged. "What's the big deal?"

"Your wife is destined—" William paused. "Do you want to keep her from making the world a better place?"

"What does that mean?" Philo's eyes opened wide.

"She'll be studying with me to hone her gifts. We'll need time together, and I want you to give us the space to do so."

Her deepest desire was to spend as much time with William as possible. In her adult life, he was the only man who'd filled her with love, hope, and possibilities.

Philo laughed. "That's downright peculiar. You just want to continue your hanky-panky."

William shook his head slowly. "There's no affair. Our relationship is on a sacred plane. I'm her teacher, and she is my student."

Philo squinted his eyes. "Humph!"

"You know me to be a noble married man. Do you truly believe I'd break my vows with a friend's wife?"

Philo sat up straight. "Are we truly friends?"

William was always so kind to Philo. He continued, "Of course. We're Masonic brothers too. I'm sure you've kept the handshake secret."

"Yes!"

"Can you keep another secret?" William asked.

Her husband nodded and put a finger on his lips.

"Katherine is destined to someday take over the Theosophical Society here in America."

He hadn't mentioned it since the day he showed her Madame Blavatsky's sketch. Katherine had assumed he didn't really believe it.

"Don't you want to help her do that? Wouldn't that make you proud?"

Philo stared at her in what could be disbelief, disgust, or some combination of the two.

"What is it you want from me? She has duties to me."

"Don't you think this is more important?"

"Maybe." Philo shrugged.

William said, "I care about you and want you to refrain from drinking."

"I can stop anytime."

"Really?" Katherine scoffed.

William eyed her.

Philo asked, "What'll you do for me if I agree?"

"What is it you most desire in the world?"

"I don't know."

"What about your inventions?" Katherine suggested.

"Of course, I want to have enough funds to procure more patents. All my grand ideas are going down the drain."

"Could that be one of the reasons you drink?" William asked.

Katherine had never thought of that possibility.

Philo nodded sheepishly.

"How many inventions do you have ready to go?" William asked.

"Twenty."

William put his hands on his head. "My heavens!"

"As you said, I'm very smart."

"Are you smart enough to stop drinking, show respect to your wife and her needs?"

Philo smiled at her. "Of course."

"Shall I draw up a pact between the three of us?"

"What would it say?" Philo frowned.

"How about if you join the straight and narrow, Katherine and I will make sure you have funds for an attorney and patent fees annually for one invention?"

"What? Don't try to sell me a dog! We already have one." Philo pointed to Spots.

William laughed, picked up his quill, and jotted some notes. "We'll also make sure you'll always have a place to live."

"Will we live apart?" Philo's bottom lip quivered. "Is that what you want?" He looked at her.

She shook her head no. She had no idea where William would get the money.

"Philo, after you sign the contract, if you behave yourself, I'll pay for the egg scrambler patent and send in the application myself as your attorney. How does that sound?"

Philo whooped. "You won't be sorry."

Chapter Seventeen

A few days later in his Nassau Street office, William told Katherine, "Don't worry about the funds. I'll have it all arranged." He handed her the contract draft and she read it quietly:

I, Philo Tingley, will:

- *treat my wife, Katherine Tingley, with respect*
- *abstain from imbibing alcohol*

If so, Katherine Tingley and William Q. Judge will:

- *finance funds for one patent attorney and application yearly*
- *provide sustenance and housing for the rest of your days*
- *arrange for necessary incidentals upon request*

She raised her voice. "I can't believe it's come to this. If I'd known how he was, I'd never have married him. He's like a little boy, thinking only of himself and obsessed with tinkering in his playroom. He won't be able to live up to this contract."

"Try to have compassion for him." William folded the document and handed it to her. "If you want to grow, you'll need to transform your doubt into faith. Does he remind you of anyone from your past?" He closed his eyes, and she worried she'd upset him.

The office walls seemed to close in on her. She didn't want to consider

William's question. She only wanted him to judge her self-obsessed husband.

"Anyone?" William asked again. "Sometimes we choose the same kinds of people to have in our lives, over and over."

It dawned on her: her own father had been a drinker too, but she kept it to herself.

"Since you aren't going to divorce, make peace with Philo," William said. "If you don't, you'll never be happy. Have you considered what you have in common?"

"Nothing!" She jumped up, opened the door, and allowed the sandalwood scent to float in from the empty room. "Katherine, please." William's voice remained calm.

"I'm sorry." She sat back down.

"Don't you both want to help make others' lives better?"

"What do you mean?"

"Isn't that one reason he's driven to invent these things?"

A month after they married, she'd realized Philo might just be a fool. It was hard to accept a different version of him, even William's.

"In your journal tonight, open your heart and come up with a list of what you admire about him. Like Madame Blavatsky, you're a strong woman, able to make it through all kinds of travails. Don't doubt your own strength, Katherine. Trust your soul."

"I don't want to live the rest of my life with him."

"If you forgive him, you might not need to."

"What do you mean?"

"If you move to that golden land on the Pacific, would he want to live there too?"

William might not be able to change the past, but it seemed he might have the power to transform the future. "I wish I'd married a man as wonderful as you." She couldn't believe she'd just said that and put her hands on her hot cheeks.

He laughed. "I'm not who you think I am. But I'm who you thought I might be."

What an intriguing riddle.

He continued, "You've shared with me about your childhood; now I'm going to tell you about mine. When you hear it, you'll be relieved you didn't marry someone like me."

"I doubt that." She smiled at him.

"What do you know about reincarnation?" he asked.

"When someone's soul comes back in another body." She'd never quite comprehended it. As a medium, departed souls had communicated with her, but she hadn't considered if any had reincarnated.

"Yes." He nodded. "Reincarnation is when a soul leaves its physical body, swirls into the ether, and usually returns to earth and enters the body of a baby being born. Occasionally, there are exceptions to this."

"I've heard if you've been terrible in a past life, you come back as an animal or even a monster," she said.

"Some from the East think that. Theosophists believe once a human, the soul only returns to a human body."

"What's the difference between karma and reincarnation?" she asked. "I've heard them paired together."

"Karma regulates the cycle of reincarnation. It ensures that an individual's actions in one life affect the circumstances in the next one. The soul bears the impression of every good and bad deed we perform while alive. If the sum of our deeds is positive, we're reborn into a higher level."

"Does it hurt to leave loved ones like that?"

"Most times a soul doesn't have consciousness. It usually vacates its body unaware of the past, present, or even the future. However, there have been rare exceptions when a child retains the astral body and memory of the old personality with knowledge and dexterity."

That was hard to believe. "How do you know that to be true? From the masters?"

"It's from all the way back to the ancients." He closed his eyes for a moment, then opened them and fixed on hers. "I have also experienced it."

Her breath caught in her throat, and she crossed her hands over her heart.

He continued, "I've told you about my childhood illness. Let me tell you more. Throughout my youth memories of another life flooded back to me in waves with vivid dreams that I lived as a rajah in an Indian palace in an earlier time guided by a wandering Brahmin. Over time, back and forth he led my soul with a magnetic light to a Celtic land, into the body of a four-year-old dying child with his family mourning around him."

William sighed. "One day I awoke from a deep sleep and looked out at the doctor and his family through the boy's eyes. I felt his soul slip into the ether and my identity merged with his. I weakly smiled as the stunned doctor took my pulse and said, 'Most marvelous. He has revived. He may live!'"

Was this a miracle, tall tale, or the story of a man who had lost his senses?

William sipped some water. "As my illness continued, I floated between two existences. At times, I was a rajah student of ancient philosophies and at others the boy. Sad and difficult, I couldn't tell which was my reality. When I lived in one time and space, I recalled the other with distant memories. Bedridden for weeks, I lingered in the Irish home. Slowly, my strength regained.

A year later I climbed out of bed into my mother's room and helped myself to her armful of books about magic and started studying things from the beyond. With our large family, no one even noticed. When they did, my parents were shocked to find me perusing those books. They didn't even know I could read."

No wonder Philo had mentioned William was sometimes called the Rajah. "How confusing for you."

"I've learned to cope."

Even though this was an outlandish tale, she remained silent. She stared into his iridescent eyes, and before her he transformed into a clean-shaven Indian man wearing an orange robe and turban. He resembled the tall man who'd walked the path above the Merrimac with her. "It's you! The Rajah."

He grinned at her and transformed back to William Q. Judge with the beard. "Yes. Show your husband this contract. Don't judge a man before he has a chance to change."

She feared Philo was not capable of changing.

That night she journaled William's story of reincarnation. Curious about the exercise he'd given her, she decided to give it a try, picked up her journal, and wrote:

Philo

handsome
dapper dresser
gifted tenor
funny sense of humor
creative in his own way

She also made a list of things she liked about William. It filled a whole page.

Chapter Eighteen

Ella, without malice, greeted Katherine at the brownstone. "Welcome, William's in his study. I'll be back later." She slipped outside and down the steps to the carriage.

A week since their last meeting, Katherine had much she wanted to discuss with him. She hung her coat in his study and said, "Ella's certainly changed her tune." Katherine took her seat across the desk from William.

"I hope someday you two will become friends. I believe you'll need each other."

Katherine doubted that very much. She told him Philo signed the contract, but last night she'd smelled alcohol on his breath.

"Has he done anything to dishonor or embarrass you?" William asked.

"He's been cordial."

"Okay. It's common for someone at this stage in their revitalization to slip now and then. If need be, gently remind him of the contract. Were you able to make the list?"

She nodded.

"Add to it. As time goes by, I'm certain there'll be other attributes you notice. Do you have any questions for me?"

This was her chance to find out what most baffled her. "I wish I understood exactly how mediumship works and where it comes from." She hated to admit she didn't know.

"The true light of mediumship is one of God's wonders. It is through a trinity of spirit, soul, and mind. One who possesses it should use it wisely and feel supremely blessed. Does that make sense to you? Do you feel that way?"

She shook her head. "Sometimes it feels more like a curse instead of a blessing. It's gotten me into trouble countless times."

"Like your father, many cast aside divine wisdom because they believe it comes through an evil instrument. Don't let that deter you. For now, embrace it as an art form given to you by the Creator. There's never been a note of true music created, a line of poetry penned, a harmonious blending of color painted that wasn't the result of mediumship."

Katherine had never thought of it that way. "Sometimes souls appear at the most inopportune times and clamor for my attention. I can't discern one from the other. I've tried to let them all go, then I feel sorry for them and am compelled to respond. If I'm overwhelmed by my life events, I can't receive readings at all, and those attending sessions are disappointed."

William nodded. "To help with those challenges, I'd like to teach you some ancient techniques handed down from the masters."

Other mediums had tried to teach her tricks, but Katherine had instinctively known more than they ever had. She hoped William could help her. "Okay."

"Are you familiar with the chakras?" he asked.

"I've heard of them."

He picked up a crystal from his desk. "When light passes through a prism, it breaks into seven rainbow colors. Each one has a different vibrational energy that affects the body and mind." He moved to her side of the desk, lined up gemstones along the edge, and displayed a chart he'd sketched and water colored. He pointed to the bottom. "Red has the longest wavelength and slowest vibration frequency." He pointed to the top. "And violet the shortest wavelength and fastest frequency." He told her the seven chakras were vortexes of energy that represented consciousness of emotional, physical, intellectual, and spiritual levels. Through them, a person moved through the lower self to the higher self.

"Some of your chakras are blocked," he said softly.

"I'm sorry," she said.

"There's nothing to be sorry about. Most people, especially those who live in the city, have jammed ones."

"How can they be opened?"

"Mainly through meditation. First we'll focus on where in the body they're located and the corresponding gem associated with each. Let's start with the root chakra." Still standing next to her, he pointed to the ruby crystal, touched the base of his spine, and nodded at her to copy him.

He continued to point out each gemstone and the corresponding chakra on his body: moonstone for sacral, just below the navel; citrine for solar plexus, above the navel; emerald for center of the chest; aquamarine for throat; blue sapphire for between the eyebrows."

He stepped aside and picked up the large purple rock. "You usually wear purple."

"Yes, I'm drawn to it." She didn't feel comfortable in any other color. Her frocks, coats, hats, and gloves were all purple-hued. She'd even had the shoemaker dye her boots and the dressmaker her petticoats deep violet. When she was young, her father had complained purple was garish for a child. Grandfather, though, used to bring her grape jam-colored ribbons and bows and whispered to her, "Live with what you love." Her favorite flowers were purple: delphiniums, hydrangeas, asters, lilacs, and irises.

"I'm not surprised this is your favorite color. Violet is the most powerful color in the rainbow. People drawn to it are unique individuals who are often intuitive and deeply interested in spirituality. Lovers of purple are said to be good judges of character and visionary, with a great need to participate in humanitarian issues."

He handed her the purple crystal she'd held in her lap the first time she'd been to his home. With tenderness, he touched the top of her head with his fingertips. She closed her eyes, and an imaginative purple spiral swirled there, and the scent of lavender filled the air.

He said, "The amethyst represents the crown chakra. It provides healing, protects one from negative energies, calms dreams, and makes one more in tune with the divine." He moved his hand away and she continued to relish the purple sensations.

"Each chakra has other things associated with them: lotus petals, aromas, planets, metals, senses, even musical notes." He handed her the chart and a sheet of paper with more instructions. "It's all right here. Take this home, memorize it, and practice breathing into each chakra. You're on your own for another twenty-one days; by then, you should have grasped it."

Amazed to hear there was a whole world she never knew existed, she thanked him but complained, "How will I survive another twenty-one days without you?"

He laughed. "Just study."

"After the days are up, I look forward to attending a Theosophical meeting."

He grasped her hands in his. "Listen to me carefully. No one is to know about our relationship. We need to keep it secret."

A lump formed in her throat. "Why?"

"There are others who believe they should take over leadership when I'm gone. I need to protect you from those rivals until it's time for the butterfly to safely come out of her cocoon."

Chapter Nineteen

New York autumn began to show her colors as green leaves changed to purple, reds, and pinks carpeting the sidewalks and streets. Six months after the blizzard, Katherine visited the mission with mixed feelings of melancholy and relief that she wasn't needed there as much anymore. Grace ran it smoothly, and many of the volunteers continued to assist.

Even though it had been two weeks since her last meeting with William, she put her energy into studying the chakras and practiced clearing her own. Now that her chakras had begun to open, at the Thursday benefit she felt more connected to the spirits communicating with her during the readings. Philo even arrived on time and sang his solos superbly. She'd added he was an *excellent cook* to his admiration list. He'd taken to fixing most meals, adding an innovative flair to the recipes, such as cinnamon and vanilla to the pancake mix, walnuts in the chicken soup, and lemonade in the tea.

After the three weeks were up, William greeted her warmly in his study. "Sit comfortably, close your eyes, and let's check your chakras."

She shifted in her seat. He guided her through some exercises and said, "Excellent, your chakras are clear, and you're ready for the initiation." He tapped the mallet on the brass bowl's edge, and it rang out. The sound vibrated throughout her body, and William began to chant. She joined in until their echoes died down.

"Stay silent as we invite the five sacred elements in." He told her earth was the first element, placed a bowl of yellow soil in front of her, and asked her to run her fingers through it. She thought she'd feel silly, but instead it brought back tender memories of her childhood at the Laurels when she'd sit on the earth and touch the dirt with her hands.

He poured water into a ceramic bowl on the desk. "The second element is water. Cleanse your hands and arms."

She rolled up her sleeves and rubbed the cool liquid on her limbs. Instead of a chill, she felt warmth.

He lit a candle. "Fire is the third element. Look into the flame."

She concentrated on the flickering candle for a few minutes, and her mind quieted even more.

He ran the tip of a white leaf bundle through the flames and wafted it throughout the room as the scent of sage filled the air. "This represents air and cleanses the space with reverence." He set the bundle in an ocean shell.

"Close your eyes and inhale with me, in and out three times. Open them, look into the flame again, and keep breathing." The dancing glow and sage scent continued to lull her, and she felt rested and protected. "Ether is the fifth element, the clear sky way beyond the clouds. It is a god-like element, and a substance that allows humans to connect to spirituality and intuition."

William slowly swirled the mallet around the brass bowl's rim until the room filled with a fascinating blend of harmonic resonances and rich overtones. "Breathe deeply as you listen to the sounds and notice any sensations that arise in your body."

"Close your eyes and repeat after me: I'm traveling to the upper world to meet a spirit guide."

He struck the bowl. "If you encounter a spirit, ask if they're your guide, and at the end of the session, take a moment to express gratitude."

He repeatedly hit the bowl over and over as vibrations loped through her chakras from bottom to top. The colors changed until she was released from time and space. Like a bird, her essence flew up through gauzy clouds until a bearded man's visage began to materialize. The kind eyes filled with love reminded her of William's. Her senses heightened, she asked, "Are you my spirit guide?"

He nodded. Her breath caught in her throat. This wasn't the gory sculpture that hung above the convent altar to beg for forgiveness, or even the angry one in her family Bible who threw down marketplace tables. She admired the eyes' beauty until clangs rapidly emanated then ceased. She bowed, descended through the clouds, and found herself back in the study in present time and space.

William set down the bowl and smiled at her. "How was it?" he asked.

She held up a finger and sipped from the water glass he gave her. "Confusing. I thought it was Jesus."

With enthusiasm, William clapped his hands. "You're blessed! He's one of the highest masters of wisdom. Many have yearned their whole lives to meet him."

She scowled. "You know how much I hate Christian hypocrisy."

William spoke softly. "Jesus didn't make Christianity. People did."

She'd never thought of it that way. In awe, she asked, "Was it him, you, or just a vision?"

"What's the difference?" William stood. "Write all you've experienced."

"Can't we discuss this more?" She wanted to tell him about the eyes.

"It's late, and I leave for Europe in the morning. I've been called to speak at the Dublin delegation and meet with Madame Blavatsky in London."

Her heart sank. "How long will you be gone?"

"I'm uncertain. Don't feel abandoned. We're cosmically connected. I'll always be with you. Remember, your truest advisor should be sought within yourself. Practice what you've learned. Practice opening your chakras and close them afterwards to seal in the power." He handed her the brass bowl. "Take note of shifts you experience mentally or physically: Are you calmer, lighter, more uplifted? Bow to yourself in acknowledgment of the self-love you have practiced. Try to meet a spirit guide again."

Before William sailed, he had a pile of books delivered to her to study. At least she knew the Holy Bible well. Growing up, each night after supper if her father was home, he'd read a different chapter and orate about it. If he wasn't there, her grandfather or mother would do so. And how different all their interpretations were.

William also sent the Bhagavad Gita, a holy Hindu book, translated from Sanskrit to English in verse form that was hard to understand. Supposedly written by the god Ganesha, as told to him by the sage Veda Vyasa, at least it had beautiful illustrations. Even though William had tried before to give her Madame Blavatsky's big tome, this time he sent volumes one and two, as well as her first book, *Isis Unveiled,* that delved into the mysteries of ancient and modern science and theology. With over a thousand pages, it was so heavy Katherine couldn't even hold it up.

She wanted to please her teacher and tried to comprehend the books, but her mind would wander and, if at bedtime, she'd simply fall asleep. He was an academic, but she wasn't. She hoped he wouldn't be disappointed that she didn't have the mind to grasp that dense material.

However, she practiced opening her chakras and prepared with the five elements. Fear overwhelmed her as she tried to journey. She sent William a cable explaining her dilemma. Two weeks later she received a reply: *Purple, perhaps you need a reason to journey. Next time, if you meet a guide, ask a question.*

That night she placed a question in her heart. Spots lying beside her, she lit sage and hit the brass bowl. After a while the sounds vibrated in her chest; she dropped the mallet onto the quilt and fell into a deep state. She drifted up through the veiled clouds. The spirit appeared again but this time it was a whole figure in an ivory robe, shimmering lights surrounding him. And she asked, "How do I use my gifts to help the world?"

His aura expanded into sunrays pointing out into the universe and beyond. She stood on a pedestal orating to a crowd. The spirit motioned to her to follow him, and she flew behind him to foreign lands and alighted in one above a great ocean. The sound of the sea mingled with orchestral music. Gardens flourished among arched gates, round bungalows, and domed buildings. Babies filled a nursery, and she felt the softness of an infant in her arms. Artists painted landscapes on easels. Across a stage in an ancient amphitheater, she directed actors from many countries in a play.

It seemed like minutes, or it could have been hours, until she thought she heard William say, "It's time to come back to us." She floated through the clouds into her own bed with Spots licking her hand. The following morning, she sent William a detailed letter of her astral journey and imagined him smiling. A deep longing to be with him overpowered her.

Chapter Twenty

January 1889

The morning of William's arrival, snow flurries ceased, and the sun shone through bleak clouds. Katherine couldn't wait a second longer than necessary to see him. She donned her amethyst-colored bonnet and heavy cloak and made her way to the harbor. She waited for the *City of Paris* to pull up at the wharf. He soon strolled down the gangplank in his top hat, holding his walking stick. Her heart beat fast as she pushed through the crowd toward him. When he stepped onto the dock, Ella slipped her arm through his and patted his hand.

Katherine froze; she had no right to be there. She turned and began to hurry away when he called, "Purple! Katherine, is that you?"

Slowly, she pivoted toward him as the married couple drew closer. Ella, in her usual black from head to toe, wore a sable coat. Katherine was distressed to see how the trip had diminished William's health. Dark circles rimmed his eyes, and he'd lost a lot of weight. The look on his face told her more than the words he dared not say; he'd missed her too.

Ella nodded, pulled his arm, and steered him away. Her big bustle caused her coat to poof out like a hassock that had stuck to her bum. He looked at Katherine forlornly. She smiled and gave him a small wave goodbye, then made her way to the mission, where she belonged. No matter how much Katherine meant to William, Ella would always be his wife. He'd connect with Katherine when he had the time. It would probably take days.

However, she was wrong. That afternoon he sent her a message: *Come to the house tomorrow night. We have much to discuss.*

When she arrived, Ella stiffly met her at the door and pointed down the hall with a large book in her arms. Ella had been a teacher when she met William, and he'd told Katherine her keen intellect was one reason he'd married her. How would Katherine confess to him she'd been unable to comprehend those gigantic books he'd sent her? As she entered his study, the toll of his journey was even more apparent. Reclined on a chaise instead of at his desk, he appeared feverish, and she hoped his tropical disease hadn't returned. As he told her about the trip, she so wanted to reach out and touch his face.

He shared that Madame Blavatsky continued to be the organization's Outer Head, Olcott president of the Theosophical Society, and they had appointed William vice president, and as American Section representative all communication should go through him. This concerned Katherine because it would add to his already heavy workload. Madame Blavatsky had also emphasized the masters warned of cyclical changes to come upon the earth in 1897 and 1898. In political, scientific, or physical changes—all combined—to prepare for the new century.

"What does that mean?" Katherine asked.

William replied, "In a transition period, the full cycle of information is not given to a generation that elevates money above all and scoffs at the spiritual view of man and nature."

That answer confused her even more. Did that have anything to do with Madame Blavatsky's prediction that Katherine might be the next Outer Head after William was gone?

Katherine continued to meet with William at his home. His fever abated; however, his stamina was still low. Embarrassed to admit to him her inability to devour the tomes, she returned each book and asked him to describe its substance in his own words. As he verbally condensed the essence, she jotted down notes, increasing her ability to comprehend the information.

After three meetings, she asked, "Have you considered some people may have a hard time understanding these dense books and their concepts?"

"Some people?" He looked at her with a wry smile.

The jig was up. She felt her face redden with embarrassment and sputtered, "I'm sorry. I'm truly interested in these topics. The way they're written is too hard for me to comprehend. When you explain them, they make sense to me."

"Why didn't you tell me when I first got home? No need to apologize. We all acquire knowledge differently."

Her shoulders dropped. "I didn't want you to think badly of me."

He sat up. "You have an astute mind and memory. You're human, aren't you?"

She smiled with relief. "Yes. If I can't understand these books, what about others? Isn't your goal to spread Theosophy around the world?"

He lay back onto the chaise. "What do you suggest?"

"As you told me, Madame Blavatsky herself described your articles in *The Path* as pure Buddha. Why don't you pen a book distilling these important concepts?"

He smiled. "Great idea. Why don't you help me?"

"I'd be honored."

Then and there they came up with chapter headings, and she typed them into his machine: "Theosophy and the Masters," "Cosmos," "Earth Chain," "Constitution of Man," "Astral Body, Passions and Desire," "Reincarnation," "Karma," "Cycles," and "Psychic Phenomenon and Spiritualism."

As the year marched on, they collaborated on his book; the words flowed freely back and forth. Her knowledge widened, her skills honed, and their bond deepened.

Chapter Twenty-One

April 1890

In the first few months of the new year, William's health wavered. Katherine encouraged him to rest but he told her he must do as much as he could before he left the earth. He allowed her to help with more Theosophical business, typing correspondence and delivering messages. Wrapped up in his enthusiasm for her presence, she'd never felt so loved.

On a warm spring afternoon, the carriage delivered her to their home. Ella answered the door and shook her head. Katherine walked down to William's study, where he reclined on his chaise.

"I'm sorry you weren't able to make it to your office today." She gently touched his hand, and he grasped hers.

He'd lost weight over the past few weeks, and dark circles ringed his eyes. "I'll be right as rain by tomorrow."

She sat beside him, still holding his hand, terrified at the thought of losing him forever. "What can I do to help?"

He dropped her hand and coughed. "Visit for a while and listen to my good news. I've received an invitation from King Oscar II to meet with him in Stockholm."

She frowned. "When?"

"I'm boarding a ship in a few days." William smiled wanly.

She raised her voice. "You're in no condition to travel. You must send someone else."

He tried to sit up but fell back onto the chaise. "There's no one I trust to go in my stead."

"Why can't Madame Blavatsky go? She's much closer."

"She's ill too."

"What's the meeting's purpose?" Katherine asked.

"Sweden's recently started a Theosophical branch, and I need to support their efforts. Some citizens are opposed to our efforts. It's to be a clandestine visit."

Katherine blurted out, "Send me!"

"No." He shook his head.

"Why not? Don't you trust me?"

"Of course I do. A woman traveling alone to a foreign country is highly dangerous." He began to cough.

She poured a glass of water and handed it to him. She waited for him to catch his breath. "No one would suspect me to be there on Theosophical business."

"Maybe if you could take Philo?"

"Can you just see him trying to sell an invention to the king?"

William laughed and began coughing again.

"I'll find another companion," she promised. "I want to go." This was a new confidence Katherine had never had around William, a confidence that surprised her.

They argued back and forth until he finally closed his eyes and relented. "Tomorrow I'll send a telegram to Madame Blavatsky and another to Sweden with the changes. The travel particulars and itinerary will be delivered to you."

With Spots as her audience, she pulled her satchel from the armoire and piled clothes on her bed. As if overnight, his pendulous feathered ears and snout had grown longer and his body sturdier.

Philo sauntered into her room and stopped short. "Are you leaving me?"

Since the contract signing, he'd been more fixated on his inventions than ever before. She didn't mind so long as he kept up his side of the bargain. On William's advice, she'd tried to be more compassionate with Philo. It had been a challenge at times; at other times, though, she'd begun to enjoy his company.

She rolled up a scarf and stuck it in her satchel. "No, dear. I'm going to Europe to meet with a king."

"Are you being funny?" he asked.

"I'm going on a secret mission." She raised her eyebrows to tease him.

"Is William going?" Philo tilted his head to the side with a frown.

"No." Katherine explained William was ill and sending her on a trip in his stead.

Spots crawled around the luggage and climbed into her satchel.

"You can't come," she scolded the dog.

"I don't want to go anyway," Philo said.

Katherine stared at him, then shook her head. "Not you. Spots. I'm depending on you to take care of him. Are you up to it?"

"Of course. But you won't be here for me to make breakfast for you."

"I know. But you'll be fine. Please mind your *p*'s and *q*'s."

He saluted her. "Yes, ma'am. I'll also mind my *r, s, t, u,* and *v*'s."

Katherine tried hard to suppress a smile, then burst out laughing.

Chapter Twenty-Two

Katherine arrived in Stockholm as the sunset washed the city in a golden glow. At the hotel she handed over William's reservation documents. After the weeks-long grueling journey, she skipped supper and fell into a restless slumber with dreams of a feather-shaped island amidst a smooth body of water. In the morning she overslept and barely had time to don a purple gown, let alone eat breakfast, before being whisked away for her audience with the king.

Outside of town the carriage drove through a grand avenue inside a park filled with blooming bluebells, roses, and apple trees. Carmine and pink garlands roped low fences around bronze sculptures. Patinaed copper roofs in the distance complemented the brilliant blue sky. She'd been impressed by palaces in her earlier travels, but the baroque Drottningholm Palace was the grandest by far.

Katherine approached the hefty woman in a black lace gown who stood on the steps between the blue-and-gold uniformed sentries. "Countess Wachtmeister?"

The countess frowned. "Yes, who are you?"

"I'm Katherine Tingley from New York," she spoke softly, uncertain how clandestine she should be.

The countess looked confused. "So?"

Katherine had a dreadful feeling in her gut. "Didn't you receive the telegram?"

"Where's William? What telegram?"

"He's ailing." Katherine handed her the just-in-case letter from him.

"What? Madame Blavatsky sent me here from London to greet him." The countess glanced at the note. "This is highly unusual. I doubt His Royal Highness received the telegram and will grant you an audience. We'd better hurry anyway."

"I apologize." Katherine wanted to go back to the hotel and hide. She didn't want to let William down, though. Her stomach growled. She wanted to ask for something to eat but didn't dare.

The countess led Katherine up the steps and through the opulent entrance. Despite the warm weather, she bundled Katherine in a long cloak, pulled up the hood, and said, "To keep you warm against the chilly palace." They traversed tiled hallways and hurried through crowded rooms filled with paintings, photographs, and furnishings.

William had shared that the widowed Countess Wachtmeister's husband had been Minister of Foreign Affairs assigned to Sweden and Norway, and that she'd lived in Sweden off and on for many years. Now she resided in London with Madame Blavatsky as her closest confidant. Katherine wondered if she knew about the sketch William had shown her.

She walked briskly, and Katherine began to perspire and kept up as best she could. She wished she'd worn her walking boots. "Is it much longer?" she asked, out of breath.

"There are 660 rooms. We're only halfway there. Hurry!"

Weary, Katherine continued to follow the countess up more stairs until at last, at the end of another long corridor, she stopped, spoke quietly to a man in royal garb, and handed him William's letter. The man slipped inside, and a few minutes later he returned with a nod. The doors opened wide, and sentries removed the women's cloaks and announced their names. Katherine's heart beat rapidly as she stepped inside. King Oscar II rose from his chair at the far end of the room. This man of royalty was regal even at sixty years old with his mustache and goatee.

The countess bowed her head, and he kissed her hand. "It's wonderful to see you, Connie."

Katherine bowed to the king. He kissed her hand too, sparking a childhood memory. Her father had forbidden her to speak to the intriguing vagabonds who often camped near the Laurels. Katherine had spied a group one day and curiously wandered over to say hello. An old woman with dark hair had lifted Katherine onto a knee and explored her little palm. "A king will kiss your hand, everything you own will transform into gold, and flocks of children will follow you."

The king's kiss, the realization that part of the premonition had just come true, and the lack of food caused Katherine to become light-headed and weak in the knees, and she crumpled onto the carpet.

"Bring the smelling salts!" the countess yelled.

The next thing Katherine knew, she was looking up at the king's concerned face. A sentry helped her up and the king led her to a chair beside his own. Head still spinning, emotions coursed through her, foremost of all embarrassment. She'd swooned in front of a king! What would William think?

After Katherine ate a pastry and sipped bitter coffee, she was able to speak. "I apologize, I don't know what came over me."

"It must be my royal presence." The king laughed.

She'd heard he had a good sense of humor. She laughed and shared William's sorrow at not being able to make the journey himself and that she was honored to be his envoy.

"Tell me about yourself," the king prodded.

She felt affection for this kind monarch, and her tongue loosened. "I grew up in a magical place called the Laurels." She reached into her handbag and handed him a book. "I understand you're fond of poetry. This is a collection of poems by our neighbor and friend. He even wrote a poem about my home."

The king smiled and glanced through it. "Would you read it to me?" he asked and handed the book back to her.

Her hands quailed. She'd read poetry aloud her whole life but had never had such nervousness before. She flipped through the pages, sat up straight, and began to read. The king closed his eyes with a peaceful expression until she finished. He looked up, "*Underbar*! *Underbar*!" He applauded. "She's charming," he said to the countess.

Katherine told him about her vision of a white city on a sundown sea where people from around the world would live in peace. As they parted, he took her hand. "I'm confident you'll find it someday. Please correspond and return to visit again. Countess Wachtmeister will tell you about our Theosophical progress and tomorrow show you some other royal sites."

That night Katherine dreamt again of the feather-shaped island in a smooth-as-glass lake but this time with an oak forest that reminded her of the Laurels. In the morning, the women bounced in a carriage along a jaggy road bordered by emerald-green grasses, bright flower-filled gardens, and tall pines. "Tell me about Theosophical efforts here in Sweden," Katherine said.

The countess shared about public lectures, group meetings, and pamphlets thus far instituted in Swedish. "I've also helped them learn to respond to press criticism," she said.

"Has there been much?" Katherine asked.

The countess nodded. "Plenty."

"How can America help?"

"They've recently gathered some five hundred titles and opened a Theosophical library. They'd like to have many more works translated into Swedish. I can't do it all myself."

"I'll see what we can do."

Out in the country, they traversed wooden bridges laid flat on the water, so low in places water splashed up between the planks. They stopped as a bridge swung open to allow sailing vessels and a river streamer to pass through. Katherine held tight while the carriage shook like a tremblor.

The road smoothed out, and the countess said, "I can't wait to return to London."

Katherine smiled. "More than anything, I'd like to meet the Outer Head. May I voyage back with you to see her?"

The countess stared at her as if she'd asked for all the crown jewels of Sweden, Norway, and Great Britain. "Her health is too delicate to receive visits from everyone. Do you have mystical powers?"

Katherine didn't know quite what to say. "I occasionally have had premonitions."

"I've many powers," the countess went on. "I'm constantly in touch with the masters."

Her self-importance surprised Katherine. William had said these communications were sacred and not to be discussed.

The countess eyed her. "Have you heard of Annie Besant?"

Katherine shook her head. "Who is she?"

"You'll learn of her soon."

The carriage pulled off onto another road and another castle came into view. A sentry opened the door and the countess started to get out. After yesterday's visit, Katherine had had enough of palaces to last a lifetime.

Suddenly, Katherine had a vision like the one in her dream. "Wait! Is there an island near here, one with an oak forest?" she asked.

The countess stared at her. "There's a trifling island, barely nine miles long and two wide. You'd be unimpressed. It's full of meager farms and old ruins."

"Please, let's go there instead."

"If you insist. I wouldn't like the king to hear I hadn't honored your request."

The countess told the driver to take them to Visingsö Island and climbed back in. The women alit from the carriage at Lake Vättern and boarded a ferry. As it departed, like in her dream, the water shone blue and smooth. As the ferry approached land, rough whitecaps rose, and heavy waves lashed the shore. At the wharf, Katherine had to hold tight to the ramp rails to get up safely.

On land, the women climbed onto a remmalag, a horse-drawn carriage. The ride down a dirt road was surprisingly gentle with the clatter of horse hooves. A farm woman in a checkered apron and kerchief waved from her doorstep. Fields of wheat blew gently in the breeze. A nostalgic feeling hit Katherine as if she'd been there before.

They rode through her dream's dense oak forest. The countess told her the trees had been planted to provide lumber for naval ships that were never needed. They visited castle ruins overlooking the lake, where four Swedish kings had resided, and another castle site constructed on property a king had conferred to a count in 1560.

At the medieval Kumlaby Church, Katherine climbed the tower and gazed across the island. Her emotions swirled. This charming island was sacred. She envisioned out on the horizon a convening of all ages from around the world filled with peace and a Parthenon-like temple overflowing with paintings and sculptures. She descended the stairs and mused to the countess, "This would be the perfect setting for gatherings and an art school."

"That's impossible," the countess told her. "It's crown property, and the only way to do that would be by decree of the king."

Nothing's impossible, Katherine thought with a smile. William had shown her that much.

Chapter Twenty-Three

William's health had improved by the time Katherine returned from Sweden, and she told him she was sorry she'd failed him.

"In what way?" he asked.

"Countess Wachtmeister never warmed to me. The only thing she said we could do to help was translate Theosophical materials."

"You met the king, didn't you?" William asked.

Katherine told him about the fainting spell and he laughed. Then she shared about the poetry reading, and William responded, "If he hadn't been taken with you, he would've rushed your visit. Write him and keep in contact."

She also shared her dreams about the island and her visit there. "What does it mean?"

William smiled. "As I said, write the king. He's wise and will understand you."

The next day she sent King Oscar a letter. She told him she believed Visingsö Island was sacred and shared her vision for an art hall and peace meetings there.

A month after the trip, Katherine sat across from Philo at the breakfast table and sipped her tea. Spots circled the rug and plopped down.

"You won't believe this!" Philo held up the *New York Sun*.

"I'll read it when I get home. I'm in a rush." She seized her toast and jumped up.

"Your friend is maligned throughout an article." Philo loved society gossip.

"What friend?" Katherine frowned.

"None other than your high-and-mighty William Q. Judge."

"He's not high-and-mighty. It's unkind to say that. He's your friend too."

"Do you think so?" Philo asked.

"Of course he is. He even told you so."

"I know, I'm sorry." Philo hung his head and popped it up again. "Listen to this. A Dr. Coues calls William an exhorter, a knave, and a phony." Philo laughed.

"That's not funny!" She slid back into her chair, reached for the outstretched paper, and read the headline aloud. Even with her strong verbal skills, she had to concentrate to keep from tripping over the words. "Blavatsky Unveiled! Tartar Termagant Tamed by Smithsonian Scientist. How the Ringleaders Work the Fraud with Bogus Mahatmas and Humbug Phenomena."

"Don't tell me that's not funny. I warned you Theosophy might be a bunch of hooey."

"From my experiences, I know it's not," Katherine said.

Philo rolled his eyes and sipped his coffee. She'd never seen such outlandish and spurious writing in her life. Professor Coues alleged William's friend Olcott in India was a buffoon and Madame Blavatsky a charlatan with unappealing physical traits. Coues also claimed she'd captured Olcott body and soul, causing both of their divorces.

Katherine tried to read the article, but Philo kept cutting in with twittering comments. Finally, she slipped the paper into her handbag and hurried downtown to William's office. Arriving, she ran up the stairs and knocked on his door. No one answered. She knocked again and called his name.

He peeked out. "It's you." He pulled her inside and closed the door. "You've seen it?"

"I don't understand." She removed her hat and gloves. His crimson face made her fear for his fragile health. Had his fever returned? She touched his forehead. He was burning up. Hopefully, it was just the stifling heat.

"I can't believe one of our own brothers would make these gross charges." William hit the desk with his hand.

She'd never seen him so angry. She opened the adjoining door to allow sandalwood scent and air to flow through. Still morning, no one was there. She poured water and waited for William to take a sip. He said, "I didn't trust him from the very start. Ages ago I wrote to Madame Blavatsky and Olcott to beware. They didn't take my heed. That Smithsonian Institution professor attended Theosophical conferences pretending to be supportive. I've never gotten along with the former priest. He practiced outward bells and astral travel at public events to garner egocentric attention."

"You've been fostering my own journeys," Katherine said.

"Yes, but in private. They're sacred. Not so others think we're special."

"What's the Hodgson report the article refers to?" Katherine frowned. "You never mentioned it to me."

William explained, "It was rejected as untrue years ago. The *Sun* shouldn't have brought it back into the light. It's quite complicated and deceitful."

"I've got all day." She sat back in her chair.

William explained that after Blavatsky and Olcott established headquarters at Adyar, in India, they traveled to the continent and left management of the site to the Coulombs, a trusted caretaker couple. Soon, though, complaints accumulated that they'd used extortion and blackmail to dissuade people from joining the Society, and the couple had to be dismissed. "In retaliation, they counterfeited letters from the mahatmas and provided them to the local Madras Christian College, saying Madame Blavatsky had paid for them to be forged. The college magazine published all fifteen."

"Why?" Katherine asked.

"The Christians wanted to thwart the Hindu and Buddhist revival we'd stimulated." William continued, "I traveled to India to investigate and discovered our shrine, a wooden cabinet, had been tampered with.

Kept pure of all magnetism, it'd been used a dozen times for the transaction of communications between masters and chela. When I arrived, in the room behind it a partly finished hole had been started and plaster had fallen on the floor. Mr. Coulomb, a carpenter, must have been fired before he could finish the treachery."

"What is the Hodgson report?"

William sipped more water. "The London Society for Psychical Research sent Hodgson, a young man, to Adyar to investigate Blavatsky's physic ability. The report received international attention. Too young and not well acquainted with psychic matters, Hodgson was entirely unfit for the inquiry. We disputed his claims, they were deemed inaccurate, and things quieted down. In fact, last year Annie Besant, a highly respected member of the London School Board, refuted the report as a tissue of lies and joined our society."

"Annie Besant? In Sweden, Countess Wachtmeister mentioned her."

"Yes, Mrs. Besant has become quite a close follower of Madame Blavatsky."

Katherine asked William why he hadn't told her about all this before. He said he didn't want to worry her and reiterated there would always be enemies in their midst wanting power. Raising his voice, William continued, "The *Sun* should have allowed me to respond before publishing such lies. I've sent a message to the editor for an immediate retraction. If he refuses, I might file suit."

"Won't that bring more bad attention to the organization?" Katherine asked.

"I'll need to confer with Madame Blavatsky. This is going to unravel her."

Chapter Twenty-Four

January 1891

The *Sun* still refused to cooperate, so William, as Madame Blavatsky's attorney, filed suit in hopes they would publish a retraction. A month later the paper still hadn't retracted, and court proceedings moved forward. Soon, though, the *Sun* requested a postponement.

Katherine had received a lovely holiday card from King Oscar, and another from Cora sharing she wouldn't be returning to the States for a while. Theosophical Society business moved along well, and Katherine and William began to plan for the Fifth Annual Conference of the American Section, scheduled for April in Boston.

On a sunny spring day, Katherine arrived at William's office. His eyes beamed brightly, and he handed her a letter. "I have the most wondrous news! Read this."

Katherine sat and scanned Madame Blavatsky's missive:

Unselfishness and altruism are Annie Besant's names. She's studied occultism with me only a few months and yet she's passed far beyond the other esoterics. Not psychic or spiritual, she's all intellect. Yet she hears the master's voice when alone and sees His Light. She's a most wonderful woman, my right hand, my sole successor in England, as you're my sole hope in America when I am forced to leave you. I'm sending her to represent me at the upcoming conference. Schedule a New York talk for as soon as her ship arrives.

Katherine's intuition churned with foreboding. There was that name again: Annie Besant. No one could be that perfect. How could a pure intellectual receive messages from a master and so quickly gain Madame Blavatsky's trust? Katherine hoped her instincts were wrong and forced herself to say, "I look forward to hearing her speak."

William frowned. "That's not a good idea."

"Whyever not? Don't you trust her?" Maybe he was leery of her too.

"It's not Annie. It's others who might be there."

Katherine stood up, put her hands on her hips, and raised her voice. "Rajah, I've been studying with you for almost three years. Isn't it time you introduced me to your colleagues?"

"Be patient. When it's time, I'll let you know."

Katherine crossed her arms. How frustrating.

"You must stay safely home," he said.

That was what he thought.

Two weeks later, on the night of the lecture, Katherine, disguised in widow's weeds, sat in the back of the packed auditorium. Yes, Mrs. Besant was beautiful, amiable, and one of the best orators Katherine had ever heard, but she was only another intellectual. Could it just be jealousy? No. The woman was putting on an act; there was something about her Katherine couldn't quite swallow.

As Annie stepped down from the podium, scores of people rushed to kiss her hand. Vain and prideful, she smiled and held it out. Not filled with the humility William had counseled Katherine to have. He was no one's fool. She couldn't wait to hear his reaction.

The next day she hurried to his office. "How was last night?" she asked.

"What did you think?" William grinned at her from behind his desk. "I saw you in the back."

"I'm sorry to disobey you." Katherine sat and looked at her hands.

"I'm sorry; it was too much to ask. I'm glad you got to hear her." He smiled. "Wasn't she astounding?"

"What do you mean?"

"Her aura. You, of all people, must have seen it?"

She shrugged. "I didn't."

"You didn't? I'm certain the membership at the convention will be enthralled."

Fearful of the popularity Annie had reaped the previous night, Katherine blurted, "You must do something to demonstrate your dominion over her, or she'll upstage you."

"What does that matter?" William asked.

"She's got power on her mind. I can feel it. Madame Blavatsky might want her to be in charge in London, but Annie has her sights set on America too."

"Don't be ridiculous." He laughed. "No one would go against Madame Blavatsky's instructions."

"I'm serious," Katherine said. "If Annie takes over international leadership, your plans for me to take over would be for naught."

"What are you suggesting I do?"

She'd seen him do it once before, but it was still almost impossible for her to believe. He was very powerful and should share it with the others. "Show them you're the Rajah."

He shook his head. "I couldn't."

"For the good of the organization, you must."

He agreed only if Annie could be part of it and warn the audience that what they were about to view was something they needed to never speak of.

Katherine hoped their strategy would work as she rode in a separate train car up to Boston for the conference. The carriage dropped her off at the Gothic-style Hotel Boylston. That evening, disguised in a large bonnet, she made her way down to the Steinert Concert Hall and found a chair in the back. Many of the Theosophical luminaries William had mentioned were there. She longed to meet them but needed to respect his wishes. Soon all three hundred and fifty seats were filled.

From the pedestal, William twirled the gavel in preparation for calling the convention to order. Katherine clasped her hands tightly in anticipation. He leaned over to Annie standing beside him and whispered into her ear. He frowned as she shook her head and returned to her chair.

Katherine prayed he'd have the courage to do what should be done. He studied the crowd, laid down his gavel, and stepped to the pedestal's side. He truly intended to show them he was the Rajah!

He said, "I'm going to share something with you. Do not ever speak to me or others about it later. It is to remain a sacred secret." He paused. "I'm not what I seem."

He began to sound *om,* the word with the triple intonation, and the delegates soon joined in. When the voices rose to a crescendo, William's bearded face mystically converted to that of a clean-shaven turbaned Hindu. Katherine's breath caught in her throat as a hush fell over the crowd. A minute, then two, passed and then William's bearded visage reappeared. Now none of the members would ever question if he was really a rajah filled with the power to lead them.

Back behind the podium, William hit the gavel and called the meeting to order. "Now our distinguished guest from London, Mrs. Annie Besant, will share a message from our Outer Head." The distracted audience conversed and didn't pay the reader any mind.

Chapter Twenty-Five

Two weeks later, on a warm May evening, William arrived unannounced at Katherine's home. Without stopping to greet a yapping Spots, he rushed past her straight to an armchair in the parlor.

Relieved Philo wasn't there, she stood in front of William and kept her voice calm. "What is it?"

He didn't respond. His eyes were rimmed in red, and beads of sweat sheened his forehead. Katherine hoped his fever hadn't returned. Spots pawed him, but William didn't even notice.

"Wait a minute." She carried the puppy to the kitchen, filled his food bowl, and fluffed his blanket. He'd soon fall asleep. Something must be horribly wrong. Could it be the slander suit?

Back in the parlor, she asked again, "What's wrong?"

William moved his lips, but words didn't come forth. He put his head in his hands. She knelt before him. "Whatever it is, we can confront it together."

Finally, he wiped his face with his handkerchief and whispered in a hoarse voice, "She's gone into the light."

Katherine put a hand on his arm. "What happened? Ella seemed perfectly fine the other day. Were you with her?"

"Not Ella." He shook his head. "Madame Blavatsky."

The name hit Katherine like a blow to the chest. She sat in the chair facing him. This changed everything. "I'm so sorry."

"As you know, she'd been ill for some time. The upcoming trial had exacerbated it. At least that will be null and void now." William's eyes glistened with tears. "How will I go on in this world without her? I don't know what she'd want me to do. Go to Europe now or stay here?"

Katherine had never seen this side of him. "What does your intuition tell you to do?" she asked.

"I can't think clearly. Please help me!" he begged.

"I'll do anything for you."

"Contact her for me."

Taken aback, Katherine paused and looked around the room. The open windows through the lace curtains cast a shadow on the low-lit turquoise walls. The chances of her being successful in communicating with Madame Blavatsky's spirit were slim to none. Katherine's own mind danced in shambles of sadness and doubt. She'd never met the Outer Head in person but had grown to think of her as an intimate.

William looked at Katherine with pleading eyes.

"I don't think I can," she said.

"You could try! You're more powerful than you realize."

Katherine didn't want to get his hopes up to then let him down. She hated to see him so desperate and finally stood. "I'll prepare. Come back tomorrow night, and we'll see what the spirit has for us."

He spoke rapidly, "Do it now."

Katherine glanced at the door. "Philo might come home."

"I don't care."

"I might fail."

"Try, please."

"Give me a few moments. I'll be right back."

She checked on Spots asleep in the kitchen.

Try to summon Madame Blavatsky? No matter how hard she tried, Katherine doubted she'd be able to communicate with the Outer Head's spirit. William was coming apart; more harm could be done than good. This might send him further off the rails and her own destiny with him. But she could not say no to him; she had to try. She filled water glasses, carried them to the parlor, and lit a few tapers. She swayed a bundle of sage through a flame and circled the room, wafting the sweet, earthy scent.

"Join me." She helped him to the oval table and took the chair across from him. His smooth large hands reached to clasp her small ones—an act she'd yearned for these past years, and the strength of their love for one another pulsed through them. It wasn't a carnal lightning strike of younger days, but instead a warm glow emanated through her body and soul. They were meant to be together here on earth, for each other, in this time and place.

"Let's close our eyes and breathe." She hoped she could be successful tonight. She began to enact the newfound powers he'd taught her to harness her skills. To activate full relaxation, her back pressed against the surface of the chair, she placed her feet firmly on the floor, followed her breath, and observed the rise and fall of her chest. Chakra colors moved up through her body until they spun into a bright pearly light on the top of her head that opened like lotus petals.

Her eyes fluttered open. She focused on the crystalline light clearing the energy in the room and throughout the whole house. A tethered root grew up from the center of the magma earth, passing through everything put there: subway tunnels, lost gardens, and Lenape Indian artifacts, up through the mansion's floor beneath her. The blue cord of energy was an anchor that kept her grounded, with light and dark balanced, feminine and masculine. She crossed a rainbow-colored bridge and walked through the carved oak doors that slowly swung open.

"Spirit." Katherine's gaze flew above William's shoulder, and she said aloud with a bold voice, "May I come into your soul space?"

She paused until her body sensed she was granted permission to continue. "Draw near, spirit, we know whoever is supposed to appear will do so." She waited in silence a few minutes, then tried again. "I'm with William, whom you know and love. Please come forward and let your presence be known."

A gust of wind blew the lace curtains into the room. Katherine described what she saw with as many details as possible, whether they seemed meaningless or not. "I have a woman in a white sari with a scarf over her head. Her azure eyes gaze with compassion. She holds an ornate urn with a dome atop it."

"That must be her," William whispered.

"Bring us precise evidence of who you are for William to recognize."

After a few moments, Katherine said, "She waves her hand back and forth, revealing a golden ring."

"It must be the signet. What does it look like?" William asked.

"A star and ancient letters are engraved on it."

Katherine listened carefully and shared with William the message she heard: "It's up to you to make sure the Society flourishes. Go now. Make certain my sacred home is protected. Stand by Olcott and the others."

Katherine continued to focus on the image; then it faded away. "The spirit is gone."

William stood. "I need to go."

"A moment, please." She held up her hand, waited for the carved door to shut behind her, walked back over the bridge, and closed the chakra colors. Then she blinked at him with a nod.

He started to speak. She held her hands in prayer position and gazed at him. He followed suit and bowed to her with a grateful smile.

"*Namaste*," they said simultaneously.

Panic filled his voice. "There's much to do. I must book my ship passage, send a cable to London, pack."

She smiled gently. "Go home. Get some rest. First thing in the morning, I'll make your travel arrangements and cable London you're on the way."

Relief softened his face. "I'm usually the one to take care of everything, and here you are taking charge. I'm so grateful."

Chapter Twenty-Six

Three weeks lapsed before Katherine received a missive from William. She sliced open the envelope with greed.

Dear Purple,

After the arduous voyage, I found Olcott in a state of paralyzing grief and piles of papers in disarray. How I wish you were here to assist. Blessedly, Annie has been of enormous support and keenly helps with administrative tasks. Individuals have come out of the woodwork insisting Madame Blavatsky chose them to succeed her. Annie and I agree her intention was for us to share the Outer Headship with her in England and me in America; however, she left nothing in writing. We're doing all we can to hold these claims at bay. Try to contact Madame Blavatsky again to determine how to proceed. Either way, write when you are able. Your words lift my soul.

Affectionately yours,
William

Katherine prayed his health could withstand such dire challenges. She couldn't believe he was still besotted with Annie even after her vanity became apparent, even after she allowed people to kiss her hand after speeches, even after she wouldn't introduce him at the conference as he'd requested. All Katherine could do to aid him was to honor his request, even though it was a long shot.

After Philo left for choir practice, she lit candles, closed her eyes, and prepared. After an hour of sitting, she was unsuccessful. She attempted again the next night to no avail. On the third night, after she crossed the bridge and walked through the doors, a breeze blew into the parlor and the candles flickered. She felt Madame Blavatsky's spirit and heard her whisper, "William's in grave danger. Must return to America as soon as possible. Move headquarters." As the voice faded, the address 144 Madison Avenue and a big building flashed into Katherine's view.

The next morning Katherine wired William a cryptic telegram: *Come home. Vision clear. US center. Address assigned.*

After a visit to the mission, she made her way up Madison Avenue and followed the numbers into the posh neighborhood. Down the street from J. P. Morgan's home and diagonal from the giant Baptist church there it was, the 144 address. The nondescript building, four stories high, would have plenty of space to expand the organization's facilities. The vacancy sign was not a coincidence, only proof she'd received a message from the beyond. She couldn't wait to see the inside and move William from the tiny Nassau Street office and meeting room.

For the fifth night in a row, Philo came in late again. She could no longer ignore the empty bottles stashed in cupboards, his lewd songs, and clothes reeking of alcohol. She should have done it earlier, but she abhorred the thought of a confrontation.

The next morning she let him sleep it off and joined him in the kitchen. He didn't seem any worse for wear. "I am the very model of a modern major general," he sang as he cracked eggs into a bowl, his hair and beard neatly brushed and a clean shirt on underneath his smoking jacket.

He poured Katherine a cup of tea and whipped up eggs with his patent prototype. "Pretty handy, isn't it? Do you want to try it?" He lifted the spiral-geared instrument toward her. "Oops!" He flipped it back into the bowl before the eggs dripped onto the tile floor.

William had counseled her to use compassion. She sat at the table, opened her heart, and kept her voice calm. "Where were you last night? I heard you come in late."

"Out and about." He poured the eggs into a pan on the stove.

She tried again. "I'm frightened when you get in so late. You might have been in an accident."

"Statistically, chances of that are slim." He laughed.

"William would be disappointed."

Philo stirred the eggs. "He's not even here."

"He'll be back. It's almost time for another installment of cash. I'd hate to see you lose that opportunity."

"I've been trying to abide by the contract. It's difficult," Philo admitted.

His honesty broke her heart. "What can I do to help you?"

He eyed her. "Maybe compliment me more often."

What a little boy. "Of course." She smiled at him. "You're clever and capable."

"What can I do to make your life better besides minding my *p*'s and *q*'s?" he asked.

She thought for a moment. "Continue to make meals and keep singing like you do. It brightens my spirits." She hoped this conversation would do the trick.

Chapter Twenty-Seven

Katherine walked up the brownstone steps, wondering what it would feel like to see William after these four long months. Ella met her at the door with a terse smile. "He's not well," she said. "I've never seen him like this."

"Like what?" Katherine asked.

"He's different. Distant somehow. It frightens me."

Katherine patted Ella's shoulder and followed her to the study. Ella, like Philo, lived outside William and Katherine's mystical union. She felt a twinge of guilt for not being kinder to her in William's absence, for not checking on her more.

As they entered his study, William told Ella to close the door and not to disturb them. As Katherine sat, he said, "I've longed for this moment. Your letters gave me great comfort at a difficult time. I wished you were there with me every day."

Her body resonated with his power. Their combined strength had only increased since he'd been gone. "I've missed you too," she said with a smile. "Hopefully, you accomplished all you wished for." Ella was right; there was something different about him, and Katherine feared for his health too. The weight loss was significant; his eyes had a dazed look, filled with sorrow and sleepless nights. She looked at the table filled with sacred objects and wished now that he was home they'd help him recover.

"How are you? How's Philo?" he said with a hoarse voice.

Her eyes returned to William. She shared about the slipup, how they'd talked it through, and that all was well now.

"I'm proud of you." William blinked at her. "The mission?"

"Doing well with the Masons' support. Grace continues to gain confidence with her management skills."

"The building Madame Blavatsky suggested?" William asked.

"Perfect for the Society." Katherine enthusiastically told him the entry hall was spacious and the rest of the building had rooms enough for staff offices, classrooms, a library, and even the printing press. The top floor quarters were full of light. "I can just picture you there ruling the roost. I'll make an appointment for you to see it. We should put in an offer right away."

He coughed. "I'm leaving for the California tour I had to postpone when Madame Blavatsky passed."

"You're in no shape to travel."

"I must. We have many members there, and as predicted, you know the West is very important."

"Send me instead!"

"No." He shook his head.

"What about the building?"

"We must wait until things die down and have the cabinet approve it. I've decided to strengthen the slate of officers here in the American branch."

"As an Outer Head, can't you just make these types of decisions on your own?"

"Afraid not. The transition wasn't as smooth as I'd hoped." He folded his hands on his desk. "Olcott and I are at odds over leadership." William told her Olcott claimed Madame Blavatsky had chosen Annie to succeed as sole Outer Head. Countess Wachtmeister agreed and claimed she'd received a message from Master Morya in the Himalayas, Madame Blavatsky's teacher, that Annie was the one. Others felt she wasn't qualified because she hadn't been a chela long enough. "At least Annie agreed Madame Blavatsky had written we're to share the Outer Headship post, with me in America and her abroad in England, Europe, and Asia. Do you remember that letter? Do you think you can find it?"

Katherine nodded. "I'll try. Wait. I'm confused. Isn't Colonel Olcott the Society president?"

"Excuse me." William started to hack, a deep resonate cough, and drank some tea. "Yes, but the Outer Head runs the Esoteric Section and truly has all the power. You can see it's not the right time to mention Blavatsky's message about buying a headquarters building."

Disappointed, Katherine feared it might get snapped up.

"Plus, nobody could deny this." William held up his hand revealing a gold ring that shone in the light. "Master Morya had it made for Madame Blavatsky years ago."

She drew William's hand across the desk toward her and studied it closer. Katherine couldn't believe it. Madame Blavatsky's spirit had worn it in the vision. The green-flecked agate with blood red veins and ancient etchings were smooth under Katherine's thumb. "What do the letters mean?" Katherine asked.

"Life and truth in Sanskrit."

"How did you come by it?" Katherine asked.

He told her Claude Falls Wright, Madame Blavatsky's secretary, and one of three people in the room, had slipped it off her finger as she passed. When he arrived in London, Claude gave it to him privately.

William carefully opened the signet's hinge. "This is a clip of her teacher Master M's hair."

"Astounding. What about the other Outer Head, Annie?"

"Evidently, Madame Blavatsky had a duplicate ring made for her without the locket."

Katherine had a sense of foreboding. "I hope this co-headship-ness will work out."

He laughed at her description, but she hadn't meant it as a joke. If Annie became Outer Head internationally, she could take over their operations in America at any time. If that happened, Katherine would never take over leadership as Madame Blavatsky had wished, and the city on the sea wouldn't come to realization.

Katherine visited William often after he returned from California. She fretted over the building, over her visions, over the Theosophical leadership intrigue, and for a while she worried William's health was getting worse again. By October, though, his fire returned, and his dedication to solving leadership challenges redoubled. He began negotiations to purchase the Madison Avenue building. Cora had decided to stay in Italy, so he'd also arranged to rent her entire Upper West Side residence so Katherine could have her own suite upstairs. By Thanksgiving, William was well enough to carve his own turkey and laugh with Philo over his latest inventions. The Christmas season was filled with carols, camaraderie, and good cheer.

Chapter Twenty-Eight

April 1893

The following year the building sale closed, and Katherine began to help pack the Nassau Street office to move to Madison Avenue. Bittersweetly, she looked around the small space and adjoining room. This was where she'd chanted for the first time and started to understand the power of Buddhism, Theosophy, and so much more.

As the year progressed, the organization settled into the new building and American membership grew. By May, over a year since Madame Blavatsky's death, the *Sun* finally printed an apology that they'd been misled and the allegations against her character had been without foundation. William was in fine health, in his element. He'd been invited to represent the Theosophical Society at the World's Parliament of Religions during Chicago's World Fair in September. Katherine helped him compose and rehearse his speech.

"I'm excited to hear the dignitaries and see the fair," she told him.

William said softly, "I'm sorry. I can't have you go."

"Why not?" she asked.

To her chagrin, he told her, "It'll be crowded. I'll be busy and can't worry about you. Olcott and others, including possible local spies, still doubt the Outer Headship, which might reflect on you. Plus, Annie's coming over for the Parliament."

There was that Annie again. Katherine crossed her arms. "I can take care of myself."

"I'm just not ready to tell the world about my plans."

"What plans?" Katherine sat up straight.

"For you to take over leadership after I'm gone," he said.

He hadn't spoken of this in several years. If he believed in her as much as he said, why did he still keep her hidden from others in his circle?

Even though she'd been pleased to hear him say it, anxiety filled her. Was she worthy? She didn't understand or quite accept many Theosophical beliefs. Was she up to the challenge and strain of the job? Even so, she wanted to continue to work with him and do what she could to help humanity. She wouldn't mention her doubts. Her desire to comprehend all she could remained, and going to Chicago would strengthen her knowledge. She would just wear a disguise.

He eyed her. "No widow's weeds," he teased. She hung her head. Had he read her mind? She'd better not disobey him on this.

Before he left, they were able to celebrate together the Society's publication of *Ocean of Theosophy.* The manuscript she'd helped him write explained the organization's tenets in a simple and clear fashion. Topics included the sevenfold nature of man, reincarnation and karma, the dangers of psychic practices, the pitfalls of pseudo-occultism, cosmic and terrestrial cycles, after-death states, the existence of highly advanced human beings, and much more.

September 13, 1893

Dear Purple,
Parliament opened a few days ago with an inspiring speech by Swami Vivekananda from India. In perfect English, he introduced Hinduism to America and called for tolerance and universal acceptance of all religions. A kindred spirit, he aligns himself with our Theosophical tenets. Annie is entranced by him. Your suggestions and edits to my speech helped make the words come from my heart and smoothly roll off my tongue. I'm grateful to you. Philo would be flabbergasted by the inventions. There's a machine that goes up many stories and down again. And a giant riding wheel taller than Paris's Eiffel Tower.
Always yours, W

How she wished she'd been in the gallery to hear William's speech. When he returned home from Chicago, he sent her a message that he had visitors and would see her as soon as he was free. The next day she saw a photo in the *Sun* of a large party held at Bayside, the wealthy Neresheimers' Long Island Estate. William was seated between Ella and Annie. A pang of jealousy made Katherine wince. She wasn't certain if it was because he was there with Ella and Annie, or that Katherine herself was not there to meet the religious royalty, including Swami Vivekananda.

A few days later William came to her residence in distress, hurried to the parlor, and sat down. "Something is very wrong. At the conference a sudden coldness came over Annie that I can't quite explain. Quite taken with Swami Vivekananda, she spent much of her time with him. At one point, I caught her staring at the original signet ring on my finger. Then she began to show the duplicate on her hand and boasted to anyone who would listen it had been Madame Blavatsky's."

He continued, "I quietly pulled her aside and reminded her she didn't possess the original, and as a comrade I advised her to be careful in statements as to the ring."

"How did she react?" Katherine asked.

"She scowled and walked away."

Katherine's intuition had been correct. That woman wanted all the power.

He said, "I've made a decision; it's past time to introduce you to one of my closest allies."

Chapter Twenty-Nine

A week later, as the sun set over the Hudson, Katherine said to Philo, "Please put on something decent."

With stains on his undershirt, he was reading the newspaper in the parlor while smoking a cigar. "Why're you so gussied up?" he asked and drank from his cup.

She suspected he had something more besides coffee in it. She'd quit arguing with him about the tippling. At least he'd been staying home out of trouble instead of coming home inebriated. William had hoped if they continued to assure him he was cared for, he'd be able to uphold the contract for the rest of his life. She began to view it as a malady and attempted to hold compassion for him.

"I told you William's bringing someone important to meet you."

Philo put down the paper and sat up. "Meet me? Who?"

"Mr. Neresheimer."

Philo's face lit up. "August Neresheimer? The diamond merchant? The man who built the castle around the corner?"

"The very one."

"He must be loaded!"

"Don't be crass." She sighed. "He's also on the Society cabinet."

Philo raised his eyebrows. "Maybe he'll be interested in one of my inventions."

"William said that was a possibility."

"He did? I'll go get natty." Philo gamboled down the hall toward his bedroom.

She picked up the cup and followed him. "I'm rinsing this in the kitchen, and you'll abstain for the evening."

He kissed her cheek. "Whatever you say, kitten."

She smelled alcohol on his breath. "Polish your pearls too." She hoped he wouldn't embarrass her tonight. As horse hooves stopped outside, she hid the newspaper in the sideboard and peeked through the curtains at the shiny black carriage. In the hall tree mirror, she smoothed down her best frock and unruly curls, and retied the plum-colored ribbon in her hair. After introductions, she led them into the drawing room. Although short in stature, Mr. Neresheimer carried a distinguished demeanor. Impeccably dressed, with wavy hair parted in the middle and a trimmed beard, he appeared to be about the same age as William, only a few years older than her.

"Philo will be out in a moment." She gave them seats and poured tea.

"Mrs. Tingley, share with me about your Do-Good Mission." She detected a slight German accent to Neresheimer's voice.

As she spoke about her mission, his eloquent blue eyes offered support and understanding. Had William also told him she was more than a chela? Perhaps he'd wanted Neresheimer to meet Philo so he could see how she lived.

Mr. Neresheimer stood as her husband floated into the parlor with a mound of papers. "Hello! I'm here." He had certainly cleaned himself up, wearing his bright blue suit, floral ascot, and matching pocket square.

"It's a pleasure to meet you, Mr. Neresheimer." Philo handed him the pile and tried to shake his hand; however, the man couldn't reach out from under the stack.

"Please call me Nere."

"You can call me Philo."

"I've heard about your genius."

"You have?" Philo grinned.

"Of course." William suggested, "Let's move to the table so we can examine the papers more closely."

Nere put the papers down, and Philo turned up the sconces. "What might you be interested in, household items, farming, fashion?"

Nere asked, "Which has the most marketability?"

"Hard to choose." Philo rustled through the papers. "They're all brilliant, if I may say so myself." He chortled and reached for a proposal. "How about the wave-making motor? As soon as it goes on the market, every oceanside town will want one." Leave it to him to choose his biggest, most hare-brained project ever.

"Sears and Roebuck might even carry it in their new catalog," William said.

Philo stood, picked up the packet, and began to read, "Let it be known that I, Philo B. Tingley, a citizen of the United—"

"Skip the preamble, please," William coaxed.

"My invention has for its object to provide a motor capable of responding to the motion of waves and so constructed—" As Philo read line ten of hundreds, Nere's eyes glazed over. William cleared his throat and nodded at Katherine.

She took the cue and cut in. "I believe Nere's heard enough."

Philo asked, "What questions do you have for me?"

"Where might I see the prototype?"

Philo's shoulders drooped. "I haven't finished it yet." Then he brightened. "Would you like to see what I've done so far?"

Katherine cringed and shook her head. "I don't think he has the time."

"Yes, I do." The diamond broker stood and followed Philo down the hall.

"I'm embarrassed," she told William. "You can't imagine what a horrible state his workroom is in." Katherine had been relieved to take over the top floor so Philo could spread out his creations and bang to his heart's content in her old bedroom.

William laughed. "Don't worry. It's all part of the plan. Nere has agreed to help us procure funding for a patent annually." Had William also told him she should be Outer Head after he was gone?

"When do you think you'll finish it?" Nere asked as they returned.

"Alas, I don't have enough funds." Philo sighed.

"I happen to be searching for an investment. Something clever like this would be perfect. I'll consider it."

"You will?" Philo began to sing, "For he's a jolly good fellow. For he's a jolly good fellow . . ."

William and Katherine couldn't help joining in too. After the couple walked the men to the door and called good night, Philo said, "How do you like that? I must be a genius after all."

Chapter Thirty

May 1894

William visited one evening appearing more tired than usual. "Purple, it's time for me to double down and introduce you and your vision to more of my faithful. It'll strengthen my power if people know I have you by my side. Also, when the time comes, they'll pitch support your way."

Did he think he was going soon? Even though she'd longed to meet more Theosophists, she had mixed feelings. Would they warm to her and accept her as worthy, or would they challenge her? Was he going to tell them about his plans for her?

"What do you propose?" she asked.

"Let's offer a sitting in your parlor and share your childhood vision."

"Wouldn't it be better if I met them casually at first?"

He shook his head. "It's imperative to demonstrate your potential right away."

On the appointed evening, Philo helped Katherine move the parlor table to the center of the room, added the lace cloth atop and chairs around. She lit candles, checked her hair in the mirror and sat at the end of the table with William to her right. As nervous as a debutante at her first ball, she clasped her hands in prayer for what would be one of the most important nights of her life. She closed her eyes, breathed with William, and invited her chakras to open.

Soon the knocker rapped. Philo introduced himself and escorted each person to their assigned seat. Even though he hadn't wanted to participate in this way, William had convinced him it would be worth his while. Katherine smiled to each as they sat. A tall, broad-chested man pushed in front of Philo and reached for Katherine's hand. "I'm Ernest Temple Hargrove, and you are?"

She pulled back from the dark energy that eddied around him like a storm of wasps. Clean-shaven with handsome, baby-faced features, his cool green eyes reflected a spark of danger. He disrupted the centered peace she'd found earlier. Was he one of the enemies William warned of?

She studied the three males in their tuxedos and two women in their gowns and jewels. Her own lavender silk felt smooth on her body, but she wore no genuine jewels. The few she'd had she'd sold off long ago. The last guest entered the room with apologies for her lateness.

"Dr. van Pelt, what a pleasant surprise," Katherine said.

"Oh, please. Everyone calls me Gertie."

Philo took the chair to Katherine's left and put Spots on the ground at her feet. Moonlight streamed in through the open window, candles flickered from the nearby river breeze, and wax scent filled the air.

William began, "I've invited you here as my trusted ones." He lifted his hand toward Katherine. "Mrs. Tingley has been my loyal chela for some time and her support has been invaluable to me. She has great promise."

"It's been my honor." Katherine kept her voice strong and full.

William continued, "Please introduce yourselves to her."

Nere smiled at her. "We've met." As promised, the diamond merchant had sent cash for Philo's prototype supplies through William.

"Elizabeth Churchill Mayer," one of the women said with melodic grace. An aura shimmered around her lovely face with large eyes and dark hair. "I studied under Madame Blavatsky in London and have been a worker for Theosophy ever since." Katherine felt drawn to her and hoped they'd be friends.

"Claude Falls Wright. President of the New York City Theosophical Society Lodge." Tall and ginger-haired, this man had been the one who'd passed William the signet ring and moved here soon thereafter. William had told her he was also Dublin-born, a fine fellow, and a great public speaker. "And here's my betrothed, Miss Leoline Leonard."

The young woman didn't appear to be the renowned beauty Katherine had heard about—until she smiled; then Leoline was stunning. Claude gazed at her, and his face lit up like a candelabra.

Claude continued, "We recently recognized each other in Boston. And instantly knew we'd been married in a past life on the banks of the Nile River." Katherine thought that was absurd.

"I'm Joe Fussell, private secretary to William Q. Judge." Katherine had delivered messages to him from William a time or two but hadn't realized he had such an official title.

"As I told you, I'm Ernest Temple Hargrove," the disagreeable man said with a clipped British accent. "As a member of Madame Blavatsky's Inner Circle, she bid me come to New York after she was gone to help William with the American Section."

Katherine resisted the urge to look at William. Why hadn't he told her about this man? Ernest? Her instincts told her he was anything but.

Hopefully, William's plan to guide Katherine this evening would work. It was a risk. In a trance state, sometimes the spirit was with her and other times not.

"Please hold hands." Golden sounds swirled throughout the room as William played the singing bowl and led them in a chant. "I'll now lead Mrs. Tingley in a meditation."

Katherine allowed her eyes to flicker, breathed in and out, and waited for her chakras' brilliant colors to reopen. She walked across the bridge, through the carved wood doors, raised her arms toward the ceiling, and said, "Spirits, be with us tonight." She listened to the singing bowl again, waiting for a calmness to set in. She waited, waited, waited to become entranced, but it was to no avail. She kept breathing, breathing, and breathing until William asked, "What do you smell?" The sound of his voice released her senses.

She inhaled. "A salty sea, orange blossoms, and roses."

"What time is it?" William prompted. His familiar Irish brogue peaceful to her ears, her chakras swirled.

Her head rose, she opened her eyes, and a vision began to come forth. A vast ocean where whales, dolphins, and other beautiful sea creatures swam. "It must be evening because the sun moves westward." Nothing else came to her, and she froze.

"Tell me what else you see." William's deep voice spoke, strong but tender.

More images flashed before her. She described the magnificent setting as she wandered through it. "Waves crash onto a sandy beach below cliffs. A forest lines a hillside. Like the Garden of Eden, fruits, vegetables, and flora grow. Light reflects off Mount Olympus-like marble buildings with pillars and columns of ancient architecture. I see glass-domed roofs that sparkle in purple and green."

"What do you hear?"

"Ocean waves, children's laughter, an orchestra playing, and voices singing. Brilliant minds discussing many topics."

"What else?"

"Canvases painted and craftsmen creating." A hand to her heart. "I see an outdoor amphitheater, costumed players in Grecian robes presenting an ancient play, sprites dancing." She swallowed, took a breath, and spoke rapidly, "Adults and children of all ages from many lands, dressed in white, living in harmony and love for learning in nature. They gain knowledge and power and spread rays of bright energy across America and around the world, throughout the universe—north, south, east, and west."

"What do you feel?"

"Love. For all mankind, for brotherhood." The beauty of the vision began to fade. "Now the sun sets over the ocean and the sky above is crimson, amethyst, orange."

"How do you feel?" he asked.

"Peaceful. On a sundown sea."

William put his hand on her shoulder. "Katherine, it is time to return to us."

Her lashes fluttered as she regained consciousness. She hoped what she'd been able to share pleased William and the visitors. They began to speak all at once, which overwhelmed her senses.

William put out his hand. "Quiet, please. Let Mrs. Tingley rest a moment."

He nodded to Philo, who brought her some water. She took a sip and smiled at each person at the table, relieved the vision had been with her.

"Claude, you go first," William offered. "What were your impressions?"

"How astounding! This is the prophecy Madame Blavatsky spoke of many times. A great school in the West, the revival of ancient mysteries. Did you hear about it from William?" He asked Katherine.

She shook her head. "I've had this recurring vision since childhood. Each time the details become clearer, as if the time for it to come to fruition is moving closer."

"That's impossible." Hargrove scowled.

"I feel in my heart it someday will come true," Katherine whispered.

Nere smiled. "She might be the one we've been looking for."

"Looking for?" Gertie asked.

"The next leader of the Theosophical Society," William replied.

Some around the table nodded their heads in agreement.

"Let's wait quietly for a sign," William suggested.

After a few minutes, as if thrown by invisible hands, pastel blossoms drifted from the ceiling and the scent of sweet peas permeated the air. Hargrove glowered, hurried from the parlor, and slammed the front door. In awe, Katherine held a spray of flowers in her hands. This miracle had not been on the agenda. Some guests were in a daze and others had tears in their eyes as they scooped up blossoms and made their way to their carriages. Philo began to clean up while Katherine walked William to the foyer and asked, "Did it go well?"

He whispered, "Better than I ever imagined. Those sweet peas were a lovely touch."

She shook her head. "Not me. I thought it was you?"

"No. Was it one of Philo's inventions?"

"He couldn't have kept it a secret."

William smiled. "It is said Madame Blavatsky did something similar once."

"Could it have been her blessing?"

"Possibly. I believe most of our guests tonight will understand and accept you. We'll need to gather others into our confidence as time rapidly approaches." Time? Did he mean time for her chelaship to be over, time for him to go into the light, time for the new century? Not wanting to ruin the dreamy sensation of the night's triumphs, she chose not to ask.

Chapter Thirty-One

February 1895

One night after the new year, Katherine's drumming heart woke her as a vivid vision leapt to the surface of her consciousness: William struggled to breathe; a coffin hovered in thunderstorm clouds; slate-colored ashes flew into the sky. He'd never complained, though recently with weight loss, hacking cough, and swollen eyes, his health had turned with a vengeance. She'd known he'd leave his earthly body before her, but it was too soon, and she begged him to take a respite. However, he refused.

The vision was a clear sign she had to take immediate action, and that day she spoke with his doctor. He shook his head, handed her a few brochures, and said, "A healing water resort might be of benefit to ease his pains."

She told William they still had much to do together. Her seven-year chelaship wouldn't be over for another year, and she wasn't ready to take over leadership. She begged him to go to a resort settlement. He finally relented only if they lodged out of town. He wanted his privacy. With their spouses' approval, two weeks later William and Katherine were on their way to Texas. She'd procured a sleeping car, but even so, the many-day train ride was exhausting.

At their San Antonio stop, Mr. Foster, the driver she'd hired to pick them up, tipped his floppy hat and directed his men with a stretcher to transport William to the back of a wagon. Katherine helped him lie down, readjusted his blanket, and climbed in beside him.

Scratching his mangy beard, Mr. Foster clicked the reins and told the mule to giddyap. Oaks lined the bumpy road toward Mineral Wells. As the morning waned, clouds blew overhead, and the temperature cooled. She huddled in her coat, removed her shawl, and placed it over William's blanket. The extra medicine dosage helped him sleep soundly.

Katherine worried she'd made a mistake bringing him here. If he died, she'd receive the blame, but no one would blame her more than herself. Too late now. She took out her grandfather's watch and held it tightly. They were here. She had to carry on. The mule pulled them forward for what seemed like hours until they reached the small town. The hand-painted sign said: *Home of the Crazy Water*.

Mr. Foster pointed to the sign and spoke in a Texas twang. "Bet you're wondering about that. Yes'm, a few years back a lady went crazy, sat by the town well all day drinking the water. Lo and behold a few weeks later she got up, danced a jig, returned to her husband and seven children, and took up housekeeping again. News spread, and soon hundreds of people from all over the country flocked here."

"Do you really believe that?" Katherine asked.

"I certainly do. Knew her before and after. Now she's writin' poetry. Yes'm, those waters heal all sorts of infirmities: tics, rashes, stomach aches, rheumatism, paralysis, and more."

Katherine didn't believe his yarns. She only hoped the water would help William. He stirred. She patted her patient's hand and whispered, "Go back to sleep, my darling."

As they passed the freshly painted clapboard Johnson Hotel, folks on the wraparound porch waved. She wished they were checking in there. Mr. Foster drove the mule through town and continued for miles, until at a fork in the road, he pulled up to a cabin and stopped. "This is the place." A rusty plow stood among tall weeds that grew in front of the peeling painted cabin with a window box hanging off it.

"Are you sure? It doesn't look like the picture." From her satchel, she found the photo of a neat log cabin with a garden and handed it to Mr. Foster.

"That's what it looked like ten years ago." He chuckled, dropped their luggage beside the wagon, and carried William to the porch. "Need anything else?"

Katherine handed him a few coins. "No, thank you."

"Good luck," he said and drove off.

The door opened, and a woman stepped outside, hands clasped on her ample bosom. She glanced down at William. "Goodness, mercy me! He does look a fright."

"Please help me get him inside?"

The woman squealed across the yard toward the barn, "Henrick! Come!"

A freckle-faced boy peeked his head out from behind the tumble-down barn and tossed down a cheroot. Katherine hoped it wouldn't catch the barn on fire. If it did, though, it might be an improvement to the property. The boy ran toward her as his pronounced cowlick bounced atop his head. She tried to ignore the dust and cobwebs as she helped Henrick carry William to the brass bed in the corner of the room. Apropos, a crazy quilt had been laid over the stuffed mattress. She fluffed up his pillows, hoping the bedclothes were clean, and pulled the quilt over him. His eyelashes fluttered. She hoped he'd continue to sleep.

There wasn't a rocking or easy chair in sight, just the brass bed, a cot in the opposite corner, and a rough-hewn table with two chairs. A narrow cast-iron tub sat on another side of the room. Not a piece of art, nor, of course, gas or electric lights in evidence.

The woman pointed to a pile of jugs inside the door. "Two dollars each if you want Henrick to fill these up. Ten dollars to carry that man down to soak."

That was highway robbery! "We'll manage." Katherine started to ask the boy to haul in their luggage and then she intended to broach the subject of the condition of the cabin with the woman. However, in a flash the boy ran up the road, with the landlady right behind him.

Katherine didn't have the energy to catch up with them. She sighed and dragged their bags into the cabin. She wanted to scour the filthy space but needed to get food going. At least the woman had stocked the larder as Katherine requested. A full jug of what she supposed was crazy water sat on the floor. She opened the jug and poured liquid into the kettle that hung over the hearth as the smell of rust and rotten eggs permeated the air. She forced herself to stick her finger in for a taste that was as bad as it smelled.

She'd never been much of a cook but was determined to make William Irish stew, hoping it might restore his body and soul. She swept cobwebs from the grate, tossed wood on it, found matches on the mantel, and lit a fire. She chopped mutton—or at least it looked like mutton—potatoes, and unidentifiable root vegetables, tossed them in the water, and stirred the mixture together. Soon the cabin grew warm and filled with a deep, sultry aroma.

As it grew dark, William shifted in the bed. She lit the lantern and fed him a few bites of the stew. Afterward, she gave him a dram of his medicine, and he immediately fell back to sleep. Bone tired, she decided to clean on the morrow, crawled onto the cot, and draped the thin blanket over her. She couldn't sleep, so she got up and moved the cot closer to William's bed. She had a need to be near him. A gentle wind blew in from the open window, crickets chirped, and a pair of owls hooted back and forth to each other. After all this time in the city, she'd forgotten how peaceful it could be out in the country, reminding her of the Laurels.

Before sunrise, his moans woke her. Her palm to his forehead, she discovered he was as hot as the fire on the grate. He'd taken a turn for the worse. She spooned him more stew and a medicine dose and held his hand until he fell back to sleep.

As it grew light, he turned and whispered through a hoarse voice, "It's time to let my soul leave this shell of a body."

"No," she raised her voice. "I can't bear the thought of losing you. We've come this far to heal you, and heal you I must."

He lingered in a state of delirium for a week as his symptoms persisted. She questioned if she was doing right by him or if she should allow nature to take its route and let him go. Daily she filled a jug with spring water from the brook behind the barn and lugged it up to the cabin. She wanted to pour it into the bathtub and bathe him, but she wouldn't be able to get him in and out of it. Instead, she sat behind him on the bed every few hours and, beneath his nightshirt, washed his bare chest and prayed to the All Powerful to restore his health.

While he slept, she sorted the correspondence and writings they'd packed. Some of the urgent business she answered herself and signed his initials for him. Confidence in her abilities to fulfill the business responsibilities began to rise. She prioritized papers to set aside for when he regained his strength—if he ever did. She wanted to walk to town to post the letters and restock the dwindling larder but didn't dare leave him alone.

After another week, when she was about to give up, his fever ebbed, and he was able to turn himself over. Mr. Foster, in his floppy hat and wagon, came by with fresh vittles and offered to post the mail. Grateful, she gave him a larger than necessary tip.

One morning at the end of the second week, William woke up and smiled at her. A few days later he began to whisper "The Laurels" to her, and back and forth they recited it together. He soon was able to dictate letters to her. She was his nurse, his amanuensis, his beloved chela. Some healing could happen in the twinkling of an eye, though this seemed to take forever.

By the fifth week, he threw his feet out of bed and stood on his own. A couple days later he walked a few steps, and by the end of that week he made it to the table and sat in a chair.

She filled the tub with mineral water, and he was able to help her get him in and out of it. Soon he was even well enough to lean on her arm and venture outside for fresh air.

Was it the waters or her prayers? She didn't know. But after eight weeks, his health had been much restored, and they were able to return to the East Coast in time to prepare for the annual Theosophical convention. When they arrived in New York, they were hit with shocking news: Colonel Olcott and Annie Besant had produced false evidence against William's communications with the masters and had filed a fraud suit against him. Katherine's intuition was correct; the woman had been posturing to take over the organization internationally all along.

Chapter Thirty-Two

A few mornings later, in her upstairs office with Spots curled up at her feet, Katherine sat in a ray of northern sunlight that shone through the window. She tried to meditate, but her mind wandered. Even though William had recovered from the edge of death, his energy wavered at a nadir, and she feared his vigor would never return. Plus, Olcott and Annie's betrayal added to his depressed state. William had been unable to plan the agenda, and she prayed he'd be well enough to participate in the meeting.

A mockingbird from outside the window broke her reverie, and she began to breathe and open her chakras. After a while, shapes shifted, a calmness set in, and a sense of euphoria engulfed her. Words, words. She grabbed her journal and pen and quickly began to write the words that turned into phrases that grew into sentences that became a whole paragraph:

> *With un-Theosophical exertions against William, America can no longer submit to such friction. At the convention, it must declare itself independent from Adyar until disrupting forces bring the fight to a close. Unless this is done, a year will pass in turmoil and the chief aims of our work will be retarded. Fix it to be well planned with no mistakes. Consult Neresheimer.*

Katherine withdrew from the trance and glanced down at the journal in her lap. The handwriting wasn't hers. Her pen held black ink, but the calligraphic style before her was bright red and neat, easy to read, unlike her own messy sprawls.

She'd received a message from a mahatma! William received letters in blue ink from Koot Hoomi, one of Madame Blavatsky's teachers who resided in the Himalayas. His mesmerizing portrait with dazzling eyes, long hair, and beard was displayed on the wall in the Madison Avenue headquarters. Blavatsky's other teacher, Master Morya, also known as Master M, lived there too, and Katherine had been told his messages arrived onto pages in red ink. This must have been from him.

William had explained the mahatmas, or masters, introduced by the Theosophical Society were living human beings but wiser with a deeper knowledge. They themselves had written they were men, not gods. An adept most high, some claimed Master M had been reincarnated from Abraham; Melchior, who'd brought the infant Jesus myrrh; King Arthur of the round table; Thomas Becket, Archbishop of Canterbury; Saint Thomas More; and others.

Only a few had received communications from Master M in the form of a letter or astral visit. Only a privileged few had met him in person. The honor of receiving a message filled her with joy until she read it again and comprehended its meaning. She wished she wasn't the one given the responsibility to share the dire command. She immediately sent a note to Nere asking him to come at once.

She greeted him at the door, led him to the table, and showed him the message.

He read it slowly and asked, "Where did you get this?"

"It came through me," Katherine said.

Wide-eyed, he responded slowly, "The masters have spoken. But it won't be enough to only separate, one or the other needs to take over leadership of the entire society. It should be centered here in America, the land of its origin, where Madame Blavatsky, Olcott, and William founded it."

"Are you certain?" Fear and excitement mingled in her core.

"Yes." He nodded. "Let's share it with William now."

"Under no circumstances must he know of this yet." She set a hand on her heart. "It would greatly upset him and might cause a relapse. The doctors have rendered a month's rest imperative if he's going to participate in the conference at all. Let's formulate a plan alone."

"Are you certain?"

"Yes." She nodded.

"I'll draft a proposal to send to specific members to garner their support and run it by Joe, as private secretary. I insist he's included."

For the next month, Katherine and Joe worked with Nere on the message to select lodge members and sent it out. The respite allowed William the power to rally for the conference. A few days before they left for Boston, Nere, Joe, and Katherine sat William down and shared Master Morya's message and the proposal.

"Absolutely not." William shook his head. "You should've notified me as soon as this transpired. I won't endorse it."

"William, the masters have spoken." Katherine put her hand on his shoulder. "You know we need to follow their guidance. We've also drafted rebuttals to the allegations made by Olcott and Annie in case anyone has concerns."

"You're saying I have no choice?" He looked sadly at Katherine.

She nodded.

"It's for the best," Nere said.

William put his face into his hands and started to cough.

In April, the American Section of the Theosophical Society convened at the Boston headquarters with eighty-nine American lodges represented by delegates in person or by proxy. At the welcome reception, William, weak but stable, sat in a chair beside Katherine.

He introduced her to other members who came over to greet them. Katherine's head swam from all the swarming before her. She waved her fan as she tried to cool herself and memorize all the names and faces.

William said, "Elizabeth's by the door. Go to her. She'll introduce you to others. Just be careful what you say."

She remembered the woman with the large eyes she'd immediately liked at the sitting when Katherine first revealed her vision to chosen Theosophists. Elizabeth now smiled brightly and said, "I'd like you to meet Alice Cleather, a dear Theosophical sister visiting from London. Alice, this is Katherine Tingley, one of William's chelas."

Alice eyed her with raised dark brows and tight lips, then whispered into Katherine's ear, "So you're the medium I've heard so much about."

Taken aback, Katherine laughed. She couldn't tell if Alice thought being a medium was a good thing or a bad one. Ernest Hargrove, who'd been at the sitting too, pushed Alice aside, his large body looming over Katherine. "How are you, Mrs. Tingley? Will you be seeing my demonstration tomorrow?"

She couldn't answer any of his questions because he just kept talking. William drew beside her, grabbed her elbow, and bustled her away. "Time to go."

"He gives me the willies," she whispered, and shook her shoulders, trying to dispel the foul sensations.

"He can be a bit overbearing. Because Madame Blavatsky sent him to us, I'm trying to open my heart in hopes he'll become more tolerable. He claims she promised him a high cabinet position if he moved here. At this point keep your distance."

Katherine planned to.

The next morning the hall was filled to capacity at one hundred. Katherine feared the proposal would be quickly voted down. She gave William, sitting beside her, a weak smile. Nere read the proposal to split from Annie Besant in London and Olcott in Adyar and have America become international headquarters. When he finished, the room fell silent, and as a Mr. Fullerton took the floor against the resolutions, she was sure it was all over. She wanted to put her hand on William's but didn't dare in public. After an hour and a half, Fullerton concluded by asserting, "Wait a month, and you'll have all the evidence needed to prove William Q. Judge guilty of the charges of fraud by Mrs. Besant and Colonel Olcott."

As Nere began to read again, she was glad they'd taken the time to draft the explanations for each of the six charges. He presented for over another hour and a half and when finished he provided his own personal statement, "Now you have heard there is abundant evidence that William Q. Judge has been under the direct guidance of the masters. When the presence was upon him, he knew well what others only suspected, that he was divine."

The crowd gave resounding applause, and the American Section of the Theosophical Society delegates voted to secede from the parent society, electing William as Outer Head for Life! Out of the eighty-nine American lodges, only five stayed loyal to Annie and Olcott. The organization's international headquarters would be located at Madison Avenue, where William's party would continue to hold the corporate name, seal, and property.

Relief filled Katherine even though she had many questions. What would this mean for her future? Would she someday be Outer Head for Life of the international organization? Was she closer to or farther from her white city vision?

Back in New York, it appeared William had used up all his strength to get through the conference. Like a balloon losing air, his health slowly deteriorated again. Along with Nere and Joe, Katherine continued to manage much of the Society business. Fortunately, within a few months William's health rallied, and he was able to resume many duties. When asked by members whom he'd selected as the next Society leader, he replied, "All will be revealed at the correct time."

Chapter Thirty-Three

March 1896

Miraculously, a year later William's health had almost fully recovered, and the astounded doctor said if careful, he still had some good years left. Katherine spent as much time with him as possible and, on the doctor's recommendation, they walked when the weather allowed.

On a sunny afternoon, William and Katherine strolled down Fifth Avenue. His walking stick, now a cane, had become a necessity instead of a fashion accessory. Katherine smiled as they passed underneath the magnificent marble arch into Washington Square Park, where daffodils, tulips, and purple hyacinth bloomed in abundance. A squirrel zipped by. The fountain splashed. A slight breeze twirled cherry tree petals, pink with beauty, onto the green grass. Life would never be more perfect.

They'd walked much farther than usual, and she asked where they were going.

"It's a surprise," he teased.

"Do tell." She straightened her lavender bonnet.

"For some time, I've been trying to get you a reading with Cheiro. He arrived back in New York from London last week."

"The palmist who met with Sarah Bernhardt, the Prince of Wales, and Samuel Clemens?"

"Yes, in Madame Blavatsky's last letter, she insisted you see him," William said.

Cheiro, a powerful palm reader, a mystic, a man renowned the world over for his spiritual gifts. He'd read Madame Blavatsky's palm, and she felt he was truly endowed. This was Katherine's life now, meeting people she had only read about in books or newspapers.

"Is Cheiro his real name?" she asked.

"His sobriquet." William smiled. "Clever because chiromancy means palmistry. He also self-identifies as Count Louis le Warner de Hamon. I hope we have luck getting in today."

In the heart of Fifth Avenue, they rode a lift to Cheiro's apartment, which was decorated like a rajah's palace. Oriental carpets and leopard skins graced the floors, tapestries hung on the walls, potted palms sat proudly, and a wood-carved ox and hand castings were displayed. William pointed to a cushioned chair for Katherine to relax in and joined the queue waiting to check in with the turbaned secretary behind a desk.

Katherine removed her gloves, examined her hands, and wondered what Cheiro might see there. She put her gloves back on. The other seats were filled with a cast of characters that might have been in a play: a mustached man in a giant derby, a rotund woman crying into her handkerchief, and another with hair the color of radishes.

A few minutes later William returned with a numbered card and sat in the chair beside her. "We'll need to wait a while."

Katherine checked the time. Did she really want to know her future? What if he predicted something dreadful was going to happen to her?

She stood. "It's such a beautiful day. Let's come back another time."

William laughed. "Don't be silly. You're just nervous is all."

She frowned. Had he read her mind? He put his hand on hers. "Please, dear. This is important. It'll give me peace of mind for your final confirmation."

Did that mean William still wasn't certain she was the chosen one? Even after all he had said and done for her? She didn't want to discuss it here and stewed on it for a while.

A half hour later, a woman in a giant ostrich-feather-topped chapeau and, despite the warm day, fur coat came from behind a brocade curtain with a sly smile on her face. Strutting through the waiting room, she waved at the group and exited toward the lift.

The secretary, a few minutes later, motioned to the redheaded woman and escorted her to the secret chamber. After a full hour, the secretary stood before William and Katherine and said, "Cheiro will see you now. Follow me."

William whispered, "As I told you, it's important you don't share our names."

She nodded. The secretary opened the curtain and led them to sit at a small table with a pillow on it. Bright electric light shone above. He exited, and from behind a screen, Cheiro showed himself. One of the most dashing men Katherine had ever seen, he had a side part that separated his full head of wavy hair above a cleanshaven face. His dark eyes hinted of mystery. An exotic talisman sparkled over his full-length satin robe.

"Thank you for seeing us today," William said.

Cheiro sat across from them. "Happy to accommodate you."

"I'm curious to know why you do what you do," Katherine said.

"So that all will know their purpose, the duties they are best fitted for, and when and how to act so they might achieve success, happiness, and greater fulfillment of their destiny."

Katherine liked that answer. "What can we expect?"

He continued to speak flamboyantly like an actor on a stage with a crisp British accent, even though it was common knowledge he'd been born in Ireland. "I'll tell you about your past, present, and future. By finding the key to the number which seems to govern your life, I can foresee what year, and in some cases what month, climax of the life's career would be attained."

"You can do all that by just looking at one's hands?"

Cheiro smiled. "After all, hands are the tools that carry out the wishes of the brain. Now, let me see yours."

She removed her gloves and slid the back of her hands on the silk cushion.

He studied them for a moment, then looked up at her with wide eyes. "These are one of the most extraordinary pairs of hands I've ever encountered."

Did he say that to everyone?

"Madame what is your birthdate?" he asked.

"July 6, 1847."

"Your small, plump hands are rounded." Cheiro looked at her left hand for a full minute, gazed up at the ceiling, and then closed his eyes. Not at all like the other palm readers she'd met who'd traced each line like a road map explaining where the future led.

He began to speak in a deep voice. "Line of sun, starts brilliantly, then stops in the beginning. Doomed in early life due to troubles with father."

Katherine glanced at William, and his eyebrows raised to her.

"You're a person of strong habits. Independent and intuitive. Dramatic nature. Flair for performances. Marriage lines stooping. Failed relationships."

No surprise there.

"Line from heart bends down to meet line of head. Sexually unsatisfied although you have no problem with orgasms."

Katherine felt her face redden.

Cheiro continued, "Line of head, disturbed below Saturn's mount. You'll go to any length to achieve your aims. The year 1897 will be one of the most important of your life."

A rock in her gut tumbled, and she said, "That's next year."

He nodded, then blinked his eyes open and scrutinized William. "If this lady is in any way associated with whatever your business is, she'll take your place and carry on that work to even greater success than you could do."

Katherine was astonished. "Do you know who I am? Did someone tell you about me?"

Cheiro shook his head. "As I said, your hands are extraordinary. May I make impressions of them?"

"I suppose so."

He rolled ink on her palms and guided her to plant them in his guestbook. "Would you please sign it?"

She signed *Katherine A. Tingley, 6th March 1896.*

"Would you like to know your Fadic death date?"

"Do you think I should?" she asked William.

He nodded. "If you wish."

Cheiro looked at the ceiling again and closed his eyes. "July 11, 1929."

That was many years from now. She'd be over eighty. It thrilled her to think of all she could accomplish with that long a life.

Even though the session ended in thirty minutes, much had been received. As the chiromancer escorted them to the brocade curtain, William turned to him and said, "It may interest you to know I am William Q. Judge and you have predicted that she is destined to follow me as head of the Theosophical Society."

Cheiro smiled and held back the curtain. William and Katherine rode the elevator down and stepped out into the sunshine. "Do you think he was really reading my hands?"

"It seems they don't directly provide him information. Only stimulate his occult consciousness. Remember Madame Blavatsky said on the masters' direct authority that 1897 would close the cycle when something major would occur."

"What exactly do you think that means?" Katherine asked.

"Possibly the Society will witness the shutting of a door and cease in its direct public forum and be influenced by those who are chosen."

He stopped abruptly and looked at her. "We approach the beginning of that new cycle. I will not be here to witness it."

She started to argue, but he held up his hand to stop her. "You'll be the one to carry it out. Cheiro's reading made me certain of it."

Chapter Thirty-Four

The following day William's health took a turn for the worse. Throughout the next two weeks Ella and Katherine nursed him in rotation until one morning Katherine was quickly summoned to the brownstone. Ella, with exhaustion and sadness in her eyes, opened the door and shook her head.

Spots in her satchel, Katherine put it down and held Ella in her arms. At this time of dying, they had made a final peace at last. "Don't know what we would have done without you," Ella murmured.

Katherine said, "Get some rest, dear. I'll take over the vigil." She picked up the satchel and made her way down the hall to William's bedroom.

Less than a year since he'd been elected Outer Head for Life, his life on earth was coming to an end. Fully dressed, propped up by pillows, plum stains arched below his closed eyes. With so much weight loss, the signet ring had been moved to his thumb so it wouldn't slide off. His cane, like a scepter, leaned beside him on the nightstand, even though he hadn't used it for days.

Spots whined, and William reached out. Katherine laid the dog on the bed, and he crawled over and curled up next to him. William lifted his arm. "Purple."

She sat in the chair beside him, kept her sobs at bay, and grasped his hand. "I'm here." Despite the fever that raged through his body, his fingers were cold.

"It's the end of my little human life. Do not be sorrowful. I'll return to take up our unfinished work in another life, in a new day."

She recognized this phrase from his own published words in *The Ocean of Theosophy,* and she added in that vein, "I hope our paths will collide again to continue our toil together."

In hospitals, she'd seen men die before, even held their hands to ease their agony, but this was different. Many of those men called out in grief for their mothers or sweethearts, but not William. With a beatific smile on his swollen lips, he seemed to wait patiently at death's door.

He blinked his eyes, now faded blue, let go of her hand, and struggled to sit up. "You must follow your life's star and make your vision become reality."

"I'll try." She couldn't think of that now. "You've been the kindest, most generous guru a student could ever have."

"And you've been the kindest and most generous chela," he gasped and caught his breath, "a teacher could ever have." He pointed to the bedside table.

She picked up his journal, held it to him, but he pushed it away. "I'm weak. I'll dictate and sign."

Even though an entry would have more credence in his own hand, she dipped the pen in ink and sat ready, like so many times before.

"I . . . need . . . to . . . go." He wheezed for air.

She wrote, *I need to go*.

"Promise. There should be calmness." He paused, closed his eyes, and gasped. "Hold fast. Go slow."

She wrote, *Promise. There should be calmness. Hold fast. Go slow.* What did he mean? She raised her voice and reread the line to prompt him to continue, "Go slow."

He didn't respond. She read the words again. Was it directed at her or the organization? At times he called her Promise. He knew patience wasn't one of her virtues. He wanted calm for the Society, but without explicitly naming her as the next Outer Head, that might not be possible.

"William?"

He opened his mouth again, but nothing came out. His breath labored. He gazed at her lovingly, then winced. Tears streaked down both their cheeks. She hoped his pain would soon be over.

He moaned and fell back onto the pillows. His eyes flickered and closed; rattling sounds emanated from his chest. Perhaps every thought and circumstance of his life was flashing vividly across his mind. She remembered the first moment she'd seen him at the mission and their instantaneous connection. Like they'd known each other their whole lives and possibly in a past one. He'd been certain they had.

He had been a kind emperor, a mentor. He doted on her and believed in her, unlike her own father, unlike anyone else in the world. His joviality had lifted her spirits, and they agreed the stars had been aligned that brought them together. He'd brought the Americans together in harmony. Would she be able to continue this assignment?

A lengthy gasp escaped from his mouth. Then the room grew quiet. Sweet illumination lit his face. She felt his wrist for a pulse. At nine o'clock in the morning just short of his forty-fifth year, he was gone.

Grief seeped into her chest. She picked up Spots and held him in her arms. She didn't know how she'd survive without her teacher. She longed to be elated for him, certain his enlightened soul would be reborn into a new babe's body at some point in time at a higher level.

Holding his hand, she recited *Psalm 23*, the rhythm beating a broken-hearted melody of love in her heart. She pulled scissors from the nightstand, cut off a lock of his hair, slipped the curls in her handkerchief, and slid it into her pocket. She needed to gain the power to break the news to Ella.

Spots followed her out of the room. Katherine froze. She'd forgotten to remove the signet from William's thumb. She hesitated, unsure if she should go back inside.

She needed the ring. Was now the right time? It felt strangely frightening to stand outside the now-closed door. A minute ago, being in the room with him had felt natural, normal, even peaceful. Could she go back? She must. The ring was too important. She retraced her steps and touched his hand, but the ring was not on his finger.

Chapter Thirty-Five

After the funeral, Katherine needed silent solitude. Wild with grief, she couldn't eat, sleep, or concentrate. Most afternoons she settled into her easy chair and just closed her eyes. Even though William had spent years preparing her, she wasn't certain she had the strength to fight those who would certainly line up against her. For him, she had to forge ahead quickly with all the power she could muster. She needed to convince the cabinet she was the one and then surround herself with trusted confidants to support her.

A few evenings after the funeral, Nere and Joe called the other cabinet members, C.A. Griscom, Henry Turner Patterson, James M. Pryse, and Ernest Hargrove, to her home. As the latter walked in, Katherine felt a chill. Introductions were made, and the group gathered around the table. Spots was in his usual place near Katherine's feet. A bouquet of roses on the sideboard scented the air.

Nere began, "Thank you, Mr. and Mrs. Tingley for opening your home to us this evening."

Philo grinned and jumped up from his chair behind Katherine. "You're most welcome!"

Katherine glared at him. He was wound up but had been warned to hold off comments unless she asked him to speak. William had encouraged her to include Philo as much as possible to support her. She hoped he wouldn't embarrass her tonight and his gadget would add ambience to the evening.

Nere continued, "Gentlemen, as executor of William's estate, I've accompanied Mrs. Judge to the bank to retrieve his will. Hargrove, Pryse, and I have searched their home and Society headquarters for designation papers. However, we've found nothing in his handwriting bearing upon the future of the Society, nor did we find anything naming directly or indirectly his successor."

This infuriated Katherine. Why hadn't William left a document somewhere with his final wishes? That would have made the transition so much easier.

"Where's the signet?" Patterson, a dainty man, tugged on his thick chops.

"We don't know," Pryse said.

"Doesn't matter." Hargrove grumbled. "Since it's known by all I'm the next Outer Head, let's move forward with that decision. And come to consensus tonight before the organization collapses into chaos. All in favor—"

Joe cut in, "Not so fast."

Katherine was relieved not everyone in the room felt Hargrove should be the one. At the funeral, he'd insisted on giving the eulogy. He'd towered above the podium with his snobbish British accent and orated on and on much longer than necessary. Having no idea of what William had meant by brotherhood, Hargrove talked more about himself than William.

"I agree. Let's move forward with appointing Hargrove to the position." Griscom smiled at his chum.

Nere looked at Hargrove and said, "Remember, William told us such a person existed and would be recognized as his successor when the time came. I don't think he meant you."

"Is it you?" Patterson asked Nere. "You're a highly qualified candidate."

"Heavens, no." Nere shook his head. "I'm certain it's not me. Besides, I'm too beleaguered by business ventures."

"What about Claude? He's a fine speaker, and he was closely connected with Madame Blavatsky." Patterson had a practical mind.

Nere looked at each member in turn. "I'm convinced William had another choice."

All grew quiet as the men at the table sat up straight. Under the table,

Spots snored loudly. The room broke out in laughter that diminished the tension. Katherine gently nudged Spots with her foot.

Nere cleared his throat. "During the last years of his life, William was closely connected in active collaboration with a New York resident who was his chela. That chela was in communication with the masters."

"Look here! Madame Blavatsky—" Hargrove raised his voice.

Nere shook his head. "Hargrove, stop. I too have personally been in association with this chela. William told me and others she had great promise. At the request of that chela, you've been called here tonight to become acquainted with the situation."

The men's heads turned to stare at Katherine, who tried not to smile.

Hargrove bellowed, "Are you daft? It's impossible for us to accept an unknown person."

"I agree we should make a choice soon." Nere kept his voice calm.

Joe said, "I can vouch for her too. Why don't we attempt to receive a compelling message from William about his wishes?"

Hargrove jumped up. "This is a ridiculous waste of time."

Nere waved him back to his seat. Hargrove looked at the others for support. Receiving none, he took his time sitting down.

"Let's at least try," Joe said, and the others nodded their agreement.

"Some of you may be aware Mr. Tingley is a brilliant inventor and has created a device for us to use." Nere tipped his head toward Philo.

This was a risk. Katherine hoped her mediumship skills would strongly be with her tonight and she'd receive a message from William's recently departed soul to share with these men.

Philo held up his innovation. "As you can see, this resembles the Ever-Ready hand torch invented a few years ago, only my invention is better. Mine uses four dry cell batteries instead of only three. I've replaced the cheap brass reflector with polished nickel, a much stronger metal."

Hargrove yawned loudly. Katherine tried to catch Philo's eye, but he ignored her and kept rambling, "I use a thicker cardboard scroll instead of their flimsy paper."

Nere cut in, "Philo. Everyone is anxious to begin."

Katherine lowered the sconces and let the glowing candles cast eerie shadows across the walls as she returned to her seat.

Philo flicked on the torch. "I have secured a red scarf over the glass for occult purposes. I've heard spirits prefer that color. The light will continue to blink." He pointed it at the ceiling as it flickered on and off like a lighthouse beacon.

The men murmured, obviously impressed.

Katherine instructed in a businesslike voice, "Let's hold hands and close our eyes." She recoiled inside as Hargrove's moist hand clasped hers. Thankfully, Joe's warm one on the other side counteracted it.

Katherine continued, "Let's inhale in and out together." She set the pace.

Katherine's chakras felt charred from Hargrove's energy. She tried to imagine he wasn't there but to no avail. She focused on breathing slowly in and out and finally her chakras began to clear. She walked across the bridge and through the wooden door. Vibrations sped from her hand to Hargrove's on her right and around to the other hands at the oblong table, swift as a racehorse. As it reached her again, Joe gently squeezed her hand as if sending encouragement.

"Open your eyes," she said.

As they did, a zephyr blew the lace curtains into the room and a jovial voice said, "Give me the torch."

Spots jumped up with a bark. Gasps were heard around the table. Katherine's heart filled with love. There was no mistaking that familiar Irish brogue. She'd hoped to receive a message from him, but this was beyond fantastic.

Philo's hands shook as the room pulsed red. He held the torch at arm's length, and the next instant it flew high over the table in circles, flashing on and off quickly. Then the light stayed on as it slowly swept across the room.

All eyes turned to the wall lit by the crimson spotlight, and a vapor began to gather.

"Phosphorescence!" Hargrove hollered. Awestruck, Katherine held her breath. The billowing cloud became more visible as it grew in volume, danced in the still air, and slowly brightened into scarlet luminosity.

"There's a face," Nere whispered.

"Whose is it?" Pryse asked.

"It's the Rajah!" Patterson shouted.

William's visage remained for fifteen seconds, then the light began to fade. "What's the matter with you? Come up, light!" William's voice commanded the torch.

So akin to a command William would have used, the room exploded in laughter. The light grew to an unusual brilliance, and the face said, "Go down."

In an instant, the light grew dim, snapped off altogether, and the torch fell onto the carpet. With the room in complete darkness, disappointment vanquished ecstasy for Katherine as she thought it was all over.

William's voice said, "Open your palms. I have a gift for each of you."

An expectant silence followed. A red ray of light flew in front of Nere and into his hands.

It moved to Patterson's, and he yelled, "An apport! Thank you, Rajah."

Grateful voices and surprised expressions continued around the table as the light scanned members' faces. Katherine held her breath and kept her hands open. Nothing dropped into them until finally, after a few minutes, something weighty and cold fell there, and she clasped it tightly. Feeling the details with her fingers, she dared not hope what it might be.

A moment later the torch fell to the ground again. "Namaste," William's voice echoed as his visage faded away.

The sconces and candlelight rose. Katherine blinked her eyes to adjust to the brightness. One at a time, each shared their sacred gifts, varying in size from tiny brilliants to those measuring two inches in length. Nere had received a giant amethyst geode broken in half. Philo laughed aloud when he displayed his piece, a red ruby in the shape of a heart. Joe showed his aquamarine, Patterson a rose quartz, Griscom a blue sapphire, Pryse a sparkling emerald. Hargrove's pieces of onyx chips were no bigger than his fingernail.

Lastly it was her turn. She opened her hands to reveal the ring. There could be no clearer sign from William.

Hargrove bellowed and leapt up. "There's trickery here! I'll never agree!"

"Are you suggesting I'm a charlatan?" Katherine asked.

"Why would he choose you? Why would he choose her?" he asked the men.

Nere calmly said, "Maybe he thought she would continue his vision, unlike others."

Katherine looked down, concealing her exaltation, and slipped on the ring.

Hargrove raised his eyebrows at Griscom, who said, "I'm not convinced either way. I suggest we not accept anything that isn't written in William's own hand."

A clamorous crescendo filled the parlor as opinions were argued back and forth. Hargrove and Griscom on one side, Patterson, Joe, and Pryse on the other. Katherine put her head on the table and covered her ears, her moment of happiness crushed. Philo stepped over and put his hand on her back.

Nere finally pounded on the table. "Gentlemen, our William would be appalled at your behavior. Let's search his rooms again tomorrow for more evidence of his wishes."

Drained after everyone left, Katherine thanked Philo for doing such a great job and supporting her. She hied up to her room, climbed next to Spots on the bed, and nestled against propped pillows. In front of all those men, she had needed to maintain her composure as if it was the most natural thing for William to appear in her parlor and give them each blessed gifts. To have seen her beloved teacher's face in the fog had been a shock.

She held her hand up to the light. The original signet designed by Master Morya for Madame Blavatsky and given to William after she passed. Katherine had seen it on his finger many times but had never held it. She studied the Sanskrit markings, interlaced triangle, and oval agate with shiny flecks and bloodred veins. Photos showed Madame Blavatsky had worn it on the fourth finger of her left hand. Katherine easily slid it on her own fourth finger. With this ring, without a doubt, she was William's chosen one, and she needed to do everything in her power to become the next Outer Head and bring Theosophy, with all its brotherhood, to the masses across the globe. And her vision of the white city on a sundown sea flashed before her eyes with elation.

Chapter Thirty-Six

The next night Nere called the cabinet back. Philo was out for the evening, so it was just the men and Katherine. At the oval table, Nere began, "Joe and I searched William's home again and found this sketch." He held up Madame Blavatsky's drawing William had shared years ago.

What a relief—this should be evidence enough. All eyes turned toward Katherine.

"That's sure a keen likeness," Patterson murmured.

Hargrove muttered, "We all know William sketched well."

"Look at the signature." Nere handed the paper to Hargrove.

"H-P-B," Hargrove read aloud.

There could be no denying whose initials those were.

"Flip it over," Nere pointed to it.

Hargrove turned it over, didn't say a word, and handed it to Griscom, who read it aloud, "Have you found your chela yet?"

"We don't know if it's authentic," Hargrove protested.

Nere held up a small diary and said, "While we were searching the Rajah's study, Ella brought this to us. She found it between William's mattress and bedstead and thought it might be helpful. Most of the pages are blank except ten that contain cryptic references."

He turned to a specific page. "As you'll see, William's X symbol refers to a chela with promise. It states X received soul messages for him from Madame Blavatsky. He also writes Purple's identity should be kept secret for a year after she becomes Outer Head to shield her from slander and persecution." He passed the diary to Patterson. Katherine's spirits were raised by this evidence.

"This shows Katherine enjoyed the full measure of William's sureness." Patterson smiled and handed it to Hargrove.

His face blanched. "How do we know for certain he's referring to Mrs. Tingley?"

"Who else would it be?" Joe asked. "He called her Purple and Promise too."

"Still, I'll never agree to it," Hargrove scoffed.

The men decided to wait two nights before making a final decision. She walked them to the door and said her good nights, but Hargrove hung back in the foyer.

Exhausted, she opened the door wider. "Goodbye, Hargrove."

"We need to talk," he said.

"Yes." She turned and looked up at him. "Please support me as Outer Head."

"Please support me," he whined, mimicking her. "Why should I?"

"Because it was William's wish," she said softly.

Hargrove's massive body drew close to her, and he glowered down into her face. "No. You somehow tricked him into falling for your wiles."

She shook inside and stepped back. "William didn't choose you, and neither did Madame Blavatsky."

He moved toward her again. "Just like you to try to dupe us with phosphorescence, apports, and flowers from the ceiling."

Angry now, Katherine moved toward him and shouted, "No earthly human could have done those things!"

"I don't care. I should be Outer Head."

"What's it going to take for you to endorse me?" she yelled.

"What are you willing to offer?" Hargrove asked.

She couldn't afford to lose Hargrove in the cabinet. Not now. He had too many followers and connections. "The organization's treasurer."

He shook his head. "Nooo," he said, rolling out the *O*'s.

"Vice president?"

He hollered, "Madame Blavatsky promised me at least the presidency. I'm not taking anything less than that."

Katherine abhorred the thought of giving him any authority, but she didn't have a choice.

"Okay." She nodded slowly. The only reason she agreed was because they both knew the Outer Head had all the power to make final decisions and the president was mostly a figurehead.

He walked out the door and slammed it behind him. Katherine made her way up to bed. As she crawled in, she felt tossed like a ship during a storm. She missed William, missed being his chela, and wanted this controversy over.

Why her? Had she been favored by William as the next Outer Head because she reminded him of Madame Blavatsky: strong, virile, dominating, mysterious, yet compassionate? Or was it because the Outer Head had shown him, through occult powers, she more than approved? Had the masters chosen Katherine too?

Being Outer Head was a colossal responsibility. Katherine wouldn't ever be able to fill William's shoes. They were so different. Without a word, he'd been able to convince people of his philosophy and his power to alleviate their woes. Would she be able to do that too?

She twisted the signet on her finger, her grief bubbling up anew. "William, how can I go on without you?"

Even though the windows were closed, a warm breeze blew through her heart, and his voice whispered, "You must carry on with your own vision to lead. I'll always be with you."

Feeling his love, her dream on the Pacific slowly reappeared, less clear than before, as if on a fog-shrouded coast. Still her vision. Still her land. She'd shift the Society's direction and create an educational and learning community where Theosophy could be practiced in daily life. Her aim would be to make Theosophy intensely practical, rooted in a deep altruistic ethic, not just for the study of metaphysics and explorations of visionary realms. Not just for the wealthy, but for the downtrodden too. Not just for

Americans, but for those around the world. That would make William proud.

As she drifted off to sleep, she mused on how she would convince the cabinet and the membership of her desire. Later, words woke her, words, words in the dark of night. She turned on the lantern, grabbed her journal, and in a daze began to write the words that became phrases that became sentences. Red ink poured from her black ink pen. Master Morya was with her:

World Crusade to Conquer the Earth

- *Reinforce William's factions abroad to establish new lodges around the world.*
- *Invade England & India where Besant & Olcott reside to claim the Society's leadership.*
- *Visit Madame Blavatsky's masters in India to gain guidance and endorsement.*

Only three goals, but all very complicated.

Katherine said to the men at the next cabinet meeting, "Imagine seeing the Celtic mounds of Ireland, pyramids in Egypt, and mahatma retreats of India. We'll spread Theosophy around the world, gather more members, open new lodges, gain positive press." To avoid stirring up controversies over authenticity, Katherine chose not to share she'd received a message from Master Morya. Instead, she decided to garner support for the School for the Revival of the Lost Mysteries of Antiquity in the West, predicted by Madame Blavatsky, and plans for the World Crusade.

Hargrove muttered, "How in the heck are you going to pay for it?"

She didn't miss a beat. "I'll invite affluent members to finance themselves on the trip and others to donate to the cause."

"What an adventure. I'll go." Patterson smiled broadly. "I believe our friend Pierce will come too." Both men had business and leadership skills and would be assets to the journey. Pierce's engineering firm and Patterson's hardware store were both extremely successful.

Nere offered to help support the Crusade, although he'd be unable to join them for any length of time.

"I'm confident Claude would be eager to participate." Patterson started to jot a list.

"What about you?" She looked at the others.

Joe and Pryse said they couldn't commit but supported the idea.

"I'm uncertain." Griscom glanced at Hargrove's frowning face.

Even though the idea of traveling with Hargrove churned her stomach, Katherine forced herself to appeal to his ego. "We need you. With your brilliance and contacts, you're the only one who can help us strengthen and penetrate across the pond. Please join us."

He smugly raised his head. "I'll consider it."

The cabinet unanimously endorsed Katherine as William's successor and signed a pact to keep her identity secret for a year at his request. They would start the convention on a united front, and Katherine moved forward with devising more of her vision. As the time approached, she felt excited but also wary. What if Hargrove changed his mind? What if the membership wouldn't vote for her without being seen?

Chapter Thirty-Seven

On April 16, Theosophical members from almost every American state and Canadian province, international figures, and the press poured into Madison Square Garden. As an orchestra played John Philip Sousa, cabinet members, including Katherine as one of the speakers, marched onto the platform and took their seats. She trembled as the music shifted to a somber rhythm while a bronze bust was unveiled. Modeled from William's death mask, as well as photographs, it truly resembled her teacher's refined hair, distinguished nose, and tender mouth. The shape of his eyes was the same; however, without the light that had shone in them, it made her miss him even more.

Hargrove struck the gavel and officially opened the meeting, reading the roster of new officers, including himself as president and an anonymous Outer Head. Nere responded to the objection from the floor on the sacredness of that person's identity to be revealed one year later at William's request. After speculative rumblings, nevertheless the slate of officers was approved.

Cabinet members and other prominent Theosophists said a few words, or lots of words. Katherine understood William's concerns about her safety, but even so, as she paced to the podium and began her speech, buried among the other ones, it seemed she deceived the membership. "Madame Blavatsky predicted the founding of an educational institution in the Western United States near the ocean. To honor her, I suggest we begin to plan and raise funds for the School for the Revival of the Lost Mysteries of Antiquity, a repository of arcane lore to be utilized for modern science, religion, and philosophy. To increase our membership abroad and search for others who may want to move there, a World Crusade might be considered."

After the session five thousand dollars were pledged, and the fourteen members of the Inner Esoteric Council were sworn to secrecy and told the identity of Katherine as Outer Head, as well as the plans for a World Crusade. At the end of the meeting, russet-headed Claude, with his beautiful fiancée, Leoline, made their way to Katherine. "We want to join you on the Crusade. As you know, we were married in Egypt in a past life and would love to see it again."

"You'd be an asset to the group, but you two aren't married in this lifetime. Traveling together wouldn't be appropriate."

Leoline blushed, and Claude said, "We've been preoccupied."

"How'd you like to be the first Theosophical wedding recipients?" Katherine asked.

Two weeks later, on the platform in the headquarters building, Katherine sat in a heavy veil and purple robe, covered from head to toe. No one could tell if she was a man or woman. It was the first time she had appeared in public as Outer Head, albeit incognito. The anticipation filled her with joy.

Leoline's face glowed, her hair piled high in the new Gibson Girl fashion, her white satin gown trimmed with seed pearls and a lace train. Claude was fine-looking in a black frock coat with gray stripes. So as not to reveal Katherine's identity through her voice, Hargrove verbally conducted the ceremony. Esoterics, the Theosophical inner section of advanced students of occultism, circled around the couple as rings were slipped onto their fingers and the sacred word was chanted. As the sounds echoed and died down, Katherine crisscrossed her arms over the couple while Hargrove solemnly read, "The Outer Head strengthens the bond between you on a spirit plane forever."

After the ceremony, there were congratulations galore. Katherine foresaw many more sacred rites in the future. She smiled beneath her veils, feeling as happy as if she'd pulled a brass ring from the Central Park carousel. She truly was the head of the Society now.

Exhausted the next morning, she could barely lift her spoon at breakfast. Philo dramatically read her newspaper articles agog with descriptions of the occult wedding ceremony and speculations about who the veiled mahatma might be.

The doorbell rang. Spots ran down the hall barking his head off and Philo stood.

Katherine said, "Ignore it and they'll go away."

Philo sat and continued to read. Then the bell began to ring again, the knocker clacked, and someone rapped on the door.

"For goodness' sake! See who it is." Katherine felt a headache coming on.

Philo returned. "It's the press. They want an interview with the Theosophical Society's new Outer Head."

"Tell them that person does not live here."

Philo went back to the door and soon returned. "They want to speak with Mrs. Tingley, the new Outer Head, and learn all about the upcoming World Crusade."

Katherine hit the table. "That Hargrove! He must have spilled the beans. Tell the press to leave." Katherine suspected he'd wanted to generate more attention to himself and take the wind out of her sails. She dragged herself up to her bedroom, but the racket wouldn't stop. Philo knocked on her door and opened it with a frown.

Katherine sighed. "Tell the *New York Journal* to send a reporter tomorrow and I'll give an interview." She wanted to manage the information. If not, who knew what they'd dig up about her: the traveling theater experiences, her father's illegal indiscretions . . .

Hargrove sent her a message: *I revealed your identity so you could be the visible leader of the Crusade.* With Joe, she composed her biographical sketch, made Hargrove sign it as president, and wired it out to the press and Theosophical membership. The publicity created enthusiastic applause from members and gained new ones, and further financial resources rolled in. As crusade fervor rose, so did her confidence that fellow travelers would remain loyal to her, that they'd be welcomed abroad with open arms by the citizens in countries they visited, and someday Theosophy would take over the world.

Chapter Thirty-Eight

Two months after her identity had been revealed, she sat on the Madison Square Garden dais once again to inaugurate the World Crusade destined to spread Theosophy around the world. Invitations addressed to Freemasons and Lovers of Humanity had been distributed across the city, and a standing-room-only crowd filled the arena. The gold etched initials ITNOTGA, *In the Name of the Great Architect,* graced the purple program's front cover.

Nearly eight o'clock on her watch; almost time to begin. She clutched her grandfather's watch and admired the signet ring, grateful for the path William had set before her, to work toward the good of all mankind. Her grandfather and William, both with her in spirit now, were proud of her for initiating this grand endeavor.

Lights blinked off and on, the arena quieted, and a string quartet began to play Mozart. As the music died down, Claude took his place at the podium and welcomed the crowd. He introduced himself and his new wife, Leoline, and invited the rest of the Crusade members to stand as he read their names. "Henry Turner Patterson, Frances M. Pierce, Ernest Templeton Hargrove, Mr. and Mrs. Claude Falls Wright, Mr. and Mrs. Philo Tingley." They waited for the applause to die down and took their seats again. Claude talked about his experiences as secretary to Madame Blavatsky and the history of the Theosophical Society.

Patterson spoke articulately about his reasons for going on the Crusade, and then his friend Pierce, a tall man with a mustache and goatee, read heartfelt words. Scheduled to go up next, Katherine stared out at the audience, trying to abate her thumping heart. She'd been onstage many times before but never with such a rousing crowd.

By the time Claude introduced her as head of the Theosophical movement, she had full command of her senses. She strode to the podium, raised her arms in greeting, and powerfully began, "When Theosophy has liberated all, the prisons will be emptied, wars will cease, hunger and famine will be unknown, and under the shadowing wings of the great brotherhood, all mankind will abide in peace, unity, and love."

She continued her speech, keeping her eyes slightly above the audience until she sensed they were rapt. The words flowed, and she lost herself in time and space. As she concluded, her body pulsated with joy, and she made her way back to her chair to rousing applause. She was that much closer to changing the world and making her vision come true.

Hargrove as the organization's president ended the program with a long-winded speech. Besides his egoism, the kickoff had gone off beautifully. At least she'd felt that way until she read the paper the following morning: *Not generally known she approached her fiftieth year, she was garbed in purple, robust and energetic in carriage with attractive features set off by a mass of dark hair—*

"Why did they need to mention my age?" she moaned to Philo.

He chuckled. "Dear, the reporter meant it as a compliment. He did say you had attractive features. And I agree." Philo kissed her forehead, which raised her spirits.

That afternoon the Crusaders rode the train to Boston for a repeat presentation at the Tremont Theatre that held two thousand seats.

On a misty morning two days later, the Crusade party boarded the SS *Saale* in New York Harbor. Its smokestacks and masts rocked back and forth as the ocean liner pulled out into the East River toward the Atlantic. Katherine planted her shoes firmly on deck and waved to the well-wishing crowd with gloved hands. She wished Nere had been able to sail with them, but his business didn't allow it. Hopefully he'd join them in Ireland.

"This ship holds one hundred and fifty first-class passengers, ninety in second class, and up to a thousand in steerage." Philo chattered on, "It can go up to seventeen knots and is 439 feet and six inches . . ."

She frowned at him, and he moved his fingers over his mouth. She'd advised him that if he kept technical information to a minimum and listened to others, they would like him more. Katherine had suggested he stay home but he promised not to embarrass her. It would be better for the cause with a husband accompanying her anyway—that was if he behaved by holding back odd comments and limiting alcohol intake.

Years ago, the last time she'd left from this port, she'd scanned the crowd for her first husband. He might have hired men to search for her and even put her in an asylum for disobeying him. It hadn't been until the shore was out of sight that she'd breathed easier. Now citizens along the water's edge went about their business. The *Saale* cruised under the bridge as a rowboat and steam wheeler passed by. Farther out, Katherine teared up as they sailed by the Statue of Liberty, remembering the day it had been unveiled. The copper had recently begun to patina to a gorgeous shade of verdigris. Gulls flew overhead as their ship progressed out into the open ocean where the sky turned blue.

She hadn't thought it appropriate to procure first-class cabins, but the others had insisted. They were the ones funding the Crusade and she had to pick her battles. To accomplish all she'd set out do, she'd need to maintain group camaraderie. She repeated in her mind the goals embedded in her psyche: spread Theosophy around the world, establish more lodges, and gain more members, including in England and India where Annie and Olcott reigned, and visit Madame Blavatsky's teachers in the Himalayas.

At dinner that night, the opulent dining room shone brightly with chandeliers, white tablecloths, and a plethora of offerings on the menu. Dapper men in tuxedos and women bejeweled in gowns chatted and enjoyed their meals. Were these the people who needed to learn hope was in their futures?

At her group's table, Philo couldn't even get a word in edgewise as Hargrove droned on and on. Patterson and Pierce appeared to courteously listen.

Leoline's beautiful eyes began to droop. She blinked them open, shook her shoulders, and sat up straight. Claude covered his mouth to hide a yawn. Hargrove bragged about the occult presentations he'd do and told a story Katherine had heard three times before. How could she listen to this pompous nincompoop one more minute, let alone for months? It was impossible to feel love and compassion toward him. He assumed the world revolved around him.

After dinner, salty sea air filled her senses as Philo escorted her to the deck. She sat on a lounge chair and asked him to get her a blanket. He returned momentarily and covered her in it. "I'm going to bed. I'll see you in the morning." As he left, she hoped he wasn't going to the bar.

She lay back on the lounge chair. Alone at last, she studied the moonless velvet sky, which sparkled with billions of diamonds, reminding Katherine of her smallness, a mere gem chip in the universe, and the billions of poor in the world. How would they reach those that needed to hear about the hope of Theosophy the most? The softly rocking ship soothed her to sleep until a baby's cry woke her.

She opened her eyes to see the sun rise over a cobalt-blue ocean in oranges and pinks. She crossed to the railing, and a stench rose from the third-class deck beneath, where the babe continued to shriek. The deck's surface below was crammed with mats. Atop were those unable to afford their own cabins who had moved outside from the tight space inside.

That had been her situation many years ago. Even though she'd been relieved to escape the States, she'd been unprepared for the squalor of steerage, where passengers were packed like pilchards, bathrooms were buckets, food was slop, and privacy was nonexistent. The grind of machinery creaked and squeaked all night. She too had chosen to sleep on deck when weather allowed.

These were the people who needed to hear of humanity. Many customary Theosophical elite tea-and-lectures had been planned for the Crusade. She'd move that day's event from the first-class floor down to steerage. The others would object, but this would be a battle worth fighting.

That afternoon drizzle dripped from the sky, so the group moved the presentation inside. She stood on a wooden crate and began her speech. “Friends, have hope! All is not lost.”

A theologian cut in with his fire and brimstone. “Sinners are eternally damned to hell.”

She spouted, “I disagree! A sinning man should have other chances through good works.”

Another man in the crowd yelled, “Hear, hear! That’s the right kind of religion!”

And so, the real Crusade had begun. She’d never been more thrilled in her life. This was her destiny.

Chapter Thirty-Nine

Over a week later, the ship pulled into the bustling Southampton port. When their train arrived in London, Katherine promptly canceled the elite tea-and-lecture arrangements and insisted on hosting a Brotherhood Supper for the poor. Furious at the change, Hargrove got into quite a row with Katherine. He'd planned a demonstration of his occult capabilities for the tea, but as Outer Head, she had the power to change the schedule.

At Albert Hall, the Crusaders fed three hundred prior to a speech for the masses. Her companions complained about the expense and insisted on limiting the number of these suppers. Hargrove especially had no idea how essential these healthy meals were for the poor, with fresh vegetables, hearty soup, fish, and bread. She compromised, and they hosted smaller salon events as well.

Katherine smiled at a newspaper clipping that read: *Mrs. Tingley is determined to break down all technical lecturing, forego Sanskrit terms, and do more heart-talking that anyone can understand.*

The Crusaders left London, speeding throughout the country and speaking in as many towns as possible. Brotherhood Suppers fared better than the elite meetings due to interrupters during the question-and-answer periods asking about the old Hodgson report that had accused Madame Blavatsky of forging letters from the masters. Katherine grew suspicious that Annie Besant and Colonel Olcott were behind the troublemakers.

In August, after visiting Scotland, the Crusaders arrived in Dublin,

William's homeland, for the Theosophical European Convention. His dear friend poet George Russell and many other influential literary figures were there to greet them. Katherine was pleased Nere had arrived to join the Crusaders too.

When she began to orate at a Brotherhood Supper, the crowd rebelled. Ireland had been Annie and Olcott territory, and folks there weren't keen to listen to the American Theosophists. Katherine wanted to gain their attention and intuitively said, "To honor William Q. Judge, we'll search on the outskirts of Killarney for the cornerstone for the School for the Revival of Lost Mysteries of Antiquity to be built in the Western United States as predicted by Madame Blavatsky. Mr. Judge often spoke of thin places where the separation between the divine and the earth are slender. He believed we've all experienced these places in our lives—those mystical, unexplainable touches with the divine that both test and strengthen our faith."

A few days later Katherine left Philo in the comfort of their Killarney inn while Crusaders, George Russell, and other Irish Theosophists, fifteen in all, were driven out on the grasslands in carts. A camp was set up below a mountain with a view of the lakes.

Katherine walked onto the damp moors with winds whispering from all directions, reminding her of the three sisters in Shakespeare's Scottish play who forewarned that something wicked was coming. Could that be a bad omen? Would she find the cornerstone? Or perhaps be humiliated in front of the others?

That night rain pelted her tent and woke her from an abyss of dreams. She pulled the eiderdown over her shoulder and tried to fall back to sleep, but a vision floated to her mind's surface. A spirit with blue eyes flew overhead above a dirt road and motioned for her to follow. They reached the shores of a distant lake with mountains above and a floral-filled meadow beyond. A path opened before her, up and up until a grassy knoll of an ancient ruin appeared, and she landed and walked toward it.

The vision flickered in her memory like a fading candle. Quickly, quickly, before it escaped her, she needed to jot it down before the sparks extinguished. Her diary left at the inn, she seized an envelope from the ground and rapidly sketched a map of the path. She slipped the envelope in her pocket and had the group awakened.

Outside her tent, the sunrise barely visible through the mist, a squall of wind blew her hair from its bindings to fly wildly about her shoulders. The campers crawled out of their tents, sleepy-eyed and dazed.

"It's time to start the day," Katherine shouted above the gales.

Hargrove stood above her. "Are you senseless? With this weather, we must cancel today's excursion."

"This isn't what we signed up for," Leoline, who never complained, said.

"Katherine, be reasonable." Nere put his hand on her shoulder.

She insisted, "I've had a vision. We're off to discover the cornerstone. Would any of you want to miss that?"

Shaking his head, Nere helped her climb aboard the first cart next to the driver. She pulled her cloak's hood up and pointed her walking stick onward as the caravan trailed behind. The cart pitched back and forth while she followed the map with her fingers. On the other side of a forest, a slow-moving stream flowed into a lake, where ducks rocked on its surface and marshy reeds filled its banks. The cart crossed a wooden plank that spanned a stream that moved up the shore to the other side, and on and on.

They twisted on the bumpy road for thirty minutes. Had she made an error? Would she be accused of taking them on a wild goose chase? Should they turn back?

The carts behind her stopped, and Hargrove called, "We've gone far enough. Obviously, your vision wasn't correct."

She would not be bullied to follow that man's orders and waved her walking stick forward.

Nere asked, "Are you sure?"

"We'll go a bit farther," she said.

They started up again and kept going. After another half hour she was about to give up when a sensation of warmth filled her chest. The winds died down and the sun shone through the mist. Just like in her dream, a purple mountain rose. The searched-for site would appear around the bend. Near a glistening lake, beyond the pines and an eagle's rookery, an ancient ruin appeared.

"Stop," she told the driver. "Here it is."

Nere helped her from the cart, and she motioned the others to join her. "This site was a sacred temple many centuries ago." Her feet followed her vision to the edge of the ruin until it told her this was the place. She reached down and brushed away the soil with her gloved fingers until they hit stone. Nere assisted, until a triangular-shaped stone about two feet long of a greenish hue appeared, exactly where the vision had shown her it would be.

She removed a glove, placed her bare palm on the shivering mass, and yelled over the voices, "This is the one. I feel vibrations." The group gathered round, eyes opened wide. Hargrove stood with his hands on his hips and a frown on his face.

"Here. Feel it." Katherine stood back as each follower put a palm flat on the stone and nodded as they felt the tremor. Afterward, she looked out over the vista to the shimmering lake and above. "A great temple once stood here, filled with ancient worshippers, and like them we're here to worship nature again."

As she instructed, the Theosophists sat in a circle around the cornerstone and observed a moment of silence. She led the sacred chant, reverberating it out into the heavens. Then, one by one, each chose a rock and laid it atop the stone with a prayer of hope for the school. They continued to sit around the cairn in awe until carts pulled up to carry them back to camp.

On the ride back, she said to Nere, "Now that the cornerstone's been found, we need to purchase the school site as soon as possible."

He blinked. "You don't even know the location."

"Remember, General Fremont told me it's in San Diego in a place called Point Loma."

"I've been to San Diego, but I've never heard of Point Loma. How can we buy land we haven't even seen?"

"I've seen it in my visions."

He laughed. "What's the rush?"

"We should dedicate the school when the Crusade reaches California. The new century's fast approaching. We need to be ready to usher it in."

"The Crusade alone will deplete our funds. Once we've built the school, how will we sustain it?"

"We'll be self-sufficient in all respects." This was another thing worth fighting for. "Instructors will work for free and be learners too. We'll charge a fee to those who can afford it. Some will welcome the opportunity to give more; some may even wish to give everything they possess. Others will be admitted who have nothing at all. At some point I see over five hundred people living there."

"We'll need funds to get started."

She looked at him directly and smiled. "If anyone can raise them, it's you. You'll be an example to others to contribute. When should you go to San Diego?"

"As soon as possible."

"But you've always wanted to see the pyramids."

"I'll go to Egypt another time. This is more important."

"Are you certain?" she asked.

He nodded. "I have other business to attend to anyway."

"Philo seems a bit weary and ready to go home. Do you mind if he goes back with you?" She didn't mention his behavior was on the verge of slipping.

"That's fine."

"Keep the organization's name secret from the press. I don't want anyone to know we're the buyers yet."

When they arrived back at camp, the sunset cast a magical spell around the campfire as the Crusaders and guests conversed and sang in jubilant celebration. Sparks flew up to the mountains, mystic woods, and the wonderous stars. Katherine's spirits lifted higher than ever before as she imagined the future.

Chapter Forty

Across the continent, newspapers reported the search and Katherine's discovery of the cornerstone for the School for the Revival of Lost Mysteries of Antiquity. The Crusaders traveled through France and Holland, where they picked up another cornerstone, and then departed for Germany. Even though it was difficult to communicate through interpreters, Katherine felt they'd made fine results spreading the Theosophical word and gathering more members.

They'd been on the road for three months since Ireland, but she hadn't heard from Nere about the property. In early September, they finally stopped to rest in Geneva. She made her way up to her suite and eagerly flipped through the mail that had caught up with her. When she touched his wire, she felt bad news was inside and reluctantly opened it: *Impossible to purchase place you name; owned by the government.*

Jolted, she threw the cable on the floor, fell onto the bed, and pressed her face into a pillow. How could she have been so wrong? All her promises and plans were based on that property. Fremont had traveled up and down the coast. Could he have been confused and the land was somewhere else? Even William had agreed Point Loma was her destiny.

She spurned the afternoon excursion, curled up into a ball, and slept until supper, then joined the Crusaders in the dining room.

Pierce said, "We found another cornerstone today."

She tried to smile, braced herself for the reaction, and read the cable to them. Most commiserated with her. All except Hargrove, who raised his eyebrows. "So much for your childhood vision." He laughed.

"Leave her alone." Patterson frowned.

"What're you going to tell the press?" Hargrove asked with a surly smile.

"Let's wait," Claude advised. "I know we're supposed to leave tomorrow, but there's a Theosophist in Geneva that would like to meet us."

The next day Katherine sat at a table in the hotel's salon and tried to frame a cable back to Nere. Stumped, she looked out at the iridescent lake with snowcapped peaks behind it.

A young man followed Claude into the room. "This is the member I told you about."

The chap handed Claude his Swiss hat and walking stick, kissed Katherine's hand, and said, "I'm Gottfried de Purucker, but everyone calls me G. de P. It's such a pleasure to meet you." His English was impeccable, with no trace of an accent. "I've been following the Crusade's feats."

She smiled at the stranger and wanted to touch his golden hair that shone in the light. She looked deeply into his eyes that sparkled as blue as the lake. A gentle rotation scrolled in her chest, and she felt an immediate connection to him. "I'm busy, but I can spare a moment or two." She extended her hand to the chair next to hers, and Claude sat nearby.

They discussed finding the cornerstone, the upcoming crusade itinerary, and her plans for the school. After a while, G. de P. rose. "Thank you for seeing me. I've already taken up too much of your time." He started for the door.

"Wait!" Katherine couldn't let him go. "Were you ever in America?" She vaguely recalled William telling her about a lad he'd met in California who might be able to handle a difficult Theosophical situation but had later returned to Europe.

He turned. "Yes."

"In what part?"

"San Diego, California."

Claude jumped up and exclaimed, "My God!"

Katherine continued, "Most interesting. Did you ever meet William Q. Judge?"

He smiled. "I heard him speak once. What an amazing man."

She stared at him. "Why were you in San Diego?"

"For several years, I worked on a ranch and ran *The Secret Doctrine* discussions at local lodges."

A chill skittered through her. This must be him. "You seem so young."

"I'm twenty-two now. My father, an Anglican minister, raised me to be one too. Instead, I became a Theosophist and have been studying it ever since."

"San Diego's a seaport, is it not?" Katherine asked.

He nodded. "Yes, it's a small town, quite a beautiful place in its way."

Her heart picked up speed. "Do you know the surrounding areas? Is there a place that has cliffs with beaches below it? I'm thinking of a land that juts out into the sea—a sort of peninsula?"

He smiled. "Why, yes. Point Loma."

"What do you know about it?"

"I've been there a few times, though the roads are very bad. It's eight or nine miles from town."

Katherine couldn't believe it. She explained her vision to him and shared the contents of the cable as well.

"Your representatives have been misled," G. de P. said. "Before I left a year ago, the government had the most southernly land. I'm not sure exactly how much. The rest is privately owned."

She asked, "Could you draw me a map—just a rough sketch of San Diego Bay, where the town lies, and more or less the shape of Point Loma?"

"I'm no artist, but I certainly can try."

She handed him a piece of paper and the pencil she'd been scribbling with. He began to draw a map with cardinal directions. When finished, he held it up and traced it with his finger. "This is the peninsula, the Pacific Ocean, and this is the steamship route into the bay entrance near Coronado Island, where there's a tourist hotel. On the mainland is San Diego's city, sometimes called New Town. Past it is Old Town, and up this curved slope is the rugged road to Point Loma."

She exclaimed, "Today you've done more for me and the work than you realize." William had said if she ever came across this youth, she shouldn't lose sight of him. "Please join us on the Crusade."

"There's nothing I'd like more." He sighed. "But I've other obligations that prevent me from doing so."

Saddened, she said, "Let's correspond."

"I promise, and perhaps there'll be a place for me at your school someday."

Woeful to see him go, she shook his hand. "I'm certain there will be."

She immediately cabled Nere: *The site of the school is exactly where I said. Government land is to the south of it. Make inquiries and buy quickly.*

Chapter Forty-One

In early October, the Crusaders left Athens and rode a steamship across the Mediterranean Sea's smooth aqua waters. As they approached Alexandria, the sun reflected brightly over the tops of the villas, mosques, and palace. Katherine effused, "Egypt! Motherland of civilization and wonders of ancient history! Madame Blavatsky penetrated the Brotherhood of Luxor Lodge here. I predict we too will make contact with masters there."

"I'm unconvinced," Hargrove sneered. "No one even knows where it is. Or if it even exists."

"I believe it's there," Katherine said. "And waiting to be found by us."

Alice Cleather raised her eyes as a wry smile parted her lips. Katherine cringed inside, not sure what the expression meant. They'd met at a long-ago conference. When the British Theosophist joined them in Rome, Katherine thought another woman on the journey would be an asset, but the odd duck watched Katherine as if assessing her every move. Besides Hargrove and Alice, the party still consisted of faithful Claude, Leoline, Patterson, and Pierce.

Katherine's patience had been challenged the last few weeks; she'd struggled to ignore Hargrove's snide comments and Alice's sidelong glances. Katherine wouldn't let them hamper her high hopes for Egypt. The ancient mysteries still to be discovered would help guide her creation of the School for the Revival of the Lost Mysteries of Antiquity.

The African continent would be different from anywhere else they'd been. In the last few countries they visited, they'd had mixed results. In

Austria, they'd made headway gathering new Theosophical members, but to Katherine's consternation, wherever they spoke, Annie Besant trailed behind and insisted the Americans were imposters. In Italy, the early architecture awed Katherine's senses with fountains, basilicas, and arenas. But due to suspicions of church and state, they'd done little more than travel through. In Greece, they'd been forbidden to lecture at all. However, before leaving Athens, they were allowed to aid a group of Armenian immigrants fleeing Turkish oppression.

As the steamer now set anchor outside Alexandria, shouting men in scant clothing paddled toward them. Katherine reached for Leoline's arm as the men climbed on deck and ran toward the passengers, grabbed at their baggage, and attempted to throw it overboard. Katherine sat on her trunk and hung on to her valise, struggling with a determined thief to keep it. Hargrove and Claude tried to push the Egyptians aside. This was not at all like the dull accounts she'd read about Egypt!

The statuesque Egyptian Cook's agent appeared, and the invaders silently moved back out of respect. Mr. Ani, with a dignified presence, bowed and aided the Crusaders off the ship and onto a skiff. After a few minutes, it reached the depot. Katherine tried to catch her breath as they waited for the train. She soon was quenched by hibiscus tea and sated with the bountiful basket of pomegranates, oranges, and bananas procured by the guide.

She asked him, "When we're in Luxor, would you take us to the Brotherhood Lodge?"

He looked at her oddly and shook his head. Many assumed secrets had been lost in time, but Katherine believed the masters had kept those mysteries alive and shared them with only a chosen few. She planned to make contact with these masters and glean how the past could aid her in helping future generations find peace and harmony. Even though some didn't believe, she was certain there was such a place. Madame Blavatsky had written of it often in her books, so it must be there. Katherine didn't know how to find it, but she would follow her instincts.

Outside the train window, the Nile endlessly passed. Palms dotted its edges and men in flowing robes led camels, laden with heavy burdens, over the sands. After many hours, on the river's eastern banks they reached the largest city in Africa, Cairo. Katherine had read that Ramses II built it upon the ruins of a great city dating back to prehistoric times.

Acacias shadowed the avenue as they were transported in carriages to their hotel. A woman in a loose gown shyly held a veil over her face. Bright-eyed children in simple garments, heads decorated in colorful handkerchiefs, played in the street.

After the group checked into Shepheard's Hotel, Mr. Ani said, "Sleep well. Tomorrow we'll go to Giza to see the pyramids."

Bellboys carried Katherine's luggage upstairs to her room. There were letters from Philo in her stack but not one from Nere. She hoped he was in negotiations for the Point Loma property by now. She skimmed the letters from Philo that described his most recent inventions in detail. Then she soaked in a cool bath, recalling the pyramid photographs she'd studied in a *National Geographic Magazine,* excited to see the actual edifices the next day. She crawled into bed for a good night's rest as prescribed by the agent.

After a quick breakfast, outfitted in sunglasses, hats, scarves, pants, skirts, and tall socks, the group was loaded into horse-pulled two-seater Victoria cars. Everyone had paired off, so Katherine squeezed onto the seat beside Mr. Ani. The drivers navigated through narrow winding roads crowded with camels, water carriers, and men toting baskets of fruit. The Victoria passed shops filled with many-hued fabrics. Katherine glimpsed a gorgeous palace, gawked at the imposing mosques, and wondered what was behind the harem balconies enclosed by latticework. Arabs, Bedouins, Greeks, Armenians, and Jews in native costumes mingled with plainly dressed, stiff Europeans and English soldiers in red-and-gilt uniforms.

As they pulled off the narrow streets, she asked Mr. Ani, "Did you find where the Brotherhood Luxor Lodge is?"

"No, madame." He shook his head.

Past a small village with low-roofed mud huts and green banks of Nile fields, the cars halted. The journeyers got out, strolled a few steps, and in silence they paused. Up ahead, the yellow-gold Pyramids of Giza towered above the desert sands, accompanied by the Sphinx. Photographs hadn't begun to indicate the sheer size and grandeur of the royal tombs. Transfixed at the sight, Katherine couldn't move; her chest whirled with awe at their beauty.

Mr. Ani said, "No one knows exactly how they were built. Herodotus, an ancient Greek historian, believed the Great Pyramid took over twenty years with the labor of one hundred thousand men."

Katherine quivered at the thought of the enslaved toiling in this heat for the ancient pharaohs. Even so, she couldn't wait to get closer. The stillness was disrupted by loud cries as a group of robed Bedouins pushed their camels toward the tourists, urging them to ride. A dignified Egyptian garbed in pale blue and yellow stripes followed.

Mr. Ani introduced the man to the Crusaders. "You're in good hands with 'the Sheik of the Pyramids,'" he said and walked away toward a nearby hotel.

A Bedouin demonstrated how to stride up to a camel purposefully on a diagonal without looking into its eyes. Katherine watched the other Crusaders mount their beasts with screams and laughter.

"Hold tight." Katherine lingered back as the camels rose to standing. A Bedouin motioned for her to climb on one. In her youth she adored riding horses, but this humped beast made her tremor with fear.

"Come on, girl, get up there," Hargrove teased.

She held her terror inside. "No, thank you."

"It's nice." Alice laughed. "You'll like it."

"Suit yourself," Hargrove said and followed in line with the others.

As if the handsome "sheik" knew how she felt, he held out his arm and offered to escort her. In spite of the disregard men of this country were purported to have for women, he seemed most courteous. He carried her umbrella over her head. In the clear, motionless air, they trod in the footsteps of ancients. This was certainly not a stroll through Central Park; a modern-dressed American lady, arm in arm with a sheik, moving through deep desert sands behind a procession of stately camels.

Saddened that Nere was missing these wonders, Katherine felt comforted to know he was on a more important task. She told the Sheik she was from New York. He asked her many questions about it and America too. She spoke with pride, and he expressed a wish to visit it someday.

"Do you know of the Brotherhood Luxor Lodge?" she asked.

He gazed at her and shook his head. "You'll never find it."

They caught up with the others near the Great Pyramid as they dismounted their camels. Pierce gave his box camera to the Sheik and requested he take photos.

The women and the Sheik witnessed Patterson, Pierce, Hargrove, and Claude begin to scale the pyramid with Bedouin helping hands.

"Claude, careful!" Leoline called to her husband.

"Certainly." He blew her a kiss.

The Sheik laughed. "Don't worry, it's only about four hundred fifty feet."

"Do you want to climb it?" Alice asked Katherine.

She gave a little laugh and held her breath until the men waved from the top while the Sheik snapped photos. After the men descended, he led the group into a narrow passage underneath the pyramid and through the king's chambers. After the others remounted their camels, Katherine followed along again on the Sheik's arm.

He asked about their travels, and she said, "One of the purposes of our Crusade is to spread peace and understanding across the world and learn of the ancients. Tell me about your own beliefs."

The Sheik smiled widely. "You aren't like other Christians we've encountered. They didn't care to understand Muhammad our prophet who was divinely inspired to preach and confirm the one God's teachings of Abraham, Moses, Jesus, and other prophets."

"Theosophists also believe in a Supreme God and the prophets."

"We aren't so different, you and I." The Sheik nodded as the caravan arrived at the Sphinx. He shifted to his formal voice and told the group, "Horus, the Rising Sun, was believed to be the conqueror of darkness, the god of the morning. Thousands of years ago the Sphinx was hewn of solid rock. It's one hundred fifty feet long and seventy-five feet tall. At one time, its head was vivid red. No traces of the color are visible now."

Katherine had imagined the lion-headed figure would be huge compared to the pyramids. Instead, it looked like a kitten. Even so, it was still impressive. The Crusaders, as if under a spell, floated in the air, holding all who beheld that majestic figure in silence. For the first time, she felt the group had aligned and they understood each other without words. Katherine thought of the hustle and bustle of the Western world, and its never-ending stream of words that generated all forms of excitement. She imagined hearing the Sphinx whisper, "If thou knoweth the mysteries of the soul, of life and death, look within and listen to the silence."

The Crusaders followed the Bedouins back past the Great Pyramid and up the road to the Mena House Hotel. Inside the former royal hunting lodge filled with colorful blue tiles, ornate mosaics, and carved wood details, the group made their way to the patio in the shadow of the Great Pyramid. There a four-string quartet played, and a repast of vegetables, legumes, squab, chicken, and lamb had been laid out before them. With a sense of rare camaraderie, the Crusaders ate heartily and reminisced about home and other Crusade experiences.

The Sheik pushed his way through the crowd to the carriages, assuming a look of sadness as he told Katherine, "A British man named Carter digs for shards at the Valley of the Kings and paints watercolors for tourists. He might share with you information about the Brotherhood Luxor Lodge. Tell him I sent you." And with that, he reached out both hands to her for a last shake and salaam.

Early the next morning they boarded a steamer at Aswan and drew upriver on the Nile toward the Valley of the Kings and Luxor. Her anticipation rose as she envisioned the sites they'd encounter there, and she hoped to locate the Brotherhood Luxor Lodge. Time passed leisurely as they sailed along. At twilight, fireflies onshore blinked in the silence. The old river spoke to her of peace, and the moon above emphasized the eloquent power of nature as well as human life.

After two days on the water, well rested as the sun rose, they disembarked on the west shore and rode horses along the river up and over hills and down through ravines to the Valley of the Kings. Stopping at a hillside door, Mr. Ani said, "The first Seti, considered a great king by his peers, established a golden heritage filled with magic, glory, and wonder. He opened quarries and gold mines, built monuments and temples."

The group followed Mr. Ani inside the deep, long royal tomb, through underground galleries, and down flights of stairs carved in the rock to a room where eerie shadows were cast on the walls. A sarcophagus lid had been removed to reveal the great pharaoh's features, lit by electricity. A silence descended on the party, an inner symphony of majestic reverence, as if they were in the presence of an essence imperishable of that long-dead ruler. Emotions spun in Katherine's chest.

The following day they explored the Karnak and Luxor ruins: obelisks, monuments, temples, colonnades, and tombs that filled her with wonder. They found Carter, the British painter, who laughed and said, "No Brotherhood Lodge here." Even so, Katherine felt the existence of old hierophants who'd left mysteries in the atmosphere.

That night Leoline and Claude stood on the Nile bank holding hands, probably dreaming of their past lives together. It must be profound, Katherine mused, for a couple to believe they'd not only spent years together but past lives as well. The only man she hoped to spend time with again in another life was William.

As she packed, a charm fell out of her bag. She decided it had probably been dropped in by the Sheik. In the palm of her hand, the Eye of Horus, like the one she'd seen in the museum, symbolized protection, health, and restoration. She'd cherish this forever. She hadn't connected with the Brotherhood Luxor Lodge. There probably wasn't one after all. Instead, she'd experienced something more profound, the silence of the desert. William had been right: the only way to bond deeply with her soul was through quiet contemplation.

Chapter Forty-Two

After an arduous journey down the Red Sea, through the Gulf of Aden, and across the Arabian Sea, Katherine and her Crusaders finally arrived in Bombay and checked into the luxurious Watson Hotel. Even though she admired the architecture and amenities, she felt no pleasure due to the poverty outside on the streets. If it had been up to her, they'd have stayed at a basic hostel and used the rest of the budget to feed the poor.

On her hotel bed she sorted through a mile-high pile of mail. First she opened five letters from Nere filled with Theosophical business updates. Then she searched the stack again until she found a cryptic telegram from him that read: *Not able to purchase property yet.* What did that mean? Had he located the land or not?

Three lengthy Philo letters included more descriptions of his recent inventions. He said he'd been minding his *p*'s and *q*'s and that Spots missed her terribly. She smiled at the thought of the two of them spending close time together. Other greetings were from Theosophical well-wishers around the world who had been following their itinerary and another from King Oscar II in Sweden, whom she'd continued to correspond with.

The next morning she stepped out on her balcony that commanded a breathtaking view of the harbor, bay, and distant hills. At the end of the monsoon season, the heat had risen, but even so, she told the *punkah wallah* assigned to hand-operate the fan in her room not to enter. She needed her privacy; plus it wasn't right for someone to cater to her in that way.

With high hopes for India, she wanted to glean as much as she could about the culture and reclaim leadership of the Society from Besant and Olcott by spreading the true Theosophy across the land of mysticism where the majority believed in the mahatmas. She also planned to visit the Himalayan lodge where Masters Koot Hoomi and Morya, Madame Blavatsky's teachers, dwelled. She'd documented the location, so it should be feasible to find it. As Outer Head, Katherine hoped to gain their endorsement and receive guidance on the organization's future.

The presentation tonight would be important and set the tone for the rest of their time in India. She'd honor William, who'd been betrayed by Annie and Olcott, and set the record straight to the British in power here, as well as Hindus, about who the real Theosophists were. William had believed in her, and she wanted to demonstrate she was worthy of the authority bestowed on her by adding more Indians to the American Section roster.

She made her way to the brightly lit dining room, where round, white-clothed tables were filled with colonial guests. Every diner had a silk-turbaned servant dressed like a character from *The Arabian Nights* standing behind them. As she approached her table, the Crusaders stared at her as the servants cleared the plates. Her servant pulled out her chair and she requested a pot of tea.

Hargrove had a smug look on his face.

"What is it?" she asked him and turned to the others, her face inquiring after Hargrove's attitude.

Patterson held up a newspaper. "There's an item in the *Times of India*."

Katherine reached out for the paper and unfolded it.

Pierce removed his glasses and said, "It's rubbish. You deserve better."

She quietly read the notice: *Kindly publish this repudiation of certain persons who are at present masquerading in India under the name of the Theosophical Society. We, the rightful Society, disclaim all responsibility for the "Crusade" now being carried out in this country.* It was signed by Annie Besant, Colonel Olcott, and other leaders at Adyar. She shouldn't be surprised, but Katherine still felt like a carpet had been pulled out from under her. She closed the paper, handed it back to Patterson, and then nodded to the waiter to bring her breakfast.

"What will we do?" Patterson asked. His bushy mustache twitched, indicating his distress.

"We shall respond," Katherine said.

"I'll write it," Hargrove bellowed. "I'll give them a piece of my mind."

Katherine said, "I'll do it." The servant delivered her eggs, toast, and jam. "After I've had my breakfast." She remained calm, spread jam on the toast, and took a bite. The others rose and left the room, except Hargrove, who remained to her chagrin.

He said, "You'll deliver the speech, but you won't be welcome."

"You keep trying to intimidate me," she said. "It's not working, Mr. Hargrove."

"I care only about the Society," he said.

"Then in that, we are aligned. I want to finish my breakfast in peace."

"I hope you realize how important tonight's speech is," he said. She kept eating her toast, further signaling to Hargrove her interest in him was at an end. Still, his words had the intended effect. She was more nervous now than before. He waited a moment longer for her to respond. She held her silence, and finally he left her alone at the table.

She dropped the toast back onto the plate. Her appetite was gone.

At the small desk in her room, perspiration dripped down her forehead as she attempted to write a rebuttal. Absent-minded and irritable, she found it as difficult to write as to fly. How could Annie be so rude? It had been a year and a half since the American Section of the Theosophical Society ceded from Adyar. Katherine's plans to infiltrate Besant and Olcott's power base were beginning to evaporate.

Katherine closed her eyes and took a few minutes of silence, then worked through the response. *The real Theosophical headquarters have always been in New York,* she wrote, *where the Society was founded. To call us masqueraders is childish. Furthermore, we constitute three-fourths of the whole membership, and if truth be told, for years we have paid the greater share of funds to upkeep the Adyar headquarters.*

That afternoon, through the hustling, bustling Bombay metropolis of the British Raj, carriages drove them toward the town hall. Five-story red-and-yellow buildings lined both sides of the wide avenue, and pillared balconies with awnings hung above open shops. Turbaned Indians in white kurtas walked along. Women in brightly colored saris carried jugs on their heads.

The Crusaders were dropped off in front of the neoclassical building embellished with a Grecian portico and Doric-style pillars. The group hiked the thirty steps up to the entrance where a British interpreter in scrubby short sleeves and knickers greeted them.

Hargrove grumbled, "Why isn't anyone from the aristocracy here to meet us?"

"I don't know, sir," the interpreter answered.

"Invitations were delivered to a list of them," Patterson said.

Alice whispered, "Could it be due to that published letter?"

Katherine hoped not.

Most times when they arrived for a lecture, they were met by a dignitary and escorted to a room to wait or at least provided chairs backstage until the audience had been seated. One of her favorite parts of any presentation was her grand entrance to enormous applause. Instead, now the Crusaders were led directly onto the platform and took their seats. Leoline helped Katherine adjust her sari. She'd hoped it would demonstrate she respected Indian customs. As the audience dribbled in, Katherine counted a few hundred. Only a few were British.

No one from Bombay had appeared to introduce the Crusaders, so Claude brushed back his red hair with his hand and stepped to the podium. No one clapped. He conducted the welcome, shared his experiences of being Madame Blavatsky's secretary, launched into his talk about Society history, and then introduced Katherine.

Stifled by the heat, she pulled her shoulders back and strode to the podium, trying to find confidence. "As Madame Blavatsky told us, the masters lit the Theosophical fire and gave the world its mystic teachings. The Brotherhood never had its headquarters in India, but moved thousands of years ago from what is now part of the American continent. The real Theosophical headquarters have always been in New York," she said, quoting the article she had written. "It spread to Egypt, then elsewhere, sending teachers to India to enlighten its inhabitants. Krishna, Buddha, Jesus, Zoroaster, Muhammad, Quetzalcoatl, and many others who could be named were members of this great Brotherhood."

She caught her stride and spoke from her heart, lost in her oration's energy. "There is no religion at the present time that has remained pure and undefiled. Hinduism is no exception to the rule. It does have an esoteric side; nevertheless, it is unprogressive and stagnant."

The already silent room somehow fell quieter. Not a single crackle of applause. Dark eyes opened wide above frowns. Katherine put a hand over her mouth. She'd made a ghastly mistake. How could she have been so self-righteous?

"Lies," a male shouted. Others joined in, and the silence in the hall collapsed into a cacophony of anger.

Katherine shuffled her papers to stall for time. Claude came beside her and held up his hand for silence. Men ran toward the stage. Claude put an arm around her and rushed to a back hallway with the Crusaders in tow. The interpreter led them to a small room barely big enough to hold ten chairs in a circle.

"Wait here," he said. The door closed, and the sound of the lock clicked.

The Crusaders took seats, all except Hargrove, who towered over Katherine. "How could you say that?"

Katherine hung her head. Her body shivered with shame for saying what she had. "I don't know."

"I'll be taking over your speaking duties for the rest of the Crusade."

She ignored him.

"Look at me when I'm talking to you," he yelled and tugged the scarf off her head.

She flinched as her mind flashed to her father, the times when she was a young girl and he'd screamed those same words at her and yanked her hair. A warning his ire might go further and she needed to get out of the way. She'd run behind her mother or grandfather or out the door to hide.

William's love was still in her heart. She didn't deserve to be treated this way. Instead of fear, fury took over. She jumped up, put her hands on her hips, and stared up at Hargrove. "Who do you think you are?"

"I'm the president," Hargrove sneered.

She hollered back, "You might be, but I'm the Outer Head."

Claude stepped between them. "Settle down, you two."

Hargrove pushed past Claude toward Katherine again. "You don't deserve to be Outer Head."

Pierce and Patterson held Hargrove's arms back.

"Hargrove, you're out of control," she yelled.

Patterson said, "Let's discuss this in the morning after you've both calmed down."

Alice put a hand on Katherine's shoulder, attempting to get her to sit down again.

Hargrove raised his arms. "There's nothing to discuss. She's a fraud. She's no gifted leader like Madame Blavatsky. Purple's put us all in peril, and not just tonight. She's such a coward she can't even ride a camel."

The room fell quiet. They could still hear shouting somewhere in the building.

Katherine felt her face flush with humiliation and allowed Alice to push her into a chair. Leoline sat beside Katherine and took her hand. Hargrove located a seat as far away from Katherine as possible, and the others returned to their seats as well.

Time passed as they waited for the echoing hollers outside of the room to subside. Finally, the interpreter knocked on the door and said the coast was clear. Leoline slid Katherine's scarf over her disheveled curls and linked an arm through hers as they shuffled to the waiting carriages. Outside, a shard moon overhead was as sharp as the pain in Katherine's heart.

Chapter Forty-Three

The next afternoon, descriptions of the incident and another scathing letter from Annie filled the newspaper pages. Had Olcott and she sent followers to incite the riot? In addition, they organized a presentation that night at the town hall. Katherine canceled their own scheduled talks for the next two days to recover from the ordeal and allow things to die down. All wholeheartedly agreed, except Hargrove, who said he would present on his own, but Katherine and the other Crusaders nixed it.

Three days later they moved forward with a planned elite tea for British dignitaries in the hotel atrium. Ushered in, they took seats at a corner table while the staff set up.

The glass-covered, gabled roof provided the perfect ambiance. Katherine began, "Madame Blavatsky said we cannot hope at once to be great, wise, and wholly strong. That falling and failing, we learn. She and the masters expected this from all of us; they never desired any of us to work blindly, only that we work unitedly."

Hargrove mumbled under his breath.

Katherine lifted her eyes to him and said humbly, "Let us put this division behind us."

He did not smile or nod his head, nor did he raise a vocal objection, so she took this as a begrudging assent.

Patterson facilitated a hammered-out agenda compromise: Katherine would share the introductory history, Claude the main speech in her place, and Hargrove the final talk. That was key because whenever he spoke earlier in a program, he took up more than his allotted time and listeners began to lose interest.

That afternoon, in the room set up for fifty, only two spinster sisters and their soldier brother showed up. Embarrassed and defeated, Katherine had the sandwiches and sweets taken to the poor on the streets and announced that the rest of their Bombay events would be canceled and they would move on. Hargrove stared at her with a smug grin.

As they began to cross the country, Hindus were courteous at their presentations. When she asked about their beliefs, she learned they admired the truth and believed in God's unity, very much like the Society. All the Crusaders except Hargrove seemed to forgive her for angering the Bombay crowd. Soon, though, they discovered Annie and her cohorts, including Countess Wachtmeister from Katherine's trip to Sweden, trailed wherever they'd spoken and gave lectures to discredit them. Press articles continued back and forth between the factions, clouding Katherine's thoughts. Again, her fellow journeyers became icy toward her.

The Crusaders relished and recoiled from the sights they witnessed as they crossed India: the City of Caves dedicated to Shiva; the magnificent Taj Mahal; the Monkey Temple on the Ganges, where cremation ghats spewed constant smoke as Hindus cast ashes in the river for loved ones' speedy passages to heaven; and the Bodhi Tree, beneath which Buddha had found enlightenment.

Ostracized from the group, no matter how Katherine tried to fully experience these sites, a pall of disappointment and loneliness had befallen her. One of the purposes of the Crusade, besides spreading Theosophy, was to develop unity with her own leaders; instead, with each stop the wedge seemed to widen.

By the time they reached Calcutta, a month after leaving Cairo, she knew only one thing would raise the Crusaders' trust in her. Even though they hadn't spoken of it after the Luxor Lodge disappointment, Katherine sensed the Crusaders were eager to head north to the Tibetan border in the Himalayas, where Masters Koot Hoomi and Morya dwelled. She wasn't certain how to get there, but she hoped as they drew closer, she'd receive guidance from them.

On their travels, she'd had little time to meditate. After checking into their hotel, she finally had a chance. As the day's heat began to lessen, late afternoon light spilled into her room. She plumped pillows behind her on the bed, closed her eyes, and breathed in and out. Outside noises began to fade, and her breathing deepened. She focused on opening her red root chakra, then spiraled the prism colors within her—orange, yellow, green, blue, purple—up to the top of her head, where white light hovered and glowed. She started from the Bodhi Tree and up through tulle veils until, through a cloudy mist, dark, glowing eyes stared at her.

"Who are you?" Katherine asked.

"Don't you recognize me?" A clear-cut bronze face appeared, with raven hair and a beard. The vision of a giant stood at full height. There could be no mistake; this was Master Morya, purported by others to be anywhere from six feet six inches to eight feet tall. Yes, he'd sent her messages, but he'd never visited her.

His deep voice echoed, "My Rajput warrior blood will not permit me to see a woman such as you hurt in her feelings. We shall meet. You alone may visit me at my retreat above Darjeeling. Take the toy train north toward the Himalayas." His body faded away.

In astonishment, Katherine's essence fell to earth. She held the message in her heart, regained time and space, moved to the desk, and reached for her pen to quickly write the words gifted to her. Had this been her imagination, or was it truly a message from Master M? How would she share her solo invitation with the Crusaders? It wouldn't help regain their affections. She had a desire to make the pilgrimage on her own, to gather guidance about her leadership and the future direction of her organization. She reread the message. Mostly illegible, she recopied it into two sections. The first one about her feelings was too personal, so she kept it separate from the rest.

That night she tossed and turned until the sky faded from black to gray to pink. In the morning, she woke early, craving outside air before the heat set in. She dressed in her thin Western frock and tied a white scarf over her hat to keep cool. Then she made her way down the wide staircase and out the hotel's front door. She couldn't believe her eyes.

Pith helmets on their heads, her Crusaders sat astride elephants. Claude and Leoline on one, Alice and Hargrove on another, and Patterson and Pierce on still another. A group of locals had gathered around them.

Patterson waved at Katherine. "Join us! The weather's delightful up here."

"We're going for a promenade," Leoline called.

Pierce laughed. "There's plenty of room. Come sit between us." He leaned back on the giant saddle. "We'll make sure you're safe."

"Yes, memsahib!" The mahout on the ground instructed Patterson and Pierce's elephant to kneel.

Katherine's pulse raced as she studied the man in front of the saddle and the mahout holding a thick lead.

Hargrove taunted, "She doesn't have the courage."

Her anger at him seethed. She strung her purse over a wrist and stepped forward.

"Put your hand on Mr. Patterson's back and place your foot on Haathi's bent knee." The mahout demonstrated. "Bend your knee and swing the other leg over."

Katherine tried to move her leg up over the elephant but was unable. She tried again and again. This was foolish, a waste of time. Patterson grabbed her arm, and the keeper boosted her up. It wasn't easy, but she made it. As the keeper raised the reins and cued Haathi to rise slowly, Katherine didn't look down and held on to Patterson's waist. When the elephant was at full height, Katherine waved from the top and the crowd cheered.

Her body swayed side to side as Haathi walked single file behind the other two beasts. Katherine smiled as if a circus entertainer. Along the road men in white turbans and short pants smiled back at her, humped cattle moseyed nearby, and inside a latticed second-story window a woman wrapped a sari around her body. Along the port road, lofty sailboat masts pointed to the blue sky. A white woman in Western attire strolled the dock, her parasol overhead.

Back at the hotel, after Katherine was gently brought to the ground, the Crusaders circled around her. For the first time in weeks, she felt a tinge of happiness. Hargrove frowned, and her elation faded. Gloom settled in as they entered the dining room for breakfast, where she'd need to tell them about Master Morya's private invitation.

The scent of curry in the air, teapots were delivered, and Alice said, "I look forward to our trip to Darjeeling tomorrow. It's supposed to be beautiful and much cooler up there."

Leoline asked, "Do you think we'll really make contact with the masters?"

All eyes looked at Katherine, and she said slowly, "I've received a message."

"What have you heard?" Hargrove's eyes grew wide.

Katherine didn't have the nerve to say the words out loud, so she pulled the paper from her pocketbook and slid it to Patterson on her right. He read it quietly and passed it around the table. Disappointment permeated the group.

"Are you sure he didn't mean all of us?" Claude asked.

Pierce read aloud, "You alone are invited to visit me." He sighed. "It's most clear. Katherine is the only one to go."

Hargrove scowled. "As president of the Theosophical Society, I'm sure he meant I should be a guest too."

Katherine waited for a Crusader to speak up. No one did, so she asked him, "If you didn't believe in the Luxor Lodge, why are you so keen to go?"

"You well know Master M's existence and whereabouts have been confirmed." Hargrove raised an eyebrow.

Katherine tried again. "Won't he be displeased if you show up uninvited?"

"I'm certain he'll be honored to have me." Hargrove's voice was filled with pomposity.

She glanced around the table for support. Patterson shrugged. Claude put his hand on Leoline's shoulder. Alice and Pierce looked at their plates.

If Katherine denied Hargrove this, he'd be wrathful at her forever for seizing a privilege he felt should be his. And yet she knew what the invitation had spelled out. She neither assented nor demurred. Perhaps karma would intervene on her behalf.

Chapter Forty-Four

In the stifling heat, Hargrove pointed for Katherine to take a seat on a bench while he bought the toy train tickets. She regretted the others hadn't been able to come. Without them, there would be no buffer between her and Hargrove. In front of her on the track, it was hard to believe the bright blue locomotive with three coaches behind was the engineering marvel it was purported to be. She supposed the twelve-foot-gauge light design made it easier to climb the steep slopes with a series of zigzag switchbacks and loops. Philo would appreciate it.

With a smile, Hargrove returned to her, holding up the tickets. "We're in luck. They just finished repairing the line that had washed out from last year's monsoons."

Lordy! Trapped with this ogre and the possibility of a train wreck. She prayed for safety and patience to keep his verbal jabs from riling her or ruining this important part of the journey.

He sat beside her on the bench to wait and started back in right away. "I'm letting you come with me because you're the one who heard from Master M. You've failed miserably from the start with that Bombay speech and the ludicrous letters back and forth with Besant in the papers."

He'd told her this many times, and she'd almost started to believe it. A squat hill-man waved them over, swung open a small door, and took their tickets as they stepped inside. There were four bench seats, with two on each side facing each other. Katherine waited for Hargrove to find his and sat kitty-corner, as far away from him as possible. To her chagrin, he stood and moved next to her. The other passengers filing in wore kerchiefs tied over their faces like train robbers.

Katherine and Hargrove bowed to the man and woman who slid in across from them. The woman wore a silk scarf over her face and snuggled a tiny baby.

"Admit it, you're a failure," Hargrove continued his bashing. "You're wasting our time and money on this highfalutin Crusade."

She tried to laugh to make light of it. "You're the one who wanted to come today."

"Of course, the master invited us," he said.

The woman across from them stared at Hargrove with large dark eyes and hugged her baby closer, the *bindi* between her eyebrows shiny red.

Hargrove continued, "Give up now. You've done enough damage—"

A piercing whistle blew. The steam engine powered up with a rumble; black smoke blew into the coach, blinding Katherine. The stench was so strong it flooded her mouth and down her throat. She pulled a violet scarf from her handbag and tied it over her mouth and nose. Now she understood the kerchiefed faces.

Hargrove coughed, yanked out his handkerchief, and held it over his mug. The hill-man jumped up and perched over the forward engine buffers. The train jerked and moved northeast slowly on the tracks, out onto a flat plain, and soon climbed into a forest. A few minutes later, the horn blasted as the engine began to pull through its first loop. Katherine held on to the seat's edge for dear life as her stomach loop-de-looped too. The train crossed over the track, switched to a new one, smoothed out, and chugged along on the side of a sheer cliff with a thick jungle below. Her breath hastened as fear began to overpower her.

Hargrove yelled in her ear, "Besant's made a laughingstock of us. I should've written those newspaper letters. You've only made it worse. I'm the only one who can—"

The train slowed with a metallic screech, as if the wheels had lost their grip. The hill-man leaned over, scattered sand on the rails, and the engine continued to move along again. The horn hooted at the next loop as they passed a water tank for nearby laborers working tea plantings that dotted the hill above. Hargrove sat back as the train zigzagged. The hill-man constantly blew the whistle and honked the horn.

As the train turned a corner, the coach hugged the mountain edge, a drop into the craggy chasm as deep as a twenty-story building. She grasped her grandfather's watch and held in a scream. If the train lost traction, it would be the end for all of them. She turned her head away from the window and found herself face-to-face with Hargrove.

He caught her elbow and said, "If you're frightened, just hold on to me."

She tugged her arm away. "I'm fine." She wouldn't let him recognize the panic trembling inside her. The train continued to move along the rim's edge. The woman across from her handed the baby to the man, and nodded at Katherine as if she recognized her terror. She put her palms onto her thighs and closed her eyes, as if going into a meditative state. Katherine followed suit, inhaling in and out until calmness began to set in as she imagined her white city on a sundown sea.

Hargrove broke her reverie. "Isn't it time you let me take over as Outer Head?"

Her calmness from the meditation didn't dissipate, and she was able to ignore him.

"Isn't it?" he poked.

She wouldn't let him ruin this moment. God had given this challenging train ride to her for a reason, and she wanted to take it head on. She turned her back to Hargrove. She admired the beauty of pines on the mountain as an eagle circled the indigo sky. After a while, Hargrove grew quiet. Did he get the hint? She peeked around. His eyes were closed.

A few miles farther, as the locomotive switchbacked and looped again, he started in again. "And you have this crazy idea of starting a school in California, of all places, on a property that probably doesn't even exist." Hargrove laughed.

"I've had a vision."

"Wasn't the retreat of the Brotherhood Luxor Lodge one of your ideas too?"

She hated to even think about it. Time and the train moved slowly until the hill-man yelled an announcement in his language. "Here comes Agony Point," a man on another bench translated loudly. "Tightest loop yet."

Wheels screeched again, and a few of the passengers gasped. Katherine couldn't see the tracks ahead, only the sheer drop below. How was the rickety old bucket going to traverse this razor's edge? The wheels groaned onward. Agony Point was not a metaphor, but the starkest reality. The hill-man in front of them disappeared, turning into the void around the narrowest bend. Katherine held on tight as their car leaned out over the edge of the mountain, pivoted, and at the last possible moment, straightened and fell back in line.

Katherine let out a tiny sigh of relief. Even Hargrove's hands quivered. They'd done it. They'd safely curled around Agony. Hargrove started to speak, but the train screeched, zigzagged backward for momentum, moved forward, and continued to climb.

Eight hours after the journey began, the train pulled into Darjeeling. As they disembarked, Katherine shivered at the drop in temperature and looked around for someone to greet them. The panoramic view encompassed the snow-covered, awe-inspiring Mount Kanchenjunga, the third highest peak in the world. To see the master would she need to hike up into the mountains on foot or ride a mule or pony cart? Perhaps he'd meet her in the village instead.

Hargrove said, "When we meet Master M, let me do the talking. I'm the only one who can save us now. You need to give up."

"Give up what?" Katherine asked, shivering at the chill. It had been so hot in Calcutta that she'd left her wraps in her trunk at the hotel.

"Outer Headship."

Hargrove had said this many times, and she was tired of it. "Don't be ridiculous. William didn't choose you."

"I'm not sure I believe he chose you either," Hargrove harrumphed.

She sighed and scanned for a carriage. "What would you do differently?" she asked.

Hargrove rubbed his arms for warmth. "I'd do demonstrations of my occult powers and teach others how to increase their own skills."

No use arguing with him. He didn't understand what she was trying to do. His statement was contrary to what William had taught her. To use her powers in private and not for ego reinforcement.

"I've got an idea," he went on. "Let's ask Master M to choose between us."

"I don't think it works that way," she said.

Hargrove smirked. "What are you afraid of?"

"Feel free to ask him, if you must."

A barefoot youth in a maroon jacket with a skirt underneath hurried toward them with a serious look on his face.

He tugged his wool cap down over his head, stopped, and bowed to her. "Welcome to Queen of the Hills. I am Ananda, chela of Master M. I'll take you in *tanga* to hotel."

Katherine bowed back. Hargrove trailed behind as she followed the chela to a small carriage with two giant wooden wheels. He opened a gate in the back, held her elbow, and helped her climb inside. Over the loose dung-smelling hay, she made her way to the back seat. Hargrove began to follow her in.

Ananda frowned and put his hands on his hips. "Who are you?"

"I'm Ernest Templeton Hargrove, Theosophical Society President."

Ananda frowned. "What are you doing here?"

Hargrove stood erect. "I'm here to meet the master."

"Were you invited?" Ananda squinted his eyes.

"I'm not certain, but—"

"I thought not." Ananda held up his hand, gave a fake smile, and allowed Hargrove to climb in.

"Who does that whippersnapper Indian think he is, treating me this way?" Hargrove mumbled. He bumped his head on the canopy rod and found a seat, avoiding the hay. He rubbed his injured forehead. "Is it bleeding?"

It served him right. "No. You'll probably have a bruise later."

Ananda loaded their luggage in back, jumped onto the front seat, and grabbed the mangy horse's reins.

"It's sure cold up here," Hargrove complained.

Ananda turned around and looked at him. "Yes, over seven thousand feet above sea. Nice and cool. Isn't it?" He handed Katherine an intricately woven pashmina. "From the master," he said. As Ananda clicked the reins and the horse moved forward, she wrapped the shawl around her shoulders with gratitude.

At the elegant Hotel Angleterre, rhododendrons graced the grounds. Ananda told her she'd be contacted the next day about the master's plans to see her. As she collected her room key, she feigned a headache, had dinner sent up to her room, and climbed onto the inviting thick mattress and under the warm bedcover. Her body still felt the zigzagging of the train, and she had a fitful sleep. The next day she took breakfast and lunch in her room as well, to acclimate to the elevation, avoid Hargrove, and await instructions from Ananda or the master. She meditated, but no communications came. During dinner, Hargrove asked if she'd heard from either of them. She shook her head.

"I've met with a guide who said he can take us up the mountain," Hargrove told her.

"Shouldn't we wait for instructions?" She couldn't imagine a stranger would know the way.

"It's been twenty-four hours. I'm ready to get there. The guide said he knows exactly where to find the master." Hargrove narrowed his eyes at her. "I'm going tomorrow with or without you."

She wouldn't let on that she too was concerned she hadn't heard anything, and as soon as possible, she bade Hargrove an early good night.

"Sleep well. It'll be a long trek tomorrow." He smirked. "I hope you're feeling up to it. I'd hate for you to miss the experience."

She nodded, wary of what the morrow would bring. In her room, she gazed up at the mountains and couldn't imagine hiking up there. As she was about to turn off the lamp, she heard a soft knock, and a note was slipped under the door. *Before sunrise, you'll be escorted.*

Chapter Forty-Five

Dressed for the journey, Katherine curled up under the covers and threw the pashmina on top. She found it difficult to sleep until the sky outside the window faded from gray to black. She dreamt of her last happy day with William, walking arm in arm under Washington Square Park's arch. His radiant blue eyes filled with love for her. Hyacinth blooms circled the fountain, and cherry tree petals flew.

It was still dark when a soft knock woke her. She quickly donned her walking shoes, curled the shawl around her shoulders, set her straw hat on her head, and grabbed her walking stick. She opened the door. Ananda put a finger to his lips and tilted his head to the room across the hall where Hargrove slept.

"Should we wake him?" she whispered.

Ananda shook his head. "Master said he is not to come."

She had mixed feelings as he led her out of the hotel. Four men in kurtas with jodhpurs tucked into tall boots waited, a hammock sling placed on the ground between them. Scrawny and thin, they clasped their hands in namaste and bowed to her. She bowed back. Hopefully, they were stronger than they appeared.

Barefooted, Ananda must not have planned to join them. Would she be safe with these unknown men? Ananda helped her sit on the tarp, and the four carriers lifted the poles on their shoulders. This would be much more comfortable than any camel, elephant, or train ride. However, she felt a bit silly being treated like a royal maharani.

Ananda walked in front of the sling and began to lead the way. Though she was relieved he would be escorting her up after all, she worried his feet would be bruised and bleeding within no time. As they began to climb, the front carriers' long braided queues bounced from beneath their turbans. The half-moon was a lantern in the sky lighting their way. A tea plantation appeared through shadowy pine trees. An owl hooted, and another hooted back. She didn't look down and kept her eyes on Ananda instead of the mountain path, just barely wide enough for the party. Sacred Mount Kanchenjunga's snowy peaks painted red by the sun greeted the morning. A distant woodpecker knocked as if trying to get someone to open a door. She spotted purple orchids hanging from the trees—a good omen.

A varmint ran in front of Ananda, and Katherine screamed. The men froze and stared at her.

"Only a mongoose." Ananda laughed, and the carriers joined in.

"I've never seen one," she said.

"First time for everything." Ananda laughed again.

The men picked up the pace. Poor men probably working for a pittance to serve her.

She imagined Hargrove awake now and his ruddy face as he discovered she'd left without him. She second-guessed her decision not to insist on rousing him. Even so, she was glad she'd meet the master alone. Free to ask whatever questions she wanted without Hargrove vying for attention. Was he trekking up the mountain at this moment with his guide? Would he perhaps meet her there? Hopefully not.

What if he discontinued his support or left their section and started his own? He'd threatened before. She didn't care—her private audience was requested by the master. Even if they fell into dire straits, without Hargrove's egocentric ways and power struggles, she'd be free to lead as she saw fit.

After an hour, light-headed and struggling to breathe, she called, "Stop, please."

The carriers set down the sling, and Ananda led her to a boulder. "It's altitude. Tilt back your head and open your mouth," he instructed and poured a sweet liquid between her lips from a bota bag. The men waited patiently for her to recover, and after a few minutes' rest she nodded, ready to continue. Soon the carriers regained their rhythm. The air grew cooler and clearer. Katherine pulled the pashmina tighter around her shoulders and sensed the teacher's gaze as they trekked toward him.

Ananda still leading the way, the carriers leapt over steppingstones, soared across a river raging with melting snow, and entered a gorge of green-grass beauty. She'd lost sense of time and had no idea how long they'd been traveling. Even when the path narrowed, she trusted Ananda to know where they were going. It concluded near a hut, and her carriers set down the sling. Legs wobbly, she stepped onto solid ground.

Ananda and Katherine poked their heads through the hut's cloth-covered door. Inside lay an empty cushion, a spent candle, and a book. Ananda shook his head with a frown. Had they come all this way for naught? After all this, what if they found no one?

Using her walking stick, she followed him up a precarious hillside trail. He told her to wait and entered a cave. Soon he reappeared, shaking his head, and they continued farther upward. Out of breath, she thought she couldn't take another step when Ananda waved at a man on a rise plowing a nearby field with a pair of oxen. The man pointed up.

A few minutes beyond, she spotted a pagoda clinging to a mountain edge, colorful prayer flags strung across it. As they drew closer, at the building's base she recognized the tall master from her hotel room visit sitting cross-legged on a bench. His garnet-colored robe was made of wool. He was whittling a piece of wood with a pocketknife.

Madame Blavatsky had met Master M when a young woman of twenty. She claimed in all the years she'd known him, even when she was an old woman, he'd not aged. Today he looked to be about thirty-five, strongly built, with an unpretentious dignity. Smiling at Katherine, a manly beauty lit up his face with an inner glow. As if in a dream, she couldn't believe she really was here with the master. He reached out his hands and had her sit on a stool beside him.

Ananda placed a tote and satchel on the ground nearby, bowed at them, and climbed the stairs to the pagoda. Together Katherine and Master M gazed up at the mountain above and sparkling lake below. "Where are we exactly?" she asked.

"In the world." He chuckled.

"I meant are we in Tibet or India or some other place?"

"Space and countries do not matter here," he answered softly.

A redheaded hornbill flew overhead. "Stunning," Katherine said.

"Stunning." Master M nodded his head and pointed the peg he'd been whittling toward the peasant farmer.

"Do you see that chela? I'm making this little plug for him. Inserted in the yoke, it will make it easier for the oxen to help. Were an army of guns firing and shells falling around him he wouldn't stir from his work. He'd be so absorbed in his task he'd hardly be aware of the noise or peril. The two beasts are unmanageable with anyone else, but with him, they're always perfectly content."

Master M paused and smiled at her with love. "Those frivolous beasts can feel the atmosphere and my chela's purity of thought. In fact, after walking many miles, his barefoot soles haven't been damaged because he doesn't dread or think about the distance. His mind is only filled with joy of the spiritual life that lightens his body."

"Ananda seems to have that ability too." Katherine took the bota bag from the tote and drank.

The master nodded. "He practices. Ananda means bliss. Soon he will live up to his name."

"I wish I could learn to go through life like that." She sighed.

"I hope you will someday too. Practice, my child."

She grinned at the thought of him calling her, a fifty-some-year-old woman, a child.

He glanced at her hand. "Nice ring," he teased.

"Yes." She laughed. He was the one who'd designed the signet for Madame Blavatsky.

A silence set in. The same silence that had touched her in the Egyptian desert. In the presence of Master M, a deep peace set into her soul with no need to converse. Just the rhythm of two people breathing in and out as the sun sparkled over the aqua lake and began to set in shades of purple. More stars than she'd ever seen dotted the moonless sky.

She shivered from the drop in temperature and lifted the shawl over her head. Master M stood. "Let's go inside."

She didn't want to leave the stars, but, cold and hungry, she followed him up the stairs and through the pagoda's carved wooden door. She took the candle he lit for her and blinked, waiting for her eyes to adjust to the darkness. She followed his echoing steps up three more flights and through a fissure toward flickering lights until they entered a room filled with candles that lit up the room like those night stars.

Sandalwood incense permeated the air. She sat on a cushion facing the master. Ananda brought her a warm blanket, wrapped it around her, and left. She wished she had a gift for the master. She reached into the tote, pulled out a fig, and handed it to him. He nibbled around the stem. Her stomach gurgled. Within no time, Ananda returned with a tray of naan and hummus. She handed him the tote, and he added the rest of the figs to the tray.

Even though famished she waited for Master M to start.

"Eat, please," he insisted. "I do not eat much in the evenings."

William had told her of the Buddhist custom of fasting, said to help maintain health. In fact, he'd grown so thin at times she suspected he'd also practiced it. She liked food too much to ever skip a meal. She dipped a fig in the hummus and enjoyed the soothing flavors. She ate her fill, sipped some tea, and nodded at the master to share his wisdom, but he remained silent and just smiled at her.

"Where's Koot Hoomi?" she asked in hopes of meeting Madame Blavatsky's other teacher.

"He's resting," Master M answered. Katherine had heard stories of masters going into trance states for months without food or water. "You must be tired too." Master M began to chant, and she joined him.

Ananda returned with a bamboo flute and handed it to him. The music hovered over her body as he began to play. Her eyes drooped. She reclined back on a thick mat, soft as a cloud, and fell asleep. Dreams of her white city on a sundown sea wafted through her.

When she awoke, flute notes still floated in the air. She opened her eyes, sat up, and smiled at the teacher. He put down the flute and handed her a warm cup of tea. Behind him, incense still spiraled from the altar with a golden Buddha reminding her of the one at the Nassau Street building.

She sipped the tea, then asked, "How long have I been asleep?" She felt well rested, as if she were years younger.

"Time doesn't matter here," he said.

She waited for him to continue. He did not, so she said, "Thank you for inviting me here. We're grateful for your guidance to Madame Blavatsky. When she passed, William Q. Judge became Outer Head, and I was his chela. Sadly, a few months ago he also went into the light." She paused, embarrassed at her nervous rambling. "You must already know all that."

"Yes." Master M bowed slightly. "You've taken over the organization's mantle to continue our vision. How fortunate for the earth's people. Let's greet the day." He led her outside, and they sat quietly in front of the pagoda as the sun rose in a plethora of pinks and purples within dove-gray clouds.

"What is it you want most in life?"

She told him of her childhood dream and that she hoped the property was in the process of being purchased. "I plan to open a school with people from all over the world, to teach the brotherhood of man, Theosophy, and to embrace nature and beauty. Am I on the right path?"

"Do you think you're on the right path?"

"I don't know. It's overwhelming. I have enemies."

He took her wrinkled hands in his soft ones. "You must learn to love them."

She thought of William's same advice and of Annie and Hargrove. "That's impossible."

"Practice sending warm thoughts to them daily. They are God's creatures. Many others will want to help you. Let them do so. Find Bacardi. He'll assist."

"Who?"

"You'll discover." They sat quietly for a while, and then he asked, "What is it you most want to know about life?"

She paused. "What is the secret to a happy life?"

He laughed. "What a wonderful question. I will tell you three things. Firstly, awake every morning and listen for birdsong. Think a beautiful thought. Find something in the silence and sweet sunlight that links you with your higher nature."

"Secondly, many waste depth in their lives by looking ahead. Instead let beaming thoughts pour into each arriving moment. Don't practice and share your powers to impress others for personal gain. It's more important to help humanity." William had often spoken of this too.

"Thirdly, the outer life is transient. The kingdom of heaven is here on earth. The gates to it are to be sought and discovered in the heart. Divinity is within yourself."

Teacher and student spoke back and forth until nightfall. She once again slept while he lovingly played the flute. At sunrise, he told her she needed to go.

"I'm not ready. I want more time with you." She wished she could be with him forever.

"Time and space do not matter here," he said again. "My child, you have much to do." Before she followed Ananda down the thin path and climbed on the tarp for the journey back to Darjeeling, Master M said, "I believe in you." He draped a talisman with beads and trinkets over her head and smiled at her with love.

Chapter Forty-Six

January 1897

While the *Empress of India* sailed from Ceylon to Australia, Katherine left the watch in her pocket and stopped counting the days. She soaked in the moments and appreciated the cerulean sky above emerald-green waters that caressed her forward. Though there had been ups and downs on the journey, buoyed by her encounter with the master, a sense of peace filled her senses like she'd never known before. Instead of preaching to the steerage poor, she spoke individually to each, asking about their lives. She didn't worry about their futures but tried to soothe and support them at the present time.

When she shared details of her visit with the Crusaders, Patterson, Pierce, Claude, and Leoline appeared to listen with awe. Alice, as always, remained stone-faced. Hargrove, without admitting the guide he'd hired hadn't come through, grumbled, "I don't believe you really found him. When we arrive in San Francisco, I'll give up my presidency and probably leave the cabinet too." She didn't care how he felt or what he did. She practiced opening her heart to him like Master M had advised in hopes one day her ire toward him might be alleviated.

After several weeks on the water, they arrived in Sydney where a wire from Nere awaited: *Found property. It's uninhabitable.*

She didn't share the message with her fellow travelers and, not daunted one iota, wired him back: *It's the place. Move forward and procure no matter what. Start cornerstone dedication plans.* Her grandfather and William had supported her vision. G. de P. in Switzerland had been confident about the location. Master M had encouraged her about it. She closed her eyes and envisioned it again; lush gardens, white buildings, and a community filled with people from around the world appeared. In less than a month, after visiting New Zealand and Samoa, the Crusaders would arrive in California, and she needed the land to be part of their celebrations. As Outer Head, it was her job to make decisions to move her vision forward.

A few evenings from San Francisco, denim clouds gathered, rain poured onto the ship, lightning flashed across the water, and thunder rumbled. Even so, she didn't flinch. Instead of hoping it would end, she smiled with anticipation as each booming applause rolled over her.

Chapter Forty-Seven

Katherine and her Crusaders stood on deck as the California coast came into view. A slight February breeze blew as a dozen pelicans in *V*-formation flew overhead in the turquoise sky—a good omen. Even so, Katherine found it hard not to worry. Had the property been bought? Had they kept her identity secret, as she'd requested? Would Philo and Nere be there to greet her?

She prayed the next part of her plan would come to fruition. Otherwise, she would be a laughingstock. At this juncture in the journey, it was important for her to impress Theosophical members old and new with generosity of spirit, courage, and grit to support her vision and perhaps encourage them to move there.

The ship sailed past the island of Alcatraz and its military prison, and she shuddered at the sadness of men incarcerated there. Juxtaposed, the sun shone on San Francisco as they drew closer, and she understood why General Fremont had dubbed the bay entrance the Golden Gate. She'd often wanted to see the former mining town built among the hills that had grown into a major city.

Her men had let themselves go while visiting the South Seas. Now, though, Hargrove, Patterson, Pierce, and Claude had dressed in suits and vests with well-trimmed whiskers and muttonchops. Beautiful Leoline, exquisite in a fawn-colored traveling dress with sable trim, held on to Claude's arm. Alice wore a dowdy black ensemble, her pursed lips curved into a rare smile.

As the steamship pulled toward the wharf, an enormous crowd waited. In shock Katherine asked, "Who are all those people?"

Pierce held up his binoculars. "I have no idea."

Katherine spotted Nere and waved at him with glee. She told the group she'd disembark first. She tugged the brim of her amethyst-colored hat toward her face, donned dark glasses, and held the railing as she made her way down the ramp.

She put her hand on Nere's shoulder as he greeted her and asked about the crowd.

"Theosophical members, people who read about the Crusade in the papers, and of course, the press."

She leaned toward him. "Have you kept my identity concealed?"

"Of course." He smiled. "A smashing idea. It's added interest and intrigue."

"You've bought the land?" Katherine asked.

He nodded. "It's done, but we need to talk."

"Where's Philo?" She looked around. He'd written he'd meet her. "Is he at the hotel?"

"He decided to stay home with Spots."

Katherine felt a pang of sadness and homesickness. Even though he sometimes got on her nerves, she'd missed his quirky sense of humor. She knew he cared for her in his own way. But probably for the best he wasn't there because of his unpredictability.

Like conquering heroes, her fellow travelers came ashore and waved to the throng. Nere greeted the other Crusaders. Leoline held up the San Diego map he handed her, and Hargrove read the prepared announcement to the crowd. "I invite you all to the cornerstone ceremony scheduled in ten days for the School for the Revival of Lost Antiquities being built by Madame Katherine Tingley and the Theosophical Society for the study of divine wisdom."

As the Crusaders posed for photos, Nere whisked Katherine away to a waiting carriage. She removed her hat and sunglasses. "The adventures we've had! I can't wait to tell you all about them."

His face fell. "Yes, I suppose so."

She paused, feeling guilty he had to miss Egypt and India that he'd so wanted to see. "I guarantee we'll go on another Crusade someday soon."

"All right." He nodded.

She could tell he didn't believe her. Outside the window, tall buildings lined the road and houses on the hills above overlooked the bay. The carriage drove up Market Street, filled with other horse-drawn vehicles.

"Is Minnie here?" Katherine asked. She didn't know his wife well but felt admiration for the true Theosophist, known for delivering food to the poor and even helping them set up housekeeping with kitchen tools and furniture.

"Yes, Aimee too. They're out shopping. That girl is happy as a clam in the mud at high tide. Even though we live in New York, she revels in the department stores here too."

"Last time I saw her she'd certainly become a beauty. Is she coming out this season?"

"She's very shy. She's not ready." He frowned. "Minnie and I disagree on the matter."

"I understand how you feel. I've always considered debutante balls demeaning to girls paraded by parents to find husbands for them." Katherine admired Nere for not pushing Aimee into an early marriage and thought of her own father who'd tried to do so.

The carriage halted as a cable car clicked and clanged in front of them. Nere said, "The property isn't what you think. As I wrote, it's a desert. No one will ever be able to live there."

"Pish-posh. It can't be as bad as all that." She laughed.

"There's no water for the community or gardens you've planned."

"No water? We'll dig a well!" she scoffed.

"San Diego is in the middle of nowhere with only seventeen thousand residents."

"As our members move there, we'll add to the population."

"There's no direct train service to the east. Riders must go through Los Angeles first."

"We'll lobby for one." She put her gloved hand on his. "I'm grateful for all you've done. Together I'm certain we'll overcome any challenges that arise." She exuded authentic confidence, but she hid doubts from her friend. Katherine needed to believe everything she said was true; she had no other choice.

He frowned. "What if it's not really the place of your vision?"

"Have faith. I wish you'd been there when Gottfried de Purucker drew the map. It was as if the Almighty One sent him to me. Don't you believe in my vision?"

Nere paused. "Of course I do; otherwise, I wouldn't have bought the property. I'm just afraid not everyone will."

"Don't share your concerns with the others as of yet."

"Shouldn't we prepare them?"

"They'll see it soon enough and can make up their own minds. Let's not dampen their enthusiasm for the cornerstone dedication." Nothing would deter her. She'd been yearning for this her whole life.

The horses clopped into the hotel's skylighted Grand Court carriage entrance overlooked by seven stories of columned balconies. "Nothing on our journey could compete with anything so grand," she said.

"The Palace, dubbed the Bonanza Inn, is the largest hotel in the Western United States." Nere laughed.

She smiled. "The owner must have struck gold."

The two followed the bellman through the tiled reception area to the hydraulic lift. Inside Nere said, "I've registered you in the Royal Suite so events can be held there."

Egad. She would have preferred something smaller. Those gatherings went on and on, and she wouldn't be able to graciously slip away. Not wanting to hurt his feelings, she held her tongue.

Overwhelmed from the hustle-bustle, she yawned as they stepped inside and said to Nere, "Thank you for all you've done."

He took the hint, left the suite, and she retired to the bedroom.

Voices from the parlor woke her. She opened the curtains, looked out toward the lovely bay, readied herself, and stepped into the parlor. Cabinet members who hadn't joined the journey, most of the Crusaders, and a few strangers gave her a standing ovation.

She waved her arms. "Sit. It's my other dear travelers who should be applauded." Circling the room, she greeted each guest, then sat in a Louis Quinze chair underneath the giant crystal chandelier.

Everyone in the room poured over weeks of speculative newspaper articles. Katherine guffawed at journalist conjectures about the property: a new harbor with a steamship terminal, a grand resort to outdo the Hotel del Coronado, or perhaps a casino to rival Monte Carlo. Hargrove entered the room. Evidently, he hadn't left her fold after all.

As the sun moved over the bay, the room became awash with afternoon light, and Nere began the meeting. "We've purchased 132 acres in Point Loma with an option to buy forty more."

"What's it like?" Alice asked.

Nere glanced at Katherine. "You'll need to wait and see for yourself."

A sandy-haired man stood and said with a strong voice, "I can speak on the topic. The beauty of the Point Loma coastline has no comparison."

"Who're you?" Hargrove asked with a frown.

"I'm Lorin Wood, a longtime Theosophist and naturopathic doctor from Delaware. Last year I bought Point Loma property and plan to build a health hotel adjacent to the land you just purchased. We'll be neighbors. I'd be happy to help oversee the school's construction until Mrs. Tingley and the cabinet can relocate there."

Katherine took an immediate liking to this doctor and began a cheer. "Hear! Hear!"

Nere rolled out the New York architects' plans. "It's a 120-feet-long multileveled wood structure."

"What's it going to cost us?" Hargrove asked.

"Only forty thousand dollars. A local firm's been contracted to build it," Nere answered.

Too plain. Katherine wasn't impressed with the drawings. She'd skip that battle for today. Plenty of time to amend them once she felt what the land called for.

Nere held up a map. "In ten days, we'll take the train south to San Diego, where we'll stay at the Brewster Hotel. The site is far from downtown. To get there, we'll ride a ferry." He pointed to the map. "Or go around the bay by carriages. If there's been rain, it can be quite muddy."

"Isn't there an inn closer?" Hargrove complained.

Nere shook his head. "No, there isn't."

Hargrove grumbled, "Who'll come all that way for the dedication?"

Katherine smiled. "Besides the press articles and advertisements we've arranged, let's have a presentation the night before in a downtown assembly hall to entice citizens not to miss the California event of the year."

They hammered out a cornerstone dedication agenda. She said speakers cannot go longer than ten minutes. Hargrove pushed back that as president he should be allotted more time. She acquiesced, giving him seven minutes at the beginning and another few at the end. Wishing he would disappear, she stood at the picture window trying to rejoice in her first California sunset.

Minnie and Aimee Neresheimer, first to arrive for the evening reception, extended warm hugs to Katherine. An emerald larger than any Katherine had seen in India rested over Minnie's heart chakra. Pink rosettes circled Aimee's collar below her heart-shaped face as she spoke. Yes, that sweet girl was too naïve for a coming out.

Nere played the piano while the San Francisco elite and local Theosophists flowed in. Others had arrived by train from around the country, including Elizabeth Mayer. As before, while Katherine spoke with her, she felt they were kindred spirits. The room teemed with excitement as visitors studied maps, plans, and photos. The Crusaders answered questions about their travels. Hargrove lapped up the added attention. With pride, Katherine smiled at the other members and would-be members who she hoped would support the school.

Later she spotted Hargrove chatting with Aimee in a corner. She worried that the poor girl must be bored to tears, but then the ingénue's giggles floated across the room at something he'd said. Odd.

After the welcome reception, the days dragged on, with speaking engagements, meetings, and teas. These tedious events were important; without the support of patrons, her vision wouldn't come to reality. So she tried to observe and appreciate the present moments. Although all she wanted to do was hop on a train and prove Nere was wrong about the property.

Chapter Forty-Eight

Ten days after they arrived in San Francisco, as she packed, she received a wire from the preparation committee in San Diego notifying her that no cornerstones had been delivered. She immediately replied: *Find local granite and have one made.*

The next morning her entourage finally boarded the train south. The beautiful ride reminded Katherine of the Italian Riviera as the train passed between water and mountains, dove into tunnels, and circled around precipices. It stopped in small towns and took the whole day. When they reached San Diego, she was surprised that electric streetlights, trolley lines, and telephone poles dotted the land. This wasn't the backwater town she'd been warned of after all. There were banking institutions, opera houses, a library in the works, and even a teacher training school.

Delivered by tallyhos—fringe-topped open coaches—to the Brewster Hotel, Katherine barely had time to change before leaving for the evening's presentation. Despite a heavy downpour, eight hundred curious San Diegans packed Unity Hall to hear about the property plans, with hundreds more turned away.

Katherine, anonymous under a large chapeau in a back row, listened to Hargrove cajole the audience like a carnival barker. "Ladies and gentlemen, tomorrow's event will include music, poetry, and an appearance by the Theosophical Outer Head. A sacred dedication for the School for the Revival of Lost Mysteries of Antiquity will occur with the placement of the ancient Killarney cornerstone and other spectacularities." She hoped he hadn't overdone it.

That night she fell asleep to a pounding heavy rain on the hotel roof. In the morning, as the group caravanned to the ferry landing, dense fog hung over the town. It sure didn't feel like a desert. Katherine, with Nere's family, pulled up at the pier where a long queue of passengers waited. Katherine didn't want to delay another moment to see the property.

"Can you take us there the other way?" she asked the Tallyho driver.

"It'll probably take longer than the ferry. I don't advise it after last night's rain."

"How bad can it be? I've just finished a world tour," she replied.

He pointed north and west. "It's seven miles through mudflats and up a steep winding grade."

Katherine told him, "I'm sure we'll be fine."

Nere said, "Minnie and Aimee, you take the ferry. I'll ride with Katherine."

As the women got out, Hargrove hopped out of another Tallyho and followed them. The rest of the group chose to wait for the ferry too. Katherine's driver sighed, clicked the reins, and started up the horses. He guided them north, through Old Town, where tile-topped adobes stood. They entered the tidal flats, partly submerged in high water, and within no time she rued her stubborn decision. Her shoes, face, and even her hat became splattered in muck. She avoided Nere's eyes and didn't say a word.

Hours later, rising through a deep canyon on a wagon-rutted road, they passed a chicken farm, and as they continued, she turned and saw the ferry crossing the bay. Maybe she'd beat the rest of them there. Even though they'd advertised in the newspapers, sent out two hundred and fifty personal invitations to prominent San Diegans, and rallied attendees at last night's event, would anyone really come all this way?

Turning left at the top of the hill, the horses pulled onto another dirt road and finally stopped near the site, where a fog bank hovered. After the tallyho dropped them off, she said "Sorry" to Nere, but he excused himself and made his way south. She heard the ocean but could barely see it through the fog. She walked the way the driver had pointed and spotted members of her group setting up the event, walking the grounds, and scaling an observation tower.

Patterson rushed to her with Pierce on his heels. "Do you want the chairs on that mound or below it?"

"They should face the ocean view," she said, hoping the sky would clear by then.

The men stared at her with laughter.

"What's so funny?" she asked.

Patterson handed her a kerchief, and Pierce pointed at her face.

She wiped it and studied her filthy dress and ruined shoes. She'd deal with them later. Good thing Leoline had carried Katherine's costume over on the ferry.

"Where do you want the banner?" Pierce asked.

"At this moment, I don't care," she snapped and checked her watch. Two hours until the dedication was scheduled to begin. Her voice softened, "You've got the diagram we worked on. You two are so capable. You make decisions." She needed to walk alone, to gather her senses.

Hargrove and Claude huddled behind a dying citrus tree. "What a god-forsaken spot," Hargrove said.

Claude sighed, "I quite agree."

She walked in the opposite direction. Could they be right? This property didn't resemble her vision at all. Scattered clumps of cactus dotted the hillsides. No colorful flowers bloomed; no healthy trees provided shade or lined a path to walk on. A scrubby bush caught on her skirt, and it ripped as she tried to tug it free.

Had she made a drastic mistake? Nere had warned her. Too late to back out now. Fingering her grandfather's watch, she tried not to panic and to stay in the moment. He'd encouraged her vision. So had William and Master M. But what if this wasn't the right place?

She whispered to them and the Almighty, "Please help me!" The words flew into the air. No matter what, she'd need to move forward and ready herself and the others for the dedication. She headed back.

At least there, all seemed under control and ready. The on-site dedication committee had spent a week on preparations. An American flag covered the podium, and cypress branches hung in an arch above it. National flags awarded to the Crusaders during their trip flapped in the breeze, and a purple banner with gold letters read: *THERE IS NO RELIGION HIGHER THAN THE TRUTH*. Life-sized portraits of Madame Blavatsky, William, Katherine, and Hargrove were displayed. When the latter had insisted on his photo being among theirs, Katherine had to hold back from blurting, "You've never been an Outer Head."

She studied the derrick suspended with ropes to lower the cornerstone into place. She made sure it worked well up and down. Hargrove had also demanded he'd be the one to lower it during the ceremony. She hoped she could trust him to do so slowly. The next part of the plan was for him to pour burning alcohol over it to create flames. He'd argued that no one would believe it was magic. She had replied, "I don't expect anyone to. It's all for dramatic effect."

Pierce handed her the souvenir program. She smiled as she ran her fingers over the purple paper with embossed lettering and flipped it open to see the etching of Point Loma printed inside. Very impressive. It had been worth the extra expense. "It's lovely," she said and told Pierce to have Leoline meet her in the tent.

As Katherine made her way there, the fog thinned to mist, the sun shone through, and the mighty Pacific sparkled clearly. That was the ocean of her dreams! This must be the land. Inside the tent, she washed her dirty face in the washbasin below the mirror.

Leoline entered and handed her the gown. "Claude needs me to help practice his speech. I need to run." Before Katherine could stop her, she rushed back out.

Katherine draped the dress on the back of a chair. Strange, Claude had given that talk many times before. Stepping out of her muddy shoes and stockings, Katherine tried to stay calm. What if no one showed up? What if they booed her? What if locals and visiting Theosophists weren't impressed?

Elizabeth Mayer popped her head inside. "Leoline told me you might need help."

"Thank heavens you're here. I'm filthy, and my hair's a rat's nest."

Elizabeth poured clean water into the bowl and helped Katherine scrub.

"Is your Mr. Spalding here?" Katherine asked.

"He's sorry he couldn't make it." Elizabeth draped the purple gown over Katherine's head, helped her step into slippers, and slipped the shined signet on her finger. Katherine studied herself in the mirror. So much depended on this; her demeanor must be impeccable. She told herself she had power, a charisma to attract, a glow that drew people within her midst to follow her. She hoped to assure the crowd that her desire to awaken the world to humanity was pure.

Elizabeth studied her. "I'm sorry the property isn't what you'd imagined."

"What do you mean?"

"It's so barren."

"Wait until we erect the school, plant trees, and occupy it. It'll be all I've ever dreamed of and more," Katherine said and tried to believe it herself.

Chapter Forty-Nine

Pierce rushed in. "There's nearly a thousand people here!" Outside the tent, the sound of waves mingled with a cacophony of voices.

Patterson followed him in, fretting. "There aren't nearly enough chairs for everyone."

"They don't seem to care," Pierce said.

Katherine and Elizabeth peeked outside as people on horseback, in rickety wagons, fancy carriages, fringed tallyhos, and even on bicycles streamed onto the site.

"The mudflats must have dried." Katherine smiled. And she'd been afraid no one would come. The acolytes, a white-robed lad and lassie chosen from a local lodge for the occasion, ran inside. The dozen esoterics, students of occultism from around the world, many of whom Katherine had never met before, entered and donned their purple robes. The special speakers and the male Crusaders came in wearing suits. She'd asked them to wear robes too, but they'd bristled, saying it would be undignified. That was another battle she'd chosen not to fight.

Katherine nodded, studied the program, and took role. "Where's Claude?" she asked Leoline.

The beauty looked down. "He must be ill."

"I just saw him. We must search. What if he fell off a cliff?" Katherine yelped and started to exit the tent.

Hargrove pulled her back in.

She tugged her arm away. "He could be in peril."

"He's not." Hargrove shook his head.

Katherine glanced at the frowns on the other Crusaders' faces, and it dawned on her. Claude must have decided not to participate of his own free will. Was he going to leave her? She'd felt he was one she could trust.

"We must begin," Pierce said.

She scanned the group. "There's a hole in the program. Alice, you speak about Madame Blavatsky, briefly mention my titles and recent history only." After she said it, Katherine rued her decision. Alice had a tendency for exaggeration and going off topic. "It's to honor Madame Blavatsky."

Alice nodded. "You can count on me."

"Let's gather." Katherine reached for the acolytes' hands, and the others circled around. She composed herself, looked up, and said, "Today we follow the destiny you've planned. Help us demonstrate the power of brotherhood and vision for this land. Amen."

"Amen," the group echoed.

She clapped her hands. "Only ten minutes each or we'll be here past sundown. Pierce, as master of ceremonies, it's up to you to keep the wheels rolling!"

"I know!" he shouted with enthusiasm.

Katherine pointed to the flap. The Crusaders and main speakers lined up on either side beneath the flagged arch and faced each other. Hargrove made an entrance and stood at the podium until the crowd silenced, then said, "Welcome to this solemn occasion that brings people from all parts of the country to witness the laying of the cornerstone of the School for the Revival of the Lost Mysteries of Antiquity. It might seem strange that the founder-directress, Mrs. Tingley, should have selected this spot, never having seen it before. But she has a vision that all must follow."

Was that a dig? Katherine nodded to the esoterics and they lined up near the exit.

A triangle clang denoted the official ceremony's beginning. The crowd hushed again while the twenty-piece San Diego City Guard band played the serene introduction to the "*Intermezzo Sinfonico*," and the esoterics glided out and stopped under the evergreen arch.

Katherine's heart pounded wildly. She closed her eyes and allowed the dreamy music to soothe her. At the fifth stanza, she pushed her shoulders back and placed a regal expression on her face as if playing Titania, queen of the fairies from *A Midsummer Night's Dream*. They expected a queen and she'd give them one!

Flanked by the acolytes, she stepped out and paused for the crowd to view her. Her back to the ocean, she faced a sea of faces. The afternoon light hit her and awakened her soul with awe. A zephyr rustled her gown, and the scent of orange blossoms filled the air.

Nere and his family smiled at her from the front row next to the mayor and his wife, who Katherine recognized from newspaper photos. The Robinsons from San Francisco smiled at her along with Dr. Anderson with his receding hairline and bushy mustache and chops. A striking man in an ascot tie and a five-gallon hat sat behind them. Another gentleman began to nod off. Others fanned themselves with the souvenir program. Katherine couldn't believe it. The 250 chairs were filled. The rest either stood behind or were perched atop carriages peering over toward the ceremony.

As the band continued to play, the children marched beside her as she glided in a stately manner down the aisle, clasping the tin box that contained a history of the movement, Crusader thoughts, a copy of the souvenir program, and other various parchments. She passed underneath the banner and colorful flags, then halted beneath the cypress arch. On the side by the cornerstone derrick, she spied Hargrove. Slowly, the ropes began to lower the two-foot stone from the arched branches toward her. Suddenly, it sped up. Before it hit her head, she ducked and shoved the cornerstone away. It flew back into the air.

She glared at Hargrove, who shrugged, grasped the rope again, and slowly inched it down. When the stone was in front of her, she applied mortar and deposited the box on top. As the music ended, the stone drifted down into place beneath the ground. She raised her arms for applause and lowered them to quiet the crowd.

In a clear voice, she said, "I dedicate this stone to the work that'll be done in the temple for the benefit of humanity and the glory of the ancient sages." She placed her palms together above her head toward the sky and brought them down to her chest to begin the ancient chant.

The sounds reverberated across the terrain as the acolytes, esoterics, and speakers joined her. A woman in a wide-brimmed hat held her hands to her cheeks as if she might faint. The man who'd earlier nodded off sat wide-eyed. Another blinked rapidly and pursed his lips, as if he'd like to join in. This was exactly the effect Katherine had intended. She had their attention now and beamed as the crowd applauded. The girl handed Katherine an urn. She took it and said, as she scattered kernels over the stone, "I ladle corn to symbolize earth."

She accepted carafes from each acolyte and streamed liquids onto the stone simultaneously. "I pour oil and wine to symbolize air, the emblem of man's breath and inner self."

The boy handed her a bowl, and she tipped dirt onto the stone. "I sprinkle loam to symbolize brotherhood." The next moment was crucial. Katherine opened her heart, willed it to work, and said, "Fire, the emblem of man's spiritual power."

Hargrove poured burning alcohol over the cornerstone, stepped back, and proclaimed, "May these fires be lighted and burn forevermore."

A crackling bonfire blazed upward from the stone. The crowd oohed. The spectacle worked! After the flames died out, the children threw flowers atop the smoldering ashes.

Each esoteric stepped to the dais and quoted excerpts Katherine had carefully selected for the occasion from: Orphic hymns, a Zuni prayer, Ralph Waldo Emerson, Confucius, Eleusinian Mysteries, the beatitudes from the New Testament, the Bhagavad Gita, and more. Leoline beautifully recited the poem "Harmony."

She handed Katherine a scroll. Katherine stepped forward, unrolled it, and read, "Today you have witnessed the laying of the cornerstone. In ancient times, the founding of a temple was looked upon as of worldwide importance. Kings, princes, and sages from distant countries gathered to lend their presence at such a time, for the building of a temple was regarded as a benefit upon all humanity. At this school, the children of all races will be taught the laws of physical, moral, and mental health. They will learn to live in harmony with nature. They will become compassionate lovers of all that breathe, grow strong in an understanding of themselves, and gain strength to use for the good of the whole world."

She paused and gazed out over the audience. "Rejoice with me, then, at this hour and in the brightness of this future which contains so much joy for man."

All stood with their hands on their hearts as a large American flag was raised up a pole and the band struck up "Columbia, the Gem of the Ocean." At this juncture, she'd requested a gun salute, but due to nearby horses it had been nixed. Hoisted in hopes it would be seen flying all the way downtown was the purple Theosophical flag, with alternating stripes mirroring the American flag and a great gilded seal.

Mr. Rambo from San Francisco's Lodge spoke about the history of the Theosophical movement; Dr. Lorin Wood, who was building the hotel nearby, read the effects of the recent Crusade from Pierce's notes; and Patterson shared about the life of William Q. Judge. Pierce told the audience Claude Falls Wright had been unavoidably detained and Mrs. Cleather would share about the life of Madame Blavatsky.

Alice pointed at Katherine and began to speak about her instead of eulogizing Blavatsky. "Madame Tingley saw the horrors of life during the Civil War, and at the early age of thirteen, helped nurse soldiers." Alice talked about Katherine's New York relief work and continued, "Until she discovered Theosophy, she felt no other existing belief could surmount the plight of millions. When our leader William Q. Judge went into the light, many accused Madame Tingley of stealing his title, but she never sought the position, she was entreated to it. Madame Tingley never claimed to be Madame Blavatsky reincarnated, as some had said."

Katherine kept a nonchalant expression on her face as she fought the ire that rose in her chest. Why would Alice bring up these issues now. Most San Diegans had probably never heard of Madame Blavatsky or Theosophy, let alone the organization's infighting. Alice's words might make them doubt Katherine's legitimacy. Good or bad, the speech might answer rumors circulating about her and push her reputation into more respectability. However, they might raise other questions about her. Gossip can be moral murder. She should lambast Alice for breaking a key rule: no one talked about her past. Like Hargrove, Alice might not be a friend, but a foe! Katherine looked at the silly goose smiling at her and realized Alice had meant well.

Reverend Williams of the local Unitarian church discussed divine teachers, and Pryse the esoteric side of Christianity. Colonel Blackmar, president of San Diego's Theosophical Section, took Katherine's hand, and talked about the local influence the school would provide. Mayor Carlson responded positively to the founding of the school. Three hours after it began, Hargrove came to the podium a second time and bid a final farewell. Horns blared, and the band played Wagner's "Fest March."

After the crowd left, Katherine paced to the cliff edge overlooking the Pacific, where she could see for many miles up and down the coast. This was the place, she could feel it, the one she'd dreamt of all these years, and she was finally here on this sacred land. Her grandfather and William's love spun within her and Master M's too. She thanked them for believing in her and for their encouragement to press on. She closed her eyes and let the cool winds caress her body.

Even though some said this land couldn't be worked agriculturally, she now imagined a garden of the Lord: a forest of trees from around the world, vegetable gardens to feed the entire community, flowers in bloom. There would be magnificent buildings in white reminiscent of ancient architecture. The children would be sweet, the adults scholarly. From all nations, living together in harmony among nature, they would gain knowledge and skills to be able to spread brotherhood across the earth. She'd traveled the world. This would be the most exquisite paradise of all.

Katherine knew she'd remember this day for the rest of her life. This was her destiny. These plans weren't from her head, only from her heart, with divine inner guidance. She felt the esoteric value of the land. She'd been called to this sacred place at this time to fulfill her long-held dream. She was finally home.

Chapter Fifty

Katherine wanted to begin implementing her vision immediately. However, much had to be accomplished beforehand: membership needed to be increased, funds had to be raised, and designs redrawn to her specifications. She boarded the train to continue the Crusade across America with plans to move international headquarters to Point Loma as soon as possible. Some in her orbit would need convincing but she felt in her soul it was the right thing to do.

Thousands attended Theosophical events in Los Angeles and Sacramento. In Salt Lake City, inquisitive Mormons were eager to learn about the organization, and in Denver members as well as curious folks welcomed the group. Besides presentations and brotherhood dinners, stops included prison lectures to tell the incarcerated to have hope for a future in another life.

A month later, as their train approached Chicago, the constant speeches, visitations, and late-night dinners had taken their toll on Katherine. Delirious with fever, she often awakened with visions that didn't make sense—Spanish-speaking men fighting on sacred grounds. She lost her voice and was overtaken by exhaustion.

One morning through a veil of sleep, strange men hovered over her. In fear, she tried to scream as they lifted her onto a stretcher and carried her off. Was she having a nightmare, a vision, or had she gone into the light?

Her throat on fire, she tried to ask where she was, but the words Katherine heard didn't make sense and she closed her eyes again. The next thing she knew, someone was putting a cool cloth on her forehead.

"Welcome back," a familiar voice said.

Katherine opened her eyes and grasped Elizabeth's hand.

"I'm glad your fever has broken." She saw Elizabeth's smile through a gauzy haze.

"Where are we?"

"In Chicago, at the Palmer House."

"I must get ready for our presentation." Katherine tried to sit up.

"It was last night," Elizabeth said. "Sleep now."

Katherine fell back onto the bed in a stupor. Newspaper in his hand, Hargrove rushed into the room. The last person she wanted to see.

"Annie Besant and the countess are on their way to the United States with a counter-invasion," he cried.

Elizabeth tugged the paper from him and pushed him out the door. "Scoot!"

"Read it to me," Katherine insisted and blinked her eyes closed.

"I'll just summarize." Elizabeth studied the article. "Their first engagement is scheduled for New York; then they'll make their way across the country and speak in San Diego last."

Katherine opened her eyes. "Cancel all future stops. Head for New York."

"You're too ill to travel."

"I don't care. I'm the Outer Head, and I know what's best."

Two weeks later a carriage dropped her off and Philo carried Katherine upstairs to her suite, where she crumpled into bed.

"Poor dear," Philo exclaimed. "You look a fright."

Even though she'd been gone almost a year, Spots jumped on the bed with resounding barks and tail wags. She nuzzled his thick hair, smelling sweetly of Philo's aftershave lotion.

Her voice reduced to a whisper, she said, "I'll just take a little nap. Wake me in an hour for this evening's event."

Philo sat beside her and took her hand. "You're not going anywhere tonight."

"I must. It's Madison Square Garden. Our victorious celebration," she rasped, coughed, and pointed to her handbag.

He opened it, pulled out a bottle of medicine, and spooned some into her mouth. "Sleep now, and we'll see how you feel later." He helped her out of her boots and tucked her into bed.

Once again confused with fever, she had that same dream, horrible visions, the Spanish- speaking men in military uniform, this time more violent, swords and gunshots. Bodies on the ground, blood in the water. In the backdrop, an oak and white buildings. If the dreams continued, she'd suggest members learn the language in case they were needed for casualty support. All of it was disturbing and cruel, made worse by the pain in her head, throat, and body.

She opened her eyes as Philo set a tray on her bed. Her throat didn't feel as sore.

"Good morning!" he sang. "You look much better today."

Shimmery sunrays streamed through the window as he opened the curtains. She sat up and realized she'd slept all night. "Why didn't you wake me?"

"I tried. You didn't budge."

"I've missed everything." Her shoulders dropped.

"And I've missed you." He grinned and plumped up her pillows.

She sighed. "I've missed you too." She leaned back on the pile and looked at him. Neat as a pin, beard trimmed, dark hair combed back, clothes neatly pressed—she'd truly missed him.

As if he knew what she was thinking, he said, "I promise I've been on the wagon, taken great care of our Spots, and attended choir practice."

"I'm proud of you." She smiled broadly.

"And I'm proud of you too. It's an honor to be your husband."

He'd never said anything like that before. Surprised, she asked, "What do you mean?"

"I've been following the articles," he said; then his eyes opened wide.

"Where's today's journal?"

"It didn't come." Philo studied his hands.

"Liar!" she teased. "Go get it."

He sheepishly brought it to her and read the headline aloud, "Battle of the Fair Theosophists Is On."

"That Annie Besant will be the death of me." Katherine coughed.

"I certainly hope not." Philo put his hands on his hips like an HMS *Pinafore* sailor sailing the ocean blue.

Another article described the previous evening's event with a copy of Hargrove's keynote speech taking all the credit for the Crusade successes. At least she'd be well enough to oversee the annual convention scheduled in a few weeks.

Chapter Fifty-One

By April she'd regained her strength, and the Do-Good Mission drew her to the East Side where factories puffed soot into the sky. Young and old, rich and poor—but mostly poor—streamed along. A mixture of languages from around the world flooded around her. She waded across the street and started to open the door, but Grace slid onto the threshold, her hair disheveled and apron filthy. She congratulated Katherine on the Crusade.

Astounded to see Grace's condition, she said, "Sorry I couldn't get here sooner."

"I heard you've been ill. Don't come in. Many are sick here too. I'd hate for you to catch anything else."

"That's silly." Katherine gently pushed past her and froze in shock. Since the blizzard almost ten years ago she'd never seen so many. Babies cried while mothers coughed, holding listless little ones. Older children slumped along the rough-hewn benches.

"They're suffering terribly. Many can barely breathe," Grace reported and pointed above. "It's even worse upstairs. The doctor said there was nothing to be done."

"Send someone to fetch her for me. I'm going up to see," Katherine said and struggled up the narrow stairs. One flight up, she covered her nose and mouth with her scarf to protect her senses from unemptied chamber pots and ailment stenches. Children's cries and coughs grew louder as she rose to the third floor.

She'd planned to go to the fifth floor and work her way down to assess the situation, but instead, drawn by wails, she stepped into the Levis' dim apartment. The room hushed, and eyes stared at her. A lad, his two younger sisters, and a tabby cat huddled together in a single bed under a paper-thin counterpane. Even though the weather was in the low thirties, no fire glowed in the woodburning stove. Bowls of congealed gruel sat atop a table.

Katherine had known this sweet family for a long time. Shocked she asked, "Where's your mother?"

With listless eyes, the boy began to cough. The children started to bawl again as Katherine moved to the next room where a kerosene lamp and a dirty window allowed little light in. The tailor she'd employed to make her own clothes, to help him make ends meet, cut cloth on a table. Juxtaposed with the squalor around them, a magenta frock with black velvet trim hung on the dressmaker's mannequin.

Katherine cried, "Mr. Levi, what're you doing in here? Your children need you. Where's Mrs. Levi?"

He ignored her, finished cutting the fabric, and handed it to his eldest daughter to stitch at the treadle sewing machine. Another girl picked up a basket of thread and began to sew sequins on a jacket.

Katherine asked again, "Where's your wife?"

"She's gone to the Lord, and the baby too."

Katherine paused. "I'm so sorry. Can you stop work for a while and comfort your little ones? It should provide you comfort as well."

"If I don't work," he said, barely above a whisper, "I won't be able to pay the ten-dollar rent to Mr. Thomas."

The children in the other room keened louder.

"What about your elder boy? Isn't he still working at the hat factory?" she asked.

Mr. Levi shook his head. "He succumbed as well."

Katherine thought her heart might break. She remembered him as such a sweet lad holding up his tin cup to her in the soup line ages ago. Before she left, they didn't have much; nevertheless, they'd been cheery living in this small apartment together. She opened her pocketbook and handed

Mr. Levi a few banknotes. He refused, but she left them on the table anyway and wished she had something more to say to ease his pain.

Downstairs again, Katherine assisted as many as she could until Gertie arrived.

"What's the cause of all this?" Tears welled in Katherine's eyes.

"Factory smoke, tight quarters, unsanitary conditions." The doctor seemed on the edge of dropping with exhaustion. "Last summer's heatwave lasted ten days; since then, things have gotten worse."

"What can we do to help these poor souls?" Katherine asked.

"They need fresh air and healthy food."

There were so many; Katherine didn't even know where to begin. There would be plenty of all that once Point Loma was established. She'd send many there by train. In the meantime, something had to be done to save as many as she could. She thought of her childhood at the Laurels in the open fields, among the oaks, along the flowing river. Maybe she'd buy a nearby property where ill children could be accommodated.

The convention at Madison Square Garden was well attended by lodge representatives from around the country eager to hear more about the Crusade. Nere suggested she allow Hargrove to give the Crusade report to appease him. Even though she feared he'd try to take credit for the trip again or mention the ghastly Bombay incident, she allowed him to do so. To her mortification, what he said was much worse: "Even though Mrs. Tingley as Outer Head was often ill and frail, she carried on. We didn't meet the Luxor Brotherhood as she'd predicted, but she did claim she'd met with Master Morya in the Himalayas. The rest of us didn't personally witness the meeting."

The delegates seemed not to even notice. In fact, Hargrove had been so long-winded that many fell asleep. Nonetheless Katherine would never forgive him for that, let alone love him as Master M had encouraged her to do. Hargrove also spouted that since the Crusade was over, it was time for lodges to focus on rituals and lecture meetings again.

Instead of refuting him, she followed his talk with, "One of William's last messages to his followers was that occult development comes best, quickest, and safest in the conscientious fulfillment of the small duties of everyday life. He strongly advocated that Society members should abstain from overt occult exhibitions for self-gratification and instead continue their work for the brotherhood of man."

As she transitioned the organization from mere intellectualism to practical philanthropy, she knew some would leave her. So far, the only Crusader who'd abandoned her was Claude, sadly taking Leoline with him. She didn't want someone to stay just because of contacts and money. The ones with deep desires would stay. She loathed kowtowing to Hargrove and wished he'd resign as he'd threatened. It frustrated her that as Outer Head she still didn't have absolute power to make decisions and had to run important ones through the cabinet.

As soon as she got home from the convention, exhausted, she closed her eyes and fell asleep. In the morning, she woke fully refreshed with ideas running through her mind. She grabbed her journal and composed reform components for a nonsectarian International Brotherhood League, a separate organization to expand her humanitarian efforts. She shared her ideas with Joe and Nere, who helped edit and perfect the document to present at the cabinet meeting the following week. She hoped they'd all support it.

Chapter Fifty-Two

Through the window, Katherine studied May storm clouds that gathered over the Hudson. Philo helped her open the lace tablecloth on the parlor table. He smoothed out the wrinkles and said, "You've got to slow down and take time to fully recover." Katherine had recently had a relapse.

"I'm fine now. I can't." She leaned on the table to catch her breath. "There's too much to do. Children in the tenements are dying. So many other needy in the world too. And I want to start building in Point Loma."

"Sit down." He led her to the chair at the end of the table and poured her a glass of water.

"I have big plans." She took a sip.

"Of course you do. But will the cabinet go along with them?" Philo asked.

If they didn't, she wouldn't be able to move forward.

As the cabinet members arrived, Philo escorted them to the parlor. When all were seated, Katherine nodded to Philo, and he headed down the hall to his rooms with Spots. She smiled at each man and opened her heart to them: Joe, Pryse, and Griscom, who'd stayed in New York and worked to keep the organization going while they were on Crusade. Patterson and Pierce, who'd been congenial and stalwart on the journey. And Nere—without him none of her triumphs would have been possible.

She stared at Hargrove. As hard as she tried, she was unable to summon positive emotions toward him. After his defamation of her at the convention she wanted to fire him. Nere had counseled her not to make enemies of Hargrove and his allies.

"Do any of you speak Spanish?" she asked.

"Why?" Pierce looked at her through his spectacles.

"I've had a vision." She didn't want to share the horrors she'd seen in her nightmares.

"That's ludicrous," Hargrove scoffed. "Just like your vision of a Luxor Lodge?"

"Let that go," Katherine told him.

Joe said to Hargrove firmly, "Let's stick to the agenda."

Hargrove looked at the sheet. "I don't see Spanish anywhere on it."

"I don't either," Griscom said.

"Maybe it's in connection to the Cuban insurrections against the Spanish," Nere said.

"Possibly." Katherine hadn't thought of that.

Joe looked at her and pointed to the agenda. "Let's move on. The Do-Good Mission."

"Not that silly little project." Hargrove rolled his eyes.

Katherine ignored him. "The situation is dire. Cholera, typhus, and even tuberculosis are running rampant. Many deaths have occurred. The children are especially vulnerable."

"What can we do to help?" Pryse asked.

Joe quickly took notes as Katherine continued, "Dr. van Pelt said they need fresh air and food. I propose we send as many as possible to the country this summer."

"Are you joking?" Hargrove cut in again and looked around the table.

"Mr. Hargrove," she said. "That's not helpful. Hold your comments until I've given my full report." To catch her breath and keep her anger at bay, she sipped some water.

"I don't call this being a visionary. It's time the Outer Headship was transferred to me."

"I agree." Griscom looked at Hargrove.

Nere raised his usually calm voice. "William chose her, not you, Hargrove. Let's move on and listen to what else she has to say."

"A summer camp, how will we pay for it? The one-dollar membership dues won't cover that." Hargrove sneered.

"Bazaars," Katherine said with a straight face.

The men laughed.

"I'm not kidding. We'll send telegrams to lodges around the country and abroad to sell castoff items to raise funds for a site to help the children. The new century is quickly coming upon us." She paused. "I propose we start a newsletter too."

"We already have *The Path*," Hargrove spouted. "And other publications as well."

"This one would be different," Katherine continued. "Besides philosophical articles, we'd share accounts of the cultures we met on Crusade and gather lodge updates. Businesses would pay for advertisements."

Hargrove asked, "What businesses would do that?"

"Lorin Wood," Patterson said.

"That doctor who owns the Point Loma land next to us?" Hargrove gaped.

Patterson nodded and passed a sketch around the table. "I received this from him just yesterday outlining plans for his health resort hotel."

Katherine beamed. "How clever. The diamond shape represents a journey to enlightenment and higher understanding."

"Healing for the patients, no doubt," Nere said. "We'll have a place to stay while building."

Katherine said, "Let's purchase those last forty acres and start preparing for habitation."

"We're back to where we'll get the money," Hargrove said.

"It'll come." She was certain.

"I believe so too." Nere grinned.

"You can't put any more of your own into this." Katherine shook her head. "You've already done enough."

"I won't." He held up an envelope. "I've just received correspondence too. Lady Malcolm has gone into the light and left a large legacy to the School for the Revival of Lost Mysteries of Antiquity."

"Oh dear," Katherine said. Lady Malcolm had recently been vibrant and enthusiastic about the vision and even expressed hopes of moving there.

"How much is it?" Hargrove blurted.

"Who's Lady Malcolm?" Pryse asked.

Patterson said, "We met her in Scotland while on Crusade."

Hargrove cut in, "Let's—"

"Stop!" Katherine held up her hand. "We must have a moment of silence for our noble-hearted Theosophist sister."

"Of course," Nere said. The group sat quietly for a few moments.

As soon as heads were raised, Hargrove said, "Let's use the funds to teach occult practices and do demonstrations. I could head it up."

Griscom nodded. "That's a good idea."

Nere held up the paper. "The document says they can only be used for the school and support of children's education."

"That's ridiculous. More money going to that dry heap of a desert." Hargrove said with a sarcastic grin, "Purple is all over the place with no focus."

Katherine said, "After our Crusade, I've seen clearly what is needed. I'm going to expand the cabinet to include people from around the country and even across the pond. And start a nonsectarian International Brotherhood League."

"What does brotherhood even mean?" Hargrove asked and glanced at Griscom.

He said, "Yes. What does it mean?"

Patterson stared at the two men. "Helping and sharing is what brotherhood means."

Hargrove rolled his eyes again. "What about the members who want to have occult experiences?"

Katherine answered, "What about the poor? Superintendent Elizabeth Mayer reported at the convention that within seven years the Lotus Circle Sunday School enrolled almost forty thousand children. The Buffalo Lodge had also shared about their home for destitute women. Backlash, though, had occurred from sectarian denominations. These programs could become the first transferred to the Brotherhood League to solve that issue."

She nodded at Joe to pass out the proposal and instructed the gentlemen to study it. The room fell silent as they began to read, and she skimmed it again too:

COMPONENTS OF THE NONSECTARIAN INTERNATIONAL BROTHERHOOD LEAGUE

1. *Educate children of all nations and prepare destitute and homeless children to become workers for humanity.*
2. *Improve the conditions of unfortunate women and assist them to a higher life.*
3. *Assist those who are or have been in prisons to establish themselves in honorable positions in life.*
4. *Help working men and women realize the nobility of their calling and true positions in life.*
5. *Endeavor to abolish capital punishment.*
6. *Bring a better understanding between so-called savage and civilized races by promoting a closer and more sympathetic relationship between them.*
7. *Relieve human suffering from flood, famine, war, and other calamities; and extend aid and comfort to suffering humanity throughout the world.*

Hargrove looked at the cabinet members and yelled, “This is way over the top. If you approve this, you’ll be sorry. I’ll quit!” As he stomped out the door with Griscom on his heels, Katherine wished for that outcome.

Chapter Fifty-Three

The cabinet majority approved the proposed International Brotherhood League, and the last Point Loma acres were purchased using eighty-five hundred dollars in gold coins from Lady Malcolm's estate. The organization now owned a total of one hundred sixty-five acres extending all the way down to the shore. Katherine's dream was becoming a reality. She couldn't wait to move there and start building, but she hadn't forgotten the Do-Good children's immediate needs.

Her scouts found an ideal property for the Lotus Home for Children not far in Pleasant Valley, New Jersey, on the banks of the Hudson River. The fully furnished brick mansion had twelve acres of woods and green grounds. Nere informed her she'd need to raise at least fifty thousand dollars to buy it and run the summer program she envisioned.

Theosophical lodges around the world responded enthusiastically to help raise funds through Brotherhood Bazaars for poor children. Each lodge developed a theme and gathered goods for sale, and, by the end of the three May dates, more money rolled in than needed to buy the Pleasant Valley property.

Gertie helped Katherine select twenty-five tenement children who'd benefit most from two months of fresh air and food. The two women escorted the children up to the home by train, carriages, and ferry, arriving in time for afternoon supper. Katherine worried she'd made a horrible mistake. The children raced into the dining room pushing and shoving to sit at a mishmash of furniture to accommodate them all. They banged on the tables and chanted, "Feed me! Feed me!"

Katherine waited to see how Mrs. Stabler, the housemother, and Reverend Williams, the supervisor, handled the chaos. He bellowed over the ruckus, "No one eats until we've had a moment of silence."

The children ignored him and continued to chant. Jasper stabbed the Levi boy with a fork. The boy hollered "You bloody well stop it" and shoved Jasper. They jumped up ready to fight.

Katherine was about to step in when Elizabeth Mayer walked into the room surrounded by an aura as if lit up by the sun. She swayed her arms gently above her head like rays and started to warble with her beautiful soprano voice. Mesmerized, the children waved their arms overhead too and joined to sing the "Happy Sunbeams" lyrics back to her. After a few measures they copied Elizabeth by holding their fingers to their lips.

She waited a few quiet beats and smiled. "Reverend Williams, please lead these lovely children through a blessing."

"Certainly, Mrs. Mayer. Children, fold your hands and bow your heads," he said in his Scottish brogue.

Magically the children obeyed. Even though Elizabeth hadn't been enamored of the San Diego property when they were at the dedication, Katherine had to do whatever necessary to entice her to move to California. Elizabeth expertly ran the summer camp, teaching the children more songs and etiquette and modeling brotherhood. After seven weeks, Gertie reported all the youngsters' health had improved.

As the children returned to the tenements, Katherine soon realized the improvements gained in their lives were only fleeting. She contacted the Buffalo Lodge and came up with a plan to start a Lotus Home there for infants and young orphans under three years of age so they could be raised from the cradle before bad habits had been instilled.

In addition, she learned Hargrove had finally resigned his presidency, stating he had pressing private business. Inwardly delighted, she hoped he'd simply disappear. However, Nere, who'd agreed to take over the presidency, soon came to her. "Hargrove is campaigning delegates to back him to seize your place at the next convention."

Even though it didn't surprise her, her anger seethed. "I vow not only to defeat him, but also to make it impossible for such a situation to arise ever again."

"I applaud your strength," Nere said. "Alas, that cur is making progress."

"Who's on his side?" Katherine demanded.

Nere hesitated. "Two cabinet members are leaning toward Hargrove and garnering support for him with delegates, and the number seems to be growing."

The news of the shifting alliances hit her like a bucket of ice water. Every time she thought she had turned a corner, something stood smack in her way.

"Who can we count on?" she asked.

Nere wrote the names of the votes in her favor. It would do—for now.

When Katherine left Master M in the Himalayas, he'd warned something like this would occur and urged her to take hold and meet the challenge. She only wished she'd asked him how.

That evening, propped up on her bed, she posed a question in her core and asked, "How?" She visualized Master M deeply. It was a longshot, but she hoped to receive guidance from him. She breathed in and out and opened her chakras until she felt them radiate with bright colors and she fell into a trance. Floating through thin, layered clouds, she imagined journeying up to the Himalayas.

Master M put down his flute and laughed. "I've been expecting you."

When her body and mind returned to the bed, a jumble of thoughts and messages whirled. She searched for paper, but only a newspaper was nearby. She tore off the margins and let the words flow from her heart to her hand to her pen and onto the scraps. After a quarter of an hour, the words ran out. She picked up the papers and read them with amazement.

Her hand had written these directives, but she couldn't conceive how any human would accept she would become the most ambitious autocrat in the world. If the convention delegates voted for this, it would seal her authority, never to be questioned again. Master M had given her a constitutional outline for the Universal Brotherhood and Theosophical Society to merge, with a complete name change and her as leader and Outer Head for Life.

Spent, she fell asleep holding the strips of paper. When she awoke, she called Joe to record the notations. She read a few fragments to him, looked up, and saw he was gaping at her. Could even reliable Joe be one of her enemies? She immediately dismissed him from the room. Was there anyone she could trust? She sent for one recorder after another and dictated a few phrases at a time so no one would learn the whole of it.

Elizabeth recommended a trustworthy ally from outside New York. Soon Iverson L. Harris, an attorney and strong Theosophist from Macon, Georgia, arrived and drafted the entire document. In secret for the next few months, Iverson, Nere, and Katherine continued to refine it. While in the open, Hargrove's support continued to grow.

Chapter Fifty-Four

February 1898

Katherine and Elizabeth bounced in a carriage down Chicago's brick-paved streets on their way to the convention. Dark clouds hovered above, promising a snowstorm by afternoon. Katherine yawned with exhaustion. During the holidays and into the new year, her sleep had been fleeting, and she'd lost weight. Hargrove continued to rally his cronies to spread the word to oppose her Outer Headship claim for himself. Why didn't others see through him like she did?

If he succeeded, her vision would never come to fruition. Even though her closest confidants attempted to assure her the new constitution would go through, she wasn't convinced. Mid-January, she'd called in a dozen of her loyalists to share the full contents of the document. They'd asked questions, and she'd addressed their concerns. By consensus they agreed to her divine inspiration and would rally others to support her.

A few days prior, the USS *Maine*'s mysterious explosion in Havana Harbor had killed 266 American crew members. Revolts for Cuban freedom from colonial rule had been going on for years and she feared the United States government had been waiting for an excuse to leap into the fray. Would this be that justification they were looking for? Was this a symptom of darkness at the dawn of the current cycle predicted by Madame Blavatsky? Was this the battle of Katherine's nightmares?

As the horses drew up in front of Handel Hall, a former newspaper building, Katherine pulled her cape's hood over her head and steeled herself to wade through the crowd streaming inside. Nere waved the driver around to the corner entrance, aided the women out, and hurried them up a side staircase to the hall's private gallery in the rear. There her New York contingent waited. Elizabeth helped Katherine remove her cape and hung it on a rack.

Katherine tugged down the black lace on her purple dress and sat on a sofa as the others, talking all at once, circled in seats around her. She held up her hand. "Let's begin with a moment of silence for those Americans recently lost in Cuba."

The group sat quietly and then she looked warmly at each. "No matter what happens today, I want you to be aware how much I appreciate each and every one of you."

Pierce put on his glasses. "Let's review the planned agenda. Nere will open with the welcome and then he'll introduce Katherine to give her rousing speech. Iverson will read the proposal, and Nere will call for a vote."

A boulder filled Katherine's chest. She could barely breathe and eked out, "My intuition tells me that strategy will fail."

"But it's all been planned," Patterson said.

"We need something stronger." She tapped fingers to her temple.

"What?" Nere asked.

She raised an eyebrow. "The element of surprise."

"Surprise?" Nere frowned.

She studied her watch. "We've only an hour. Let's quickly designate a Committee on Resolutions, composed of you in this room and other loyal delegates in attendance from across the country."

"Interesting," Joe said.

"We'll bring them in here, read the document and garner their support."

Nere nodded. "I see. After the welcome, I'll invite the whole group of you onstage for approval of the new committee. Iverson will read the proposal and immediately call for a vote."

"Is that legal?" Elizabeth asked.

Iverson said, "I believe it would hold up in court."

The room agreed, and they spent the next quarter of an hour choosing names from the attendee list. Then they ushered in the new committee members and shared the proposal. San Franciscan Dr. Anderson's reaction pleased Katherine to no end. His eyes filled with tears of joy, and he said, "My highest hopes have been that after twenty-one years of work by Madame Blavatsky and William, at last we'll have an organization to protect the work they gave their lives for."

As the group filed out, Nere pulled a chair near the open doors and bade Katherine sit. "Wait here, and after the proposal has been approved, you can make one of your grand entrances up the aisle."

Katherine observed the delegates filter into the assembly hall, which had recently been remodeled to house the American Conservatory of Music. The high ceiling held up by Corinthian pillars soared above the three hundred delegates in attendance. Hargrove strutted in with his cronies, smug as a boxer who'd already won a fight. She loathed him now more than ever, and as hard as she tried, no matter what happened, that would never go away.

As Nere welcomed the delegates, she closed her eyes, attempting to visualize the sea and her white city for calmness. However, her body veered inside as if careening on that toy train again, and her breath caught in her throat with fear. It would be excruciating to listen to the vote. She needed fresh air, she needed to breathe, and she needed to be surrounded by nature. She'd done everything she could to make it happen—happen for her grandfather, William, Master M, and all the people whose lives would be improved.

In a daze, she grabbed her cloak and descended the grand stairway toward the exit.

"Ma'am, may I call your carriage?" the doorman asked.

Katherine shook her head and stepped out into the beauty of a Chicago winter and kept walking. A strange peace fell over her, and for the first time since William died, she felt an untethered feeling, almost as if she could soar. She thought of the people she'd fed at the mission, thought of the progress she'd made on the Crusade, thought of her vision of her city on a sundown sea.

As snowflakes kissed her shoulders, she felt William's love envelop her, and she whispered to him, "I've done all I can to carry on the path you've laid out for me. It's up to the Great One now."

She stopped in the drifting snow, took gloves from her cloak pocket, and pulled them on. Behind her, she knew the constitution proposal was being read. She waited, and after a while, distant voices grew louder and louder from an open balcony. Passions were voiced and objections shouted down. Votes were called for and rejected. Echoing again and again.

Light glistened off icy Lake Michigan, and she moved toward it. Wind howled, and the snow began to pile high, reminding her of the winter of 1888, her fortieth year, the day of the Great White Blizzard. The day the starving women and children called for soup outside the mission in their threadbare clothes. The day she'd first seen William in his warm woolen coat and fur hat. Had he already known then she'd someday be Outer Head? Maybe even leader for life? She'd done her best to please him, improve lives, and inspire others to let their egos go and focus on giving to others.

Church bells tolled in the distance, and the snow let up. She had no idea how long she'd stood there when a Himalayan yeti covered in snow turned and stared at her with beady eyes. She stepped back as Hargrove raised his arms toward her. Just in time, his friends pulled him away, and they kept going.

She shivered and heard far-off voices call her name: Nere, Joe, Iverson, and more.

Elizabeth embraced her. "There you are. You're wanted."

The group escorted Katherine back into the building and rode the elevator up. As they entered the music hall, her name resounded over and over, up into the high ceiling created for orchestras.

"Madame Tingley! Madame Tingley," they chanted, louder and louder with hand claps in between the words. "Madame Tingley!"

Katherine floated up to the platform as if on a cloud and accepted the laurel wreath presented to her. All there rose to their feet in adoration. Instead of pride or elation, she felt a sense of gratitude and calm as William's love continued to surround her.

Hargrove's faction had lost: 299 for and 24 opposed. Not only did the organization have a new name, Universal Brotherhood and Theosophical Society, but Katherine was now recognized as leader and Official Head for Life. Now she had the full power to implement her plan and move headquarters to Point Loma!

Chapter Fifty-Five

After the convention, Katherine wired Dr. Wood to start clearing the school site. She wanted the building finished before the following year's convention so she could dedicate it then. Two months later the land was ready, and he planned to start construction. The design still didn't resonate with her, and she sent him a telegram: *Under no circumstances are you to begin. I'll be there soon to oversee.*

The next morning, with a spring in her step and thoughts of seeing the property again, she followed the scent of frying bacon to the kitchen.

Philo twirled eggs with his whipper and poured them into the skillet. "Have a seat, my love." His words were more amorous than usual. She worried something was amiss.

He served breakfast, sat, slid the newspaper across the table, and said, "Bad news."

The headline read: CONGRESS DECLARES WAR ON SPAIN. The Spanish-American War was starting. Her nightmares of battling soldiers had come to realization.

"I must assist." She stood up.

"But you're on your way to San Diego."

"I need to push that all aside."

"That's silly. Why?" he asked.

"The seventh component of the International Brotherhood League is to relieve human suffering resulting from flood, famine, war, and other calamities."

At headquarters that afternoon, she gathered up her cabinet and got right to work. Time was of the essence. She sensed the organization's help would be needed soon. Within a week, the one hundred and fifty lodges had been wired to send money for medical supplies, the War Relief Corps was established to coordinate the accumulation and distribution of goods, women members were recruited to make bandages, and Sisters of Compassion, a dedicated group of women to learn nursing skills, was instituted. Gertie planned to train them but had fallen ill herself. At the optimal moment, Dr. Herbert Coryn, recently relocated from London, walked into headquarters and started instruction immediately.

By June, American troops were sent to Cuba to defend their neighbors. By mid-July, the Spanish surrendered in Santiago, leaving thousands of American soldiers in fever-ridden areas. She knew the American military hadn't had time to prepare for the massive return of ill and wounded soldiers as they arrived back home, and she was ready to help.

To provide returnees medical care, the War Department set up camps at various disembarkation points along the Eastern Seaboard. When Katherine learned soldiers were on their way to Montauk Point, Long Island, she gathered her team and set off.

Chaos reigned as her caravan of carriages and supply wagons arrived. Crows flew over the dock as fevered and wounded soldiers trudged off a carrier.

"I'm Katherine Tingley with the War Relief Corps come to help," she told a Red Cross worker unloading men off the carrier. "Where's the hospital?"

"A few miles up the beach," the worker replied and pointed. She greeted a man as he disembarked and directed him to keep walking.

Katherine shielded her eyes to view the long line of men trekking up the hill. "Why is it so far away?"

The worker ran an arm across her forehead. "Can't serve them all here. Plus, the War Department's afraid yellow fever might spread to civilians."

Many wealthy citizens owned estates along the shoreline. Katherine directed her caravan to move that way.

"No use going there. No women allowed," the worker hollered.

"That's absurd." Katherine shook her head. A young man staggered off the boat, took a few steps, and dropped to the ground. Another and then another soldier did so too. She recognized these toothpick-thin soldiers in slouch hats, flannel shirts, and knotted neck handkerchiefs as members of Theodore Roosevelt's Rough Rider Cavalry. Newspapers had reported many in their brave regiment had been killed.

"Help them!" Katherine cried to her Sisters of Compassion in the first carriage. They jumped out and ran toward the boys as a double-decker ambulance halted nearby. They loaded the soldiers on it, and horses hauled them off.

"Move our wagons there." Katherine shouted orders like a sergeant, thankful they'd rehearsed this at headquarters, and pointed to a smooth area on the beach nearby. "Quickly! Set up tents." Within no time, the seven tents were erected, cots opened, the last of the supplies unloaded. Aprons on, nurses joined Dr. Coryn at the dock as he helped and selected soldiers for their hospital.

The rest of the afternoon, as soldiers collapsed, Katherine's team rushed down and carried more up to her outdoor intake tent. The men were given wine, milk, and meat, patched up and released, or placed in a hospital tent. As darkness fell and lanterns were lit, all sixty beds were filled.

Kerosene fumes and sweat permeated the main tent. Patients' moans and cries rang out, mingled with the nurses' gentle tones of soothing calmness. Katherine held a soldier as Dr. Coryn reset a broken leg. She carefully removed another man's hat, oozing with blood, cleaned the wound with carbolic acid, and stitched the lacerated forehead, hoping it wouldn't get infected.

Above a young man's cot, Dr. Coryn whispered to Katherine, "He's not going to make it."

She moved to the lad and held his hand. His eyes blinked open; he stared at her and pleaded, "Please, ma'am. I don't want to die."

Her mind flew to the boy who'd perished in her arms during the Civil War. A sharp pang within her rose at the uselessness of combat horrors between men. She tamped down her anger to concentrate on saving this one's life.

"What's your name?" she asked softly.

"Tim."

"I'll do what I can, Tim," she said.

His fiery forehead reminded her of William in the Texas cabin. She removed Tim's kerchief and shirt. She bathed him, wishing she had some of that crazy water. She didn't care what the others thought as she intuitively sat behind his back and held him in her arms. This was not how Dr. Coryn had trained them. Katherine closed her eyes and matched her rhythm with the boy's own breathing. She pressed on his chest and concentrated on his heart chakra, willing it to cool with energy and love. After a few minutes, he fell into a sound sleep, and she felt a twinge of hope that he might survive.

For the first two days, the team slept in shifts. On the third evening the clamors of pain inside the tent grew unbearably loud. Elizabeth's bright soprano voice began to sing a lullaby, and soon the other nurses and able patients joined in as well. The soothing song filled the tent, and it became an evening ritual.

As time passed from days into a week, the workers steadfastly toiled and a divine power glowed within Katherine. Even though her eyes drooped with exhaustion and her body ached, she couldn't stop. Elizabeth begged her to get some sleep, but she declined. There was too much to be done. After two weeks, some patients recovered enough and were sent home to their families; others, including Tim, lingered. Nurses comforted some of them as they transitioned into the light.

Three weeks later the tent began to bristle with excitement as a mustached man in uniform entered. Someone yelled, "Attention!" Patients sat up straight and others tried to crawl out of bed to stand at attention.

"At ease, men. Looking good. You've given so much for our country."

"Who is it?" Katherine whispered to Elizabeth.

"Why, it's Colonel Theodore Roosevelt."

"Bully for you, boys!" Roosevelt laughed.

He took off his hat and shook Katherine's hand. "Mrs. Tingley, you've done much for my boys, who've been through hell and back. You're certainly an angel of mercy."

"Sir, I thank you. All Americans should act in concert with brotherhood."

Chapter Fifty-Six

By mid-September, a month after Katherine began serving the soldiers, she was finally home. Soft sunset light filtered into her room as Philo tucked her into bed and kissed her forehead.

"Good night, Mrs. Tingley. A soldier's angel," he quoted the newspaper headlines. The article was an exaggeration because her whole team had worked as hard as she had.

As Philo closed the door, she caressed Spots's curly back. In the silence, her emotions flashed with the woes she'd witnessed in the tents. Heart shattered for the heroes who had lain their lives down so willingly and unselfishly, she grieved over boys gone from the earth before their time and others who'd survived but would never fully recover. This wasn't what the Spirit intended, and she vowed through the Universal Brotherhood and Theosophical Society to facilitate peace between nations.

In an exhausted stupor thoughts tossed within her mind. What steps were next for the International Brotherhood League? The new century rapidly approached. California summoned her to start building. However, many traumatized and injured men unable to work would need aid to support their families.

Well-rested the next morning, she read in the paper that Americans had appointed Emilio Bacardi as the mayor of Santiago. Master M had recommended she find the Cuban to help her cause. She'd soon learned, though, he was part of the rum family and had been imprisoned by the

Spanish for aiding the rebels. Now freed, as mayor one of his first acts was to reduce his salary and employ women at city hall. As a freethinker, activist, and art lover, he was someone she'd like to know.

By the time she made it to headquarters, her focus was crisp. She checked on the patients in the temporary hospital who'd been brought from Montauk. Fortunately, most were ready to go home, including Tim, whose mother was on her way.

Katherine wired Mayor Bacardi a friendly missive asking if Cuba had any specific needs. Then she had Joe draft a Brotherhood report to President McKinley, proudly stating the International Brotherhood League had aided almost nine thousand men in hospital tents.

No matter what she'd do next, whether go to California or send gifts to Cuba, she'd need to raise more funds. She couldn't ask the lodges for more.

She'd coordinated many benefit performances but had never directed a full-length play. In her earlier days in Europe, she'd watched Andre direct and had had a desire to do so herself. Besides raising funds, perhaps theater could be a way to express Theosophical tenets as well.

She searched the headquarters library and found plays by Shakespeare, Euripides, Sophocles, and Aeschylus. She pushed a stack in her satchel and took them home to peruse. That night she enjoyed reading *A Midsummer Night's Dream* again. During this sad time, the comedic romance and theme of true love wasn't appropriate to produce now. *The Eumenides*, by Aeschylus, father of tragedy, dealt with the ethics of resignation, truth, and the ultimate triumph of justice.

As Katherine read, her mind effervesced with costumes, sets, and Theosophical members she could cast in specific roles as gods, goddesses, and mortals. Most members had never acted. However, many were strong orators with stage presence. The possibilities were endless. Within a few weeks she established the Isis League of Art, Music, and Drama as the producing entity and began casting.

Soon she also received two special replies:

Executive Mansion, Washington September 24, 1898

Dear Madame: Thank you for the report concerning the effective work of the International Brotherhood League. I'm glad to know of such good results in its labors among the sick and wounded soldiers and sailors. Assuring you in my hope that it may continue to be abundantly successful.

Very sincerely yours,
United States President William McKinley

In addition, he sent out a War Department notice to the commanding generals of the US military forces in Cuba, Puerto Rico, and the Philippines authorizing cooperation between the armed forces and the International Brotherhood League.

Emilio Bacardi's reply stated: *My citizens are starving, dying of fevers and broken hearts. If you would come with your Brotherhood League and aid us, we'd be grateful.*

She immediately applied for transport to Cuba as rehearsals for *The Eumenides* continued.

In November, she watched from the wings as *The Eumenides* was performed at Carnegie Lyceum, an eight-hundred-seat theater to rave reviews. The money flowed in not only from ticket sales, but from the publicity it generated for her organization and their cause to travel to Cuba.

Chapter Fifty-Seven

February 1899

Katherine felt torn as the USS *Berlin* pulled from the dock, bound for Cuba. This mission kept her from moving forward with Point Loma, but on the other hand, suffering Cubans were in dire need and lives were at stake. Even though the treaty between the United States and Spain had been signed in December and the funds raised, transportation had been denied to her. Frustrated, she'd written directly to President McKinley, and he'd authorized her War Relief Corps passage on a Navy transport.

Loaded down with one hundred and fifty supply boxes, Dr. Coryn, the Sisters of Compassion, and a few Puerto Rico-bound soldiers, the ship sailed from Florida through the cold night on rough waters. Hours after sunrise, they arrived in heat- and humidity-filled Santiago.

A young man helped her off the ship. "Señora Tingley? I'm Santiago, your translator," he said in perfect English.

He must be named after the city. "Where's Señor Bacardi?" she asked.

"He'll see you *mañana*. I'll to take you to your hotel."

Her entourage followed him up cobblestone streets. The bullet-holed buildings evidenced bloody battles had taken place there. Soon a departed soul whispered a message to her. "*Por favor, dile a mi mamá—*" Her mind struggled to interpret the words, and she rued she'd not dedicated herself to increasing her Spanish skills. Caught up in the war effort, it had been a while since she'd had spirit communications. As she continued up the road, more pleas entered her and even though it made her heart ache, she needed to ignore them. She had to focus to give aid to those remaining on earth.

Her team checked into the small hotel, ate supper, and rested. In the morning, dark clouds threatened rain. Lightning flashed, and thunder roared on distant hills. Katherine ran into the street and greeted Santiago. "Where are we to set up our relief work? We must get our resources from the dock and inside before the storm."

"Follow me." He led her to a handsome mansion on Delores Plaza. Inside the building, the smell of mildew, moldy cheese, and rotten food permeated the air. A mouse nibbled from a dirty dish on the long wooden table; a tabby cat chased it away, rattling plates and knocking down empty liquor bottles.

Santiago said, "Pardon the mess. Spanish officials evacuated swiftly." His dark eyes reflected a deep sadness. It was obvious he was recovering too.

It began to drizzle outside, and she hailed an American soldier passing by to help. Santiago and the soldier corralled army wagons, and as soon as the last of their supplies and luggage were delivered into the mansion, the deluge hit.

During the storm, her team and local volunteers scoured the building top to bottom, sweeping the black-and-white floor tiles, clearing the tables and furniture. They stocked the pantry and settled luggage in the upstairs bedrooms. Dr. Coryn hastily coordinated the setup of the hospital on the ground floor.

After the downpour, word spread, and within no time hundreds of Cubans crowded the plaza where her relief workers handed out food. Dr. Coryn and the Sisters of Compassion did intake for patients suffering from infected wounds, starvation, and yellow fever. Although the process was smoother than the chaos of their first day on Long Island, grief permeated the makeshift hospital because many patients had lost loved ones.

That afternoon, Mayor Bacardi with his Samuel Clemens mustache, wire-rim glasses, and elegant wife, Elvira, visited to ensure all was going well. Katherine and Santiago joined them in the kitchen, where they were served shortbread and drank café con leche.

"*Muchas gracias* for coming and bringing so many goods," Emilio Bacardi said.

"A ton of rice is also on the way," Katherine told him. "I'm glad Master Morya recommended I contact you."

Emilio frowned. "Who's that?"

"One of Madame Blavatsky's teachers."

"I don't know either one of them." Emilio shrugged.

She shared with the group about Theosophy and her plans for Point Loma.

"I'd love to visit someday," Emilio said. "Sounds like paradise."

"You must." Katherine nibbled a cookie.

Suddenly, above Santiago's shoulder a uniformed soul in a military hat with medals across his chest whispered to Katherine, "Tell my son I'm proud of him."

"Did you have a father in the war?" she asked Santiago.

He nodded and murmured. "God rest his soul."

Bacardi said, "General Antonio Maceo was one of our greatest war heroes. Without him we wouldn't have gained our freedom."

Katherine looked at Santiago. "I'm certain he's proud of you." An idea began to percolate in her mind of how she could help Santiago heal.

Santiago introduced Katherine to Señora Beltrán, a local war widow who'd come to volunteer with her young son, Ricardo, and ten-year-old daughter, Carmen. Katherine observed the children go from bed to bed with kindness, pouring water for patients. Señora Beltrán picked up a crying infant from a crib and began to sing a Spanish lullaby.

Over the days, the War Relief Corps served with dignity and grace. Katherine nursed as many as she could. Some hospital patients were saved from starvation, recuperated from fevers, and were released; others lingered. Many had gone into the light while her team held their hands to ease the transition.

A month after they'd arrived, their supplies had dwindled, and the hospital began to empty. Bacardi said, "We're filled with gratitude to you."

"I believe it's time for us to get back home." Katherine yearned to return to America. However, sadness and loss subsumed the island.

"Your people have endured so much. What can we do to provide some hope before we leave?" she asked.

"How about a grand fiesta to celebrate freedom from Spain?" he immediately replied.

She grinned. "*Un día de libertad*."

On the appointed day, to music by the American Military Band, two thousand children marched into Delores Plaza. Bacardi's daughter, costumed to represent the American goddess of Liberty, posed on a platform while Carmen Beltrán represented the Cuban goddess of Liberty. Orchids were scattered at their feet. Trees were planted to represent the United States and Cuba. Bacardi gave a rousing speech about freedom and the friendship between the two countries, and the fiesta continued into the night, ending with a rousing fireworks display.

As Katherine packed the next morning, it was difficult to say goodbye to Señora Beltrán and her children.

"Why must you go?" Carmen asked.

The convention was scheduled in a month. "I must return. There's much to do there."

A vision appeared above the family's heads of a man in a straw hat holding a rifle. He whispered to Katherine, "Tell *mi familia* I love them and will always be with them. Even if they're in a distant land."

Katherine's eyes grew wide as she realized this message was for her as well as the family. "What did your husband look like?" she asked the señora.

"Tall, with a thin mustache." The widow set a finger on her upper lip.

Katherine nodded. "How would you all like to come to America with me? To study at a very special new school?"

"*Sí!*" The children clapped their hands, and the señora gave Katherine *un gran abrazo*.

On the return trip to the United States, four Cuban children, two women, and translator Santiago Maceo joined the group. Katherine planned to educate them in Point Loma in hopes that someday they'd return to the island and spread brotherhood across their homeland. Cubans were a kind and patient people, deserving the help of all true Americans.

Chapter Fifty-Eight

Two years after the cornerstone dedication, Katherine finally arrived back at the Point Loma property. With Spots in her arms, she stood on the cliffs and inhaled the salty tang of the sea. The wind sang a duet with the crashing waves that shifted in tidewater on the sandy shore.

In less than two weeks, the Theosophical Congress was scheduled to take place. To add significance to the gathering, she called it a congress instead of a convention. This would be different from any convention the members had ever attended. She'd wanted this to be a time to encourage members to support her vision. However, there wasn't much to entice them with. On the adjacent property, Dr. Wood's hotel was finished, but she'd had to put off building the school and planting gardens on the barren land. If they weren't impressed, her dream would fail.

Restless as the Pacific, she felt the familiar pull in her chest. She closed her eyes and imagined the future like she'd done so many times before: buildings ornamented the land, children and adults in golden light performed music and plays, artists painted luscious landscapes, and intellectual conversations flowed. A place where people from all countries could be brought together. Children would learn to be strong and noble, and to find their true selves. Peace and justice would radiate from here around the world. With the beginning almost within reach, doubt nicked her. Even so, she was determined to move forward no matter what.

She set Spots on the ground. Over ten years old now, he slowly followed her up toward the grassy knoll where the cornerstone had been dedicated. She shook her head with chagrin. Beside the original Killarney stone that had been delivered a month after the ceremony, other blocks selected by Crusaders and more sent by Theosophists from around the world had been tossed in a massive heap.

Farther up, just over the ridge, she hiked in front of the rutted road that paralleled her property and ran south down the peninsula through the government land. She'd been told an old lighthouse perched high on a hill there, and a new one had recently been built below it. She paused to venerate the sparkling San Diego Bay with the city beyond. She looked forward to enhancing the residents' lives, from mayor to merchants and especially the children who would become an integral part of her community. Far off to the east, snow-topped peaks shone in the light, smaller than the Himalayas, but nonetheless reminding her of Master Morya and his sacred home.

As guests arrived, she knew they'd see these views and embrace her vision. No sooner had she thought this than her old familiar worry crept in. They weren't ready. Where would the tables go? Did they have enough chairs? Why wasn't any of this work being done? She walked north toward the hotel. Pounding emanated from the diamond-shaped, three-story building as workers rushed to divide rooms to house congress visitors.

She entered the open inner courtyard and said to Pierce, "Have the workers stop that racket. It's time for the cabinet meeting."

He yelled over the noise, "We need every minute, or we won't be ready."

"It shouldn't take long."

Pierce made his way up the stairs, and the noise soon stopped. Workers set up chairs in the open courtyard. A slate-colored cloud passed overhead, and she hoped it wouldn't rain. She took a seat in the center of the semicircle and put Spots in her lap. Patterson greeted her.

Iverson walked toward her holding a young lad's hand.

"Who are you in that handsome Lord Fauntleroy suit?" she asked the blond-haired boy.

"It's me, Mrs. Tingley! Iverson Harris, Junior. Haven't you heard of me?" His accent was an entertaining southern drawl. He bowed and straightened his blouse's lace.

She laughed. "Of course. How old are you?"

He pushed back his shoulders. "Eight."

Her eyes opened wide. "Weren't you afraid to come all the way from Georgia?"

"Not I. Father asked Sister and Mother if they wanted to come, but they were the ones afraid. I'd examined orange grove pictures in my schoolbook and thought it would be a great adventure to see them."

Katherine couldn't help smiling. "Has it been an adventure so far?"

He nodded. "Oh yes. I loved riding the train, and here I got to see the mighty Pacific. I want to know more about Theosophy too."

Her heart filled with joy. "Really? What do you already know?"

"Mrs. Elizabeth Mayer, head of the Lotus Circle Sunday Schools, visited Macon. I got to give the welcome speech. She told us to be good and true and care about each other and everyone in the world."

"She did, did she?" Katherine met his father's proud eyes above Junior's head.

"Yes, she's so smart." He bobbed his head. "I hope to meet her again someday."

"You will. She'll be here soon, maybe even with her friend Mr. Spalding."

"The baseball hero? I'm not surprised he likes her. She's very beautiful."

"Junior!" his father reprimanded.

"That's true indeed!" Katherine laughed.

"May I pet your dog?" Junior leaned over.

"Certainly." She held Spots toward the boy.

"Sweetie, sweetie," Junior cooed and gently stroked Spots's back.

"We need to start our meeting. Would you take Spots outside?" Katherine lifted the dog to the ground.

"May I?" Junior looked at his father, who nodded.

Junior clapped and called, "Let's go!" Spots slowly followed Junior outside.

Katherine said, "What a delightful child! He's exactly the kind of boy I've dreamed of having here."

Iverson raised an eyebrow. "We'll see."

Joe joined them with his notebook.

Katherine asked, “Where’s Nere?”

“He sent a wire with regrets.”

“Did he say what’s detained him?”

Joe shook his head. “No.”

Katherine hoped he was all right. A few weeks ago, when she saw him in New York, Nere had lost considerable weight and had dark circles under his eyes. “What about Dr. Anderson?” she asked. “I thought he planned to come down from San Francisco.”

“He sent a wire saying he couldn’t leave his practice just yet.”

Joe studied his notebook. “The hotel is fully booked!”

“Where will we put them all?” Patterson asked. “There’s not even enough rooms for us.”

Katherine remained calm. “Delegates can bunk together.”

She held up a finger and closed her eyes while the men waited. She opened them and said, “We’ll erect tents.”

“Where’ll we get them at this late date and the manpower for setup?” Patterson asked.

She insisted, “Ask folks from the San Diego community to assist. Think of how rapidly we set up camp on Long Island. You can do it.”

“The water supply is minimal.” Pierce frowned.

“What about the windmill?” she asked.

Patterson said, “It doesn’t work.”

She smiled. “Every morning able-bodied men, including you, can go down the road and hand pump it. We need to build a stage for the ceremonies and performances.”

“Where do you want it?” Pierce asked.

“Up near the cornerstone.”

“What about the pile?” Joe flipped a page in his notebook. “There are eighty slabs in all. Some of the delegates who sent them will be coming.”

Katherine announced, “Erect two pillars. One in remembrance of Madame Blavatsky and the other for the Rajah.”

The men slowly nodded their heads in agreement, although they didn’t seem too pleased.

She smiled at them and stood up. "Let's put our hearts and energy toward this. For the good of the organization and humanity, we need to show Theosophists from around the world our sacred property is worthy of not only a school, but also our headquarters. We cannot delay. Gentlemen, I believe in you and your capable hands."

Chapter Fifty-Nine

Seven trumpet blasts filled the air. From behind the makeshift stage, Katherine shouted a mantra, "Truth, light, liberation!" Iverson Harris joined in, then Patterson and Pierce, and still more, until all five hundred conveners from a dozen countries in the temporary grandstand chanted, "Truth, light, liberation!"

A few days earlier, guests had begun to arrive by ferry and small launches and shuttled up the steep grade. Even a steamship filled to the brim with Theosophists glided into the Silver Gate Bay entrance, flying the Theosophical purple-and-gold flag on its mast. Others rode tallyhos along the dusty road around the bay.

Katherine, in a royal purple gown, now paced to the podium and indicated for the delegates to sit. Hair blowing in the breeze, in her most illustrious voice, she regaled the crowd, "Welcome to Lomaland!" She paused for applause and foot stomps. "Consider what might come to pass if on this temple hill a great school should rise to educate children in ancient harmony. We'll have orchards and gardens that heap our tables with fresh fruits and vegetables every day of the year. And daily we'll be blessed with this!"

She turned and opened her arms as the sun began to drift over the Pacific in shades of lilac and rose. In silence, the audience witnessed the colors fade as the sky darkened to indigo blue. Above the two recently erected pillars, the Theosophical and American flags were lowered, and a lantern raised and lit.

Katherine continued, "Theater has been used since primordial times to pass down many mysteries Madame Blavatsky described in *The Secret Doctrine*. Reprised from our sensation at Carnegie Lyceum, we'll enthrall you with the very pearl of the great legacy of ancient Greek dramas left to the world. Tonight, a cast of over a hundred, many of whom are local San Diegans, will perform *The Eumenides* for you!"

She hiked to the grandstand's center and sat between Junior and Elizabeth. Torches lit beside the stage enhanced the eerie setting as the ethereal sea behind surpassed any theater setting the Outer Head had ever experienced. Thus, nature lifted Katherine out of the trivialities of the real world into the magical scenes that began to unfold one after the other.

Junior yawned and laid his head in Katherine's lap. She placed a hand on his shoulder to safeguard his sleep from the terror of the Furies that haunted and hunted Orestes in their shambolic wigs and hoary ethereal costumes. Katherine had cast the play well. Santiago as Orestes, in the cave of the oracle, found his huntress asleep and snatched time for a repose. The Furies awoke in the dark and howled and howled.

Katherine smiled. During rehearsals that week, she'd told the Furies to scream louder and louder, but they'd barely squeaked. She'd entreated them to project their voices louder than ocean waves and up and over the distant mountains. Still, they could not be heard. Finally, she'd told them to howl. At that instruction, they'd made a great noise so loud everyone on the hill had stopped what they were doing and stared. Then Katherine had told them to go back to their tents and save their voices.

She stirred Junior in time to see the most dramatic moment of the play. He rubbed his eyes that soon grew wide as two white steeds pulled an ornately painted chariot onstage with Alice as the shining Athena. Tall and resplendent in a Roman helmet, with a shield in one hand and reins in the other, Athena's powerful wisdom changed the Furies from seeking revenge into messengers of beauty and peace. Alice as Athena didn't resemble the dowdy Crusader one iota. She'd been transformed into the goddess of justice.

As the players bowed and the audience rose to their feet, the applause continued so long Katherine thought it would never end. Women wiped tears from their eyes. A few handkerchiefs went toward men's eyes too. Others were quiet, almost prayerful, while their friends shouted and clapped. Finally, the applause softened, the voices became a mellow murmur, and the audience began to mingle.

Katherine turned to Junior, who was holding Spots. "What did you think, my young friend who came all the way from Georgia?"

"Wow, Mrs. Tingley," he replied. "That's the most spectacular thing I've ever seen."

Katherine smiled, patted his head, and quietly enjoyed all that she had rendered. The only twinge of sadness was in wishing William could have seen it all.

Softly, almost imperceptibly, she heard his voice whisper, "I have."

A star dotted inside the waxing crescent moon as it rose. The festivities lasted until midnight, when a solemn cornerstone rededication commenced, and fifty miles away atop a mountain, a bonfire lit for the occasion was visible all the way to Point Loma.

For ten days, the events continued. Some of Madame Blavatsky's and William's ashes were strewn beside their pillars, and Katherine knew she'd always think of him when she walked by. The Isis Conservatory Orchestra performed with Elizabeth conducting. Lectures on the mystical interpretations of Wagner were discussed and selections from his scores played. And to great applause, a reprise performance of *The Eumenides* was given on the final night.

On the last day, as Katherine said goodbye to the Macon delegates, tears gathered in her eyes as she looked down at Junior again in his sweet Lord Fauntleroy travel suit.

He suddenly piped up, "I know what you want most right now, Mrs. Tingley."

"What?" She smiled.

"You want me to stay here."

How could he know exactly what she was thinking?

"If you really want me to stay," he said, "I'll stay!"

His father took the boy's hand. "Don't be silly. What will I say to Mother when I get home and you aren't with me?"

Junior raised his voice. "Tell her to come here and bring Sister too."

Katherine laughed, handed Junior a tiny American flag, and sent him to lead the closing procession toward the cliffs and down to the beach.

She looked into Iverson's eyes and said, "What a dear. Won't you let him stay while we're on tour? Dr. Wood will watch over him. He can be enrolled in the small Roseville school down the hill until we open ours in a few months."

Iverson said, "It's always impossible to say no to you, Katherine."

Chapter Sixty

Junior remained at Lomaland while his father, Katherine, and other cabinet members departed on a lecture tour. She hated to leave. Membership had risen to eight thousand, and it was imperative to gain even more supporters to raise funds to build and run the school.

At the end of August, before boarding a ship to England, she dropped off Spots with Philo and tried to see Nere, but he was indisposed. What was wrong with him?

In September, the group attended the Sweden and Norway Branch Convention in Stockholm, hosting a reception in their suite attended by her letter-writing friend King Oscar II. In October, they appeared at the European Congress of Brotherhood held at the Royal Pavilion in Brighton, England. As part of the festivities, Katherine planned a jubilee celebration as her organization took over Madame Blavatsky's London property. At the event, sadness crept into Katherine's happiness. She so wished she'd met the hierophant in person.

In New York, before she headed back to Lomaland, Nere finally came to see her. When she opened the door, fear overtook her, as the poor man looked to be at death's door. She led him to the parlor and asked, "What is it?"

He slumped into a chair. "We've suffered a grave tragedy. Aimee has married Hargrove."

In shock, Katherine sat down and put a hand on her heart. "What?"

Nere's eyes filled with tears. "The knave asked for my blessing and had the audacity to request a dowry. Evidently, he's spent all his inheritance."

"I can't believe it. Poor Aimee. And Minnie?"

"My dear wife is brokenhearted. We begged Aimee not to marry him, but she claimed they're in love and had been married in a previous lifetime."

"For heaven's sake! Right out of Claude's playbook."

"She wanted me to give her away." He shook his head. "But I refused to even go. They married in January and sailed to England right afterward. He's trying to start a rival society."

"That's dastardly." She paused. "But that was before the congress. Why didn't you tell me?"

"I didn't want to ruin the celebrations for you."

Had Hargrove married Aimee for retribution, or was it a foolish ploy to get Nere to change his allegiance to him?

"Nere, you're a shambles. Join me in California. You could play the piano and sing every day. Your passion for music will heal you."

"Perhaps a visit would be warranted."

Later that evening she asked Philo, "Why aren't you packing? Our train leaves in the morning."

"I'm not compelled to move to California just yet."

"Why not?"

"I'm busy here with my inventions."

"Don't you want to see the property?"

"You're the leader now. I'll write and support you from afar."

Her first reaction was disappointment. Then relief set in that she wouldn't need to worry about him while she focused on construction and opening the school. Despite their earlier troubles and his quirks, she'd grown fond of him, and he showed admiration and care toward her in his own way. She'd miss him.

Chapter Sixty-One

February 1900

On Katherine's first morning back in Dr. Wood's hotel, she woke at sunrise to the sound of waves crashing on the shore and twirled the signet ring on her finger with hope. Almost a year since the Point Loma congress, at long last she'd relocated the International Brotherhood and Theosophical Society headquarters from New York to Lomaland. While gone, she couldn't wait to return and welcome in the new century there. Lucky for her, most citizens and newspapers agreed the new century began January 1, 1901, instead of 1900, and that worked in her favor. She'd have plenty of time now to plan and complete the school's construction and open it before they celebrated.

With a smile, she looked out the window at the ocean, put her hand out the window, and felt the dewy air. She donned a casual frock, opened her wooden jewelry box, and pulled out the talisman Master Morya had given her in the Himalayas. She'd kept it safely hidden, waiting for the right time. Turning the pouch upside down, she fingered the beads and trinkets, added the Sheik's scarab amulet that symbolized protection, and draped the talisman over her head.

With Spots beside her, she strolled in peace above the cliffs. Seagulls flew overhead through blue skies and into cumulous clouds. She held up her skirt to avoid catching it on a scrubby bush. This bare land didn't worry her like it did others. Some locals claimed when natives lived there it had been a forest. She'd also heard the soil was so rich, and the air so pure, all one had to do was throw a seed on the ground, allow fog and rain to drip, golden sun to glow, and the pip would take root and grow. With her dream closer to reality, she wouldn't allow the undertaking to overwhelm her. As she implemented her vision, she'd need to be true to her dream, stay firmly on course, and motivate her followers to be dedicated to it as well.

Elizabeth and Junior, hand in hand, walked toward Katherine. Junior broke away and ran toward her. "Mrs. Tingley! Spots!"

As the two women embraced, the lad bent down and cuddled the dog.

"Junior, run along. It's time for Dr. Wood to take you to school," Elizabeth said.

"Can Spots come with me?" Junior asked.

"Would your teacher like that?"

Junior frowned and ran toward Dr. Wood's office.

The women laughed, and Katherine said, "Thank you for moving here."

"I'm the one who's grateful. After the congress, I couldn't think of anywhere on earth I'd rather live." She paused. "I don't want to alarm you, but I've heard grumblings from the men."

"About what?"

"Concerns your visions are too highfalutin and not even possible."

A lump formed in Katherine's throat. "Like what?"

"Ancient architecture, hundreds of trees planted, flowers in a desert. They're afraid you're making decisions on your own without consulting them."

"My ideas have been given to me by the Great One. It's up to me to lead." Katherine's emotions wafted from embarrassment to anger. "If I were a man, they'd say no such thing. Only that I had ambition, power, and strength." She hoped someday women would be admired for those traits too. Occasionally, some of her plans sounded extraordinary, but that was the point. They'd show the world Theosophy's power, the beauty of ancient wisdom, and the force of living in community with nature. "What do you think?" she asked.

Elizabeth put a hand on Katherine's shoulder. "I agree on most of your points. However, you know you can be dictatorial. Pace yourself and allow cabinet members to have more input. Lead them to where you want them to go."

Katherine didn't have time for this lecture. "The meeting's starting soon."

"Wait. One more thing," Elizabeth said. "The men want to know where the money will come from. And personally, I do too."

"Don't worry. It will be provided." Katherine patted her hand and walked away.

Elizabeth was right: Katherine needed the men to support her ideas. The way to do that would be for the cabinet members to think they'd thought of them. She couldn't do it all anyway. She'd ask for their opinions, give them more responsibilities based on each of their interests and strengths, and enlist them to help with those. She'd search for humility, step back, and channel her softer side.

She climbed the observation tower and studied the rise where the school would be built. The pillars where the ashes had been spread stood tall. The Theosophical and American flags waved at her in the gentle wind, setting off a fluttering in her chest. She froze. Something felt off. The dedication committee had selected the school site before she'd even been to California. Light-headed, she grasped the observatory handrails. That wasn't where the school should be built. It was sacred ground, holy, dedicated ground to honor Madame Blavatsky and William.

Her heart chakra swirled as a vision arose. Over the pillars, a green sphere as big as a rodeo ring floated in the azure sky and moved north. As she watched in awe, it landed atop the hotel. The globe burst, and she came out of her trance. Dr. Wood had chosen the perfect spot. That was where the school should be.

She touched the talisman hanging on her chest and closed her eyes. The school and all new construction should express the sacredness of home and place, receptacles, and expressions of a divine source. Her imagination drew building outlines in detail. She was no architect and would need professionals to listen and draw sketches and artisans to carry them out.

Determined, she carefully climbed down the tower stairs and walked toward the hotel to meet with her men in residence and share the recent vision. She'd let go of her forthright ways, be patient, and encourage them to participate in the decision-making process. Katherine entered the makeshift office where Joe, Patterson, Pierce, Iverson, Dr. Coryn, and Thurston, a new member and owner of the American Screw Company, assembled around a table in the chilly courtyard. She took a seat at the head of the table and pulled her shawl around her.

She steadied herself for the challenge ahead. "It's time to start building, in earnest."

"I agree." Pierce unrolled the plans. "We're ready to begin." He pointed to the drawing. "Here's the cornerstone, the front of the building, and here's the ocean."

Patterson nodded. "Wonderful."

She hadn't liked them when she'd seen them in San Francisco and didn't like them now. The men looked at her expectantly. She started to speak, thought of Elizabeth's warning, and smiled. "It's very nice and would have an excellent vista." She changed the subject. "Shouldn't the children's dorms be built at the same time so we can start the school right away?"

"Won't they live in the school?" Pierce asked.

"It'll take months to finish the school building." She toyed with her talisman and chose her words carefully. "Might it be prudent to repurpose what's already been started?"

The men gaped at her in confusion. "What do you mean?" Patterson asked.

"Follow me." She stood and led them out to the inner courtyard. The energy here was superb. "Isn't this a fine space? Maybe this could be the school."

"But we already dedicated the School for the Revival of Lost Mysteries of Antiquity." Joe pointed over the hill.

She flipped her hand. "We can build there later; plus, isn't the School for the Revival of Lost Mysteries of Antiquity quite wordy? Our children won't even be able to pronounce it."

"It is a mouthful." Thurston laughed, and the others joined in.

"What about this diamond-shaped building?" She turned in a circle and looked up at the sky.

A cloud passed overhead, the sky darkened, and the temperature dropped. "What about the weather?" She knew the exact answer but kept quiet to let the men talk it out.

"We could put a roof on it." Patterson squinted.

Pierce shook his head. "It'd be too gloomy without outer windows."

"How about a few skylights?" Patterson suggested.

"The ceiling would be too low." Pierce frowned.

Katherine thought of the meditation room in London. "Those of you who visited Madame Blavatsky's garden, what would she envision?"

"A dome," Patterson said right away.

Joe groaned. "Those are costly."

Pierce said, "And difficult to build."

"But beautiful. We could call it the rotunda and have lectures, performances, and celebrations in here." She gazed dreamily around the space.

"Aren't we getting ahead of ourselves?" Joe raised his voice. "We don't even own it."

"I'm sure Dr. Wood will sell to us. I'll speak to him."

"We already have these plans." Pierce held up the drawings. "You'll need an architect. I'm only an engineer."

"You're a remarkable draftsman; you can do it." She smiled at him.

"Where would the children sleep? In the hotel?" Thurston asked.

"For now. Eventually, I'd like them to feel as if they're living in homes. Any ideas?" Katherine held her breath.

"What about cottages or bungalows?" Pierce suggested. "To pick up the pace and move the male students in as soon as possible, we could design them with canvas until funds are raised to fully build them out." He was getting the hang of it now.

"Pierce, draw up plans, and we'll meet again tomorrow. That's all for today." She stood.

"Wait! How will we pay for it all?" Joe asked.

She paused to let them speak.

"We'd discussed charging for tuition and board," Patterson said.

Joe added, "And a residency fee for adults."

Katherine added, "Only for those who could afford it."

"Of course," they all chimed in.

She continued, "Joe, contact Nere to see if there are more funds in the coffers and for his thoughts. Tell him we need him and encourage him to move here with Minnie as soon as possible." She wished he were here. If he participated, others would be encouraged to do so as well.

"What about Dr. Wood?" Joe asked.

"Don't worry. I'm sure he'll be happy to sell us the hotel. Leave it to me."

Chapter Sixty-Two

Katherine found Dr. Wood organizing roots in his musty apothecary cellar. She stuck her head in and said, "Let's talk in the sun."

He stepped out, wiping his hands on a rag. "What's up?"

She said, "We need to open the school, and I'm concerned it'll take too long to build. Your hotel would be ideal. Would you consider selling it to us?"

He laughed. "Not only will I consider it, but I'd be delighted. In fact, I'd been thinking the same thing and will sell it to you at a nominal fee."

Nere sent word he'd held back some of Lady Malcolm's bequest earmarked for the school. In addition, he committed a generous amount for residential donations for a sunset suite in the hotel for himself and Minnie. Katherine designated rooms with an office, parlor, and living quarters for herself there too.

Within a few weeks, one hundred local workmen covered the property like ants. They cleared the coastal sage scrub to prepare for the bungalows and residential cottages. Reconstruction began on the hotel, now dubbed "the Homestead." Arches were added to the arcade porch that surrounded the building, and the third floor and outer façade were finished off. Katherine had envisioned white buildings of gleaming marble or at least limestone. However, convinced the time and expense to import would be prohibitive, she settled on wood siding covered in stucco painted to resemble stone.

She walked the property, filled with gladness as her vision began to take shape. A Romanesque gate was built on the Homestead's entrance road, and an Egyptian gate led to the southern Camp Karnak tent row that provided temporary housing for members of her handpicked literary staff. A makeshift dreary box of a building was expanded into a refectory with windows to take advantage of the views. The hexagon-shaped Lotus Bungalows were in process and would soon house boys. The girls would continue to stay in the Homestead until their bungalows were erected across the road to the east.

One day at the end of April, Katherine closed her eyes with a sense of inner peace as the sunset caressed her face. She opened them as a purple orb sprang from the sea, soared, and landed in front of the Homestead. She'd received a message. The Homestead required a sister, a temple with an amethyst glass dome to light the night skies alongside the emerald dome, as beacons of hope to let all know Lomaland was a sacred place of peace and brotherhood.

The cabinet scoffed at the expense, so she ordered the Madison Avenue building and Pleasant Valley Lotus Home to be sold. By the end of the month, west of the Homestead, she laid the cornerstone for the Temple of Peace.

A rabbit crossed her path as Katherine made her way down the hill. Clouds cradled the early half-moon as the sun moved over the ocean and the sky darkened. In summer at the Laurels, fireflies blinked off and on like Philo's torch. Fireflies didn't glitter in Point Loma, nor did forests surround her.

She inhaled the salty air and allowed her body to feel what could be: paths tamped down to wander on, seeds sprouting with flowers, and trees from around the world all the way to the cliff's edge. She not only wanted people of all nations to join her, but international representations from nature as well. Maybe even fireflies could be imported to thrive here also. Without a doubt, the orphans who had just arrived would blossom here too.

Pink buds had begun to bloom on Dr. Wood's Casa Rosa and someday would cover the whole building. Katherine tingled with anticipation as she stepped inside. She walked past the infirmary and down the hall to the nursery.

"*Buenas noches.*" Katherine nodded at Señora Beltrán.

"It's a good night, Señora," the widow said. "*Los niños* are doing well."

Katherine smiled at the kindly woman. The Cubans had all acclimated well and were assets to the new community. Señora Beltrán was splendidly fitted to supervise settling in the first batch of ten orphan babes under the age of two who'd arrived by train with their godmothers from the Buffalo Lotus Home.

Katherine strolled the row of white metal cribs, greeted each caregiver, and cooed at the neatly wrapped babies down for the night. One bundled infant in a blue blanket wailed. Katherine lifted the sweet one into her arms, sat in a rocker, and moved to-and-fro until the room fell silent once more. This was her chance without parental influence to raise newborn souls before they'd learned harmful thoughts and habits. She'd promote physical, mental, and spiritual enlightenment and well-being so they could reach their highest potential.

Carmen, Señora Beltrán's daughter, feeding a baby in the crook of her arm, came over.

"I see you're helping your mother." Katherine smiled. The first time she'd met her in Cuba, she knew Carmen was special.

"Yes, they're sweet."

"How old are you now?" Katherine asked. She needed a companion to assist her. Someone she could trust. With her kind disposition and grace, perhaps Carmen was the one.

"Almost twelve."

Katherine smiled. "How would you like to live with me?"

"*Qué?*" Carmen's eyes grew wide.

"Be my helper."

Carmen nodded.

"Let's talk to your mama tomorrow evening."

The next morning Pierce came to Katherine. "The city inspector rejected our pumphouse permit." For the rest of the day, one problem after another was reported to her: the school was scheduled to open in two weeks, but the grounds still needed clearing and the last of the paperwork had to be filed with the city. Katherine had vision, but she had little patience for bureaucracy, so she delegated it all.

By the time Carmen and her mother walked into Katherine's office before sunset, she had a throbbing headache and a mountain of fears about the future. However, Carmen's bright face and kind eyes made that all disappear.

She smiled at Katherine as her mother began to speak in rapid-fire Spanish. The girl translated her mother's stories into English almost as quickly as the woman talked. The long and short of it was that she loved living there, was grateful to Katherine, and if her daughter could ease her life, that would be good.

Within a few days, the final inspections were complete, and the paperwork came through. On a bright shiny morning two weeks later, Katherine's heart rejoiced again for another day she'd longed for. The school was being officially opened with the first five tuition students: Iverson Junior, now ten years old, and the four daughters of Walter T. Hanson, the executive of a large Georgia cotton concern, also from Macon, ranging from ages two to eight. The small crowd gathered in front of the Homestead for the ceremony. Dr. Gertrude van Pelt—Gertie—had moved to Lomaland to be the school headmistress. Dr. Wood and his daughter Ethel, the first teacher, Iverson Harris Senior and his wife and daughter, the Cubans, the cabinet members, the tots, and their godmothers completed the group.

Katherine began, "Families and friends, I dedicate this school Raja Yoga, meaning kingly union of mental, spiritual, and physical development. I'm throwing off the shackles of traditional education. Each child here will be taken as precious, wonderful, and unique. The present system of thirty to fifty students per overworked teacher is lethal to national welfare. Those little lives, different by heredity, environment, and individuality, are given a curriculum that demands they be alike as peas in a pod."

She smiled at Ethel Wood and continued, "No two children are alike;

therefore, as we grow, no teacher will have more than a few students to instruct at one time. They'll be given their own recreational time, close to nature, an opportunity to restore their own poise and spiritual equilibrium. May this school be forever blessed."

At dawn the next morning, the children, dressed in their uniforms, along with housemothers, the orphan toddlers, caregivers, and staff, stood outside the Homestead again. Master M had told her it was important to rise and greet the new day to make every minute count.

"Good morning, darlings," Katherine said. "Follow me." She led them up the incline to greet the sun. The children chattered like little birds. Katherine put a finger to her lips and whispered, "*Shh.*"

The children smiled and copied her. In the silence, they watched the night lantern being taken down and the flags raised. They made their way to the crest of the hill as the shiny sphere peeked over the mountains to the east in a bright orange hue.

"Let's welcome the sun." Katherine raised her arms toward the bay.

Adults and children alike lifted their arms.

"Repeat after me," Katherine ordered. "Rise, oh sun!"

The children copied her, and the others joined in too. "Rise, rise, rise!"

Katherine lowered her hands, and the adults did so too as a smattering of clouds began to lift over the city and the sun shone above the mountains in a multitude of crimson hues. Slowly, it moved over the city and sparkled over the bay.

"Start our day in glory." She raised her arms again, and her voice rang. "Send peace, peace, peace out to the world!"

"And send money," Joe said, leaning toward Katherine.

The money would come. She chose to ignore him and marched the group down the hill, past the almost completed bungalows, beyond the kitchen garden bursting with fruits and vegetables. During breakfast, Katherine put a finger to her lips. She knew it would be difficult for the children and even adults to remain quiet, but over time they'd appreciate it.

Her first silent meal after her father sent her to the convent had felt different too. No brothers teasing or kicking her under the table or grumpy father yelling. As she chewed, the sweetness of blueberries had burst in her mouth with surprising freshness. The oatmeal underneath had a cinnamon flavor she wouldn't have noticed if she'd been conversing. The anxiety of speaking with the other girls had been alleviated, and after a while she'd felt closer to God for his delicious food.

Chapter Sixty-Three

A few weeks after the school opened, Katherine and Elizabeth walked the cliff path as the fog lifted to sunny skies. "I've got something to tell you," Elizabeth said.

Katherine put up her hand. "First I need to share this dream I can't get out of my head. A man wearing a giant crown flew on a steed over the bay, landed in front of the Roman Gate, and galloped toward me. His gloved palms held golden orbs. When he squeezed them, coins rained down at my feet. Whatever could it mean?"

Elizabeth laughed. "If the orbs were the size of baseballs, my news might be related. A.G. and I are getting married."

"That's wonderful news!" Katherine put her hand on Elizabeth's shoulder. It had been a long time coming. Albert Goodwill Spalding and Elizabeth had been childhood sweethearts. Her parents hadn't approved and insisted she marry George Mayer instead. His business schemes had shifted them from one town to another, through one idiotic, money-losing venture after another: gambling, jewelry stores, a newspaper rag. The automatic coffin had been the final straw. She'd gathered up their children and moved to live a separate life.

When she encountered A.G. again, he'd become a baseball hero; his sporting goods business had taken off too. Their attraction reignited. Now that his invalid wife had passed, they were free to marry.

"Will you give us your blessing?" Elizabeth asked.

Katherine hugged her friend. "Of course. You're soulmates after all."

"He's visiting soon. May we have the wedding here?"

"That would be our first." Katherine smiled.

"I hope after he sees the property, he'll want to enroll all our children and move here. Please help me convince him."

"I'll try." He wasn't a Theosophist, so it might be a long shot.

"Don't you see he might be the man from your dream?"

Katherine laughed. "Actually, he's the man of your dreams."

A few weeks later she was watching the workmen erect the dome scaffolding around the Homestead when a shout came from the Roman Gate. A.G. rode toward her on a giant black horse. He jumped down in front her, doffed his bowler hat, and from his pocket handed her a golden nugget.

"Where'd you get this?" she asked.

"I panned for it. I'm in Califor-ni-a after all." He guffawed as the workers gathered around to see the baseball hero.

"Here, son. Take care of Tiny for me." He handed the horse's reins to Santiago, who chuckled and walked the steed toward a water trough.

A.G. waved to the men and glanced around. "Where's my Lizzie?"

"Class will be over soon. I'm so glad you've come."

"Said she wouldn't marry me unless I visited." He laughed again and gawked up at the scaffolding. "What's that?"

"We're installing a glass dome," Katherine said.

"How big?" he asked.

Pierce stepped over and shook A.G.'s hand. "Only eighty-five feet across."

"Only!" A.G. laughed again. "There's no telling what else you'll do, girl."

"You'll have to wait and see," Katherine teased. "Want a bird's-eye view of the property? Pierce, excuse the workmen for the day with pay." She led A.G. into the Homestead, across the rotunda, and up the grand staircase to her suite. "As you can see, we're still getting settled," she said, embarrassed by her office's messy condition. William's rolltop desk from New York was scattered with papers. Floor-to-ceiling shelves were jam-packed with books and knickknacks from around the world. Paintings and framed photos sat on the floor. Other possessions had found their way into her sleeping quarters next door.

“A smashing ocean view,” A.G. said as a steamship made its way south on smooth waters toward the bay entrance.

She smiled. “The temple in front of us is almost complete; it’ll also be covered by a glass dome. Small offices will circle the top, and an arched covered bridge with a veranda will connect these two buildings.”

“This must be costing an arm and a leg!” A.G. said.

She never discussed financial details, so she simply said, “Our members have been generous.”

Fortunately, Pierce joined them and continued, “We’ve sold off assets to fund the temple, which will cost twenty thousand dollars. We’ve spent around three or four times that amount already on other buildings. You may have heard we received a bequeathment from Lady Malcolm. More people are moving here and those who can afford it pay room and board.”

A.G. forehead crinkled. “Where’s everyone sleeping now?”

Pierce said, “Some here in the Homestead and many in tents. Do you see the Lotus Bungalows for boys going up? We’ll soon need more residences as the enrollment grows.”

“Gardens and trees will provide colorful landscaping and shade,” Katherine added. She led him to the south and pointed down to the large canyon. “Imagine an outdoor amphitheater where Elizabeth’s musicians perform with the Pacific as a backdrop. One of my most memorable sights while on Crusade had been the ancient *teatro* in Taormina, Sicily, overlooking the Mediterranean.”

His eyes lit up. Katherine had his attention, but then he frowned. “San Diego’s such a small town.”

“The population is growing, with plenty of real estate investment needs.” Katherine raised her eyebrows. “In fact, I might even have a small proposition for you.”

“Really?” Pierce asked.

She led them past the Neresheimer Suite and pointed north. “Below is Ocean Beach, False Bay, and another village called La Jolla, meaning ‘the jewel.’”

“Sparkles like a jewel.” A.G. grinned.

She nodded to a knoll on the other side of the entrance road. "Can you picture a magnificent home right there and you and your family living among us?"

"I thought you were starting a school here," A.G. said.

"We are, but my dream includes people of all ages from around the world, rich and poor, settling here. All will be learners."

Elizabeth and Junior waved while walking toward the Homestead. Katherine and A.G. made their way down to greet them.

"Lizzie." A.G. kissed Elizabeth's cheek, and she blushed like a schoolgirl.

"I'm Iverson Harris, Junior." Junior held out his hand.

A.G. shook it. "I'm Albert Goodwill Spalding."

"I'm honored to meet you, sir." Junior bowed. "Sorry, I've gotta run."

Junior shook A.G.'s hand again and sprinted back down the hill.

"Lovebirds! Walk with me." Katherine led them to the possible site. "Stand here." She placed them on the mound and stepped a few yards away.

A.G. took Elizabeth's hand, and the couple gazed out at the sea. "Katherine wants me to build you a mansion here," he said.

Elizabeth smiled up at him. "Would you consider it?"

He shrugged, and she turned him east. "Do you see the building tops? If we go up three stories, we'd have a clear shot of the city and bay."

He nodded. They circled back toward the ocean, and he slipped his arm around her waist.

Katherine gave them a few more moments, then joined them and tilted her head toward the cliffs. "This could be like your own estate with a golf course and horse stables."

A.G. stared off into the distance and laughed. "Why not?"

Elizabeth's eyes twinkled. "Why not indeed? Could we have a dome too?"

"Why not?" Katherine said. "A.G., would you throw in some sporting equipment for the school too?"

"Why not?" He laughed. "Let's get the wedding underway. I've got to return to Paris for the Olympic Committee. Commissioner business is demanding."

An agreement was negotiated with A.G. He'd enroll his children, provide funds to build more Lotus Bungalows, and build his mansion. Since the couple would be traveling for the foreseeable future, the school would lease the mansion as another boys' home.

Chapter Sixty-Four

August gave way to September as autumn swept in. Cool air kept Katherine's mind clear and full of the beauty of each day. In the east, leaves would have changed to fire colors by now and started to drop. She'd need to import some of those trees here to remind them of the changing season.

A supplement published in the *San Diego Evening Tribune* included eight pages of photos and illustrations of the buildings in progress. Her quote read: *The Raja Yoga School, meaning royal union, will emphasize the balance between physical, mental, and spiritual growth.*

All seemed well until a series of articles published in the *Los Angeles Times* alleged: *Instead of practicing theosophia—divine wisdom—vile spookery ran rapid at the crank institution.*

Where did they get that foolish information? Katherine had wanted the building details finished and the school curriculum to take effect before visitors could be greeted. However, cabinet members insisted it was imperative to remain open to the public, or it could be misconstrued that they had something to hide.

Fog hung low over Lomaland one November morning as Katherine hurried from breakfast at the refectory and past the boys' bungalows. Artist Reginald Machell, Madame Blavatsky's devoted chela, had the genius to carry out the details of Katherine's vision and had arrived late the night before. She stepped inside the Homestead as Carmen escorted him down the grand staircase to the rotunda.

With his trimmed dark hair, Roman nose, and square chin, Katherine barely recognized him. When she'd seen him in London, he'd sported a long, scruffy beard. She welcomed him and said, "Come outside. I want to show you around."

"First this is for you," he said. Carmen and Katherine stepped back to view the artwork he held up. There it was—*The Prodigal, The Kingdom of Heaven Is Within You*—the mystical painting Katherine had longed to have here. The double wooden frame had two paintings within it. On top in purple and gold, a bearded man with a glowing heart and wings was mourned by three women. Below it, a carving in the frame read: *The knowledge of it is a divine silence and the rest of all the senses*. In the lower painting sat a man studying in the dark. *I will arise and go to my father* was carved into the frame below it.

Carmen carried the artwork up to the suite, and Katherine led Machell outside. Voices erupted from the Roman Gate as a group of tourists jumped out of a tallyho. Patterson tried to herd them to follow him, but they fanned out in all directions. Soon she'd need to train a sheepdog to help.

"What's going on?" Machell asked.

"Tourists. They come every day now." She didn't mention how their presence grated on her. She moved on and explained the Homestead had been built as a hotel but was theirs now— part school, part residential facility.

Hand under his chin, he studied the building. "I see you've created a dome like Madame Blavatsky's meditation room. It doesn't feel finished, though."

"No one's been up to the task. I waited for you." She knew what she envisioned but waited for his reply.

He said, "I see a flaming heart, like Madame Blavatsky's urn, and smaller ones on the diamond points as well."

That was exactly it. "Can you take care of it?"

He nodded. "It'll be a challenge. I'll need a glassblower."

"Certainly. Let me show you the progress on the temple." She walked him around the Homestead toward the ocean. A couple from the tallyho group walked in front of Katherine and Machell and stepped inside the open building.

"How bizarre," the man's voice reverberated off the walls.

"I think it's marvelous," the woman scolded him.

"What do you think they do in here?"

"*Shhh!* They'll hear you." They exited and walked down the hill.

Katherine grimaced and resisted the urge to follow and tell them about her vision.

"I'm glad we could keep Madame Blavatsky's headquarters private." Machell shook his head.

"We all need to feel welcome. As you can see, we need doors as soon as possible," Katherine said.

"What did you have in mind?"

"They should be filled with grandeur to enlighten folks that they're entering a sacred space. Would you sketch a few designs for my approval and supervise a woodcarver to create them?"

"It would be my honor," he replied.

A few days later she found him in front of the temple in an apron, leaning over a giant plank of wood atop sawhorses. Oak scent filled the air as he chiseled into the wood.

"What's this?" she asked.

Machell stepped back. "The doors."

"Won't they be too tall?" she blurted, then hoped she hadn't offended him.

"They'll only be twelve feet tall. You wanted a statement."

"Where are the plans and the carpenter?" she asked.

"I'm carving them myself by working directly into the wood, as if painting a picture."

"Are you sure? I can be persnickety." This was risky.

"I'm certain they'll suit you." His fingers grazed the wood as he spoke. "The lilies are for purity. This will be a dog to represent fidelity—because you're so fond of them." Machell looked at her with adoration.

She needed to let go and trust his powers. "Can you finish them by the new year?"

He nodded with a smile.

Twelve-foot doors! Such grandeur made her woozy.

Chapter Sixty-Five

January 1901

On New Year's morning, the full moon, a pearl in the velvet sky, shone in her window, waking her from a vivid dream. As a child, Katherine floated down the Merrimac in a dory. A storm whipped up. Her tiny hands held tightly to the boat's rim. Afraid it would capsize, she was about to give up. Sunrays parted through thinning clouds, the colossal waves pacified, and she felt victorious. Surely a good sign for the first day of the new year.

Master M had warned the turn of the century would bring many challenges. She found that hard to believe since things were going so well. Lomaland had settled into a relaxed routine: morning sun ceremonies, silent meals, lectures and lessons, music, and athletics for all students.

Twenty men, thirty-five women, and thirty-seven children lived in harmony with nature. Perhaps the women were drawn to her because she instilled in them freedom from society's restraints. In addition, she provided a few females safe sanctuary from cruel husbands. The sound of the waves at night soothed the women to sleep; morning fog softened their brows worried by past sorrows.

In addition to silly *Los Angeles Times* articles, gossips had been spreading tales about Lomaland, but it didn't worry Katherine. Whenever someone new moved into a neighborhood, people talked. Within no time, San Diegans would embrace the Theosophists and appreciate all the good they had to offer the community as well as the world. Still, she needed to be wary.

New Year's Day remained a busy one. Along the temple walls, she planted ivy cuttings Machell had brought from Madame Blavatsky's Garden. Young and old alike lined up along the property and marched down the hill toward the cliffs, where olive trees waited to be planted on the edge overlooking the ocean. The ancient ceremony involved the naming of each tree as it was settled into the ground and covered with soil. Afternoon festivities continued with picnics and walks along the beach. At the evening celebration, Nere and his orchestra played an assortment of classics. Katherine felt pride as Carmen performed a mandolin solo on the instrument brought from her native land.

At the podium, Katherine said, "The fresh air and beauty of the surroundings have done wonders for all of us. Applications continue to arrive. Even though I'm not sure where we'll put them all, I've faith all will be provided." She shared plans for a bright future. She announced three agricultural objectives: increase the yield for Point Loma tables, provide horticultural education for students, and contribute useful information to the world at large. The crowd cheered with every new announcement, and Katherine felt buoyed by the spirit. Behind that elation, she tried not to be concerned about Master M's forewarning of impending challenges that could ruin the success of her vision.

Katherine finished her speech. "*Buenas noches*, my darlings. As you fall asleep tonight, send loving kindness to every living thing on earth."

By February, more bungalows were constructed. On Sundays, Katherine offered lectures open to the public in the temple. The Spaldings arrived with a carload of elegant furniture and a double-seated Locomobile, the first on the property, to tour special guests in.

However, at the next cabinet meeting a few days after the Spring Equinox, Joe held up the paper. "The *San Diego Union* has announced Colonel Olcott plans to orate at the Hotel del Coronado about 'true' Theosophy."

"Bah! True Theosophy. What does that old fool know about truth?" Katherine had tried to love this enemy, but it had been impossible. Stories and lies had continued to circulate about them in the neighborhood. She certainly didn't need more. Olcott would spread more rumors to ruin Lomaland's reputation. This must be what the master had warned about.

"Annie Besant must have sent him," Nere said.

"I'll call and have a little chat with Babcock, the hotel manager." Joe stood and left the room.

Katherine sighed. "Let's continue. It's past time to formalize sightseeing tours."

Patterson and Pierce agreed and were given the task to work up a plan.

"Sunday lectures have been well received," Thurston offered. "I recommend you publish a book with your tenets to dispel rumors and gain members and income."

"That's a wonderful idea," Katherine said. "If only I had the time."

"Blavatsky and Judge found time," Dr. Coryn said.

"I'm not them."

Thurston said, "I'm happy to help."

She swished her hand in the air. "Feel free to start on it. Include stories and poems from the children too. I'll add something later."

Joe returned. "Colonel Olcott will not be speaking in Coronado."

"How did you manage that?" Nere grinned.

"I asked Babcock how he'd feel if his guests were no longer welcome here for tours."

Katherine tried not to smile. Trouble eliminated.

But within a few days, Olcott's talk was rescheduled at the opera house, and Fisher, the owner, refused to cancel.

Katherine frowned and said, "I can't wait to hear what he has to say."

Nere looked aghast. "It's not advisable for you to go."

She had the final say and told Joe to schedule a rebuttal for the following night.

In the late afternoon on the day of Olcott's talk, with Carmen by her side, Katherine rode the carriage down to the pier and took the ferry across the bay to New Town. As they traveled up D Street, Katherine pulled her hood over her head, and Carmen tucked in her unruly curls. They climbed out onto the sidewalk and stared up at the Romanesque building with two million bricks surmounted by a turret that towered five stories high above them. Katherine had admired the second largest theater on the West Coast when she first came to town, but she'd never been inside.

Hand in hand, they walked across the mosaic-tiled lobby and up to a private loge hidden behind lush ivory-and-gold drapes. Katherine gaped at the three tiers of boxes and the bas-relief details. She'd been in many grand theaters on the East Coast and while overseas, but this one was just as impressive. What she wouldn't do to own one such as this! She imagined the lectures and entertainments she could present.

Only a third of the fourteen hundred seats were filled, and she tried not to gloat. But then she began to worry. What would he say to debase her and the organization? In William's photographs, Olcott had looked old, but now, years later, he appeared as ancient as Methuselah. Using his cane, he limped onto the bare stage, and his gray hair and beard rolled down to his knees. Only a few audience members clapped. Tomorrow night when she spoke here, she'd decorate the stage with flowers and potted palms and fill all the seats.

Olcott's decrepit voice could barely be heard as he gave a dull history of Theosophy. Pats on his own back included that he'd revived and united the Hindu religions of India with Japan's Buddhism. What a bunch of burning-hot bamboo-shoot curry. Carmen reached for Katherine's hand as he harangued Lomaland. The thing that especially stuck in her craw was when he said, "Tingley's a fraud, a swindler. She's hypnotized captains of industry to do her bidding."

What a liar. She'd never hypnotized anyone in her life. The whole talk lasted less than an hour. As they returned to the bay, Katherine asked Carmen what she thought.

The girl said, "Don't worry. No one listened to that ugly man."

Katherine wished she believed it. Only time would tell what damage had been done.

Seals barked as the ferry slowly sailed across the bay. High on the Point Loma hill, the amethyst and emerald domes glistened in the darkness. Katherine's counteractive talk the next night spun in her mind.

The next morning Joe came to her. "Bad news. Fisher has canceled your presentation."

"Why?"

"He wouldn't say."

"Well, I'm saying this: someday I'll buy that building and push him out."

Olcott left town, and Lomaland rumors expanded: they swam in the ocean nude and mistreated children. Katherine had been an exotic dancer. She tried to ignore the falsehoods, but they finally took their toll, and she fell into bed shattered.

Chapter Sixty-Six

As Olcott rumblings died down, the beauty of spring gardens helped soothe Katherine's soul while she walked the grounds in veneration. By summer, even though they'd instituted tour guides, the property became overrun by gawkers and talkers, disturbing the peaceful ambiance of her vision. Some days they had as many as a hundred visitors. It must be another one of the challenges Master M had warned her of, and she decided to meet it head on by welcoming these strangers with grace.

One day, Katherine learned they expected an especially large group, so she hiked over to the Roman Gate to tag along as two dozen guests alit from Hotel del Coronado's tallyhos. Remarkably, these tourists gave up a day rollicking on the beach and gliding on sailboats.

Ten other visitors joined the tour too. The guests paid the recently established ten-cent fee to keep the riffraff out. Pierce and Iverson Junior in their khaki uniforms took turns reciting the welcome greeting and guided the group toward the mansion.

Pierce said, "Our largest residence is being built by Albert Spalding, the baseball hero, for his wife, Elizabeth. It's octagonal, with three stories, and will be topped with a purple glass dome."

"Why don't you build me a house like that?" a woman asked her stout husband and the group laughed.

As they walked over the rise, someone hollered, "Look at that view."

The group stopped, and the large man asked, "Do they catch fish out there?"

"Certainly!" Junior replied. "Lions of the Sea, some weigh a thousand pounds. I haven't caught one yet though." The group chortled at the joke. Katherine was proud of how eloquent Junior had become at eleven years old.

A somber man in a dark suit pointed down the slope toward the cliffs. "And that?"

Junior explained, "Mr. Spalding's golf course. Next to it, his stables are going up."

They walked on. Pierce stopped and waited for the group to gather and said, "The Homestead's glass dome encloses our rotunda, with a circumference of three hundred feet and a height of eighty-five. Those flamed hearts are twenty."

"What are they for?" the man asked.

"Beauty." Katherine said with a sly smile.

It wasn't time to go into the esoteric value with these strangers. "Go inside, take a seat."

Junior led them up the steps and through the arched arcade. The somber man glanced around and started down the hill away from the group.

"This way, sir," Katherine called.

With a stern frown, he turned and followed her into the rotunda. Restful shades of green from the dome reflected on the guests as Carmen played her mandolin. The man bypassed the chairs and started up the grand staircase, but Pierce intercepted him.

Students in international folk costumes sang "Happy Sunbeams" with hand motions. Elizabeth had taught it to them the last time she'd visited. Tourists clapped as the children bowed.

"Aren't they just darling?" a lady in a big hat said, and the woman beside her nodded.

Pierce shared, "We teach a well-rounded education, and music is a major component of our school. Everyone here sings and learns to play the piano and other instruments they're drawn to. We emphasize selflessness, brotherhood, and spreading peace around the world. We've started a bee farm and will soon establish a silkworm cocoonery, and we have a weather program—"

The somber man asked, "When do you indoctrinate children into Theosophy?"

Pierce didn't miss a beat. "We don't teach Theosophy until a student asks for information."

The hefty man stood up and started to walk away. "Enough of this mouth-flapping. I wanna see more." His wife grabbed his elbow, pulled him down, and told him to sit.

"Who's paying for it all?" the somber man scowled.

"Those who can pay for room and board do. Others are free," Pierce answered.

Junior held up a pink form. "We don't use money here. We write things needed on these forms, they're collected on Fridays, and we pick up items later from the Lomaland Department Store. Such as thumb tacks, shoestrings, a new overcoat—"

"Is it true you think William Judge's soul has been reincarnated into Spots the dog?" the somber man asked. Who was this man, and how would he know about William and Spots?

With a straight face, Junior said, "Human souls only go into humans. Not animals. Some Eastern religions believe that. But we don't."

"Demonstrate one of your rituals," the man prodded. Katherine had told tour guides if asked about occult practices, not to share. They were sacred and not to be discussed.

Junior said, "If you want to know more about Theosophy, please attend one of Madame Tingley's Sunday talks. All are welcome here regardless of their beliefs."

The fat man called, "When do girls learn to do the blanket hornpipe?"

Junior had a confused expression on his face. Pierce turned radish red.

Oh, my stars and garters. Katherine hurried to the front of the room. "After marriage, like all virtuous girls. Now follow us for the rest of the tour." A lot more information was usually imparted, but to avoid more inane questions, she pulled Pierce and Junior aside on the porch and whispered, "Skip the temple and keep moving." She didn't want bad energy anywhere near her consecrated space.

Junior called, "Want to see where I live? Follow me." He strolled them down a path bordered by pink ice plant. Roses and kaleidoscope-colored seeds from brotherhood lodges around the world had started to bloom. The palms and pines they'd planted had begun to grow too.

Guests stepped inside the bungalow and Junior said, "Welcome to our cozy Lotus Bungalow. It's twenty-four by thirty-four feet in diameter."

Pierce shared, "Six to twelve students are grouped in each home by capabilities and age. An expert parent lives with charges day and night. As you can see, beds are in cubicles, and each bungalow has a toilet and bath facilities. The central place in the middle is for study, classes, and music practice. Every bungalow has its own piano."

"Here's my bed," Junior said. "Each morning we get dressed, make our beds and sweep the floors."

"Don't you have maids?" a woman asked.

Junior said, "Everyone here works. The man at the gate might even be the richest of us."

"All the adults, including me, are learners here too," Pierce interjected with a smile.

"It's dark in here. What about electricity?" the somber man asked.

"We have kerosene lamps for evenings." Junior held one up.

"Don't they stink?"

"We leave the windows open."

The group laughed.

Junior smiled. "The city is scheduled to install electricity next year." Katherine had delayed the process by insisting all wires be put underground because it would mar Lomaland views. She'd experienced the Great White Blizzard of 1888, when all the New York City wires collapsed. Even though it didn't snow in San Diego, one never knew when disaster would strike.

"Don't you children get cold?" a woman asked.

Pierce said, "Our weather is temperate. Soon we'll finish off the canvas with wood."

The bungalow seemed stark. Katherine would have floral paintings hung inside.

Pierce answered more questions. "Girls stay in the Homestead. A building for young ladies thirteen to sixteen years of age is being built. We'll add more bungalows as children continue to arrive from around the world. Students whose parents live nearby visit together on Sundays."

"How can the mothers abide it?" the woman asked.

"It's all for the good of their children," Junior said with a smile.

They walked farther south. "What's that big excavation?" someone asked.

Junior said, "That's going to be America's first Greek amphitheater. Hopefully you'll return when we begin to offer concerts and plays for all to enjoy."

Katherine had insisted it be perfectly situated, as if it leapt from the sea. Due to the canyon's shape and soft soil, little digging had been needed. She'd been elated when it was determined it could be made to seat three thousand. The group strolled along the avenue where pepper trees had been planted. She couldn't wait to see their little pink berries. On their way back to the gate, the afternoon sun beat down and the somber man started to climb the Spalding mansion's outer spiral staircase.

Katherine rushed over. "Sir, get down."

"I want to see what's up there," he said and kept climbing.

She tugged at his pantleg. "It's not connected to the roof."

"Why not?" he asked, landing back on the ground.

"Why do you think?" she said mysteriously with a raised eyebrow. Fortunately, the observation tower had been taken down. She couldn't wait to see this obnoxious group go.

Chapter Sixty-Seven

A few days after the tour, Katherine started to receive anonymous threats in the mail: *You're up to no good. We know what you're doing there. You will burn in the fires of hell for your sins.* Katherine began to believe there must be a conspiracy afoot.

The next day Pierce joined Katherine on the Homestead porch overlooking the Lotus Garden. "I have bad news." He held up the paper and said, "Reverend Wilson of the First Methodist Church preached an anti-Theosophy sermon. The *San Diego Union* has published it."

She took the paper from him and read, "'Theosophy as a Modern Substitute for the Religion of Christ.'" She continued to read quietly, then said, "Preposterous. He has no idea who we are."

"That shallow and ignorant man has no notion of what love and brotherhood means," Pierce said.

"We should be patient with doubters." Katherine closely studied the minister's photo next to the article. Dark hair, stern face—she couldn't believe it! "Pierce, look." She handed him the paper.

He put on his glasses. "Isn't that the man from the tour group? The one who asked all those pointed questions? He was a spy!" Pierce's face was red with anger. "I'll have the men sentry the gate day and night, patrol the grounds, and build a six-foot wall around the property. We've got to fight!"

"We have to write," she said. Two days later the paper provided an equal amount of space for their denial that concluded: *False fear of the Supreme has so weakened man's spirituality that he's lost the courage to attack and subdue his brutal selfishness.*

The following Sunday Reverend Wilson preached his rebuttal to Lomaland's rebuttal from the pulpit, and again it was published. *This reincarnation is very funny. The ego is sexless; therefore a man may be his own grandmother, any woman her uncle. The absolute fatalism of this system makes it repugnant to free men.*

Lomaland responded to this as well: *The doctrine of reincarnation was once believed by Christians and Jews alike. In Matthew, Christ said of John the Baptist: Elias is come already, and they knew him not. In Luke, prophets Moses and Elijah, long dead, were there with Jesus. God's voice came from a cloud and said 'This is my son chosen, listen to him.' This shows the divinity and humanity of Jesus.*

For the next few weeks, the editorial columns were filled with dueling perspectives.

"This war of rebuttals is ludicrous," Katherine cried whenever another paper was brought to her.

All was quiet for a few days until the *Union* printed a document signed by Reverend Wilson, eleven other Catholic and Protestant San Diego clergymen, five from out of town, and a YMCA secretary. The Unitarian minister was the only one who abstained. The conclusion stated: *Theosophy is the antithesis of Christianity. It's a system of pantheism that admits and tolerates all gods. These principles leave no room for religion or ethics. This fatalism doctrine is destructive. Its denial of the Fatherhood of God leaves no real basis for brotherhood.*

"Enough is enough!" Katherine proclaimed. In the *Union*, she challenged the clergymen to debate her representatives: *Theosophy Isn't the Antithesis of the Teaching of Christ.* A condition of the challenge was that Reverend Wilson wasn't to participate because he'd offended the Lomalanders too deeply. The clergy willingly accepted, and the Fisher Opera House was booked for the following Sunday. However, the ministers soon backed out, certainly pushed by Reverend Wilson to do so.

Katherine chose to move forward, and she'd have both sides debate the topic by having a Lomaland resident, Reverend Neill, a former Presbyterian minister and Christian scholar, represent the Christian view. The first night a standing-room-only crowd filled the theater, and he said, "We all need Christ's divine nature."

Dr. Coryn defended the Theosophical position. He assured the crowd that Theosophists maintained divine wisdom was not only compatible with religions, including Christianity, but basic to them. "Theosophy is not antagonistic to Christianity. Its mission is to rescue it from confusion and obscurity and to give the people the correct interpretations of Christ's teachings. Theosophists accept God as taught by Jesus."

When asked if Jesus was the son of God, Dr. Coryn replied, "All the men in this room tonight are also the sons of God, and the women are all his daughters." The well-attended discussions were extended to continue for a month of Sundays.

Then Katherine received another anonymous note: *Mrs. Tingley, I have documents about you that I'll give to the Los Angeles paper to be published. How much is it worth to you to have them suppressed?*

This threat must be from more than just the clergy. Could it be Hargrove, Annie Besant's contingent, or another group? "That's it!" Katherine hollered. "I'm speaking at the opera house myself."

On the appointed evening, clothed in a white sari with her talisman around her neck and signet ring on her finger, she rode a carriage to the opera house. It dropped her at the backstage door, and she made her way to the wings. Evergreens and flowers decorated the stage with her young Lomaland ladies on the platform dressed in Grecian attire. After the violin solo, Katherine smoothed her hair, pulled the scarf over her head, and walked out onto the stage to soft applause.

At the rostrum, she smiled as the lights lit up her face and emanated her aura to float down toward the audience and up into the balconies. "I've done nothing wrong but try to make the world better. I'm here this evening to share with you the power of Theosophy. We are not a religion, nor try to be. Theosophy, after all, includes Christianity and the teaching of all the masters, including Jesus, as well as Buddha, Muhammad, Moses, Abraham, Confucius, Zoroaster, and all ancient wise ones of the past. We believe in the positive works of these great men of the world. We believe in the goodness of all mankind. I'm certain deep in each of your hearts, you agree."

A murmur spread across the audience, and she detected a few hisses from one side of the room. Her talk continued for over an hour. When she finished, some cheered and applauded, but others made a beeline for the exits. Was this how it would be? Would there always be people she couldn't reach?

"Don't be silly," she heard William's voice say. "You know you can't reach everyone. Trust yourself. If you believe, the right ones will follow. As you did me."

Chapter Sixty-Eight

The Spalding home construction had been completed. Even though Machell continued to carve interior details, Katherine moved a few boys inside. Devil winds had blown the Lotus Bungalow canvases off, and rain drenched the homes. Post-haste, workers were rebuilding them with wood siding.

With more space for children now, she sent a cablegram to her friend Emilio Bacardi, inviting him to choose Cuban war orphans to come to the Raja Yoga School at the organization's expense.

One day in mid-September, Katherine waited in front of the Homestead as Emilio and his wife, Elvira, walked down the hill with the children in tow. She couldn't wait to meet these new darlings who'd made the long journey from Cuba by ship and then New Orleans by train.

As they drew closer, concern hit her. Hadn't Emilio read her cablegram? Couldn't he count? She'd asked him to handpick twenty-six children, but almost forty walked toward her, and quite a few appeared to be over the twelve-year-old age limit. Three of the boys were as tall as the nearby pines that had already shot up from the earth.

As the Bacardi couple gave her hugs, she composed herself to greet them. Each child stepped forward and said their names with a curtsy or a bow, and Katherine smiled. Through their beautiful dark eyes, she could feel the sorrow in their souls.

After the children were fed, bathed, and tucked into beds, Emilio and

Elvira accompanied Katherine up to her Homestead suite. She didn't want to offend him but had to ask, "Why did you bring so many?"

"What do you mean?"

"I requested twenty-six, and you brought forty." She tried not to sound angry.

"*Lo siento.* I couldn't help it." He looked at her with his own sad eyes. "So many need help. We couldn't decide." He reached for Elvira's hand.

Katherine understood from her time at the mission a desire to help all who needed it. Hopefully, the elder boys hadn't acquired unbreakable habits. They'd been brought to her for a reason. She'd love them all just the same, follow her intuition, and help them find peace within themselves to do their best.

Some of the children had to be taught how to brush their teeth, comb their hair, and bathe. One girl with tuberculosis required isolation and special care. Within a few days, though, they all seemed to settle in nicely.

Emilio and Elvira stayed for three weeks. But as soon as they left for their island, things began to unravel. The girl in the infirmary refused to cooperate with Dr. Wood and his nurses. Katherine had to step in and talk to her about not infecting others.

The three boys complained about the school uniform and wanted to wear the dirty clothes they'd arrived in. Perhaps they were homesick. Sensing bigger battles with them in the future, Katherine had their things washed and permitted them to put them back on.

She was right. Within another week, these boys declined to participate in the morning ritual, go to school, or join the afternoon calisthenics and sports activities on the amphitheater grounds. They also seemed to be addicted to unclean speech and lying. She spoke with them individually and prayed their attitudes would change. Rumors about Lomaland continued to eddy. If word got out about these boys, it would further tarnish their already precarious reputation.

And to make matters worse, she received another threatening letter: *All your black past is in hand from the time you lived in Newburyport, Massachusetts, as Kitty Wescott. How much would you give to have the matter repressed?*

Have your representative meet me Friday next, at midnight, at the Roseville Ferry Landing with cash before it's too late.

She read the letter to Nere.

"There's nothing to worry about," he said. "You've nothing to hide."

Her gut roiled. Yes, she did. Kitty Wescott was her maiden name. She'd talked often of her beloved grandfather. However, since her name had changed each time she'd married, she'd felt safe that no one would learn about her acting years. Also, if word of her parentage came to light, it could change everything. She couldn't tell Nere about her father's nefarious past.

Nere took the letter from her and told her he'd take care of it.

Chapter Sixty-Nine

The morning after Nere went down to the landing, he told her no one had been there. The blackmailer remained a mystery.

On a foggy morning in late October, Katherine watched as cypress trees outside her window rocked back and forth, as if shaking their heads. Usually, she liked the quiet shifting of dewy dampness but this morning she felt a sense of foreboding. Were more naysayers and perils on their way to put obstacles on her path? She didn't have the strength to combat more.

Carmen knocked and set the tea tray on the bed. "Morning, Madame."

"I'm exhausted and will forgo this morning's sun service. Tell Pierce to carry on." Since the clergy debate, she'd moved the morning ritual away from prying eyes down to the amphitheater.

Carmen stood with her hands behind her back. "*Lo siento.* Do you need anything else?"

"Where are the newspapers?" Katherine asked.

"They didn't come." Carmen looked away.

Katherine raised her eyebrows. She could tell Carmen was lying. "Go get them."

"The men said you shouldn't have them."

Katherine stared at her. Carmen left the room and sheepishly returned with the papers.

Katherine took a sip of tea, read through the *San Diego Union,* and then turned to the *Los Angeles Times* headline: OUTRAGES AT POINT LOMA, WOMEN AND CHILDREN STARVED AND TREATED LIKE CONVICTS. She crumpled the paper and threw it on the floor. "How could they print such blatant lies? How could they imagine such poppycock?" She pressed her hand over her heaving chest, trying to force the anger to abate.

"Carmen, please hand it back and leave me." Katherine put out her arm and began to skim the article: *Though situated on the most beautiful place on earth, the colony is a place of horror. Armed men guard the inmates and lock them in cells at night. The children are starved, taken away from their parents, and never allowed to see them.*

Mrs. Leavitt, who'd recently relocated to Los Angeles from San Diego, told the *Times* a Mrs. Holbrook had been forced to work in Lomaland fields and was locked up at night. Her husband had to come from the east to rescue her from the "roost" with the aid of an armed officer. The woman now hovered on the point of death from the abuse. That was ridiculous! Katherine had never even heard of these women.

The next section was even more bizarre. Mrs. Leavitt claimed Mrs. Neresheimer had told her she'd forcibly been separated from her husband and lived alone in a little tent on the grounds. What fiction. Minnie occupied a Homestead suite in luxury, and Nere had begun to have a private home constructed for them near the cliffs.

Mrs. Leavitt described midnight pilgrimages with both men and women in robes carrying torches to a hill, where gross immoralities were practiced by disciples of spookism. It was true Katherine conducted private ceremonies on the cornerstone's site. Everything else was a pack of lies. They served healthy meals, and anyone was free to leave whenever they wished.

The group tried to convince Katherine to sue for libel.

She replied, "Madame Blavatsky said there was a reason people did evil and they needed compassion. Master Morya and even Jesus told us to love our enemies."

"This is not just evil. It's malicious," Dr. Coryn said.

Katherine recalled the chaos when William sued to protect Madame Blavatsky's name. "A suit would bring even more negative attention upon us."

Pierce raised his voice. "You need to defend yourself. You need to protect your—and our—good name."

Good name? Since she'd been a girl, she'd never had a good name. Her desire to help others had often been misunderstood.

"All who've visited us know these rumors aren't true," she said.

"Then let us call them on the stand and let them prove it." Nere touched her arm. "You have done nothing wrong. What are you afraid of?"

Everything. Her father's sordid, illegal ways in Newburyport, her time on the stage. "Give me a few days to consider."

She left the meeting, pulled up her hood, and walked the grounds, the fog so thick she could barely see the sky's crescent moon. Like the distant islands, her future was invisible too. She breathed in and out and summoned the divine to help guide her decision. Her instinct was to fight back, but what was the higher power's desire for her? If she sued it would take time and finances needed to service Lomaland. However, if her reputation continued to be sullied, it would drive people away.

While passing the boys' bungalows, she peeked inside at their innocent sleeping faces. Their lives would be enhanced by a Theosophical education, and as they grew, they'd be the ones to take brotherhood far and wide and spread peace and justice to all. She was certain if her philosophy spread throughout the world, poverty and war on earth would end unto eternity.

Two days later, buried in the last page, there was a notice in the *Times* that Mrs. Leavitt admitted she'd never personally been acquainted with Mrs. Holbrook or Mrs. Neresheimer. She'd only repeated what she'd heard from San Diego neighborhood chitchat. However, the damage had been done. Katherine acquiesced and entered a libel suit against the *Times-Mirror Company*, the *Los Angeles Times*' parent company, and its owner and editor, Harrison Gray Otis, asking for fifty thousand dollars. Hopefully, it would stop him from publishing more falsehoods.

On New Year's Eve, before the setting sun, she walked the property and reflected on the past year. As the master had predicted, 1901 had brought many challenges. She'd had many accomplishments as well. One hundred students were now enrolled in the school, and almost two times that many adults lived on the property. More devout and gifted Theosophists were on their way. Edith White had agreed to be the Art Department chair, and she would soon be joined by artists Leonard Lester and Charles Ryan. Henry Edge would arrive soon to be the Boys' Department headmaster. William's spirit continued to bless her undertaking, and she gave thanks to God for bringing them together in their coinciding slice of time on earth.

The Spalding home had been dedicated as Lotus Group Home Number One. Four more bungalows had popped up from the ground like mushrooms for even more boys. The nearby music pavilion, an elevated platform with a pyramid roof and open sides, had been erected for performances and gatherings.

The Karnak House for the literary staff above the cliffs had been finished, and across the road five bungalows for girls had been constructed. Hundreds of trees were planted. Even though Miss Sessions, who helped set out the trees, warned the three acres of mulberry would never survive, Katherine insisted. She planned to start a cocoonery to raise silkworms. Girls would be taught to spin silk, make fabric, and sew clothes with it. Numerous ship captains reported using the Homestead and temple's lighted domes as navigational aids, as they were much more visible than the lower lighthouse at the end of the point. And Lomaland was San Diego's number one tourist attraction.

Chapter Seventy

January 1902

New Year's morning dawned bright and clear. Even before the sun peeked over the distant mountains, the sky lit up with a golden glow, and the Pacific lay quiet. Katherine announced a day of pleasure to dedicate the Temple of Peace. This would be the best year of her life. The clergy had quieted down, and she'd soon be vindicated by the newspaper suit. Then she'd be free to continue her Lomaland vision.

As Katherine made her way across the Homestead porch, a hummingbird darted from here to there, sipping nectar with his pointy beak. The garden, from roses to heliotropes, from pansies to poinsettias, was dewy and fragrant. She called good morning to the adults gathered below the bower-decorated temple, hurried up the sloped staircase, and waved to the children waiting in the Lotus Gardens. Boys clad in neat uniforms and girls in white with flowers strung through their hair marched behind Junior toward the temple with flying banners and song. She'd never heard such harmonies. Voices from around the world blended in international rhapsody.

Patterson and Pierce helped Katherine open Machell's carved doors. Adults followed the youths up the steps and took chairs arranged in an arched formation. Urns bursting with flowers and potted palms adorned the platform. Nere played the piano as the children continued to sing from the stage. Sadness over his daughter Amiee's marriage to Hargrove had begun to dissipate. Some heartaches all the diamonds in the world couldn't heal, but the power of music and teaching seemed to be helping. As his health steadily improved, Katherine found joy in seeing him smile again.

She paced to the podium from her front-row seat and said, "Just two years ago this property was a barren wasteland. I looked out over the sea and imagined a City Beautiful for the children, and here we are today with over one hundred of you living here. With elation, I dedicate this Temple of Peace to you. The truest temple is built within our hearts; however, this shrine is an outer expression of that love to humanity."

She continued to share her hopes that the artist in each would be infused with happy usefulness within the sacred space. In the future she saw thousands more children coming here and over time growing beautiful, strong, and true. "It is your example they'll follow. You have it in your power to be a light unto the world. Life is joy!" She returned to her chair with gratitude.

Pierce slid beside her and whispered, "The eldest Cuban boys are nowhere to be seen."

"Where could they be?" she asked.

"We'll find them," he said and slipped out.

To violin and piano duets, sixty children presented tableaus based on beloved stories including "The Doctor's Visit," "Sail Ahoy," "Little Miss Muffet," "Cinderella," and "Sleeping Beauty." Miss Wood, the teacher without training, only strong natural instincts, had done a superb job coordinating the effort.

After the patriotic finale, Carmen presented a bouquet to Nere. "To our beloved music master. For all you've done to teach us." Tears of joy sparkled in his eyes.

Junior stepped to the podium next and handed another bouquet to Katherine. "This display is a gift of brotherhood, symbolic of the courage, power, and fearlessness of our friend whom we all love because she dares to tell the truth."

Behind her happiness was the nagging worry about the Cuban boys.

The children marched to their homes in song, and the adults moved slowly to the Homestead's wide porch. Katherine sat on her peacock chair beside the handsome Robinson couple, who'd traveled from San Francisco with Larona, their infant daughter, for the occasion.

Marion said, “Roses in January!”

Alfred smiled at his wife. “She sure loves roses.”

The children raced down the path toward the sea. “Where are they going?” Marion asked as she jiggled the mewing Larona.

“To the beach for explorations,” Katherine said.

After tea was served, the poor babe continued to whine. “How old is she?” Katherine asked.

“Two months.” Marion sighed.

Concern swept through Katherine. She appeared too tiny to be two months old. “May I hold her?”

Marion passed her to Katherine, who placed a hand on Larona's slowly beating heart. With a tug on her emotions, she felt an immediate connection to this lethargic soul not long in this world. “Has she had a fever?”

“A slight one.” Marion shook her head. “The doctors don't know what's wrong.”

Alfred sighed and reached for his wife's hand. “She wakes at all hours of the night. We've tried three nannies.”

“They've all resigned. Maybe afraid of what might happen,” Marion spoke softly.

Katherine thought if Larona lived here in the nursery with a loving godmother, she'd surely thrive.

Pierce came up the steps toward Katherine. “Any luck with the boys?” she asked.

“Still looking.” He shook his head and returned the way he came.

“What boys?” Alfred asked.

“Ones playing hide-and-seek. It appears they've hidden too well.” Katherine didn't want to raise more worry. “How about a tour?” she said. “Leave Larona with me. She's sleeping now.” Katherine motioned George Gowsell, the Lomaland forester, over. “Please show Mr. and Mrs. Robinson the grounds, including Casa Rosa's health center and nursery.” Katherine smiled at the couple. "You must see our godmothers, who devote their whole hearts to our babies."

The next morning Pierce came up to her Homestead office. The sound of hammers and saws echoed up from the rotunda. They'd been at it since dawn. Maybe building desks between the pillars for the Theosophical press hadn't been such a good idea after all.

"Where were the Cuban boys?" she yelled over the racket.

Pierce shouted back, "Smoking on the cliffs."

"What?" She couldn't hear what he said. Pierce pantomimed smoking.

She opened her mouth to speak. The cacophony from below rose again, so she wrote on a piece of paper: *What did you tell them?*

He took her pencil: *To put them out and join the group.*

She wrote: *Ask the workers to stop for the day. I can't think.*

Pierce wrote: *They won't finish in time. In a few days we need to move from the downtown rental.*

She'd just need to make do. The next day she looked in on Miss Wood's classroom, but the Cuban boys weren't there.

"They haven't been here for a week," the teacher said.

"Ethel, you're a gem," Katherine said. "I'm sure our Raja Yoga system will win the way to prepare them to be a credit to Cuba. I'll get them here."

Carmen brought the three boys to Katherine before supper. They slouched before her with messy hair.

She asked, "Are you happy here?"

Victor, the tallest, who already needed a shave, said, "No."

"Why not?"

He shrugged and rubbed his scraggly whiskers. "*Es estúpido*."

"You aren't." Katherine felt sorry for the boy. She opened her arms to him, but he stepped back.

Carmen told her, "Señora Tingley, I believe Victor meant school is stupid."

Katherine felt her face redden. "Go to class and learn what you can." The boys nodded; however, she sensed they didn't plan to go and sent them off for a late supper.

Chapter Seventy-One

"Let's take these down to the library." Katherine handed Carmen a pile of books and grabbed an armful for herself. It was early February—way past time to organize the suite.

"Madame, you keep sorting, and I'll carry them down in batches," Carmen said.

"No. It'll go faster if we both do it," she insisted and led the way out of the room.

Spots jumped off his pillow and slowly trailed them to the grand staircase. "Be careful, Señora," Carmen warned.

Arms full, Katherine descended a few steps, couldn't see, and lost her balance. She screamed as books flew and she tumbled down the steep stairs, landing in a heap at the bottom with a loud crack.

Carmen threw down her books and ran to Katherine. "Are you okay?"

Katherine nodded and tried to sit up. Dizzy and in pain, she winced, lay back, and breathed deeply, trying to dissipate the agony. Press staff crowded around her. Gertie van Pelt, teachers, and pupils ran out of their classrooms and huddled around her too.

"Don't move! I'll get Dr. Wood." Junior ran outside.

Spots curled up next to Katherine, and a small girl started to wail.

"Come here, little one." Even through her pain, or maybe because of it, she reached out to the child and hugged her.

"Where does it hurt?" Gertie sat beside Katherine and took her hand.

"Everywhere."

Dr. Wood arrived within minutes with his black bag. He reached for her leg, but she shrieked, and he stopped. "You must've broken something. Gentlemen, carry her to her room."

Four men carried her upstairs. Carmen pulled back the bedclothes, fluffed Katherine's pillow, and the men laid her gently on the bed.

"Rest now," Dr. Wood said.

She closed her eyes in excruciating pain, unable to discern the doctor's hall conversation.

Dr. Wood returned. "You know I usually only use herbal remedies. In this case, we all agree it's necessary to use something stronger." He removed a tincture from his bag and deposited a few drops in a glass of water on her nightstand. "We'll start poultice treatments right away."

Everyone left except Carmen who sat quietly by Katherine. The agony was so terrible she feared she might die. How could she have been so stupid as to fall down the stairs? Why hadn't she listened to sweet Carmen's warning? That dear girl would never say *I told you so.* This was the worst possible time to be laid up. There was so much to be done. After a while, the medicine started to take effect. She floated in and out of consciousness until she fell into a deep sleep.

The next day Dr. Wood reapplied poultices and asked how she felt. She eked out a smile.

"You'll take the medication daily and continue bedrest until I give the okay." He gave her another dose, lifted Spots onto the bed, and left.

Katherine stroked her dog's smooth back. "Honey, we're both getting old."

A few days later Minnie Neresheimer sat beside her. "How're you holding up, dear?"

Katherine said, "I can't just lie around. I have so much to do."

"Maybe this is God's way of telling you to take a break, no pun intended."

Katherine didn't smile.

Minnie asked, "Would you like me to read to you?"

"No, maybe another day. I'll just rest."

Minnie patted her hand. "Good idea. You'll soon need to prepare for the suit."

That blasted suit! It had been months since her lawyers had filed, and there still wasn't a court date. She hoped Otis would finally see his errors and settle out of court.

A few minutes later Carmen told her Mr. Pierce wanted a word.

"The Cuban boys have been making rude comments to Miss Wood and using foul language. What shall we do?" he asked.

Katherine wished she could fly down to the school and reprimand the boys herself. "Have Dr. van Pelt move them to a male teacher's class and have Nere add them to the choir. If they don't shape up soon, we'll ship them back to Cuba. Bacardi should have never brought them to me—" She was rambling, her mind muddled from the medicine. She'd cut back on it soon. She closed her eyes to let Pierce know he was excused. She couldn't think. She couldn't meditate. She couldn't stand it. Her medicated mind spun with the commotion echoing from the rotunda; press typewriters, classroom clamors, even outside noises drove her senseless.

On Monday, a week after the fall, her swelling and pain had diminished. Dr. Wood examined her and gave the bad news. "You've badly bruised your hip and probably fractured a foot. You'll be laid up for quite a while." That was what he thought; she vowed to be healed in no time.

Carmen finished brushing Katherine's hair, and Joe entered the room. "Has a trial date been set?" she asked.

"No. I've got news, though. Fisher won't be able to hang on much longer. It's likely the opera house will go on the market."

"Jump on it." She smiled. Finally, some good news! "Find out what you can and give me an update. Let's put in an offer before anyone else snaps it up. What about the barley fields?"

"Nothing yet."

"Let's buy them too. I want our Theosophical holdings to go all the way to the bay!"

Joe shook his head. "Katherine, it's not even for sale. Plus, we could never afford both properties."

"It's all part of our destiny." She raised her voice. "The resources will come."

He looked at her strangely. "You're overwrought. Are you still taking your medication?"

Had she been blathering again? She yawned. "I'm tired now. Look into both."

"Don't get your hopes up," he said and walked out the door.

For weeks, Katherine lingered in bed, still on the medication.

Philo sent her a letter:

Dear Kitten, I'm sorry about your accident and hope you're feeling better. I'd train out but I'm in the middle of creating my best invention ever. It's taking up all my time and energy. You know I care about you. Love, your husband, Philo

He'd included a detailed patent sketch. She couldn't make hide nor hair of it. In addition, he'd sent her a caricature he'd drawn of her lying in a bed with a frown on her face, messy hair, and bandaged leg slung up into the air, with enormous toes sticking out in a hilarious way. That made her smile. He'd watercolored the coverlet purple. She told herself it was probably best he wasn't there to see her in this state anyway.

By the end of February, a month after her fall, Joe told her the barley fields' owner wanted to sell and the opera house was going on the market too. He emphasized again it was impossible to buy both. She told him to go away, and she'd think on it.

That afternoon she received a letter.

Dear Madame Tingley:

Marion and I have decided to move to Lomaland with Larona. Is there a cottage available with a sea view? Do you know of a Point Loma property we can purchase for rosebushes and to raise my prize chickens?

Sincerely, Alfred Robinson

She told Joe to wire Alfred about the barley fields and send Nere to her.

"We must have the opera house," she told Nere. "It will be a money-making investment. We wouldn't need to pay rent for Sunday evening presentations; we could perform Greek and Shakespeare plays there and continue to book traveling shows like Fisher. The Isis Conservatory could hold classes there, and they could rent out rooms to others. Someday we might even host an art gallery inside."

"You've convinced me." Nere smiled. "I'm happy to loan the organization funds for it."

Within a few weeks, they bought the opera house for seventy thousand dollars. She had Joe hire a manager, honor all current bookings, and keep the cash flowing in.

Voices and the grating *clickety-clacks* of typewriters from downstairs continued to float up to her room. Finally, she asked for Pierce. "I can't concentrate here. I need you to build me a house."

"But we fixed this suite to your desires. Press will be moved as soon as our South Ranch is finished. Are you taking your medication?"

She glared at him. "I've considered this for quite some time. I need privacy and peace."

"Do you have a location in mind?" he asked.

"The eucalyptus grove north of the Spaldings'. Draw up plans as soon as possible."

One week later he returned and rolled drawings out on the coverlet beside her. "These are grand," she said. "Let me see the inside depictions."

Pierce flipped over the page, and she frowned. "The stairs need to have a sturdy handrail and shallow risers."

"Seven inches is standard size." He frowned.

"Make them five." She never wanted to fall again. "As you well know, archaeologists have discovered ancient Mayans built pyramid steps shorter to match their small statures. I insist you do the same. Start as soon as possible."

Chapter Seventy-Two

Two months after the accident, May weather warmed the day. Even though Katherine's foot ached and she couldn't put weight on it, she decided to wean herself off the medicine. Dr. Wood agreed and prescribed crutches, fresh air, and stress avoidance.

Carmen carried Katherine's chair out to the flourishing poppy field above the cliffs and helped her limp out on crutches. "Leave me, dear," Katherine told her.

"Wave if you need me." Carmen said while she adjusted Katherine's sunbonnet.

Under the sapphire blue sky and golden sun, Katherine gazed out at the rumbling sea, attempting to let nature soothe her soul. She breathed in and out, trying to meditate, but worries intruded. Nere had told her the Cuban boys were doing fine but she suspected that might not be the case. Pierce hadn't started building the north house for her yet.

Worst of all, the *Los Angeles Times* continued to spread yellow journalism rumors about her and Lomaland and used all sorts of tactics to delay the trial. Otis conducted a poll to determine how San Diegans felt about him to ask for a change of venue. It was his own fault locals were prejudiced against him for calling it a backwater town. The venue change had been denied. Lawyers reapplied, and time had dragged on. Now the date had been set for the end of the month. She'd feel better within the next two weeks and planned the opera house dedication for the positive publicity it would create.

On the appointed day, the carriage drove her by the front to see the

Fisher Opera House sign over the arched entrance had been replaced by a sign for the Isis Theater, but even so, her throbbing foot, the rumors still filling newspapers, and the upcoming trial had set a pall over her emotions. Her carriage pulled around to the back door before the audience flowed in. Carmen helped her hobble with crutches to sit onstage surrounded by the mass of plants and bouquets like a wilted rose instead of making a grand entrance.

While the children performed and others presented their speeches, she worried she'd trip and fall on her way to the podium. She imagined nasty headlines: Tingley Takes a Tumble, Former Fisher Flops as Tingley Falls Face First, and later, if her new business venture didn't succeed: Isis in Crisis.

Instead of speaking at the dais, she chose to orate from her seat. "This isn't simply the dedication of a building; here souls will find an atmosphere conducive to the well-being of mankind. We'll come together to understand ourselves, make the theater a new center, a new joy, and a new divinity for all time." She'd planned to say much more, but exhaustion overpowered her. She only wanted to get home to bed. She nodded at Nere to reprise the music and perform the finale.

In the morning, she woke with a cold and a swollen foot. She stayed in bed and read the papers. Her spirits lifted to see the *San Diego Union* didn't mention anything about her. Glowing reports praised the ambiance and music. But she frowned when she saw the *Los Angeles Times* piece that sniped at everything from the new name to her ill appearance.

Over the course of a few days, her congestion worsened, and Joe came to her. "Otis's lawyers have applied for a continuance. Evidently, many of his witnesses have declined to testify." Katherine smiled.

Pierce entered. "Some of Minnie's jewelry is missing!"

"Not her emerald pendant, I hope." Katherine had often admired the piece.

"I'm sure it's just been misplaced," Joe said.

"The Neresheimers have looked everywhere. What should we do?" Pierce asked.

She blew her stuffy nose and closed her eyes. A few nights before, while the couple had been out late at the theater, Katherine had heard voices in the hallway near their suite. She now remembered they'd been speaking Spanish. "You'd better search Victor's bungalow."

Pierce returned an hour later. "You were right. We found the pendant, a string of pearls, and a diamond ring underneath newspaper in the cockatoo's birdcage. Do you want to talk to Victor? His amigos were in on it too."

"Like this? I'm still in my bedclothes." She tried to raise her voice but started coughing. "Have Nere speak with them."

After supper, Pierce ran in with a wild look on his face. "Victor pulled a knife on Nere!"

She put a hand on her chest. "Is he okay?"

"He's only shook up. Should I contact Sheriff Jennings?"

"Send Nere to me." If parents found out about the incorrigible boys, they'd withdraw their children from the school, papers would have a field day with it, and Lomaland's reputation would be marred even more. She'd hoped nurturing would evolve them into higher selves. No matter how much love and affection they'd been given, it had been to no avail. Had early trauma affected them so deeply? Witnessing war atrocities? Or had negative inescapable karma enveloped their psyches?

Katherine said to Nere, "We've done all we can. The boys must be sent back to Cuba. We'll need to get the sheriff involved. Have it occur quietly—and soon, before the trial."

"Give them another chance," Nere pled. "Let me try again. Mario has begun to show signs of courtesy and musical talent."

"To keep everyone safe, they need to go," she said sadly.

Nere hung his head as he left her.

Before they could move forward, George the forester visited her. "May I move the boys up with me to the top corner of the property? I'll keep them occupied with tree maintenance, athletics, and a few academics."

"Are you certain? It's a big responsibility." She'd observed George had a special way with others.

He said, "You often speak of spreading kindness. Ten years back someone gave me another chance, and I'd like to offer one to these boys."

Touched, Katherine accepted his proposal with the caveat they were no longer to have contact with Raja Yoga pupils and warned if they misbehaved again, they'd be sent back to Cuba. And on top of it all, she'd just sent Gertie to Cuba to escort more orphans to Lomaland. She had been right to insist only younger children be chosen.

Chapter Seventy-Three

Autumn had cooled, and as the winter solstice approached, sunlight shifted to shorten the days. The crescent moon, a Civil War saber, hung in the evening sky. Carmen helped Katherine drape her purple sari while preparing for her usual Sunday talk at the Isis Theater. A far-off coyote howled below the Egyptian Gate to the south. Katherine shivered.

Joe knocked and hurried in. "Elizabeth called. She's with A.G. in New York to greet the Cuban children. They've been locked in an Ellis Island cell."

Katherine sat on the bed. "What? Why?"

"A board of inquiry has been called to deport them."

"I'm sure they'll be let go soon. Are the children all right?" she asked.

"The authorities won't allow the Spaldings to see them, but Gertie is with them. The *New York Sun* reported thousands of Santiago Cubans protested with hate-filled slogans and burned American flags. They claimed the orphans were taken without permission and ordered our government to return them or else the Spanish-American War would reignite."

"That's impossible." Katherine didn't want Carmen to hear more about this trouble in her homeland and said to her, "Please tell Dr. Coryn to speak in my stead tonight."

As soon as Carmen left, Katherine said, "We're Cuba's friend. It's hard to believe they'd demonstrate against us."

"What shall we do?" Joe asked.

"Call the Spaldings. Have A.G. do all he can. I'll contact my lawyers and

Mayor Bacardi." If Katherine got on a train now, by the time she arrived all this would be solved. Plus using crutches continued to be a challenge, and the libel trial, after another postponement, was scheduled to begin in a few weeks. She'd need to manage this situation from afar. After a sleepless night, she received a reply cable from Bacardi that the orphans had left Santiago under the most pleasant of circumstances. Who would make up such a story? And why?

By the end of the day, he cabled a letter of support from himself and other Cuban dignitaries. It should do the trick, especially the part that read:

> *In the name of our people, we demand the Cuban children be instantly released to Dr. van Pelt to proceed to Point Loma. Without her being subjected to meddling or outrageous interference. We've cabled the Cuban minister in Washington to protest to the Immigration Board.*

San Diego's mayor and school superintendent also sent epistles to the board praising Lomaland and Katherine. A.G. took all the letters to Ellis Island, but the children still weren't released.

Elizabeth called the next afternoon to tell Katherine a hearing by the board of inquiry had taken place, conducted by none other than Commodore Eldridge Thomas Gerry, New York's founder of the SPCC—the Society for the Prevention of Cruelty to Children.

"That old coot?" Katherine said. "He wasn't ever in the navy, and his title's from yachting. In New York, I witnessed him pull children from their parents just because he could."

Elizabeth told her, "He pontificated horrible accusations against Lomaland and asked A.G. the most ridiculous questions. Does Madame Tingley consider herself the second coming of Christ? Does she say little lotus buds marry and produce children? Is Spots a reincarnated human soul?" Katherine would have laughed if it wasn't such a dire situation. "A.G. countered if all that were true, he wouldn't have enrolled his own children there."

Elizabeth continued, "The board refused to allow his attorneys to cross-examine witnesses or call in their own because it's a hearing, not a trial. The Immigration Board still recommends deportation."

As the hearing dragged on, papers were rife with rumors and gossip against Katherine. Anyone who wanted to testify against her was allowed to do so. She expected attacks by rival Theosophists. But the clergy, the *Los Angeles Times,* and now Gerry's SPCC with similar lies? It was all too much. Certain there was a conspiracy out to destroy her, she ended up back in bed, flat on her back with body aches.

As she read the articles, she realized her worst fears had come to the forefront: A testimonial letter written by her first husband, who'd been dead for years, said she'd been an unfit wife and he'd been forced to divorce her. A landlady stated Katherine and Philo sold faith cures and were evicted for nonpayment of rent and scurried away with creditors on their heels. A Lomaland bookkeeper she'd let go for alcohol consumption said, "If anyone goes against her, she uses occult powers to seek revenge." A smidgen of truth was mixed in with the exaggerated lies.

Katherine's lawyers received an Otis trial delay and contacted California Governor Gage to request an official, unbiased Lomaland investigation. President Roosevelt himself sent Frank P. Sargent, United States Commissioner General of Immigration, to San Diego to conduct the inspection.

In a tizzy, the cabinet wanted to roll out the red carpet, but Katherine nixed it. She said, "Aren't you proud of all we've accomplished? Let's treat him like any other eminent visitor we've had." She wasn't as confident as she sounded.

The day before Sargent was scheduled to arrive, Joe came to her again. "I've just gotten word Gerry has directed the San Francisco branch of the SPCC to train down here and take all our children away."

Katherine commanded, "Go to city hall and apply for a restraining order against those San Franciscans. Then gather prominent San Diegans and start a local SPCC branch for precedence."

She wished to conduct the inspector's tour herself, but since she was still using the horrible crutches, she decided not to. So Junior guided Sargent around the property, ending at the Homestead. The wind had picked up, so instead of meeting with Katherine on the porch he was to be escorted upstairs to her office.

She fingered her grandfather's watch and waited. This would be the most important interview of her life. She could lose all the children. As Sargent entered with his neatly parted hair, toothbrush mustache, and cleft chin, she rose slowly, holding on to the sofa's side. She shook the large man's cold hand and slid back down. He sat in the chair she proffered him as Junior stood behind him at attention.

"That will be all," Katherine said. Junior smiled at her with encouragement.

Inspector Sargent didn't turn around and thank the boy as he left. That wasn't a good sign. He didn't need to be kind, but she hoped he'd be fair and impartial. She tried to keep her hands from shaking as she poured tea, placed a cup in front of him, and offered sugar and cream. He shook his head, opened his notebook, and jotted down notes. Light reflected off his glasses as he scanned the room. He wrote again in his book.

Fortunately, while Katherine had been laid up after her accident, Carmen had finished straightening the office. Sargent studied Machell's esoteric painting and scribbled again. Expressionless, he scrutinized her and jotted. He cleared his throat and began, "You've been accused of being financially irresponsible, creating a vile atmosphere, and being morally incompetent. I've studied the books with Mr. Neresheimer."

"I'm sure you've seen all's in order and we have the means to provide for many children." She kept her voice steady.

The inspector said, "The tour provided me with many interesting eyewitness facts and impressions." He patted his notebook.

Like what? she wanted to ask. "I hope you were pleased with what you've seen."

He stared at her. "I'm left now to determine if the third accusation is valid—that you're morally incompetent."

Tongue-tied, she stared back at him.

"Well, what do you have to say for yourself?" he asked.

She took a sip of tea and nibbled a cookie. There had been so many lies spoken about her; she worried she'd never be able to erase them from this man's mind. "About what?"

He sighed loudly and flipped through notebook pages. "Why aren't the children allowed to talk to each other?"

"They are at specified times. Did you eat with them in the refectory? They're taught to eat properly, to fold their hands after every mouthful, chew well, and eat slowly. It promotes digestion. A healthy body is the vessel for a properly functioning mind. God is always calling out to us. If we aren't quiet, we won't hear him. Do you ever need silence to think?"

He wrote the entire time she talked.

"Is it true you lock up the children at night?"

"Of course not," she blurted, then quieted her voice. "Each child lives in a warm home filled with other students their age and a loving adult."

"If a child is bad, what do you do?"

"Sadly, children through the ages have been labeled incorrigible and punished. Lomaland children aren't punished. I believe all are born with goodness, and the staff provides a path to let that emerge. They're taught self-control and alertness and to have self-respect. A little one having a bad day might be told to look in a mirror to see how unappealing that is. Occasionally, a child will be separated from the group for a few minutes. That's all. Our Miss Wood sometimes even plays the piano to soothe misbehavior."

Sargent kept writing in his book. She had to stop rambling. She folded her hands and looked at him.

"I saw some children doing menial tasks," Sargent said.

"Yes, everyone here has duties. The children garden, sweep, clean, assist with the elderly, and do kitchen labor."

"Do they do anything for fun?"

"Learning is fun. Don't you think? We teach art and music as part of the curriculum, which the students doubly enjoy. School is over by one, and afternoons they bathe at the beach, play tennis, baseball, and basketball. Our faculty are accomplished in their fields and have other responsibilities as well, like leading nature walks, directing gardening projects, and providing private tutorials."

"I notice there wasn't a line item in the financial records for staff. How do you pay them?"

"We provide room and board and anything else they might need. In fact, many of them pay us to live here. Some have given all they have."

"One last question. Do you hypnotize or use occult means to receive money from men or to cause revenge?"

"No, sir." She kept her voice calm. "A true Theosophist conducts their life as though each moment is the most precious. They keep an endless festival in their heart and live with joy of service to others. I sense you live that way also." Katherine smiled at him.

He closed his notebook and frowned at her. Then he stood up and shook her hand. "Goodbye," he said and walked out the door. Her emotions plunged. All was lost. The children on Ellis Island would be sent back, her students here rounded up, and she'd be shut down.

The following day Sheriff Jennings stood by as the San Francisco branch of the SPCC showed up at the gate, were shown the restraining order, and told to leave.

For a week, gloomy clouds outside Katherine's windows blew around Lomaland to match her mood. A few days passed before Elizabeth called. "They're free!" she said. "Sargent submitted a five-page report to President Roosevelt stating he'd observed healthy children, immaculate buildings and grounds, with a physician always on duty. And that the learning capacity of even the youngest impressed him by reciting poetry and speeches with perfect diction and obvious comprehension. And he recommended their release."

What a relief! After almost two months of incarceration, the Cuban orphans had been freed. Word was out that Commodore Gerry planned to nab them if they touched New York soil. So A.G. chartered a yacht, collected them at Ellis Island, and shepherded them to a New Jersey train station. They were safely on their way to California.

Chapter Seventy-Four

On Tuesday, December 16, two weeks after the Cuban children reached Lomaland, Katherine woke in a Brewster Hotel room as Carmen put a breakfast tray on the bed. "Time to rise. The carriage will be here soon," she said and opened the curtains.

"I can't." Katherine felt ghastly and hadn't slept a wink. The strain of worrying about the orphans and the impending trial had hampered her health. Recently, suspicious characters spotted peering over Lomaland's six-foot wall had made her fret even more. Were they *Times* agents? She had the girls move from their bungalows across the road back to the Homestead's safety. Pierce's request for police patrols had been denied, so her men remained vigilant.

For a year, she'd wanted this trial to start. Now that the day was here, she felt trepidation. Even though Otis and his *Times-Mirror Company* were the ones being sued, she'd been warned his attorneys would try to make it seem as though she were the one on trial.

"Your lawyers say you must." Carmen grasped Katherine's hand and helped her sit up. With her head still congested and a throbbing foot as big as a whale, she wanted nothing more than to lie back down. Outside the window, the distant Cuyamaca Mountains were covered in snow. She wished she was up there far away. If she lost this case, she'd be abandoned and have nothing left but the eternal sea, dying gardens, and empty white buildings.

Carmen held up Katherine's purple suit. "It's your favorite."

It wouldn't be appropriate to look so fancy, and besides, it was too constrictive for the long day ahead. She shook her head. "I'll wear the black frock."

Carmen squinted with a confused expression. "You've always told us to look our best."

Katherine's face softened. "It'll be fine. You'll roll my hair nicely, like you always do."

Carmen twisted a bun at the back of Katherine's head and pinned a simple hat atop it. A man-sized sock was the only thing to fit over her engorged foot. She leaned on a crutch, and they made their way to the lobby. Drizzle fell as the carriage collected them at the hotel entrance and drove the few blocks to the courthouse.

Katherine hobbled along the slippery footpath, into the building, and up the stairs.

"Today's the day," Joe greeted them with a smile as he took her arm, and with Carmen on the other side, they escorted Katherine through the double doors. The spectators turned and stared at her. She focused on her foot and winced with each step. The front of the room seemed a mile away.

A familiar pair of shoes caught her attention. She glanced up and returned Philo's wave with a dip of her head. What was he doing here? Had he come to testify against her? Was that why he hadn't replied to her recent letters? Had Otis's men appealed to Philo's craving for cash? He knew many of her secrets, had even been the cause of some. How could he betray her in this way after all she'd done for him? She'd made sure Nere took care of the annual patent applications, as William had promised.

Joe helped her sit in a thick padded chair at the plaintiff's table, and Pierce pulled up the matching footstool for her injured leg. Embarrassed, she felt like a character in a Molière play. From the other table, Harrison Gray Otis glared at her and chewed his walrus mustache. He'd often been quoted as saying: *Everybody liked to see somebody else kicked below the belt.* And kicked her he had. After he set his sights on someone to abuse, he never let up.

She wanted to love this enemy, but after all he'd published about her, it was impossible. Yellow journalism was his specialty; selling papers made him rich. How had the cabinet convinced her to sue him for libel? There was no way she'd ever win a case against such a powerful man represented by the five most prominent attorneys in the land.

Her reputation was on the line, and Lomaland's future teetered in the balance. She had to remind herself that was why. She didn't care a hoot about the fifty thousand dollars she'd requested.

Judge Torrance nodded at her from the bench. She'd heard he was modest, mild-mannered, and fair. With his neatly trimmed beard and kind eyes, she had a warm feeling about him, until he gnawed on a mouthful of tobacco and expectorated it with a *ting* into the cuspidor under his bench. Dear Lord!

All afternoon her attorneys excused a potential juror only to have Otis's lawyers excuse another. They argued San Diegans would be partial to Madame Tingley and shouldn't be allowed on the jury. How was a jury going to be found with all the slander against her? Many believed everything they read. Without making progress, the court adjourned for the day. Carmen guided Katherine to the carriage and climbed in beside her.

"Hello, honey." Philo jumped in too.

"What are you doing here?" Katherine snapped.

He blinked. "I came to support you."

Relief set into her body. She hadn't seen him in over two years, and they'd parted on good terms. Why had she thought he'd deceive her? It seemed as if she didn't trust anyone anymore.

"I apologize." She put her hand on his. "It's been rough. Thank you for coming."

"Word is after Otis took one look at you, he told his attorneys his goose was cooked."

"Had he expected me to wear a tiara and a purple robe?" Katherine smiled at Carmen.

They laughed and Philo proceeded to describe his newest invention, a whirligig of sorts. His detailed explanations with hand gestures made Carmen giggle sweetly. These elucidations used to bore Katherine, but she found them refreshing after the day's grueling jury disputes. Even so, she declined his dinner invitation and ate alone in her room.

By the end of the next day, a dozen bewhiskered men from the backcountry had been chosen for the panel. One was so large he could barely fit into his chair, another wore an eyepatch, and another had flowing hair down past his shoulders like Wild Bill Hickok. These rural jurors lived close to nature; perhaps they'd be sympathetic to some of her practices.

On Thursday, Frederic R. Kellogg, her New York lawyer, stood in front of Otis and began the opening statement to impart the burden of proof, "We shall prove that on October 28, 1901, Editor-in-chief Harrison Gray Otis and the *Los Angeles Times* published an article wickedly, maliciously, and with intent to injure, disgrace, and defame the plaintiff." W.J. Hunsaker provided the defense's opening statement. It turned out none of the women in the article had agreed to testify, so he spouted a lot of mumbo jumbo about Katherine's supposed practices.

J. W. McKinley, her Los Angeles attorney, chosen because he ranked number one on Otis's hit list, stood and stroked his slate-colored beard. She wanted to crawl under the table and hide as he read and filed twenty-one evidential clippings dating back years with disparaging remarks against her: *She was a hypnotist who bilked the rich, brainwashed disciples, and hosted all-night orgies.* Otis had even printed: *I'll destroy the city beautiful on the hill.* At the end of the day, she returned to the hotel, refused to eat, and collapsed into bed before the sun had set.

The following morning McKinley stood and shouted, "I call General Otis to the stand."

The large man jumped up, his long coat wrinkled, and plodded to the stand. His eyes gleamed daggers at McKinley. Her attorney would really give it to him. No matter what Otis said, it would all be lies.

McKinley asked, "Sir, what is the circulation of the *Los Angeles Times*?"

Otis sat up smugly. "Twenty-eight thousand."

"And what is its overall worth?"

"Almost a million." Otis smiled at the jury.

"No more questions, Your Honor," McKinley said.

Was that it? Katherine thought this testimony would go on for hours. His attorneys chose not to cross-examine. Otis scowled at them as he made his way back to his seat. Were they afraid he'd perjure himself? Torrance chewed, spat under his bench, and nodded again to her table.

Kellogg patted her hand and whispered, "We've decided not to call you today after all."

"Why?" she asked.

"It's not necessary."

Her attorneys questioned Joe, Nere, and Pierce, and each shared how the article was false and greatly affected Katherine's health and demeanor. Otis's lawyers chose not to cross-examine. His lead attorney, Samuel M. Shortridge, the silver-tongued orator of the Pacific, in his fancy striped suit with a diamond-studded tie pin, called Louis B. Fitch to the stand.

Her former bookkeeper avoided her eyes as he made his way to the witness stand and was sworn in. He scratched his bulbous nose and answered the first question, "I have no conflict with Madame Tingley. I have a citizen's duty to tell the truth. Though a woman of great executive ability and charisma, she's very changeable. Told me she'd had powers to stay in the spirit world but chose to be reincarnated into this world to relieve the suffering of all mankind."

As Shortridge asked Fitch questions, Katherine's attorneys objected time and again, but the judge allowed Fitch to blather on for hours. That man would say anything to make money to buy his whiskey. Would the judge and jury really believe his absurd fabrications?

On McKinley's cross-examination, Fitch admitted he'd sent letters to San Diego clergy, Commodore Gerry, and Mr. Otis offering to sell evidence against her. At the end of the day, Judge Torrance struck most of Fitch's statements from the record.

She returned to Lomaland for the weekend, drained but hopeful the judge was on her side, and perhaps the jury too. However, on Sunday, the *Times* published all of Fitch's stricken testimony with these headlines: *Sacred Dog Spots Slips His Collar: Canine Possessed of Departed Man's Soul. Fitch's Deposition Hot Stuff.*

On Monday, her attorneys accused Otis of misconduct. The judge let it slide. He must not be on her side after all.

Shortridge called Henry Ruethling, a short, reedy man with oily hair and buck teeth, to the stand.

"I saw plainly the woman had impure intentions," he said.

Katherine wrote a note and passed it to McKinley: *Never seen him in my life.*

Shortridge asked, "What do you mean by impure?"

"Her suggestions were of a physical nature."

"What do you mean?" Shortridge raised his eyebrows at the jury.

"No woman would directly ask a man to do such a thing."

"Explain, so we all understand." Shortridge rolled his hands toward the witness.

Mr. Ruethling paused, then went on, "I understood it as a desire for sexual intercourse."

Voices from the spectator gallery erupted. Katherine hung her head in mortification.

The judge hammered his gavel and spat into his spittoon. "Silence!" He glared at the defense table. "I've had enough! A party has a right to appear without the courtroom converted into a place where people can slander others. Step down, sir."

Shortridge called another witness. "Tell the court your occupation and city you reside in."

"I'm a detective from Boston."

McKinley jumped to his feet. "Objection! This man isn't on the witness list."

What had he learned?

Torrance asked, "What's the nature of the testimony? If this is more information about Mrs. Tingley's past, I'll disallow it."

"But Your Honor—" Shortridge raised his arms.

The judge told the detective, "You're excused."

What a relief.

Griscom, Hargrove's minion, testified he'd been on Mrs. Tingley's cabinet for several years and witnessed her mysterious incantations many times. "She's hoodwinked many to believe she has special powers and took over leadership of the Theosophical Society by nefarious means." Katherine heard Hargrove's words in Griscom's declarations.

Shortridge called Dr. Anderson from San Francisco. He stared at her defiantly as he walked to the bench. She didn't understand. As one of her most avid supporters, he'd even cried when she shared her plan to add the word *brotherhood* to the organization's name.

He began his testimony, "I've seen men of wealth, education, and high social position humble themselves before her, wearing long gowns and ridiculous hats. I stood by her as long as I could but had to leave to retain my manhood." He claimed she starved the children. He said she was fat, erratic, and a megalomaniac. These insults were more than a prick. Other testimonies, even though damaging, had been quite silly. Anderson's, though, were downright hurtful.

The judge told him to describe what he'd observed, not the conclusions he'd drawn. Nevertheless, Anderson continued to ridicule her. Time and again her attorneys objected. The judge sustained some and overruled others.

Despite his reprimands, counsel for the defense produced more witnesses testifying against her. After days of unsubstantiated allegations, Judge Torrance tried to refocus the testimony. "We're only here to determine if statements made against Mrs. Tingley in the October article are true or not." He raised his voice. "We're not here to decide if Theosophy is a correct philosophy. I do not care what it is, and the jurors oughtn't either. Court is dismissed until after the new year." After two weeks of legal sparring, she was relieved for a break.

Even though most of the testimony had been struck, newspapers all over the country continued to publish libelous allegations over the holidays. Usually, Christmas was her favorite time of year. This yuletide, nothing could raise her spirits. Not the beloved music, children's pageant, or Machell dressed as Santa handing out presents. Not even Philo's efforts could cheer her. One saving grace was that right after Christmas, Pierce and the workers completed building the North House to her specifications and moved her possessions there.

Last New Year she'd predicted 1902 would be the best year of her life. Instead it had been the opposite: the fall down the stairs, her illness, the Cuban boys a danger, the orphans in Ellis Island, and now the Otis trial. Didn't anyone realize the good she was trying to do? She felt like Sisyphus pushing a boulder up the hill.

Chapter Seventy-Five

January 1903

On New Year's afternoon, Katherine greeted the adult residents as they gathered in North House's drawing room. Outside the picture window, through the growing eucalyptus trees, the setting sun painted fuchsia and violet watercolor clouds above the sea. Her furniture had been arranged for the occasion and extra chairs brought in. Soon she'd embellish the room with paintings, photographs, and lace curtains.

"Katherine has a gift for each of you. Hot off our press," Thurston said as Carmen handed out copies of *The Mysteries of the Heart Doctrine*. "For sale this week, it should help fill the coffers and increase Theosophical understanding." Katherine hadn't contributed much to it but was proud of the book that explored the teachings of ancient wisdom, esoteric Eastern philosophy, and mystical traditions of the West. She hoped it would help readers understand the true nature of how the heart could be used as a tool for spiritual growth and transformation.

Joe opened the front door. "Katherine, we have a surprise for you too."

A bright light encircled the man who stepped inside. She hardly recognized him, as tears sprang to her eyes, and she stood. "Gottfried de Purucker!"

"Everyone calls me G. de P.," he said softly with outstretched hands and made his way to Katherine. She hadn't seen him in five years, but they'd corresponded often. Handsome with his wheat-colored hair, he must be about thirty now.

"The one who drew the Point Loma map in Switzerland?" Elizabeth asked.

"The very one." G. de P. smiled.

"Is it true you translated the entire New Testament from Greek at fourteen?" Nere called.

"My Anglican minister father was quite strict." G. de P. nodded. A chorus of welcomes echoed throughout the room.

"How long can you stay?" Katherine asked. Her visions predicted he might be her chosen one. She'd need plenty of time to prepare him to continue her legacy.

"Forever." He gazed into her eyes. "I've agreed to be your private secretary, if it's okay with you."

She hugged him. "I'd be delighted."

"More good news," said Alfred Robinson as he reached for his wife's hand. They'd recently moved into a Lomaland cottage. "I've purchased the barley fields. We'll plant roses and begonias and build a mansion there. Maybe someday Theosophists will own property all the way to the bay."

The room cheered.

"Not if we lose the case." Katherine sat down and lifted her sore foot up on a hassock. Carmen put Spots on her lap.

"Why would we lose?" Elizabeth asked. "It's obvious those men are lying."

Katherine sighed. "Some people are idiotic enough to believe those falsehoods."

"The judge and jury are smarter than that," Nere said.

"When I testify, they'll learn the truth."

Dr. Wood said, "The strain would be too much. Can't we say she's too ill?"

"I need to set the record straight once and for all." If she didn't and they lost, she'd regret it for the rest of her life.

"It will open things up. The defense will have no choice but to cross examine you." Philo said.

She raised her voice. "I don't care. Otis has been bullying people for far too long, ruining reputations and lives. It's got to stop."

"Not necessarily by you it doesn't." Joe shook his head.

After the group left, Katherine pulled herself up the short steps with the sturdy banister. Carmen helped her to bed and left for her room next door. Through Katherine's dormer window the waxing crescent moon appeared closer than ever. Ocean waves were louder here than at the Homestead. As she tossed and turned, a pair of owls hooted from the eucalyptus trees. Court would resume in the morning.

Chapter Seventy-Six

Even with the windows open, the jam-packed courtroom was stuffy. Women fanned themselves, gentlemen loosened their top buttons, and reporters' pens were ready. Philo smiled at Katherine near the front of the room, which was filled with Elizabeth, Pierce, G. de P., and many more Lomalanders.

Her cane shook as she limped to the witness box supported by Kellogg. He patted her hand and whispered, "You don't have to do this."

"I must." Katherine held her grandfather's watch in her lap and studied the signet ring. She prayed the spectators, judge, and jury would believe her.

Kellogg glanced at his notes and asked, "When you saw the October 28th article headlined 'Outrages at Point Loma, Women and Children Starved and Treated like Convicts, Thrilling Rescue,' how did you react?"

She tried to keep her voice from quivering. "I was very much shocked and suffered immensely."

Defense attorney Hunsaker objected, "The answer is immaterial."

Judge Torrance mumbled, "Overruled."

Katherine continued, "Unable to concentrate, I could only work half as much."

"When former members, local ministers, and the Society for the Prevention of Cruelty to Children criticized your ways, why weren't you affected? What was so different about this article?"

"If the stories were sensational, I told my secretary not to bring them to me. But the headline 'Outrages at Point Loma' caught my eye. I read it three times, and my shock was so severe that I couldn't recover myself. The horror of my children being starved in dungeons I could not eliminate from my mind. Those false descriptions gave me horrible nightmares, and I couldn't sleep for weeks."

"Thank you for your honesty." Kellogg sat.

Shortridge stood, removed his glasses, and asked, "Mrs. Tingley, do you consider Spots to contain the spirit of William Q. Judge?"

She'd been advised on cross-examination to stay calm, answer questions, and hope Judge Torrance kept the lawyers in line. "Spots is a special pet. I never told Mr. Fitch that Mr. Judge's spirit had entered my dog."

"But Fitch stated your members exhibited reverence toward the dog."

"I've never seen evidence of that. We love all our animals. In reincarnation, Theosophists believe once a human soul, always a human soul."

Shortridge changed the subject. "Did you make out a diet list for babies?"

"No, I only made suggestions to Dr. Wood to put cream into their meals to make them more nutritious and feed them every half hour instead of every two."

"And how did you discover this theory?"

She looked at the jury. "In my work with poor children on New York City's East Side."

"Did you on any occasion withhold food from a child for any length of time?"

"No."

McKinley stood. "Your Honor, unless counsel thinks of changing his diet, we're wasting time."

Laughter rippled through the courtroom. Torrance raised his gavel, and the noise quickly abated.

"Madame, have you ever been compared to Confucius, Buddha, and Muhammad?"

"No." She shook her head.

Shortridge raised an eyebrow at the jury and continued, "Are your people sunworshippers? Do they not get up in the morning and go out on a hill to worship like idolaters?"

She paused. Shortridge dabbed his forehead with a silk handkerchief. "Answer the question."

"All of us at Lomaland get up in the morning. Some very early. I have no doubt everyone sees the sun, but we don't worship it."

More laughter ensued, and this time Torrance thumped his gavel and insisted on order.

Shortridge asked about Greek gowns, pagan rituals, and armed guards. Her attorney's exceptions were all overruled, and she declaimed each. Then Shortridge raised the topic of separating children from their parents.

She said, "Parental love is important to a child's development. Raja Yoga is based on a home-school system. Most parents see their children on Sundays. Whenever they want to see them, all they do is ask."

"Didn't you tell Dr. Anderson that parents dote too much on their children, which stunts their spiritual growth?"

"I only remember telling him parents reported being delighted with the success of our work."

Later that afternoon Shortridge seemed frustrated by her calm answers and asked, "Do you send thought waves to your followers and the world?"

Katherine nodded. "Pure thoughts only. They make for a better world. I even send them to you and Mr. Otis in hopes it will improve your lives."

Shortridge replied, "That is, madame, if you ever had a pure thought."

The gallery filled with voices, and the judge banged his gavel, spat tobacco, and glared at Shortridge. The lawyer asked, "Why have you brought so many children to Point Loma?"

"What can be so wrong about raising children with healthy food, fresh air, and nature? Every child is a genius if rightly trained to use their gifts in the service of others." She turned to the jury. "I know some of my methods might seem odd to you, but I've brought the children here for a higher purpose."

"What purpose is that?" Shortridge raised his arms.

"To prepare them to go out into the world, do good for humanity, and be warriors for peace and justice."

He squinted at her. "Who asked you to do that?"

She intuitively responded, "I was chosen."

"What did you say?" He put his hands on his hips.

She raised her voice, "I was chosen."

Shortridge prompted. "Louder so even those in the back can hear you."

"I was chosen!" She had spoken her truth.

He smirked. "By whom?"

She paused and spoke to the jury again, "Some call it a higher power, others our Creator, and still others God."

Shortridge gawked. "No more questions, Your Honor." He took his seat, and Katherine was escorted back to her chair. At the end of the afternoon, which was further interrupted with numerous objections—of which there had been seven hundred in the total trial—the testimony concluded.

The next morning Kellogg spoke for over an hour in support of Katherine, refuting the slanderous lies and asking the jury to compensate her distress by requiring the defendants to pay the full fifty thousand dollars. He ended with, "It's not enough that a merely nominal recovery may vindicate the plaintiff's good name. Great issues are involved here. Katherine Tingley, as a worker for humanity, is demanding justice, at your hands."

Shortridge gently erased beads of sweat from his forehead with his silk handkerchief, rose from his chair, and pointed his glasses at the jury. "If, gentlemen, you believe in the Christian religion, your duty is clear. If you believe in the family circle and the hearth and fireside, your duty is plain." His voice rose. "If you believe in the institution of marriage of one man and one woman, your duty is clear."

He stopped and eyed each member of the jury. "In the name of society and civilization and in the name of the Savior of Nazareth, I ask for American justice. Christian society is at stake. The time will come when this case will be regarded as a blessing because it caused the abandonment of Madame Tingley's doctrines and power. She is an enemy of all that is good, noble, and pure in our lives." After his four-and-a-half-hour tirade, he sat down, and the court was adjourned.

In the morning the judge turned to the jury. "As you make your determination, do not take into account whether you believe Theosophy is a correct philosophy or whether Mrs. Tingley's ways are appropriate." He raised his voice. "Your only job is to ascertain if the article libeled her, and if so, what is the amount of compensatory damages she deserves."

A few hours later the jury returned to the courtroom, and the judge was handed the verdict. He scanned it quietly, looked up, and frowned at Katherine. She held her breath, ready for the devasting news. The authorities would take the children and close her down.

The courtroom was so quiet, a pin would have been heard if dropped. The judge chewed his tobacco, spat, and read aloud, "The jury finds the *Times-Mirror Company* and Harrison Gray Otis guilty of libel. They are to compensate her in the amount of seventy-five hundred dollars."

She didn't care that the amount was much less than requested. The jury believed she'd been treated wrongly—that was what mattered. Otis slumped and grimaced at her from the defense table. She nodded at him, and her heart opened with compassion. He turned and walked down the aisle. As relief set in, she thanked her attorneys, and her beloveds rushed to congratulate her.

Chapter Seventy-Seven

Miraculously, a few days after the verdict, the fog lifted from Katherine's body. Her fatigue vanished, and she walked without crutches along a Lomaland path. Her world was full of wonders. Lamblike clouds soared above the aqua ocean. Along the buildings' outskirts, century plants and pampas grasses swayed in the breeze. Quail scattered from within terra cotta–colored buckwheat. As twilight descended, the flags on the consecrated hill were lowered and the lantern raised. Roses, begonias, and sweet peas bloomed in the Lotus Garden. As she approached the temple, evening dew fell on her shoulders like angel kisses. She stepped through the open doors as the glass dome filtered an ethereal lavender glow throughout the space.

"Congratulations on the win," the boy lighting the lamps called. He crawled down the ladder and moved toward her with a hug.

"Thank you, Junior," she said.

"Mrs. Tingley, I'm thirteen now. Would you please stop calling me that?"

"Iverson, you've grown so tall." She reached up and ruffled his sand-colored hair, light from spending time in the airy sun. Remembering the first time she'd seen him, in his little Lord Fauntleroy suit, she laughed. Could that have been almost four years ago? Her first student resident, he'd always be Junior to her.

She smiled at him. "You're the ideal Raja Yoga student." She tried not to have favorites. With him, she couldn't help herself.

"You've taught us to do our best." He smiled.

"I hear you're the best in reading, spelling, and typewriting."

He shook his head. "I don't think I'm any better than others."

Her mind flashed ahead in time, and she saw him as a handsome man taking dictation from her. "Would you like to be one of my secretaries someday?"

"I'll say." He beamed and hugged her again. "Anything else I can do for you before I go?"

"Leave the doors open." She wanted to feel the ocean breeze.

"Adios," he said, folded the ladder, and carried it out.

This was the first time she'd been alone in the temple, and she gently circled the sacred space. The roar of far-off waves provided the music. Purple sequins of light danced down upon her from the cupola. Her body shifted into a calming peace.

In the room's center, the ornate chair Machell had carved for her beckoned. She sat comfortably on the pillow, held her grandfather's watch in her hands, and closed her eyes. Breathing in and out, she began to loosen her blocked chakras. At the ruby root, she began to swirl up the rainbow prism colors to open her vortexes. Below her navel, energies of creativity and passion twirled up through moonstone orange. Next the golden yellow of a newfound confidence spun.

Her heart opened to a luscious green as she honored the brave parents who believed in her school and enrolled their young ones with her. She smiled at the beloved Theosophists who had relocated here to continue their own learning and skills, to share their gifts with each other and the children, and to serve humanity. Love in abundance surrounded her.

She even felt love and compassion for Otis. To have spread such hate and vindictiveness to humankind, he must carry so much misery. Chances were he'd never find the beauty in others, but she prayed he would. She sent love and compassion to Hargrove and prayed someday he'd let go of his self-love and adoration. She directed love, compassion, and forgiveness to her father. He'd never understood her and treated her as he had out of fear for her future. She prayed his spirit soared in peace.

The aquamarine blue of the throat chakra twirled with happiness because she'd spoken her truth. She was chosen! The third eye expanded as intuition and clairvoyance opened. She saw the future of Lomaland becoming the center of the world, with fifty white buildings, gardens grown into lavishness, and trees turned into giant forests. Artists created, musicians played, children thrived. She saw herself directing plays and hosting music concerts. She envisioned the children and their children's children as they reached a higher level of existence. Peace would rule the world with goodness and grace. She was chosen.

She felt William's presence. His hands spun circles of crown halos on top of her head, like he had the first time he'd touched her. Without words, he communicated mystical oneness with the universe. Her body vibrated and hummed. She remembered all those years ago when he told her she'd been chosen.

One with the universe, she heard flute music, and a voice whispered softly in her ear, "Expand."

Nothing would stop her now. She'd spread Theosophy and multiply Raja Yoga schools across America and the world to blessed lands. Cuba came to mind; Bacardi would help. The beautiful island of Visingsö in Sweden—she'd send another letter to King Oscar. She needed an East Coast presence. Not New York, too dense. Newburyport. She'd do everything she could to buy the Laurels and create a center there too. A flicker of a childhood memory of the day John Greenleaf Whittier rode across the Merrimac in his dory to visit with his poem to share. The beloved words now formed on her lips:

From these wild rocks I look to-day
O'er leagues of dancing waves, and see
The far, low coastline stretch away
To where our river meets the sea.
The light wind blowing off the land
Is burdened with old voices; through
Shut eyes I see how lip and hand
The greeting of old days renew.
O friends whose hearts still keep their prime,
Whose bright example warms and cheers,
Ye teach us how to smile at Time,

And set to music all his years!

Her emotions freed, the opportunities were endless. She saw it. Justice and joy spreading throughout the world because of their work. Eventually and into perpetuity, the evolution of humanity expanded higher and higher. She'd leave the earth, but her spirit would know it was so. Her long-held dream had become a reality. It radiated from this Temple of Peace, in a white city, on a golden land, beside a sundown sea.

Lomaland—Beyond the Book

Over time Katherine accumulated five hundred acres, extending north and east toward the bay of the original site. Construction continued with the addition of South Ranch that established a lumberyard, carpentry, plumbing, blacksmith, paint, and machine shops, a bookbindery, and printing, photograph, engraving and tailoring departments, a storeroom for Theosophical Publishing, and a mailing section. Across the road, on the corner of what is now Talbot and Catalina, forty wooden-floored tents were erected, complete with a kitchen and dining room, to accommodate visitors. Nearby a three-story pavilion with billiard parlor, music room, and hall were also built.

By 1905, a building was moved by horse and buggy and positioned north of the amphitheater. It was used as a Theosophical headquarters and became Katherine's residence as well. Over time, more than fifty houses, cottages, and bungalows spanned the land. To the north of the Spalding house were the athletic fields with baseball, basketball, tennis, archery, and an eight-hole golf course. By 1910 electric underground wiring began.

The grounds continued to flourish. Seventy-five acres of oats and wheat were planted as fodder for the stables and dairy. Soon over 22,000 trees thrived, with forty acres of unbroken forest that stretched up the slope from the ocean to the Homestead. By 1910, 40,000 trees had been planted, including eucalyptus, palms, peppers, pines, olives, citrus, and avocado. Half of the Eastern trees didn't survive, including the mulberry trees. Prize-winning orchards loaded their tables every day of the year. At one time, Lomaland provided half the fruits and vegetables for all of Point Loma.

Lomaland's population peaked in 1910 at five hundred residents, three hundred of whom were students. By 1919, enough pupils had finished high school, and the Theosophical University was chartered. Twenty-six nationalities were ultimately represented in the Raja Yoga student body. Until 1924, thirty-seven percent of them came from homes that could not pay for the children's education or board.

Lomaland became San Diego's hub for arts and culture. Over one hundred and fifty publications came from their printing press. The Women's Exchange and Mart sold textiles and crafts to the public and produced women's and girl's uniforms and theatrical costumes. Greek and Shakespeare plays including *A Midsummer Night's Dream*, with original music and costumes, were performed in the amphitheater and at Isis Theater with proceeds going to the Raja Yoga schools. Renowned visual artists flocked to Lomaland. At the 1915 Panama-California Exposition, Lomaland had a significant presence, showcasing their beliefs and exhibiting notable artists Leonard Lester, Maurice Braun, Edith White, and Reginald Machell. Braun established an art gallery in the Isis Theater and founded the San Diego Art Guild with White in 1915.

Many summers Katherine delegated responsibilities to Lomaland staff and traveled throughout the world, accompanied by her secretary Iverson Harris, Junior, and other members. She bought property in Cuba including San Juan Hill and opened three Raja Yoga schools, sending Carmen Beltrán and other Lomaland teachers and Cubans to run them. Due to financial strain, the schools began to scale down in 1909 and completely closed in 1912. Katherine set up Westcott Corporation in Sweden to lease royal property on Visingsö Island, and she also received permission to purchase more land with the stipulation that it could not be sold. There, she built a Greek Parthenon-like building to house artworks, hosted a summer school, and, in 1913 held an international peace congress.

She also attempted to start schools in England and Minnesota, but those didn't come to realization. For years she tried to buy the Laurels, where she had grown up, for an East Coast headquarters and school. It was unavailable, so instead she purchased the Dexter Mansion overlooking the Merrimac River in the town of Newburyport. In 1920, she inherited money from one of her brothers and finally bought the Laurels, performing *A Mid-*

summer Night's Dream there. Shortly before her death, she sold the property to Frederick Mosley. The land is now located in Maudslay State Park.

Katherine's outreach efforts expanded with prison visitations, anti-war, anti-capital punishment, and anti-vivisection crusades. Her greatest reform movements were her campaigns to end war by sending letters to President Woodrow Wilson and US governors, directing peace parades, pageants, and speeches, and writing resolutions. In 1915, she hosted a peace parliament at Lomaland at the beginning of the Panama-California Exposition, and Lomaland residents led a march to Balboa Park.

Alfred and Marion Robinson's infant daughter Larona was enrolled at Lomaland from 1904–1909. The couple developed the barley fields into half a city block of gardens, cultivating ornamental plants, particularly begonias. Along with Kate Sessions, they cofounded the San Diego Floral Association. In 1910, Larona died of a heart ailment and a bereft Alfred broke off all ties with Katherine. In 1912, the couple moved into their new fifteen-thousand-square-foot Italian Renaissance–style mansion, Rosecroft. Alfred originated lath houses to grow tropical plants in temperate climates. In a 1912 *Sunset* magazine article, he wrote that a "Palace of Lath" should be built for the Panama-California Exposition; this inspired the Botanical Building in Balboa Park, which has recently been restored. After his death in 1942, the estate was sold and the new owner opened the garden and lath house as the Begonia Gardens, a popular tourist attraction through the 1960s. In the 1970s, the property was sold again, and the garden area was subdivided for residential use. The original mansion is privately owned and listed on the National Register of Historic Places. Other historic homes built during the Lomaland era across Catalina in what is called the Wooded Area continue to be residences, including Sunnyside as well as Rosecroft.

Elizabeth Spalding continued to be Katherine's close friend and confidant. Albert Spalding had a profound effect on San Diego. In 1907, he was the driving force to pave the road that ran from downtown to Lomaland all the way to the lighthouse. He joined other civic-minded businessmen to purchase the site of the original presidio, created a park along the edge of

Sunset Cliffs, helped organize the 1915 Panama-California Exposition, and developed the Loma Portal neighborhood. The couple raised racehorses and collected art, books, and Chinese fine furniture. With their family, they lived in the mansion until their passings. To Katherine's dismay, she did not inherit funds they had promised her.

Leoline and Claude Falls Wright divorced, as did Aimee and Ernest Temple Hargrove. Hargrove tried to establish a splinter Theosophical Society to no avail, never remarried, and became an Episcopal priest, serving at the Chapel of the Comforter in Greenwich Village. Philo eventually moved to Lomaland and resided in his own small cottage the rest of his days.

By 1926, financial strain due to cash flow and court judgements forced Katherine to take out bonds and sell the Isis Theater, some oceanfront property, and land east of Catalina. Her memory and health began to decline. In 1929, staff begged her to cancel her summer trip to Europe, but she refused. In July, a car accident occurred in Germany, and instead of being transported to a hospital, she insisted on being taken to Visingsö, where she died at eighty-two years old.

Gottfried de Purucker, who'd drawn the map of Point Loma for Katherine in Switzerland, became the next leader. He was a man of great knowledge and compassion but did not possess Katherine's panache. After the stock market crash, Lomaland was never able to recover. South Ranch was abandoned to the US government to cover unpaid taxes. After the Great Depression, during World War II the property was used for temporary war housing. In 1942, the campus was sold to a developer. The Theosophical Society staff and remaining students moved to Covina and later Pasadena.

The new owner planned to use the buildings and site for a housing district for five thousand people. However, due to limitations in the property transfer agreement and the dangerous condition of the buildings, only three hundred patrons were allowed to move in. When the developer died in 1950, the property was purchased for Balboa University, which soon affiliated with the Southern California Methodist Conference, changing its name to Californian Western University. Artillery activity during the war had weakened and cracked the glass and wood of the buildings. The Temple of Peace caught fire in 1952. Luckily the doors were saved and are now on display at the San Diego History Center, along with paintings by Lomaland artists. The Homestead was judged too far gone and was demolished in 1953.

In 1968, Cal Western changed its name to United States International University, and by 1973 relocated to Scripps Ranch, then in 2001 merged to form Alliant International University. Pasadena College moved to Point Loma and was renamed Point Loma College, then Point Loma Nazarene University, and remains at that location today. In 1987, PLNU developed a master plan with the city to save some of the original buildings. In 1994, the headquarters building was moved across Pepper Tree Lane and rotated one hundred and eighty degrees. The School for the Revival of the Lost Mysteries of Antiquity cornerstone site remained a sacred spot for many years but now a parking lot and building sit there. The headquarters building, North House, Spalding Mansion, Casa Rosa, and a few other structures remain and are used by the university. The Greek amphitheater is still a stunning site overlooking the ocean, and many of the trees Katherine planted continue to thrive.

Author's Note

I grew up in Point Loma, near Madame Tingley's Lomaland. Though she's been gone nearly a century, the tales about her life—and what took place on the property—still echo throughout the region. I've always been intrigued by the mysteries surrounding her. Was she really a medium and clairvoyant as some claimed? How did she build a thriving Theosophical community, complete with lush gardens, a school, and an arts colony, on what was once barren land? And did she truly believe her husband had been reincarnated as a turtle?

A novelist's job is to place obstacles between the protagonist and their deep desire—and Katherine's childhood vision of creating a white city had plenty. Even though this is a work of fiction, I felt compelled to be as accurate as possible—quite a challenge because many references had conflicting information. With secrecy, gossip, and yellow journalism, it was impossible to determine timelines and truths. For instance, some sources said Katherine stayed at the convent three months and others three years. Between 1868–1880, there is little documentation of Katherine's life. Lore states she spent time overseas in a traveling theater troupe. According to research she met General Fremont on his deathbed, and others believed it was at President Lincoln's second inauguration. No one knows exactly when Katherine and William met. Stories report it was in front of the Do-Good Mission as a storm ensued.

The major characters in the book were all real, except Grace Gergen, Katherine's assistant at the mission, and I tried to capture their physical appearances and personalities. Little is written about Philo. One interviewee account stated he didn't have a moral compass, and another claimed he was a very fine gentleman. I didn't find evidence of a contract but was able to locate some of his patents online.

In several instances, I tightened up and shifted event dates and facts for the sake of the story. I pushed back the 1888 marriage of Katherine and Philo by a few months and also their residency in Cora's Upper West Side mansion. I introduced Dr. Gertrude van Pelt and Ernest Temple Hargrove earlier in the novel than I believe they met Katherine in real life.

For inspiration, I walked the Lomaland property near my home; traveled to Newburyport, Massachusetts, where Katherine grew up; and visited New York City. I scoured court testimonies, archival documents, newspaper articles, letters, photographs, passports, ship logs, and interviews, and listened to oral history from Kenneth R. Small, whose parents grew up on Lomaland with Katherine. No biography has been published about her, though copies of her talks, speeches, and quotes are available. I found *The Gods Await* the most enlightening. *Captain P. L. Westcott and his Children,* compiled by Ron Irving at the Newburyport Public Library, enabled me to understand her youth.

The following publications about Lomaland were the most helpful: *The Dawn of the New Cycle* by W. Michael Ashcroft; *California Utopia: Point Loma: 1897–1942* by Emmett A. Greenwalt; *Images of America Point Loma,* published by La Playa Trail Association; *White City on the Hill: The Building of the Theosophical Society on Point Loma, California, 1897–1942*, a thesis by Bruce Coughran; "The Many Trials of Madame Tingley, Parts 1-5," *San Diego Reader* by Jeff Smith; *The New Century, a magazine dedicated to the Brotherhood of Humanity,* Volume 1, 1897–1903, edited by Katherine Tingley; and *Theosophical History Occasional Paper Volume XV Revisiting Visionary Utopia: Katherine Tingley's Lomaland* by Kenneth R. Small. *The Kenneth R. Small, Universal Brotherhood, Theosophy, and Lomaland Archival Collection* provided a wealth of information and photos. Theosophical references I used most were: *The Mysteries of the Heart Doctrine*, prepared by Katherine Tingley and her pupils; *The Ocean of Theosophy* by William Q. Judge; and *The Path: A Weekly Magazine Dedicated to the Brotherhood of Humanity, Theosophy in America, and the Study of Occult Science and Philosophy, and Aryan Literature,* Volume 1, 1886–1887, edited by William Q. Judge.

To learn more about the Spaldings, I read *Baseball in the Garden of Eden* by John Thorn. *A Victorian Lady's Guide to Fashion and Beauty* by Mimi Matthews guided me to keep styles authentic.

To become familiar with occult activities, I pored over the following books: *The Mahatma Letters to A. P. Sinnett from the Mahatmas M. and K. H.*, transcribed and compiled by A. T. Barker; *William Q. Judge: Letters That Have Helped Me*, compiled by Jasper Niemand; *This Is Spiritualism* by Maurice Barbanell; and *Forty Years a Medium* by Estelle Roberts. Beyond perusing publications about metaphysical practices, I interviewed experts, sought firsthand experiences by attending mediumship readings, and undergoing trance journeys led by a shaman.

Katherine did indeed do mail-order correspondence, held private seances, and conducted benefits to raise money for her charitable causes. A psychometrist, she touched handkerchiefs for large audiences while blindfolded. At some point, after she started studying with William, she no longer presented public demonstrations. William may or may not have hypnotized her. Lore states Madame Blavatsky did send him a sketch and that after she died, she relayed messages to William through Katherine. Some of the communications with Master M are documented, and others I imagined. After William's death, extraordinary events convinced the cabinet that she was the chosen one. I'd read accounts of ectoplasm soul apparitions and apport giftings, which inspired me to create the scenes with sweet peas falling from the sky and William's spirit visitation. However, I found no evidence of any paranormal events after William's death. After founding Lomaland, there's no evidence Tingley engaged in mediumistic activities, either publicly or privately. However, there are accounts and anecdotes of her psychometric and intuitive abilities, including premonitions of her own death.

Acknowledgments

First and foremost, my heartfelt gratitude goes to Corey Pahanish, whose belief that Madame Tingley should be the subject of my next novel set this journey in motion. I am grateful to Iris Engstrand, my inspiring professor at the University of San Diego, who first ignited my fascination with California history so many years ago. A special shout-out to Rich Farrell, coach extraordinaire, for encouraging me to aim higher than the Himalayas and pushing me to see this novel through to completion. And to the ever-wonderful Judy Reeves—her steadfast encouragement and support have meant the world to me.

My profound thanks to Kenneth R. Small, whose generosity had no bounds. He made his Lomaland archives available to me, shared unpublished oral traditions, and tracked down key evidence. Deep gratitude goes to Bruce Coughran, who patiently answered my seemingly endless questions, walked the grounds with me, and shared his thesis. I am also grateful to the following fervent historians who helped me connect research dots: Elizabeth Courtier, Eric DuVall, Dwayne Little, Kitty McDaniel, Bonnie Nickel, Phil Johnson, Julie Sarno, Chelsea Snover, Jonathan Stone, Stephanie Williams, Michael Yee, and Beth Zedaker.

I'd like to offer a genuine thank you to the welcoming Massachusetts residents who uncovered and shared invaluable details about Katherine Tingley's childhood and family history: Sharon Spieldenner at the Newburyport Public Library; Sierra Gitlin from the Museum of Old Newbury, who located and hiked me to the Laurels' location; Susan Herman at the John Greenleaf Whittier Home and Museum; and Ross Varney and his congregation at the Belleville Congregational Church. In New York City I'm grateful to the workers at the Tenement and Transit Museums and the Grand Masonic

Lodge. I'm also grateful to Katy Phillips and Ronald Teague at the San Diego History Center for their support.

My admiration goes to Brooke Warner and her She Writes Press team for their invaluable guidance and support these past ten years. I am in awe of Jenny Q at Historical Editorial for her kindness and keen eyes. Thank you to Jessie Glenn and her dedicated team at Mindbuck Media for getting the word out. I am grateful to Amy Hesselink at La Playa Books and Nancy Warwick at Warwick's La Jolla and their staffs for championing my books and for their enthusiastic support of this new one.

Thank you to my San Diego writing community, especially Susan Gembrowski Baker, Madi Bucci, Rebecca Chamaa, Jennifer Coburn, Kristen Fogle, Adam Greenfield, Dean Nelson, Brendan Praniewicz, Tania Pryputniewicz, Jennifer Silva Redmond, Elizabeth St. John, and Marlene Wagman-Geller, and everyone at San Diego Writers, Ink.

A special thanks goes to Debra Atkins for joining me on the East Coast research adventure. Many hugs go to the following friends who have cheered me on and didn't complain these past five years when I told them no, I was too busy: Sandy Baine, Karen Begin, Jerry Buckley, Pat Fitzmorris, Holly Foster, Tom Haine, Rob Hutsel, Phil Johnson, Joan Mehnert Kegler, Seth Krosner, Dottie Laub, Lisa Laube, Carol Leimbach, Leslie Meads, Tanya Peters, Cathy Pilkington, Linda Roper, Drew Schlosberg, Carre St. Andre, Trish Shushan, Stephanie Tsuruda, Patti Wassem, and Alan Ziter.

I am forever grateful to these spiritual guides who helped me on this path: Megan Cochran, Lynn Cooper, Ashley Davis, Minna Lopez, Banoo Partovi, and Janice Zwail. Lastly, I'd like to thank Katherine Tingley for catapulting arts and culture into San Diego, blessing the beautiful property, and making the world a better place.

About the Author

photo credit: Daren Scott

JILL G. HALL is the author of the award-winning Anne McFarland series about women searching for their place in the world connected by vintage finds. These dual timeline novels, *The Black Velvet Coat, The Silver Shoes*, and *The Green Lace Corset,* are bestselling book club favorites. Hall's poems and personal narratives have appeared in a variety of publications and on her blog Crealivity, the art of practicing a creative lifestyle. Her tenure as an educator spanned over twenty years, incorporating the arts along the way. She holds a doctorate from Northern Arizona University. She is a past board president and instructor at San Diego Writers, Ink. She also practices yoga, loves to garden, and enjoys spending time in nature. A native San Diegan, she resides near the Lomaland property. To learn more about her go to: www.jillghall.com.

ALSO BY JILL G. HALL

The Anne McFarland Series:

The Black Velvet Coat
The Silver Shoes
The Green Lace Corset